VESTA, (

Vesta

Coming of Age

VII.2

William Hard24Get MacHinery

Vesta

ISBN: 978-1-7334746-0-3
ASIN: B07X2HC6FX

Thanks to the Dawn Mission and those good people
At NASA, JPL and CalTech

Cover Image: NASA/JPL-Caltech/UCLA/MPS/DLR/IDA 17 September 2012 10:29:19

Janet, Ben and Josh

Without your keen understanding

I would have been lost

VII.2 Table of Contents

"The dinosaurs became extinct because they didn't have a space program.
And if we become extinct because we don't have a space program,
it'll serve us right!"
– Larry Niven

"Prediction is very difficult, especially about the future."
Niels Bohr

Preface

Chapter 1

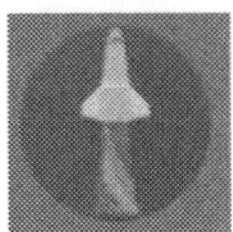

This novel is for Young People of all ages.

Welcome to Vesta, a hard and soft science fiction story. A fun read. An engaging tale set during mankind's colonization of the solar system, sprinkled with nuggets of life's experience. None of the ideas are impossible, but many are new. It is written with a certain pragmatic optimism that only surviving the future can bring. If you want to berate civilization's hard climb and imperfections, focus on depressing news, or blow up the world, there are plenty of those kinds of stories. Vesta is about standing upon the foundations set in the past, the struggle to survive today, and the quest to grow into the future.

Within the narrative you can mine for gems. It introduces leading edge technology and projections of today's science, as well as a possible explanation for dark matter. It proposes the root causes of human behaviors based upon humanity's past survival. It recounts the experience of living within a submarine and inside the space shuttle to reconstruct the issues which would confront the space cultures of the future. Survivors laugh at death, and the book contains humor throughout.

Finally, and most importantly, Vesta contains a message: Given guidance, opportunity and responsibility, people thirteen years old can successfully become adults. Many of the ancient cultures allowed this, and today's society is doing our youth a disservice by not allowing competent individuals becoming adults with full rights at that age.

In addition, a road map as it were, is included, suggesting a path that today's people could take to strengthen mankind's chance of future existence. By colonizing the solar system, humanity and life itself is given additional assurance of not only survivability, but for the opportunity to achieve our potential.

Evidence indicates that despite all the terrible problems of the world, we are not necessarily doomed. Additionally, despite the incredible growth and achievements from our small beginnings, we are not assured a future. This can be summarized as follows:

Although nothing in life is guaranteed, but if we work hard, and work together, we have a chance, which gives Reason for Hope. Hardworking pragmatic optimists like their chance.

Bring Life to the Universe

and Bring the Universe to Life

"Science, my lad, is made up of mistakes, but they are mistakes which it is useful to make, because they lead little by little to the truth."

– Jules Verne

"The future you shall know when it has come; before then, forget it."
Aeschylus

Prologue
Chapter 2

Like a worn stone ballet slipper, the old 'roid tumbled slowly in the cold outer reaches of the belt.

A point of light, a slowly dispersing puff of dust, a new orbit with only Clotho, Lachesis and Atropos watching,

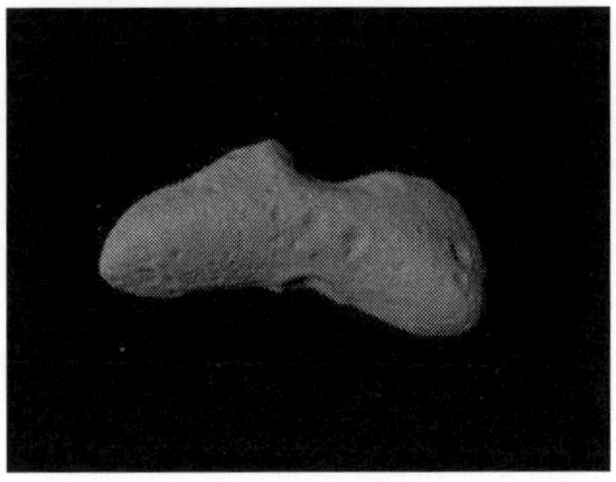

Toe over heel, toe over heel,
tossed across the Stage of the Universe.

Life is a Gift.
In our uncertain world,
The Future is not Guaranteed.
However, if We Work Hard Together,
We have a Chance, and that is
Reason for Hope

"Looking at these stars suddenly dwarfed my own troubles
and all the gravities of terrestrial life."
- H.G. Wells

"There is no grief which time does not lessen and soften."
Cicero

Encounter

Chapter 3

In war, sometimes there are mistakes.

A Freeman Habitat spun about its axis as it moved slowly through the sparse rocks of the outer belt, its years of use showing in the ungainly modules patched hither and yon as the need arose. Its indispensability was also obvious from the heat and noise generated by the family within. Scones! The smell of hot baked scones wafted through the bio compartments of the Johnson family home.

Neely Johnson was at the mid-compartment workbench cleaning dust and grime from a pancake fan when he was interrupted by the senior mechman, Ner0 Aqua.

"Sir, can I bother you for a minute?"

"Certainly."

"I have been bothered by a slowly accumulating anomaly: about 0.5 % of the deep rock entering our sphere can't be accounted for and it concerns me."

"Ner0, I am not familiar with that database. Drill deeper"

"Well, it's a small number, but typically we track two decades tighter than that, down to about 0.008% of the total mass."

"Is it important?"

"I don't know, I just don't know. I will have to think about the ramifications. I..." He stopped.

"Well, you ponder it and tell me when you figure it out, I know you'll get it." Ner0 sat there staring at the bulkhead.

Mr. Johnson turned back to his work.

"Dad?" A voice on the intercom.

"Yes Chris?"

"I was having the old boy help me get Sabrina's playhouse set up when he had a fit, he just stopped working."

"What did you do?"

"I've put Sabrina into the 'house, 'cuz it's almost finished, and tried talking to him. All the backside indicators seem fine, but he doesn't respond to anything."

"Damn these old Freeman Houses anyway, if it's not one thing it's another. Hang tight. I'll get Ner0 to come help you bring the old boy around."

Turning around to where Ner0 sat, Mr. Johnson started:

"Ner0, would you..." but then noticed Ner0 was still pondering the wall. "Ner0!" He interrupted angrily, but there was no response.

As Mr. Johnson got up a lurch sent him sprawling into the workbench and caused Ner0 to tumble to the deck, alarms began to ring from the main console. "What the...?" escaped his lips as he staggered back to his feet. The intercom blurted: "Dad, did we have a breech?" as a shriek wailed from the kitchen while Mrs. Johnson's scones and cooking wares went flying.

"Ner0! Neeer0! Snap out of it, we need you!" There seemed no response although a look of anguished helplessness seemed to emanate from Ner0's' eyes.

Christopher Johnson staggered into the main rooms the habitat continued its drunken tumble: "What's happened?" "I don't know, we could have had an explosion, or we could have lost a pod. You go to the compensation panel and I will go to the alarm and indicator system."

Using handholds, they crawled to their stations, trying to create order from chaos. Drill training prevailed and within moments they had eliminated many potential problems. "Son, things don't totally make sense, but there doesn't appear to be an explosion. Maybe we lost a pod, we sure have a wobble... but there is no indication of lost services."

"It calculates to about 15 tonnes of shifted mass to echo ring, level five. I'm pumping the fish tanks to rebalance, both trim pumps should have it stabilized in a few minutes." Already Mr. Johnson noticed an improvement as the loose ends slowed their skittles across the deck. "Echo ring level five? If I didn't know better that would mean someone docking with us."

Just as he spoke the dock-lock began its cycle. "What the...?" again escaped from Mr. Johnson's lips. "What is it?" Mrs. Johnson asked shrilly as she emerged from the galley. He replied. "I don't know, but someone is visiting us without our knowledge."

Noise continued to radiate from the dock-lock, bumps, thuds, long silences, more thuds, more silence, then finally, the inner door started to cycle open.

The inner room of the dock-lock was dark, and an immense cold began to suck the heat from the room, however there wasn't a loss of air to a cold space rupture, and Mr. Johnson wasn't sure what was happening. Just as he decided to approach the now fully opened door, an object began to emerge.

It was dark as space itself, like a huge shipping box roughly 2 meters on a side, hard to see because it reflected so little light as it scraped along the habitat's deck into the room. It was followed by two more similar shapes, slightly smaller and somehow irregular. They were some sort of mech, although what type Mr. Johnson had no clue. As the first box approached it radiated the bitter cold of deep space, hoar frost forming and spreading a filigree of crystals across much of the object surface. The ice created enough contrast on the face of the mech that Mr. Johnson observed gouges and smeared metal corners obviously created by grinding collisions with other metallic masses.

The first mech started to withdraw and the second was approaching. It was unclear how they moved across the floor, but the surface was being scoured and an irregular grinding sound emanated from beneath the objects. Now the second object started to recede, and the third box approached. The boxes were forming some sort of dance on the floor and Johnson looked down. The floor now was severely scratched, and an oval pattern had emerged. The cold in the room was being matched by a tightness and cold in Mr. Johnson's heart.

A disembodied voice scratched: "Posit ... mate ... in three."

What manner of mechs were these? How many generations

removed from their ancestors that last had contact with humanity were they? Were they still sane? Were they ever sane?

"Who are you?" Mr. Johnson demanded, using anger to cover up his fear.

"Two..." the broken/cracked speaker continued… "...we be pocked ... ellipse..."

Two? But there were three of them, perhaps one was a servo. Mr. Johnson immediately understood the pocked analogy, reference to the cratered surface of each mech, now almost wholly covered with ice. But the ellipses? Was that the dance on the floor?

"What are you doing here? What do you want?" cried Mrs. Johnson.

"One ..." the crackle and static was even more distracting "... Know you Vand...dekken?"

"What is Vandecken?"

"Know you Faulkenbird...Rime...Rokeby?" crackled the voice.

"I don't know what you're talking about. I don't understand you." Unintelligible crackle was the only response. "I am pleased to be your host, but you are condensing our precious water vapor on your surfaces. Would you be so kind as to exit-dock and we can continue this discussion by radio at a more comfortable distance?"

Mrs. Johnson began to panic. These mechs, these things! They had no right to be here! "Get out!" Shrieking "Leave, leave right this minute!" "Neely! Get rid of these things!"

"Leave we must." Grated a rusty voice "Ye..ss" echoed another. "Move one, no..no, move two, no one Kasperov." The vibration increased and the communication still sounded like a broken radio, unused for years, no, centuries.

Static, the three mechs stopped their motion, the grinding sound shut off abruptly. In the sudden silence Mr. Johnson could hear his heart beat loudly against his ears.

A sudden heat broke out from beneath each of the mechs, Mr Johnson could smell burning. “Hey, what are you doing!?” screamed Mr. Johnson. “Quit that you MechMonsters!” The floor was starting to glow cherry red in spots.

The voice crackle broke the silence: “Zero ... game .. end.” The three mechs suddenly dropped from view as the floor detonated beneath them.

The Johnson family didn’t hear the explosion that ripped apart their Freeman Habitat, they were being sucked along with much of the loose items within the station and hurled into the vacuum of the solar system. The Habitat was violently shaken by the differential forces created by the escaping gases, twisting, folding and finally ripped apart. The wriggling objects soon becoming inert, to be slowly scattered through the sparse rocks of the outer belt. Death comes to all, whether the individuals were alive two million years in the past, or two million years in the future, or now.

The shudders within the ruined shell of the habitat slowly dampened out, the uneven wobble no longer rotating around the designed center. Off center thrusts caused by leaking fluid tanks jostled the hulk, and vibrations came and went as harmonic resonances caused by the enormous energy of the habitat’s destruction chased each other around the remaining structural members.

Wedged between two twisted frames was the inert form of Ner0, shoved into the v-notch by the outgassing, prevented to follow the rest of the habitat into free space. Its sensors still recorded its environment, even though the motor system was paralyzed.

Atmospheric pressure was non-existent, ambient temperature was plummeting, local gravity was surging above and below norm as the uneven wobble caused uneven centrifugal forces. The creaks and groans, bangs and pops of the habitat could be felt through the structural steel, and behind all that, almost obscured by all the noise, were vibrations which triggered a number of selective focusing functions. These programs and routines created a cascading effect akin to human panic, until a crescendo of orders and commands were crisscrossing through Ner0, louder and Louder. Finally, perhaps due to the receding interference of the three MechMonsters, a looped subroutine was rerouted, a relay popped, and Ner0 stirred, stilled, then lunged free of its confinement.

Hand over hand, Ner0 crawled along through the wreckage, laminates separated from base metals, indicator lights flickering on small independent sources, red, orange, yellow, green, blue, indigo and violet!!!!! His optical sensors were failing. His legs were gone! No....they are there...just no feeling, no strength...he drug them along, heavy lifeless weights, getting heavier and heavier...he had to keep pulling ...hand over hand...he must press on....and on ....and on....there was nothing else to do...on, on ...on....so tired. Power was ebbing, emergency power reserves were being consumed... ...will he make it ...how far? Where is the end ...a tunnel with no end...on and on...forever? An eternal tunnel...that's what he's trapped in ...or how it seems.

How long is a roll of toilet paper? How many would go from one end to the other? Ahhhhh!!! He's losing his mind.... what are these thoughts.... a trash can for the empty toilet roll... for some reason he must place the expired toilet roll in the receptacle ... he fumbled groggily with the roll ../ it was tangled with some wires.. cold so cold...he joggled and pushed... for some reason...there, it was aligned, he pushed...

Comprehension came suddenly, as the emergency power source surged through his depleted supplies, the twist-lock plug from his abdominal cavity took the DC current through heavy cables directly to his body loads. LVP relays were reset, one after another and additional systems were brought back online.

There was a nagging memory, RAM that was closed to being wiped, important but unknown. What was it. Ahh, the vibrations in the background noise, could he find them again, he listened, but the vibrations were gone. The habitat was quieting down, he should be able to discern that weak signal, but it seemed to have stopped... No, there it was again, weaker, quite weaker. A rat!! It'll chew the wires and then ...

Acoustic noise transmitted by steel, his attention stirred to even higher sensitivity. Sabrina! Sabrina crying! The hull was vibrating with tiny wails. Sabrina was alive somewhere. Where? Follow the signal! But the signal had gone. In the low light of the distant sun reflecting off the carnage, Ner0 tried to resolve his problem. He must complete recharge. But Sabrina must need him now, perhaps she was dying and that was the cause of loss. What to do... what to do... He thought furiously as the recharge coursed through his capacitors, remembering suddenly that Chris said he placed Sabrina in the "doghouse", the Johnson's personal slang for the shuttle. Perhaps she had survived the catastrophe in there.

Where there's life, there's hope, and Ner0 hoped that Sabrina's silence meant exhaustion rather than, well Ner0 didn't want to think about that. Thinking about bad things sometimes made them come true. His charge was sufficient, he estimated, for the journey through the metal jungle to the doghouse, as long as didn't encounter too many detours. Murphy said what could go wrong, will. But everything went wrong today. But he didn't dare wait any longer. There was no right way, just some awful chances. He hesitated again, as was the wont of his sort, steady but poor problem solvers. He tried to see a way clear through the decision tree, but again came to a series of dead ends. What to do...what to do...

Mr. Johnson always said when in doubt, pick one. So, he picked, GO! Low battery be dammed. He disconnected, spotted the place where the shuttle ought to be in the dim light and the tangle of wreckage, spinning overhead as the hulk of the habitat wobbled, a monstrous gash of empty space where the floor used to be between him and his objective. Could he climb to it in time? Would the shuttle's emergency power supplies still be charged and accessible?

Calculating the jump proved to damnably difficult. Trying to plot a trajectory using a centric polar system wasn't working, who could tell where the center was now? And those random failures of outgassing tanks jerked the wreckage this way and that. He finally resorted to calculating a straight-line relative bearing jump which simplified all sorts of assumptions, but had, he hoped, a high enough estimate of success.

He leaped! A small bundle of stray wires he hadn't seen swung into his path and he swiped at them to clear his path! A small bump. They started to tangle into his right arm, but he jerked back and was free. Now he was spinning slowly around, and the opposite wall was closing in! His back started to face the circling bulkhead and he faced into outer space! He struggled, then snapped his arms against his body causing his rotation to increase as he started to glide past the opening.

Just in time he was able to swing his arms out and grab a dangling pipe as he went by. His momentum pulled him away causing a great strain on his grip and the pipe bent around letting his feet dangle out of the hole. Luckily, the pipe didn't break, and he was now on the other side near the shuttle. Hand over hand he crawled back into the wreckage, then along the shattered bulkhead to the shuttle bay.

At the bay door, he found it to be wedged ajar, but he couldn't fit his body through the opening. In the high contrast shadows cast by the emergency lighting he found against the deck a mangled star spanner which he took and used as a pry bar in the opening. A memory of Mr. Johnson saying "The right tool for the right job" caused an ironic mental shrug inside Ner0. With a grate, the bay door groaned a further 50 centimeters open. Pausing, Ner0 noted the effort had depleted his power reserves substantially, then he felt it!

He could feel Sabrina clearly through the metal now, she must have heard his efforts, and was crying again now. Success if he could only get through the door and get recharged. Looking at the opening again, he decided to try to force his way in. Placing his feet into the opening, he back down into the shuttle bay, contorting his middle body to clear the door and doorjamb.

He was in! Yes, there was an emergency recharge station next to the EAB source. And the shuttle looked undamaged. Checking his internal clock, he realized only three hours had passed since the explosion, and with the shuttle intact, he decided he could afford to recharge at the emergency station. He struggled over to the equipment locker where the emergency socket was located, absently noting the bent over sheet metal and other damage done by a ruptured high-pressure air hose which was visible behind the bulkhead.

Connecting his electrical leads to the power supply he immediately felt more capable. He searched for and found emergency Comm connector and patched in. Routing to the interior of the shuttle, he could pick up audio of Sabrina snuffling, and passed back a reassuring message to the eighteen-month-old: “You’ve been found, Sabrina, it’s all right. This is Ner0 and I am right outside your door. I will be in momentarily as soon as I fix a few things.”

He was mightily confused when the toddler stopped mewing and let go a howl and commenced to scream. He tried to calm her over the intercom, but his words just fueled more and more sobs. Scared and frustrated at his failure to still the child. He finally unplugged and went to the shuttle’s lock.

Cycling through the lock seemed to take forever while hearing the infant’s crying, the inner door finally started to open. Inside the shuttle, Sabrina turned and lunged for the figure as soon as the light was strong enough to see him. "Unka Agwa! Unka Agwa! I want mommy!" Her diapers were askew, and she tripped before she got to him and began crawl.

"Stop! Sabrina, stop!" Yelled Ner0 noticing the frost forming on his body. "Don't touch me honey, my body will hurt you!" But the youngster refused to hear and continued to crawl towards him, and he backed away, not wanting to freeze burn her little fingers. This continued, Sabrina with eyes squeezed shut blindly groping for comfort and a panicked Ner0 tripping as he backed away, all the time muttering calming words to her.

By the time she trapped him into a corner and grabbed him, his legs were covered with an insulating skim coat of ice, and although she let go of him immediately and began to wail again, she wasn't hurt.

Ner0 turned and approached the food storage locker, which with the awkward acceleration caused by the spinning habitat was now located at a 30-degree angle from "down". Carefully opening the door, he found much of the contents scattered inside the cabinet, still he was able to grab a sweetened energy bar and also a juice pack. Pushing the litter back inside, he was able close the door.

Poking a straw into the juice Ner0 turned back to the red-faced Sabrina who was curled up with her eyes shut in a corner. He placed the straw into her mouth, and she began to greedily suck on the box rocking to herself. After a minute of racking drags on the fluid, culminating in empty slurps, she rolled over on her other side and seemed to fall into sleep. After a minute a deep shudder shook her body, but she didn't open her eyes, and relaxed back into sleep.

Ner0 watched her concernedly for a while, then decided she was safely asleep and went to the shuttle's control couch. Plugging himself back into the recharge circuit, then to sensor-bionics, he began an assessment of the craft. Although the craft was intact, it seemed to have suffered from lack of maintenance. That's right, he thought, Chris was working on it before the arrival of those...those...those things. Those three things, he thought. Those three MechMonsters. Yes, they must have been Mechmons, based upon their evil killing. But he was getting sidetracked, where was he? He must continue the review of the shuttle's capability. Power and life support: 85%; mechanical integrity: 99+%; fuel 15%; navigation and computer systems: 99+%; uh-oh - communications: 0%.

He looked over; the STRAT-40 transceiver was missing from its console position. Chris must have been working on it. He looked around; it wasn't in the cabin. Bad news he thought, Chris must have removed it to the habitats work bench for repairs. He thought back, that was one of the areas missing from the vessel when Ner0 recovered from his catatonic state. He noticed that the ice had melted from his body in most place and he was dripping.

That caused him to divert down another thought train, why did he freeze up prior to the arrival of the MechMonsters? Could they have crippled him? He never had heard of such a thing, but they must have, it couldn't have been a coincidence. Maybe it was a good thing he was missing comms; he sure didn't want to signal them that something had survived their attack. They might come back. He didn't want them back. He must escape with Sabrina.

Power, Life support and fuel were low. How long could life support last on emergency levels? The computer took his input, just his own nominal energy needs and Sabrina's requirements. It spat out a 2000-hour contingency plan, which was better than he had up until now, but his and Sabrina's needs weren't high, hopefully he could stretch things. Food for Sabrina? The answer was around 90 days if spread to emergency rations. That wasn't the limiting factor.

He shied away from what came next but had to face it. He didn't know anything about navigation, but if he couldn't radio for help, he would have to take Sabrina to someone.

Looking up, he saw Sabrina staring at him with silent big eyes, not making a sound. "Hello, Sabrina, how are you?" She didn't answer, not a sound. "Sabrina, are you OK?" She still just stared at him, as if her infant personality had suffered a shock it could not bear and had been drowned. He reached out carefully and said softly: "I'm here, Sabrina, you aren't alone." She didn't speak, she didn't move, she let him put his hand on her arm. He slowly pulled her towards him, and she came.

He lifted her up and sat her on his lap, and she slowly settled her head on his chest. She stayed there, unmoving, not uttering a sound. Speaking carefully, as carefully as he could, he said: "We're leaving here, Sabrina, we're going home." Then softer, as he recalled Mrs. Johnson "We love you." She stared up at him with her big amber eyes. Then she shut her eyes and held onto him with a tight grasp. He rocked her until she fell asleep. Tears slowly fell out of her closed eyes, but she never did speak again.

Knowing how long he had, he then called up the Belt Almanac to discover where he could put to. He found that the Johnson habitat was at the neither regions of the belt, and the fuel-time equations could not reach any human occupied 'roid in time. He ran the calculations again and again, but the answer always came up the same. Insufficient fuel, not enough time. He considered spending time searching local space for Comm parts, but knew he wasn't a repair-mech. Suddenly, an idea came to him, perhaps there were mech inhabited sites nearby he could travel to, and to human space.

Returning hopefully and somewhat fearful of a negative answer, he began the search and calculations anew...preparation and elimination of all unnecessary mass...1900 hours travel...very little fuel for maneuvering at the end, must rely on proactive support at Hektor, hidden in Jupiter's Trojan Asteroids, the Mechsite...the Citadel...

Sometime later, he told the listening but forever quiet child: "We're leaving now Sabrina. With a little luck, we will get you back to your people."

Greater Understanding
Better Morals
Genuine Purpose
Real Hope

"Being like everybody is the same as being nobody."
Rod Serling

"I can't imagine a person becoming a success who doesn't give this game of life everything he's got."
Walter Cronkite

Wild Bi1l Graduates

Chapter 4

A gaggle of mankind hovered about the stodgy government offices while elevator music played the latest electro-swing: "Next!"

Wearing a flowered Harpo hat, and a big red nose, the thin and fidgety male Gentleman Mech in the front of the line moved quickly from his position to the agency's counter wondering why this was the only remaining manually administered government function in the Federation.

The mech raised a pastel green eyebrow the shape of a pistachio strip of toothpaste as the agent turned a cold shoulder and to her screen, pulling up data files. When the clerk continued to ignore him, the mech began his best Marcel Marceau impression, building an impregnatable glass wall with the flat of his palms. He began to push and strain against the imaginary glass.

Without even turning her head, "Nice try clown, but you can't hurry the ship of state."

At the word "clown", he froze, and his's cherry red glassine lips trembled in the corners. While still rigid, his heels began to twitch, then bounce maybe 1/8" off the deck as his smile grew and grew. With enormous effort he pushed away the invisible glass window and leaned slowly across the counter as if in a gale and tried to see the clerk's monitor.

"Back off bozo!" She swung the image away from his sight. "I'll be ready when I'm ready, not a nano sooner."

He reluctantly pulled himself erect, and stood there shivering with caged energy, camera irises cranked wide open, staring, intently trying to read his future.

Finally, "Name and particulars"

"William Hard24Get MacHinery, Mech III, 221A Baker Street, behind the Crow's Nest, Fremont, Vesta, United Federation of Asteroids, UF of A."

"OK, bucket-brain, whatcha want?"

"Tell me."

"Tell you what? The number of stars in the Pleiades? There are seven sisters"

She was tormenting him. "Please tell me, tell me my future!"

"OK, OK..." she smiled and left him off the hook, "Let's find out." She waved her optical bar scanner across him like an old timey fairy god mother, with a final soft tap on his chrome pate: "You sir, my fine mechanical friend, have passed your citizenship exams and…"

"Yessssss!" was the involuntary hiss. She smiled, the more they were tortured, the happier they ended up, she thought.

Not missing a beat, "... are promoted to Mech II and now eligible for additional training and grooming for several fine careers. Would you have any particular path in mind?"

"Would I? Would I!"

"No dearie, it's a glass eye, not a wood eye. Doctor told me I would be better looking with it. Glad you noticed though… So, what is your heart's desire?" She was enjoying herself now.

Standing up tall, he proudly announced "I am a mech with a sense of humor, I'd like you to know." He honked his red nose. "I wish to be a comedian."

She stared at him for good five seconds, finally she sighed: "There are a thousand clowns out of work on Vesta, and you want to be a comedian." She could hardly keep from smiling. "Are you joking?"

"With all seriousness," giving her his best dignified look, at least as good as he could with the plastic eyebrows and red nose, "I am not joking, I wish to be a comedian."

"Alright, let's see what the authorities have to say." she was scrolling the screen.

She looked up, "Sorry, no openings for comedian."

"What!?"

"Sorry."

"What about Clown?"

"Nope."

"Cowboy?"

"No! Closet employment by category, sorted alphabetically is cop… Welcome aboard Detective Second Class MacHinery."

"Well I'll be…"

"We're done here chrome-dome. Will you please fill out this satisfaction survey? Please indicate my name, here, it puts me into running for a vacation to Antiope. Thank you."

"Next!"

Damn he thought.

The mech forlornly wandered away aimlessly, ground up by the gears of civilization.

Truth and Understanding can be divided into Three Systems

"Stuff your eyes with wonder, ... live as if you'd drop dead in ten seconds. See the world. It's more fantastic than any dream made or paid for in factories."
– Ray Bradbury

"Man does not weave this web of life. He is merely a strand of it. Whatever he does to the web, he does to himself."
Chief Seattle

Detective Lieutenant George Sealth
Chapter 5

Where Boy grew up was a world of wonders, ancient forests of ponderous trees, wearing their burdens of moss and lichen, glens where the fawns were known to kick and dance, grandmother orca shepherding her tribe past the village in the clear green waters, their shadows floating over the beds of white anemones, of Raven, the Trickster, from whom his family was descended.

Grandmother was revered for her knowledge of the whole world and the histories of the people since their release by Raven. Grandfather was teaching him the transformations: from the changing seasons; to how to call the Spirit of the Elk during their rut; of the secret of making fire from the transformed wood.

The People knew the spirit world, the transformations of magical beings into animals or even people. Spirit Ravens like the Trickster had ears, as well as a deep call like a gong, unlike the squallous caws of the bothering crows, and could turn into human form like the other Spirit Animals and visit the village unbeknownst. Salmon himself, when he returned from the sea, transformed every year into Dragonfly, Frog, and Forest.

He himself had been surrounded by a pod of orca just last season, visited perhaps even by the Spirit King himself and planned to take their totem as his own when he became a man. The flowers of wild rhododendrons and currents brought joy to the longhouse in the late Spring, and the painted panels and carved posts of his lodge made a snug home with stories and plays to fire his imagination during the long nights of the wet season. Oh, the world around the village was full of wonders.

The knock came at the door. "Come in Lieutenant, close the door behind you."

"You asked to see me Sir?" Detective Lieutenant Sealth of Earth Union Police was a lightly built man, perhaps six foot and a hard one hundred and seventy pounds, dark eyes and long black hair, a dancer's grace when walking. He looked around the office evenly, noticing the commendations, recommendations and awards that highlighted the walls of Department Chief Captain Alberto Schnicht, with a photo mural of Christ the Redeemer atop Corcovado Mountain in Rio de Janeiro behind the Captain.

"Yes, thank you Lieutenant, please take a seat." Captain Schnicht said pointing to a relaxing looking rattan chair at the right front of his large office desk, facing ninety degrees away from the Chief. The chair was out of place and at odds with the other furnishings of the office which were dark wood and black leather, but most likely a comfortable reminder of Brazil and a keepsake for the office's occupant.

As George settled into the chair, the basket of the seat flexed and relaxed to conform to his weight as well as any of the modern "active" furniture pieces he had ever used. Immediately, the Chief stood up, waving George to remain seated, and walked over to his panorama, then turned back to the Lieutenant, "I asked you in today to discuss an operation whose topic and background information should not leave this room. Do you understand?"

George was interested, "Yes Sir." He knew that this interview would have an important basis: Lieutenants do not get called in to see the Chief on a whim. His demeanor and sincerity reflected his basic nature and he relied upon them to sustain him through this interview as they had throughout his career.

The Captain continued, "We, that is, the Earth Council, then passed to my office, have been invited by the Federation to provide a Criminal Forensics Attaché to their staff in the major Belt. After a significant search, staff has recommended you."

Yes, this was interesting, "Have they explained why they want such an Attaché?"

"The overt explanation is that they wish to expand the continuing cultural and political exchanges that maintain the peace and harmony between our two cultures. We think that they have grown to the point that crime is becoming a serious issue in their society and they want to pick our brains for solutions."

As usual when dealing with upper staff, politics and agendas were present, but as normal, hidden. Letting his legs relax and stretch out somewhat, as to give a sense of 'We are part of this together'. "So why me Sir?"

"Well, it has been obvious for some time that the Belters have overtaken us with regards to electronic and nano technological capabilities, and whoever we send will be searched and bugged like nobody's business. You, on the other hand, have challenged the system by going unaugmented your entire career, and would be impossible to detect electronically. I have reviewed your record and it amazing what you have been able to accomplish without assistance." The Captain turned towards George as if to charge him to explain.

Pulling his feet back in and sitting taller, “Thank you Captain, it has been a trial. As you must have read, I am from the Pacific Northwest Coast of the Americas, and I was told by my Grandfather that I embody a spirit from a race of heroes, although, I wouldn’t know myself.” A small smile accompanied this statement to remove the brag.

“One of my earliest coaches taught me that with a lot of practice, and significant patience, a person can train muscle memories that naturally augment one’s responses and speed up reflexes. This can be done in martial arts, but also in other facets of life. Build enough so-called subroutines and I can respond to many events comparable to the guys in the office who are indeed augmented.

“Their natural responses are faster once they enter into known territory, but there is a small delay when encountering new events while their mind and their augmentation have to query each other and decide on an action. This way I can keep up.”

“Interesting.” The Chief returned to his chair and sat down, obviously contemplating what George was telling him.

George turned to him, leaned forward and continued: “Another attribute I have that is unusual is I only need an hour and a half of sleep a day. Another Native Coach taught me a meditative style that eliminates most worries, and it makes this short period of sleep as restful as what most people get in eight. When I went to college, the doctors wanted to study me, but I didn’t have much time. Even though I have more hours, my days are quite full.”

In the back of George’s mind, he was evaluating the idea of space travel to the belt, it appealed to him, it appealed to him a lot. “Since I don’t sleep much, and even though I am only twenty-five years old, I have the experience, and hopefully, the wisdom of a fifty-year-old.”

The Chief Captain Detective stood up again, “Lieutenant, I have made a decision, I am going to send you to the belt.

“One of the major asteroid centers is Vesta, with a population over four-hundred million. We have arraigned to have you stationed there. This is an older community and are not as obsessed with mental electronic direct links as the younger colonies. In addition, it appears they are having problems which are hobbling their communications systems, and some of their augmentations have been disabled. This will allow you to integrate more easily within their society

“You will go as a liaison, but also as an overt observer. The Belters will know you are there to gather information, and will hide what is sensitive, but I want you to observe, I want you to come back and to report to me.

“I want you to focus on the economics of the Belt, they are out-competing us in manufacturing, and Research and Development, and we want to know how, and why. It isn’t clear and we don’t know how. On Earth we have the natural sustenance of the mother planet and they have to fight the elements, or lack of, for every inch.

“It just doesn’t add up in our calculations. Perhaps you can make a discovery. So, while you are there, you will be our unaugmented camera and recorder. Do you understand?”

The Lieutenant stood up again, “Yes Sir, I understand.”

“There is one more element that seriously concerns us. There appears to be millions of AI machines in the belt, of unknown motivation and uncertain capabilities. I don’t know how the belters trust them.

“Our intelligence has sensed military buildup within these so-called mech sub civilizations in the gas giants and the Kuiper belt, and even the belters themselves are gearing up. Our operational analysts show the belter military patrols are longer and further out than before, and seem to focus on a nexus near Jupiter called the Trojan asteroids.

"There appears to be a stronghold on the asteroid Hektor called the Citadel, which is orbited by a ten-mile diameter asteroid made of iron called Kenny. They must have run out of Greek names or something.

"Can you imagine how many robots you can make from a thousand cubic miles of iron? Can you understand our concern and fear?

"This is the reason for all our clandestineness. Anything, anything at all that you can find out about these rogue robots is of supreme importance. Do you understand the importance of the secrecy of your mission, Lieutenant?

The Lieutenant stood up again, "Yes Sir, I understand."

Changing his conduct as if he hadn't mentioned rogue robots, the Chief came around the desk "If you don't have any questions, stop by the Adjutant's desk, and he will direct you to your formal briefing team and get you outfitted. Please, this is of planetary importance, if you feel impeded in any way, or need additional support, come to me directly."

Stepping forward to shake the Chief's hand, George was mildly surprised at the magnitude of the assignment, but pleased it didn't look directly dangerous, yet highly interesting and important. More significantly, he was going to be able to grow his career, and like it at the same time, he hoped. "Thank you, Sir, I will do my best."

1. Universal Truths

Stars Exist without the intervention of Mankind

"That's the greatest thing about wikis:
they combine the best features of democracy and autocracy.
Everybody has an equal say. But some got bigger says than others."
Paul Di Filippo

"Tell me and I forget, teach me and I may remember, involve me and I learn."
Benjamin Franklin

Fremont University Orientation

Chapter 6

Followed by their mech companions, the two youths were jit-joting, a style similar to speed skating on Earth, under the arching ceiling of Tiger Walk towards the TAP, the HUB and home.

Our story begins on Vesta, some thousand years into the future. It has taken longer than expected to settle the Solar System, but life in the asteroid belt is in full swing. It appears that many dreams of the past have been realized: Earth's economy and environment are stable, and it is a time of prosperity. The population of the Belt Federation is almost twenty times that of earth, expanding rapidly with almost unlimited space and free energy. Dealings between Earth and Belt are basically friendly but limited due to the high cost of the gravity well and consists mostly of informational commerce and exchange.

It also appears that many dreams of the past have not been realized: there is no time travel, no psi power, no Faster-than-Light travel, and other intelligent life in the Galaxy has not been found.

As a great man observed: it is the best of times, it is the worst of times.

The Belt is a magical place to grow up, there are wonders everywhere! Artificial intelligence is no longer artificial, and the Races of Man are splendid indeed! There are Mechmen, genetically modified Spacemen, Hivemen, eMen, and Borgmen, all living within the society of the Belt. Do you want feathers, blue fur or a tail? Done! Do you want instant access and memory augmentation? Universal traits! A new Religion of Hope is raising its head! Old Religions are remade. Do you want harmony and a strong society? Join a hive! Do you want independence and individual responsibility? Be a Cowboy in your own ship/habitat in the outer reaches! Dress as you please and have anyone, or no one, as your friend. There is Freedom in the Universe!

It is also a time of dark secrets and creases. The Races of Man do not naturally trust each other, and suspicions are an undercurrent. There is a federation Space Navy on patrol, and cops and robbers back home. Unconfirmed sightings of ghost ships are the stuff of legend. Concentrations of strange Mechs lurk in the orbits of the Gas Giants. Hidden in the Kuiper are stories of dark dealings, pirates and slavery away from the light of the sun, and the Cowboys are too independent to care. There is Freedom in the Universe!

This is a story of a few young people, Jon and W0ody, Cat and the Blue Brothers, KaiLin and Abs: Coming of Age on Vesta.

Tiger Walk was the main connection between Fremont University, the birthplace of the liberation of the Mechmen, and the University of Vesta, the first brick and mortar University in the United Federation of Asteroids. The dome of the upper chord of the Walk was back lit from the high soffits that provided the general diffuse illuminations for the many who commuted in this urban setting. The middle third of the tunnel below their feet was dedicated to the mass transit infrastructure of vacuum trains, trams and individual jitneys that plied the local byways for the incessantly mobile population. The lowest third provided the volume for the utilities: the water, light, electrical, and chemical energies that all life required, and finally the disposal of waste being sent down to the lowest Sumatra levels.

They were passing the kiosks and brightly lit storefronts that beckoned the curious with the tailored advertisements beamed at the passerby's optics and sensors, all tastefully muted since the Lady Bird stamped her foot. Along with the other released kids the two youths bounded down thè causeway followed by their crèche mechs, jit-joting around the more sedate older students who most likely were visiting the shops along the arcade. The tunnel's broad slightly convex ceiling overhead was strewn with banners and advertisements of all colors, shapes and illuminations, stretching the full one-hundred-and-fifty-foot width of the street.

Turning left at the TAP Path tunnel access, they moved on towards the Fremont Transit Node. Other students: bright chrome mechmen, stylish women wearing this season's flair, borgmen engaged in active conversation with themselves, buffed out he-men, men of all kinds were streaming towards the HUB as the commute was underway.

So, what do you think about FU's Prep School, he narrow-beamed KaiLin, *Is it awesome or what?* They were passing an older section with its quaint flashing neon and LED strobes, yellow sequential arrows pointing and directing them to this or that shop catering to the university crowd. It sure was easier to ignore, Jonny thought, than the images that were laser painted on his eyeballs whether he wanted them or not, the one time he was able to visit the Zone with his dad. Even so, ROOMS AND CAVES FOR RENT, LEASING AGENT INSIDE did catch his eye.

Wow, he conjured up in his mind a ManCave of his very own when going to the U. *Slow down* cautioned his judge, first things first. Better forget it for now. He would never be able to afford it while going to school. The tension and stress were mounting as he approached his final exams and manhood. Prep school is the essential gate to success he thought.

It's pretty intense she responded, *all I can remember are the large rooms, tons of people and friendly faces everywhere. I was introduced to a million people but cannot remember any names.* She ended with a Victor Borgia click-pop-smiley face and briefly looked over her shoulder.

He glanced sideways at her, still amazed she still hung with him. She was glancing around to see if she knew anyone or who was wearing what. Remembering her in that swimsuit during Spring Break made him realize they weren't kids anymore. *Yeah, more lights, more options, more everything, than we have back in Helena.*

Totally different than Ender's Academy, that's for sure. Glad we're done with classes, just the finals and ceremony left, yahoo! Her hair was dark, almost jet black with deep blue highlights cascading down past her shoulders with swirls and loops, swinging with a slight bounce around the edges as she travelled.

Jonny sometimes couldn't take his eyes off her. She had subdued makeup accenting her nearly naked lips and mild eye shadow of faint manganese violet marking her as the adult she so much desired to be.

He knew that Kai was impatient, frustrated that the required classes hadn't lined up with her birthday, delaying her exams. She couldn't wait for tomorrow to run its lazy path towards her, she wanted to sprint to embrace it, sink her hands into it up to her elbows, towards freedom.

Whatever happened to Abs? He was supposed to be here with us. Frowny guy.

He sent a cryptic stating something popped up, he beamed smiley guy, watching her between jot avoidance tactics. Even though she had completed the coming of age ceremony last month, she hadn't added any body ornaments with exception of the small sapphire nova jewel on the outside of her left eyebrow, which was fine as far as Jonny was concerned. Jonny would be delayed for his ceremony until his birthday on September 27th, by then he would have passed the summer prep school and could challenge the citizenship exams.

They had to slow down as the crowd thickened at the Abalama Street intersection and Jonny was looking into a space of huge blobs of slowly moving light like molten rock contained within crystal cylinders placed under glass chandeliers, *You know, University of Vesta is supposed to be less personal, but a lot many options. Doesn't your sister go to UV?* A rousing techno edition of the classic *"Keep yourself Alive!"* blared from the shop while the blobs vibrated to the beat which was harmonized all across the spectrum.

The two mechs, E^{3}Ching and W0ody, hung back a couple of paces listening, but not engaging their crèche-mates. W0ody had grown up with Jonny and wore a custom work apron, covered with all sorts of jigs and utensils forming a kind of a kilt of tools hanging from his barrel body over his short legs, while E^{3}Ching was smooth like the dolphins that they had seen at the beach. Ching was sporting her/its gloss black look with the subdued blue highlights, matching KaiLin's, like waves breaking across a galaxy.

Yeah, she's been there three years and is majoring in Character Rig development. Jon didn't know what that was but was too embarrassed to ask and didn't have time for a mind search.

Should we talk to her?

No, she's my older sister and thinks she knows everything. Checking out the crowd with her eyes.

So, Jonny, I have been wondering: what are you going to do when you finish school? Jonny looked up to see Kai staring at him expectantly, that small quizzical way she had raising her brow just one millimeter. It caused him to pause, her attention made the world a little brighter. Calmly her right lip slowly showed a trace of a Mona Lisa smile.

They had to come to a stop and wait for a FEDEX truck to complete backing into an alley, as it struggled, stopping, coming back out partway because it made the wrong turn adjustment on the second carriage, then pushing back in. Some yahoo mech in a flame orange vest was trying to direct traffic but instead was being slowly pushed into the alley ahead of the truck.

They started off again, his thoughts were a little stuffy, she was so nice. *I don't know, Sometimes I dream about being a rock miner and finding the motherload somewhere, or playing professional battleball, but it looks like I won't be big enough.*

The TAP was ablaze with shops and kiosks. A white enamel mechman was dominating a corner with what appeared to be a set of bagpipes crossed with a synthesizer, loudly accosting the passersby with its noise.

I sure would like to be part of the mother planet's space elevator project, but it doesn't look like it will start anytime soon, maybe not in my lifetime. When Jonny stepped past, he noticed the “musician” was wearing ear plugs.

Jonny, don't be a goof, who wants to go to Earth? It’s nothing but a big ball of dirt, covered with dirtmen. Smiley face.

Tentatively: *I don't know, I just want to visit.*

Well, I want to travel outbound, she stopped at a tony travel kiosk, with close-ups of Io erupting streaming across the entry, *visit exciting places, go to the Caves of Antiope* (Engineering NOTE 1), *see the rings of Saturn up close, maybe Jupiter, then get involved with the entertainment industry, set some styles, meet famous people, own some bling, impress all my friends, maybe go to the stars, discover an alien civilization.*

Wow, sounds cool, but there aren't any aliens. Smiley face.

Sure there are. They stood and watched as the display changed and showed the jungles of Antiope with its giant girlaughs, heffalumps, helifiknows and other fantastic dinosaur recreations.

Where? We haven't found any evidence. They started up again.

Yes, there is. They've been hiding. The Church of Scientology Renewed has collected all those recordings of abductions, you know.

Yeah, sure they did. How come they don't release them? I mean, just nothin' since Heinlein and Hubbard made the bet. With no cross streets they moved faster, with fewer arcades and more commuters heading towards the HUB and FTN. W0ody and Ching kept up effortlessly as was the way of crèche mechs who had over a decade of proximity with their human friends, W0ody's belt chiming with the movement.

They began jit-jotting again as the commute sped up, eventually entering into a smooth jive. *The government is suppressing it, they've lost another probe out in the Oort and they say it was intercepted.*

Intercepted? Where did you hear this? Jonny turned his head away as Kai swept her gaze across him. He didn't want her to think he had mooneyes.

The WET site I saw last night says it's true, and made a compelling case for aliens not wanting mankind to visit the stars. We are not good enough. That's why we haven't these thousands of years.

No, it's because it's hard to do. My dad says the devil is in the details. It's easy to dream, hard to build.

Well, it's true, we haven't gone, and our probes are missing. They were passing the pit where a new complex was growing, the distant welders like stars on the outside. *So there.* Smiley face took away the sting.

Jon glanced in the deepening cave as they went by but couldn't get any details except for size and the ubiquitous wafting scent of hydraulic oil. It was huge! *Com'on Kai, that's silly, do you really believe aliens are hiding here in the solar system?* They had to begin slowing down as they approached the HUB and the glitzy businesses began to reappear.

Sure, you betcha. Look at the pyramids. Gotta be, we can't be the only ones, and there have been so many sightings for thousands of years.

Reducing their travel to a walk, they passed under the beltway into the HUB, and then merged onto Brazoria Rail Way. He loved to verbally spar with her, she was so sharp and quick and took him seriously, *OK, but my dad is a ten-ninety and says "Show me", as in: you walk away and let me look without you looking over my shoulder, I will check it out without interference.* He looked at her directly into her eyes: *Where do you think they're hiding out? The Fermi Addendum is pretty compelling too.*

Could be they've been here all the time, the Icky reptiles that run the world since before time. Or it could be the Oort, or maybe teaming up with the Mechs out in the Trojans. You know, they say Kenny has disappeared. They recommenced jit-joting towards the NODE.

Kenny has disappeared? Surprised guy, *Is that true?* Kenny was the most massive and famous of the solid metal asteroids formed during the consolidation of the protoplanets discovered in Jupiter's L-4 Lagrangian Point.: *I bet it isn't true, just that no one wants to visit that far out, because with the war rumors coming from the Trojans, so no one wants to go out to check.*

Or maybe the Skips have a cloaking device? But is hard to imagine the ability to disappear a 10-klick rock. Jonny only noticed that Migh Way turned out to be an alley as a cargo handler filled it to the overhead with black and red 55-gallon drums. They passed Resnik Park with its fabulous singing trees and glowing flowers on their left. The notes of a barber shop quartet could be heard as they went by.

Kai began to skip and sash shay turning her jit-jot into a kind of a dance, totally shifting gears as only she could do. She continued: *Or maybe, I will stay closer to home, the Antiope Wunderland sounds awesome! Flying and ancient animals and oceans and clouds and weather! We could all go together, and then after school start a destination spa to capture all the toureestas. Jonny, we could do so much, what with your hard work, and my artist skills and Abs' money, we could be rich.*

Yeah, with Abs's money, we could be rich. He actually gave her a smile with that comment.

No, you goof, with his money we could be rich and doing something important. Jonny, you have to dream big! Mom says enjoy life when you're young.

They paused for a yellow cab turning right onto High Drive: *My mom says life's a bitch, then you die.*

Oh Jonny, that's not right. We could be neighbors forever, and be surrounded by friends, and have discussions every evening like we talked about. The ancient Greeks created a fabulous civilization by sitting around with Plato and Socrates just tossing out ideas until the good ones remained.

That sounds wonderful, I have always thought loyalty is the foundation of friendship, and friendship is the foundation of life. Living with one's friends is the ultimate goal and we could do it together.

Would you like Abs there too? KaiLin was suddenly serious, watching carefully, not smiling, a little furrow between her eyes: *You seemed to have drifted apart after he moved away.*

Crossing Goa Way, he responded, *Of course, I want him around, he's my best friend. He only had to move away because of the money and the divorce. It hurts him more than us. Once we all achieve manhood and citizenship, we can make all our own decisions and find a place to settle and work. Like you, I want a home where I am surrounded by friends like Abs, where we can discuss and plan like this always*

Woody whispered a tightbeam to Jonny *"Stop talking Jonny, this isn't about you. you can't learn anything by talking." Boy howdy,* Jonny thought to himself, *why was it so hard to stop trying to be a Topper? Why did W0ody have to act as his conscience?*

Noticing his distraction, Kai beamed *What was that all about, Jonny?*

Oh, W0ody was just commenting on how well thought out your ideas were, and maybe you had more ideas about how this group could work? They had to wait at a signal while the cruisers that were going up and down Wright Way slowly strutted their stuff.

Kai's mood shifted instantly... *We'll all have to finish finals and graduate the Academy, duh, then we will all go to Prep together.*

FREEMONT

HUB and City Center

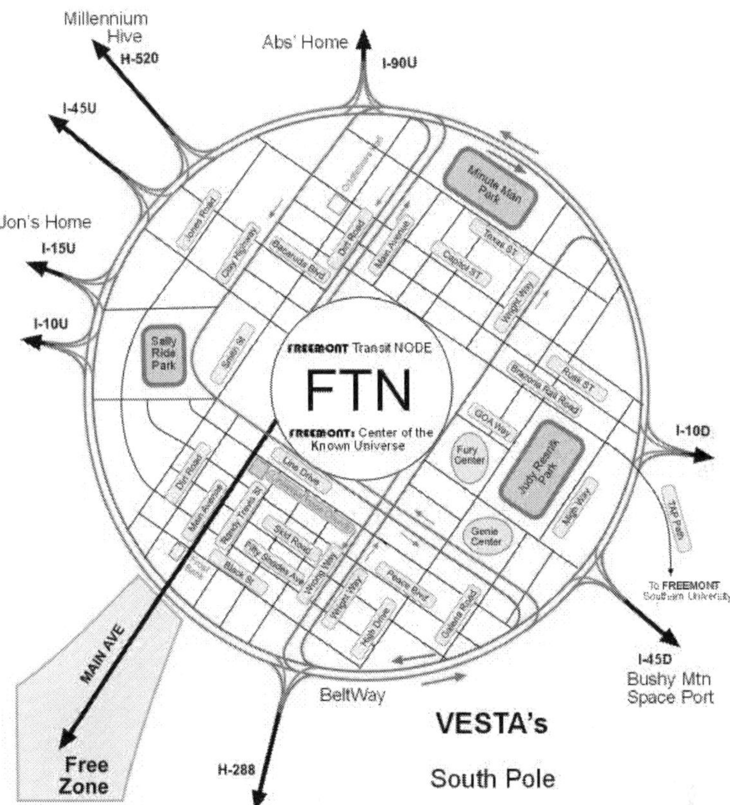

You need to complete your coming of age ceremony on your birthday, Jonny, to catch up. We need to combine our talents and fields of study and create our own dream team from the get-go.

Abs says he wants to fund a glamorous naturopathic medical clinic combined with a high-end spa-fitness center and attract all the wealthy with leading edge treatments. We can offer nano- and genetic treatments for buffing up clients without resorting to regimes and workouts, as well as offer the latest in cosmetic surgery.

Woody and E[3]Ching stayed close. KaiLin confided: *First thing I am going to do is get a labret made from a miniature self-contained biosphere.*

Are you sure? Those seem to get in the way.

Sure as a fart on a finger tug, they are all the rage. Abs says I can be CMO and meet all the clients and I want to be cherry when I chat up the patrons. He says Krage will focus on the medical degree, Obee will take business classes and you will run the gym.

Wow, when did you get together? He never talked to me about it. The signal changed and they could see the NODE entrance in the distance.

Last week when we sneaked into the Zone.

He turned his surprised face and looked at her, astonished by her illicit activities: *You sneaked into the Zone, wow! How?*

Don't you worry. Abs says we will be famous. He met Shak the superstar and asked him to be on the board of directors. We can meet him and all the Vid stars like the Prince and the Mother and the others that are so well known they only have one name. We will have the best toys and clothes and be the envy of our school.

Stepping around a lagging pedestrian, and while watching the play of emotions across KaiLin's face, Jonny collided with a citizen. *Damm, I should've jotted when I jitted.* The bare-chested person was a he-man with a shaved skull topped by a queue of dark brown hair and wearing half-face Iridium Glasses. He was covered with a multitude of black tattoos of the Suri gang style and was staring a Jonny with an impassive look, stock still, menacing.

“I'm sorry sir”, Jonny muttered out loud while repeating the apology via the common band. Still, the man did not stir. Jonny started to step around to his left, but the man suddenly moved sideways to block his move. Jonny stopped; he didn't know what to do. He couldn't see the man's eyes.

KaiLin came up from behind and looked past the man: *What's wrong Jonny?* She tightbeamed.

Don't know. I bumped this fella, and now he won't let me pass. Jonny started to his right and the statue moved exactly the same amount to block. Jonny stood fast, beginning to get very nervous, here in the big city without his parents. They weren't that far from the docks or the Zone.

“I apologize again, sir. May I pass?”

Nothing.

KaiLin walked around to stand next to Jonny. “May we pass, kind sir?”

Nothing

Then, from nowhere, the statue started to laugh uncontrollably. Jonny and KaiLin jerked backwards in alarm. The man continued to laugh uproariously, bending slightly at the knees and waist, becoming gangly-crazy, but as Jonny and KaiLin continued to back up he started to wave his arms about, eventually signaling them to stay even though he could not stop his chortles. They backed up another step to put more than a body length between themselves and this madman, who at this point was choking out “Wait, wait, wait” while he got himself under control.

By this time a small crowd had stopped to watch this play unravel.

"You've been pranked!" the apparition yelled as Abs whipped off his dark glasses. "It's me, you fool!" and the laughter began anew as a red heat crawled up Jonny's face. Damm! This is worse than awful, and KaiLin here to watch his foolishness and fear.

Abs had a hard time getting himself contained, *You should have seen your face! My glasses recorded the whole thing! It's hilarious!*

It's not funny! Jonny beamed, *Not funny at all!*

He started around, but Abs stopped him. *Aw man, it was so funny, you were so serious, LOL, you will like it after you cool down.*

Yeah, right Jonny intoned, *like anyone likes being made fun of.*

Aw, it was funny and you know it. Anyways, you guys wanted me here for the orientation, so here I am!

Abs, KaiLin beamed, *where were you, we have been here since nine, and its four o'clock now.*

I was getting ready to startle you. And it sure was worth it! I knew you would cover for me, so I spent the afternoon getting tricked out.

Abs, John beamed angrily, *this wasn't funny at all.*

Aw Jonny, you're such a sourpuss. You should have seen Obee. When I pranked him, he started spitting out so many of those words of his in that crazy language that the translator couldn't even keep up! He was frothing!

Abs, I'm disappointed in you, growled KaiLin, *how are we going to become adults and start a business if you can't be serious?*

Hey guys, lighten up. We only go around once, and we can be serious after all the tests and ceremonies. Right now, I have a few months of freedom and I am working on our project twenty-four-seven, broken up by some small fun ideas. So, lay off. KaiLin, I will apologize to Obee, OK? You OK Jonny boy? No hard feelings?

Yah, no hard feelings, but don't do it again, OK?

OK, OK, never that prank again. But keep your head up, I am still going to have fun. I will just figure it out. Let's keep going to the NODE, I know you need to get home. KaiLin? Can you come over tonight? We need to review the program concepts I had developed. I can get a car to take you home when we're done. How about it?

I'm not sure Abs, I should talk to my mom about the orientation and had planned to start studying with Jonny for the end of school exams. You should come.

As they entered the NODE from the Brazoria I90-U entrance, Jonny noted the scanner's and detector's silent but almost invisible green beams were doing their sweeping thing without the color changes that indicated warning issues. Jonny thought about what Kai and Abs were discussing. Jonny had a small start of anxiety, Abs was smarter than him and sailed along on natural talent but wasn't into slogging through basic memorization to build foundations, no sir, not him. And it would cut into his quality time with Kai.

Come on Kai, its Friday night, no school tomorrow, we can get some wicked work accomplished. Dad's team sent me a killer proposal, but I want you to look at it in its rough state for the big picture before we polish it up. Jonny won't mind going to study alone, after all, it's just mind-numbing repetition. Let's go. You can give it a shot, OK?

Abs, I'm not sure, I will check with mom, but no promises.

Great! Hey Jonny, Kai and I are going to take the 90-U express up to the Snowman. I know you and W0ody need to continue to the 15-U, we'll split here. Kai will see you at school next week, OK?

Well, OK, I just thought... boy, this wasn't working out.

Hey buddy, sorry about the prank, I'll make it up to you. I will see what I can do to help with the space elevator thing. Perhaps get us a tour of the Luna Labs or something after first quarter of college. How does that sound, huh?

Sounds great Abs, but you know I can't afford anything like that. Jonny noticed he had unconsciously started to fidget and put a clamp on it. He was getting uncomfortable.

Don't you worry, I'll get you covered. Hey Kai, let's roll. We've got places to go and people to meet, and we're all the better for it.

No Abs, I checked, mom agrees with me, I need to go back to Helena with Jonny to study.

Kai, come on... it'll only be a little while.

No Abs, you finished a year ahead of us and don't remember the effort necessary to cross the finish line. We have just a week left at the Academy and we should be focused. You are free, so enjoy it. I need Jonny to help me with my math, only fifteen percent pass on their first attempt, I won't be able to do it alone. Jonny's ears perked up on what KaiLin was saying.

Please Kai? His huge grin was infectious, Jonny almost told Kai to go ahead.

Abs, no.

KaiLin, one more please? Another dazzling smile both to KaiLin and to Jonny. *The chauffeur can get you home.*

No Abs! Can't you take no for an answer?

OK, OK. Can't blame a guy for trying.

Thanks, we have to go.

OK, you two lovebirds, Jonny and Kai looked at each other a little bit scandalized, *get on home. I will set up the biggest party you will ever see to celebrate your Academy Graduation. Be ready to rock and roll guys.* With his overwhelming good humor and smile he gave Kai a hug and Jonny a wink, and without further ado, turned and strolled towards the I-90U entrance.

The two mechs looked at each other and mentally shrugged, then became one again with their focus on KaiLin and Jonny.

Wow, I thought you were gone.

They turned left toward the I-15U concourse, mixing back into the crowd staying to the right of the big tunnel.

I will be glad to help you with math, he continued, *but I really need help with language arts. Why did they make us read Lord of the Flies anyways?* They passed the H-520 where Jonny sometimes worked doing electrical service with his dad and the 45-U and H-405 before coming to the 15-U which was their passage to Helena Crater and home.

Jonny, let's get home and get some sleep. Saturday will be here soon, and we could get a good four hours of study in after your work with your dad, OK? Then graduation will be a piece of cake. She gave him that quirky stare and a gleam.

Yep, let's do it. I'll need it. Thanks Kai, he thought without beaming, as he looked into her dark eyes. The mechs, as usual, were quiet.

2. Personal Truths

That each of us individually perceive through our senses and believe to be true.

"We get too soon old and too late smart."
- Kelly Freas

"Good character is not formed in a week or a month.
It is created little by little, day by day.
Protracted and patient effort is needed to develop good character."
Heraclitus

First Day of Work

Chapter 7

[1865] Nikki ducked his head and scrunched his right shoulder forward as if to ward off the bothersome noise the other students were making, Herr Doktor Professor Reichsfreiherren had just demonstrated another wonder! Couldn't those creatures just shut up? He focused again on the table where the invisible hands were moving the toys about again.

Perhaps the little metal soldiers were actually motivated by tiny internal windup clock springs? No! The Frieherr would never stoop to such! He had stated that the "forces electrique" were uncommon, but natural. Nikki carefully wrote down and drew the symbols and equations Herr Professor presented to the class. His mother's native tongue was a sweet whisper in his ear compared to this Latin, Croatian and German he had to learn.

At least the mathematics was clean, it was beautiful how the calculus took the many disparate reckonings and folded them up like Russian Dolls into four simple statements. He could almost see them dancing in his mind. He knew he could dance them if he strained hard enough.

Oh, there was work to do. Ignore the gibbering from his classmates and their fascination with girls. Push away the drama, he was not going to be like they, he was going to discover miracles, he was going to be famous, he was going to make his father, mother and uncles proud!

Jonny trailed as his father stumped along the access tunnel towards the air handling yard. Pops' articulated joints were hissing steam and smelling slightly of the hydraulics that kept him limber. W0ody, Jonny's crèche-mate, attended quietly and slightly behind. Their first day of work following the last class of public school, with only exams ahead.

Pops, we got to get you a new harness, that old body of yours smacks of last century Gothic. Jonny tightbeamed: W*hen I become a man in September, I want to use my first pay to help you out, OK? It makes me tired just looking at you.*

A slight squeal accompanied Augustus's movement as he swiveled his head towards his son, his gray goatee sliding across his breastplate: *Jonathon, save your money for your own needs, this old body has plenty of klicks left in it. Besides, the lacquered surface is all composite and provides PPE for me when in the high voltage substations. You are going to get tired of the standard Personal Protective Equipment you're going to have to wear. I like my custom shell, thank you very much.* They continued down the basic corridor, finally coming to a stop in front of the garage entrance proclaiming "Authorized Personnel Only!"

The Millennium Hive had recently been established here on Vesta, and construction within Lucilla Crater providing a spike in employment for many of the trades, including the Miller family: electricians.

Surely you could upgrade to any number of smooth MODs with smaller and lighter electrical-mechanical elements rather than that steam pack on your back, W0ody noted while Gus palmed open the access.

W0odrow Wilson Miller was a squatty male Mech about four and a half feet tall, a broad rotor with staves for a body. His motive force was hidden beneath a kilt of tools of all sorts which hung in layers about the lower skirt of the staves, nothing more like than a woman's ancient bustle. When excited, his lower body would suddenly rotate independently of his torso causing the tools to swing out with centrifugal force. W0ody was, by all accounts, infatuated with motors.

Ah W0ody, you will find that Humans can sometimes perform better than Mechmen in the electrical industry. Gus's body covering of simulated cherry red leather and non-magnetic copper/ brass, as well as the pistons and gearing, was a sight to behold compared to the austere surroundings of the newly completed atmosphere distribution center on level Mike. The Hive was noted for its efficiency and utility and did not show the vibrant displays of color and character that was common throughout the Belt Federation. Millennium's focus was on fiscal strategies and raw survival within the ever expanding economies of the solar system. In their hive minds, pretty was for the slow and trampled.

Gus continued as they started entering the air handler rooms. *These steam pots of mine are immune to EMP, which is a known hazard when working in the high voltage, high amperage and high power distribution systems required by modern civilization.*

There is nothing like some yahoo paralleling two gigawatt generators out of phase and creating electrical fireworks to light up your eyeballs and short circuit your neck connector. These curios continue to work in that environment, because they are chemically derived and ignore EMP, just as the human body does. As the team crossed the foyer and the occupancy sensors brought the lighting up to spec, Jonny pointed out a suspended fixture swinging in the airflow surrounding the electrical cabinets ten aisles over, creating a moving cone of light in the dark distance.

Shutting the access, Gus broadcast on the local WET "*The problem with high tech: the unintended consequences*." He marched over to a holding locker and keyed it open, pointed out tool belts and a ladder. A tiny relief valve lifted on his right leg and Jonny watched as fluid gurgled back through the transparent flex lines back into the storage tank on Gus's back. *Take some zip-ties out of the bin and secure both ends of that luminaire to the threaded rod attached to the ceiling. Do not stand on the top rungs of the ladder, you can get seriously hurt. Get a tall enough ladder so you do not have to. Don't want today's effort end up on a Tube broadcast.*

Why can't the bots complete the work?

The voltage and magnetic fields created by the substations under our feet in level November interfere with their coding.

As they started on their job W0ody remarked out loud so it wouldn't be broadcast and overheard… "Why did the Mechman cross the Code?" "Why?" "To show the 'bot it could be done!" "Ah man! You're sounding more and more like Wild Bill." Holding the stepladder for his human brother, "I got to practice on you Jonny, there is so much to learn before I can make jokes like Bill." When at the level of the light, Jonny slipped zip-ties around the ends of the fixture, then looking at the threaded rod that hung from the ceiling to the tops of the cabinets below, and supporting what looked like horizontal ladders carrying pipes, he was tempted to swing out and hold to the ladder by one hand and secure the ties with the other at arm's reach. But...

Looking down, Jonny asked, *Hey W0ody, hold tight to the ladder, would you?* Jonny cast a glance at the sharp edges and corners of the pipe racks and cabinets as he began to reach out. W0ody below called out *I've got the ladder, but are you sure you want to hang over that far?*

Jon looked down, and looked across, and down again. What a bother! It's gonna be a pain to climb down and readjust the ladder, if he could just reach out a little more to connect the tie, but that takes two hands, he wondered if he could do it with just one hand. He set the tag end of the tie between his fingers and the snug pushed into his palm, and reached out to wrap it around the all-thread, he manipulated his fingers slowly until the end was in his palm with the snug, as he attempted to place the end in the snug with his pinky, the whole thing snapped out of his hand and sprang across the aisle to the next cabinet set. Bother!

W0ody commented in a casual message, *It may be possible to move the ladder a few feet*, he paused, then yelled "Then we might finish the job in a timely manner!"

Jonny stared at him angrily, knowing W0ody was right. He bounced down the steps and jostled the ladder over a few feet "Satisfied?!" Swarming up the ladder again, he was able to attach the supports without having to lean out and was done in moments. Clambering back down, then taking a deep breath, a slow wry smile crossed Jonny's face *Thanks.*

As they were stowing the gear, Augustus called, *OK guys, fun's over. Did you hear me call you?*

No, but we were sharing jokes out loud.

OK. Maybe it's a dead spot, but it seemed as if comms went down for a minute.

The real job for today is to pass control wiring on aisle fourteen between all the racks and cabinets over to the PLCs along the wall for future controls and alarms. I will show you how to terminate the cables. He laid out some wire terminal blocks and strands of CAT cable and opened a toolbox with an assortment of cutters, snips and test equipment. Selecting a stainless tool that looked like a spider mouth part attached to a screwdriver handle, *This is called a punch-down, the cabling carries very fast data flow and requires reducing interference to a minimum. It fits this, which is a one-sixty-six block.*

The small pistons at Gus's elbows were sliding in and out as he proceeded to unwrap a small amount of wiring from the bundle, while the tiny fluid filled hoses jumped as the poppet valves opened and closed. *To accomplish this, we cannot have more than one half inch of loose wires, otherwise it picks up static.* Gus placed the loose blue wires into the small cradles of the one-sixty-six. *We need to unwind the stranded pairs just that amount, then lay them across the terminals. The punch-down will strip the insulation, nestle the conductors into the landings and trim the excess away all in one step.* The punch-down gave a small snap as Gus forced it down onto the block, and a small amount of cable ends popped away to the floor.

Reminds me, Jonny, here are some safety glasses, neither one of you want to scratch your optical lenses, so W0ody, safety lens down... Go ahead and practice on this block until you feel comfortable, then I will get you started.

OK Jonny, you first.

Thanks. His first attempt did not trim the ends *Perhaps you need to hold the tool more vertically,* W0ody offered, but by Jonny's third attempt, he seemed to be getting the idea. Out loud and sarcastically he quipped, "your turn Sherlock."

It's Sherlock 'Ohms, to you, Jonny Watt, W0ody beamed, making another one of his electrical puns.

W0ody pulled his punch down tool out his belt loop and brought it to the one sixty-six block, he used the index finger of his left hand to control the small wires, and with his right he proceeded to trim and snap the wires into place. A bright light from W0ody's miner's loop illuminated the work and was followed by three quick snaps as he made the rest of the connections. Gus had watched quietly from a short distance away.

OK guys, Jonny grab your tool. Inside of the locker next to the tool crib are boxes of wire that you are going to need. Grab the ones that say CAT Infinity on the outside and bring two over to the first rack in aisle fourteen. They gathered their material and followed over to the mentioned rack which had been opened on locking hinges.

Inside they saw on the left a column like the one-sixty-six block, but rather than twelve inches long it extended up six feet. W0ody and Jonny looked at each other. “I think I'd rather be in school,” W0ody muttered.

Dad, why can't the nanos do this? Jonny had a hard time keeping the complaint out of his transmission. *Because, like the 'bots, the magnetic fields mess with the communal CODE of the nanos and next thing you know they're weaving sticky webbing traps outside someone's door. If they miss even one out of a thousand, it could cause catastrophic damage. So, it is up to us.* As Gus started pulling the CAT from its box, his backpack APU kicked in with the demand on fluid function, the chemical reactions increased the temperatures and pressures, causing momentary steam leaks in the carapace. It was always so wonderfully archaic Jonny noted. Dad then slid the bundled conductors gently into the rack through a hole in the top.

Note that the stranded pairs in the cable are color coded, and they match colors on the terminal block on the inside of the door. He handed Jonny the punch-down.

Dad, there must be over a hundred of these wires.”

One hundred and twenty-eight to be exact.”

Why do we have to do it? You said work was fun for you.

As it is written: ***‘Life must work to sustain Life’***. He began showing them how to lay the CAT in the channel behind the block and turn it into the cradle.

I guess work is satisfying for me, because I have accepted the repetitive part of it. Perhaps ninety percent of what I do is recurrent, and when I was your age it took me a little while to accept that, since everything I did up to that point was new. But upon reflection, work has a lot of repeated steps, and I learned to relax and just do it. The learning and excitement occur over a longer period of time, so the repetition becomes my Zen part of the day. Then it isn't so hard.

In school they say if we don't enjoy our job, we should search for one that we like.

Matching the blue-white pair to the blue-white cradles Gus demonstrated the punch, his shoulder joint hissing *The blue-white pair can carry 48-volt power as well as data.*

With regards to school, sometimes what they teach isn't quite right. Each vested group in our society is called an estate. The fourth estate is the news media, the fifth is the educational industry. The educators don't realize the job market doesn't exist for people to enjoy: farmers don't grow food and give it away for free because they're bored, they do it because they can trade their hard work for the hard work of others, and everyone benefits.

If you end up working with people you like and work you are suited for, you can ignore and actually use the humdrum. I'm sorry, this is a topic I feel passionate about, and I probably have talked your ears off.

W0ody pulled out his punch down again and began on the remainder of the first cable under Gus's watch. Jon stepped behind him and opened the door on W0ody's back, exposing the magnifying monitor. Jonny could see what W0ody was seeing, as the photomultiplier's output was repeated there.

Gus also had his oculars shifting and sliding one over another until he had an optimum magnification and focus on the mechkid's work. *But Dad, my teachers point out all the successful and happy people that we should aspire to.*

They also say don't end a sentence with a preposition. As he stood the small turbines in his knees were slightly audible as they sped up and down the spectrum. *Anyways, ask them if they enjoy grading homework, and if not, why aren't they successful artists?* W0ody had completed the first cable and Gus tugged on it to verify it being secure.

As Jonny crouched down to do his first set, he said dejectedly *Dad! It's gonna take forever for us to complete this job! One-hundred and twenty-eight times fourteen plus the runs to the PLCs plus the punch downs there. I'm gonna be a dead man before we are finished!*

Gus watched gently from behind Jonny's side and asked, *W0ody, did you record the time of your work? "Yessir." Would you calculate the time necessary to complete the project?*

I estimate three months plus or minus a week. It's only a SWAG though.

Well Jonny, here is your first weekend job, and it will be easier when you find a rhythm rather than fight. You know what makes it easier?

Grumpily, *What?*

You and W0ody get paid every day for your time. You will be done in September when you can become a citizen, and you will be able to make your own choices. So, I'll be over by the PLCs cutting software and Ladder-logic for the systems if you have questions or problems.

A word of advice Jonathon: It takes about three years to get good at a job, and not to feel inadequate somewhat. Give yourself that amount of time before quitting, quitting on anything.

With a laugh out loud, "And, remember, this builds character!"

As his dad walked away like a soft tea kettle, Jonny muttered "This makes school look like fun."

Small chunks of colored wire began to fly, *But you know, we graduate the Academy soon, finish up work and Prep School by the end of summer, pass the Citizen exams, bank some scratch, become free men, and hang out with KaiLin, Abs and the gang. Can't get much better than that.*

You can say that again brother.

3. Modeled Truths

are the best available descriptions of **Universal Truths** that have been independently examined, developed by consensus, and shared.

"The capacity to learn is a gift; The ability to learn is a skill;
The willingness to learn is a choice.
- Brian Herbert

"Whoever walks with the wise will become wise, but the companion of fools suffers harm."
Solomon

University of Vesta Orientation

Chapter 8

KaiLin and Jonny joined the cohort exiting Lander Hall Auditorium and headed up the Cougar Crawl towards the TAP and home. *That place is huge! There must have been thousands, all waiting to gain entry to the University of Vesta.*

They say UV has over one-hundred-thousand students on campus and a million telecommuting.

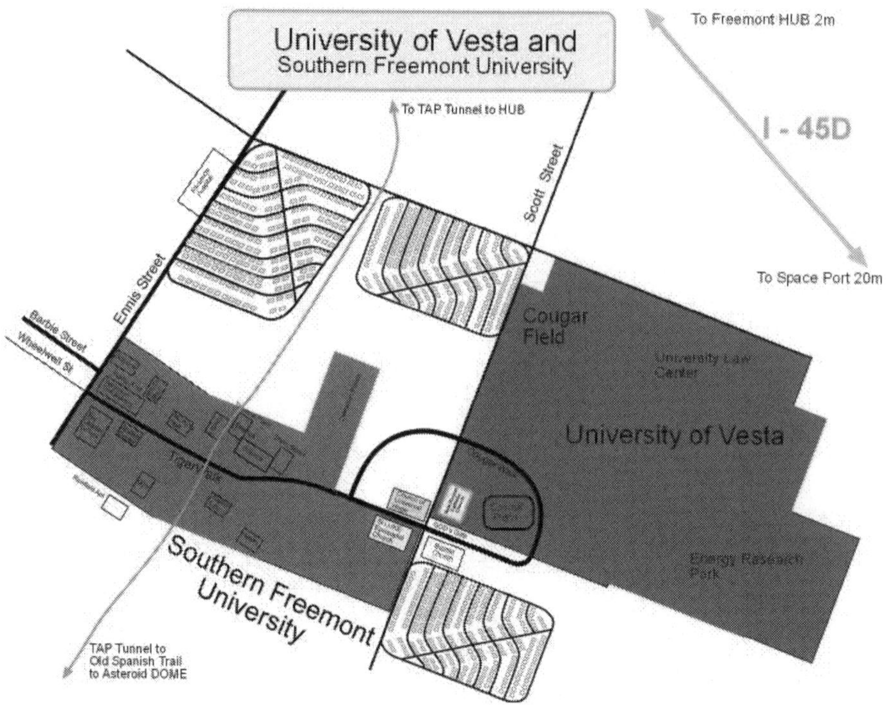

The Drexler Law School was on their right and the Fly Slamma Jamma Fraternity annexes on the left with their boys hanging out the windows, cat calling everyone in sight. *Well, that's what you get when you have the best reputation in the Universe.* The two mechs reduced their distance from their friends. You never know.

Solar system, Jonny, solar system. We don't know what's out there. She reached back a hand so they wouldn't get separated in the hustling mob. Jonny took an extra skip to step up and catch her hand momentarily. It was comforting to have a friend amongst the newness.

Now the calls were joined by air horns and yells of *"Fresh Meat!"* and *"Frosh Meat"*

You're still on that "There's aliens amongst us" kick?

Striving for attention, the bored jocks started dropping from the windows and trampolining back up doing layouts and gainers, followed by half baronies to land balanced on the windowsills.

Kai made a face at the noise and wrinkled her nose: *Sure, although there are more important things to worry about, like Wednesday's finals and Friday's Graduation.* One ambitious mech decked out in a black and red squirrel wing suit and an unexpected set of reindeer antlers on his head was doing a stately fall from the ceiling, spinning sedately count-clockwise towards a kiddy pool on the lawn as the rest of the house was shooting him with single shot lasers. Each time they connected a loud bell would clang.

Well, if we study as effectively as we did last weekend, we should be more than ready. They were finally clearing Greek Row and were approaching the boundary to Fremont University and U of V. Jonny let Kai's hand go, she seemed not to notice while glancing around.

Kai slowed down and turned to him. *To be honest, I'm not sure if I can. I'm losing all my motivation this week. School's becoming a drag, I'm tired of it.*

Aren't you excited about finishing up and getting your citizenship?

They were in front of the sororities, *Yes, but no. I want to be an adult, but I guess it's like wanting but not caring, you know?*

Really? You don't care?

Not really Jonny, I mean, I don't wake up wanting to get up, I dread it. It has finally it hit me that mom and dad broke up. I lost all my get and go, as dad used to say.

We've only a week left; you can do it!

I am not sure, not sure at all.

Come on KaiLin, you can't mean this, after all we've been through.

She was waving at someone she recognized on a balcony, *I know I'm supposed to like it, and get energized, but I just can't. The only thing I like to do is hang with Abs, he's fun to be around and has the coolest stuff. School is what I'm supposed to do.*

But Abs took a year off so he could graduate with us. You could study with him.

That's not fair Jonny. Abs is so smart he doesn't have to study. I have to. And when he gets all energized, he can sit and study forty-eight hours straight.

I'm sorry about this Kai, is there anything I can do?

No, I just have to handle it is all. Suck it up, you know.

They went on without talking for a while.

Finally, KaiLin, *Jonny, let's turn after the Interurban Guys onto Evanston where the two schools join. Abs showed me a shortcut home last week.* Jonny felt a twinge of anxiety at the mention of Abs and Kai together. He hushed it aside.

OK, where do we go? Walking between a Baptist Church on their left and a New Roman Catholic Church, they turned right and began to travel into the lessor parts of Fremont. They soon passed the Rocket Lounge and the famous statue in front of Lenin 'n Things. The crèche-mechs were taking in all the details to sort out later in dreamland. W0ody's torso spun around a number of times.

Right up there at the end is a private access called God's Gate that connects the campus to Scott Street and the TAP. Abs said a number of religions bought the tunnel, and anyone can pass for free if they are willing to spend ten minutes with one of the preachers. We get to pick which one. Saves about a half hour on the trip back. Let's give it a try. She gave Jonny a warm smile and walked closer with him.

As they approached the cul-de-sac, Jonny observed that there seemed to be about ten different denominations, from the One hundred and Forty Fourth day Adventist, to the Revised and Reformed Church of Scientology V, Old Fellows Hall, Church of Hope and others he barely recognized.

Jonny, do you have a preference which one we pick? She smiled again at him.

Each small gate had its own clergy and lineup of gate applicants, the Churches of Hope and Understanding had the most, while the Adventists and Old Fellows had none. Jonny noted the rest had two to five people waiting at the gate. *Do we go through one at a time or twos or each group gets to go together, do you know?*

When Abs took me through, we went in as a larger group. Do we want traditional or something off the beaten track?

Anything except The Church of Hope. I know their Mantra. You go girl.

With a wry smile she led him to the arched entrance of the Church of Understanding as the initial group passed through: *Let's go here, this is where Abs took us last time. It was so inspirational.* Jon paused for a second after she said this, then continued on. The priest or pastor or whatever, Jonny thought, was a borg comprised of two heads, one a trim and handsome older woman, and the mech person just a smooth silver ovoid with hints of character where the mouth, nose and eyes would go. The mostly human body had perched upon a tall stool with her/its legs tucked under the seat

As they approached, the borg got off her/its chair and nodded both heads in greetings: *Welcome Strangers, to the House of Understanding. May I assist you towards your serenity? My name is Angel,* said the human part. *I divine that the two mechs behind you are part of your group, and possibly crèche mates.*

Motioning to W0ody and E³Ching, *Come precious children, so you too can be included in our simple talks, my name is Michael,* the mech part softly intoned.

With a slight twist of her torso and dipping of her head Kai looked at the borg and said out loud: *May we use your passage to return to the NODE, Honored Zee?*

Certainly, my children, but before you pass, we invite you to be our guests so that we may break bread in our companionship. Five seats slid out of the floor, one behind each of them, the method of extrusion was undetectable to Jonny. A plate of wafers was lowered from overhead, its support also invisible. As he sat, he was startled by a huge shape moving to their right. Michael noticed his jerk and softly stated *That is but our friend, T'za. He has adapted the body of a troll for his journey.*

T'za completely filling an archway with just its head and shoulders, a small People's Scout spaceship snuggled under its left arm. Hair like seaweed covered its right eye down to the floor, while the left observed them blindly from a blank milky globe. It began to ponderously scratch its scalp with an enormous fingernail the size of a shovel, creating a small shower of who-knows-what falling to the dirt.

I guess you don't have to worry about thugs, Jonny quipped.

No. Angel said, *we don't.*

Children said Michael, *what do you know of the Church of Understanding, sometimes known as Grok?*

Not much, replied KaiLin, *and my apology gentle savants, I am KaiLin, this is Jonny, and our companions are W0ody and E*^{3}*Ching.*

I heard the Groks are mysterious and are a bunch of mystics, announced E^{3}Ching. Jonny was surprised at the Kai creche-mate's interaction; it was out of character for KaiLin's sister.

That's a good start. The Church of Understanding tries to perfect our relationship with an infinite universe. Since we can see and feel only what our senses tell us, even the stars only exist as our eyes and nerves interpret, Kai gave Jonny a look, *and our infinite universe is mysterious in so many ways, we start by looking within ourselves, unconstrained by logic and science.* Jonny looked back at Kai, who gave him a minute lift of her brows, then returned her attention and continued observing the borg intently.

How do we do that?

Good question Kai, Michael responded, *we must follow the seven-fold ways which emulates the known dimensions of the Universe.*

The first way which is all we need to discuss today is self-medication, I mean meditation, Jonny had heard of mech-heads making Freudian slips, but had never heard one. Michael continued, *which is initiated in the temple and then followed daily for the rest of your lives. You will then discover the basic truths behind the Spirituality which is the foundation of the factual Universe.*

How do I learn to meditate? Jonny was startled at KaiLin's intensity.

As I said, Michael repeated patiently, *you will be taught in the Temple. It is one of the mysteries of our faith.*

Who do I see about going to the Temple?

You can apply at the Church in person, but you must be a citizen.

I have to wait to be a citizen, why?

Because you have to be able to legally obligate yourself to keep our secrets safe, as well as participate in adult rites. Children cannot.

So, when I gain citizenship at the end of summer, I can apply? John and the mechs were motionless during the interaction.

Yes, my child.

We will be there.

We will be here waiting for you. Michael and Angel followed them as far as the entry arch as they said their farewells.

Wow, I am surprised, this sounds so right, I have always known the Universe was spiritual. What more do you want from us?

Nothing my child, you are free to go.

I'll be back. Jonny noticed T'za was observing them intently under its eyebrow. Could it be one of the fabled Animen?

We look forward to that. Goodbye our children.

Making their goodbyes they parted from the monk. Jonny was amazed at the way Kai had become vitalized, so different than just minutes earlier and her funk about school. It was if she was being lit up from inside by some kind of light.

As they continued down Evanston, it turned into the Scott tunnel heading towards Abalama Street. Kai eyes darted about looking at their surroundings, *Wow, Jonny, we really need to get our citizenship examination passed. That holy man back there has opened my emotions to something needed.*

Really, in what way Kai?

Well, there must be a brazillion religions, and I haven't heard them all. Mother's Hellfire Church is strict, and the Universal Hope Church you belong to seems good, but this Grok business, it sounds like the real deal for me. She paused breathlessly, *When Abs took me through last week, I didn't really pay attention. I can really relate to the emotional and spiritualty basis Angel talked about. I really want to learn it.* Kai brushed his hand as they started jit-jotting down the passage as the crowd began to spread out, followed by their shadows.

Jonny was surprised at her intensity and change in demeanor.

She continued and unconsciously caressed his hand again.

So, let's get focused on our studies. I know I can force myself to work super hard at the prep classes if you work with me. She paused, *I think we ought to apply to Fremont University, we should be able to maximize our talents there.*

Jonny was acutely aware where KaiLin had touched him. His skin rang with the memory. *Copy that. How'd you do on last week's placement exams?* They had come upon Abalama Street with all its yellow cabs grabbing students too lazy to jit to the Hub or the Zone.

Well, I found out that I am in three legally mandated protected groups ... she continued on as Jonny thought *Those tests were the stupidest things he ever endured*, but he couldn't say that…

She continued… *I did OK for class placement. I found that I get benefits for being human, and I am not sure what that means...*

Jonny was suddenly inundated with the strong smells streaming from Borneo's Civet Java. His stomach started to rumble at the thought of dinner at home. Let's hurry, he was reminded.

...Yeah, the tests were such a bunch of bull. John had to smile to himself. *But you know, the orientation and the monk back there have gotten me to thinking.* They had hit the TAP and turned right past the glass lava lamp and chandelier shop Jonny had noticed before, and there was the pet shop.

Thinking, thinking about what?

The TAP was full of sundry shops and crowds they had to work around. *The school said they had a class on the Introduction to Philosophy, what is the Universe, stuff like that. It would help me understand these religions.*

Yeah, that would be cool. Dad and I often have long talks over dinner about that kind of thing. There sure are a lot of ideas to consider. Look at that, the bagpipe mechman was still there.

Really? This last week is the first solid time I thought about these things. Mom never talks about much except how to act around people and how to follow the Commandments. The shops thinned out and they were able to speed up, which then slowed their conversation as they focused on not running into anyone.

Well, that's important. What Pops really shares with me are bad attempts at humor and things to help build my "character".

The HUB was just ahead already. *It has got me to thinking, really thinking: Why are we here? Who is God? Does he/she/it exist? Why do people need things?* The azure glints began to sparkle again. The beltway was just ahead.

E^{3}Ching and W0ody came abreast as the tunnel morphed into the Brazoria and Jonny began nervously looking around for Abs to punk him again. *Boy, when you do something, you go all the way. Those are the big ideas.*

Talking about big ideas, have you thought about an overmind, are we all are part of the imagination of one, perhaps the overmind is me? Goa Way was then behind them.

They continued their passionate discussion of life as only young people can, while they worked their way home. Jonny stomach was starting to cry for dinner.

Thirty minutes later they had left the mass transit at the Helena Transit Node and traversed the Last Chance Gulch. Jonny surreptitiously looked over at Kai, curious about her obvious attraction to the Church of Understanding. *Sounds interesting, so you and Abs have talked since you were there first?* He watched her with a twinge of apprehension.

It is very honest, you connect with all your emotions and inner senses, learn their positive and negative attributes, practice controlling them. It's not at all like Universal Hope with its emphasis on proving what is real and practicing responsibility. She looked both ways when crossing Day Road, actually named after the Day family, a band of early settlers. A knot of hunger was forming under Jonny heart, amplifying his small worry.

Abs says there are steps, or levels, of attainment. The highest level that can be achieved while still here in the 'physical plane' is called the Natural. Naturals are responsible for great poems, great music, fiendishly freaky entertainment. Almost all advances in culture are generated by people of the Church of Understanding. I bounce when just thinking of it. Kai was almost bounding down the street towards home, her eyes had become dilated and darker as she talked. *Did you know it is the only Great Religion started on Mars?*

Jonny, I really want to talk to you about all this. Do you think you can come over? We can learn about all those things we keep thinking about. My mom won't be there. They stopped at the corner of Knight and Lincoln Roads, their homes on the next block.

Actually, as we left the University, Kai, I made the decision to be responsible and start studying for our examination as soon as I got home. Can we do it right after finals? They stood looking at each other right on the corner, their mechs waiting.

Once again, her gaze pinned Jonny motionless: *My mom has been invited by an old school chum to Saint Andreas for a private viewing of her latest show until midnight. I will be alone and really would like you to come over.*

Aw, Kai, how can I grow up and make adult decisions, and then abandon them within fifteen minutes? I promise I will come over Wednesday after the last final, OK? He couldn't break away from her eyes, so alive, so reaching out.

Come on Jonny, don't be so square. We could do stuff, you know? He didn't know, he was confused, and unknown emotions were starting to hammer him. The knot under his heart was solid and beginning to hurt.

I can't quit studying yet Kai! And, my stomach is killing me and if I don't have dinner soon, I'll fall over. I'll call as soon as I am done. He was pulled in two directions, visit the slightly forbidden, or, stay with his responsibilities.

They crossed over to their block and approached their homes. Kai began to doddle. *Aw, Jon, we could talk about he-men and wo-men, and those kinds of things. Marriage, kids, you know. What we can do when we are citizens, what we might do before then.* They say that a girl's eyes are pools that reflect her soul. He could well believe it.

Wow, that sounds sweet! But my body's starting to shake, I'll call right after dinner. They stared at each other on the sidewalk, hesitating. Then, Kai made a decision.

Ok, Jonny, Ok. We will talk after finals. You're right, I need to be focused too. Let's get together tomorrow when my mom's home and go over our notes, OK?

He stared into her eyes, a tightness like a rock in his chest, acid crept up into his mouth. *I'm sorry, but the body sometimes fails when the spirit is willing. I feel like I have been hit with an elbow in Battleball, OK? I will call you after dinner.*

OK.

As it is said the poems, sadly, the roads they travelled diverged on this day.

Dedicated to the protection of Humanity, and the Colonization of the Solar System

"Home is People"
- Robin Hobb

"Every great dream begins with a dreamer.
Always remember, you have within you the strength,
the patience, and the passion to reach for the stars to change the world."
Harriet Tubman

Grad Ender Academy

Chapter 9

Here was where he, Aleks, was born, here was the jewel of the Aegean Sea, surrounded by deep blue waters, a harbor protected from both storm and raider by the ring and reef of neighboring isle Aspronisi, with only a small opening for Phoenicians and other sturdy sea-traders. The citizens had even repelled the Pharaoh's attempt at Satrapy, dropping the mighty howrse-hair rope across the gap and archers firing a continuous torrent of arrows at the melee below until the Egyptians sued for peace and withdrew. Here was a pleasant and comforting climate, nurturing both persimmon and olive, safe and secure, with centuries of peace and fair trade and enlightened governance, culminating in the pinnacle of mankind, where advances in thought and invention were continually nurtured. Aleks lived here in a comfortable white plastered home with his family and father who was the King's Master Maker and Smith. Oh, the laughter and companionship which defined his family built the memories and strong foundations which sustained Aleks throughout his lifetime.

The auditorium at Ender Academy was over 100 feet high with banners of ancient accomplishments and vanities in red and greens or blue white and reds hanging down the walls. Scalloped sconces created warm indirect lighting while spots from the projection rooms highlighted the podium. It was another graduation day for the most recent cohort of youth here in the Helena Crater complex.

The gathering within the hall was making a low murmur as Jonny and W0ody waited just in front of their mom, the human nervously bouncing his heel on the rug. People were still filing in, softly chatting with each other, hugs and smiles from those obviously longtime friends.

W0ody, I hate these ceremonies, we already passed our exams. Why are we here? Jonathon was slightly irritated and excited at the same time, making this wait uncomfortable.

Chill out meat stick; I think they are trying to teach us military rule three in the new sim-game: War Hero.

What?

You know, hurry up... and wait.

Yeah, right. Thanks tin-can. The WET announced it was time to begin to get into their assigned places. Jonny looked over his shoulder at his mom and pop moving to stand with the rest of the audience. They were so archaic, his pop with his carmine leathers, brass buttons up and down the seams, his mom in her girdle-teddy, button-down high-top shoes, black widow stockings and garters. It was never clear if Pops needed the pistons and augmentation from a mining accident, or just had worn them forever so they were a part of him. Well, never you mind, look forward, don't look back. He took a long breath, this was an important step to become a man; he longed so much for his freedom.

The students began to line up in their Home Room Groups, each brushed and scrubbed as clean as can be. Jonny couldn't recall seeing W0ody's tool belts so neatly organized, hanging smartly below his barrel body about his legs. He couldn't stand the uniform he was required to wear, maroon and gray, marking him as a student. He would have rebelled, thrown a real hissy fit, except he knew it was going to be over soon, as in, today!

Sighing, he followed W0ody over to the group surrounding Mrs. Tinknocker who was attempting to shepherd her group into some semblance of order, a difficult task due to the amount of chattering and fidgeting everyone in this herd of kittens were doing. Smiling warmly towards them with fondness and understanding for their situation, she initiated the student center command to secure their WET access and paint all their optics with colored lasers, allowing them only to see their feet and designated position on the flooring within the ceremony's choreography.

As the kids shuffled to their right locations *Class*, she group-broadcasted, *No talking, you can tightbeam, but your privilege with be withdrawn if you step away from your place.... Thank youuuu.*

Jonny couldn't help but twitch. He looked around to see who all was in place, W0ody, of course, was on his right, and he saw KaiLin, E^{3}Ching, Krage, Tink3r, and Obee, but there was a gap where Abs should have been. There was Obee's mech-buddy Art!. *Where's Abs?* he tightbeamed Kai, *Don't know, saw him earlier today for a soda at the WaySafe. He said he was waiting for his dad, his mom's not coming.*

Glancing outward, Jonny verified his mom and dad in the audience, *Wow, that's too bad about his mom, why can't his parents get along?*

Don't know for sure, but with my mom here, my dad won't come. He blames her for everything. I guess the Smythe's are the same way. She turned to look at him, her dark hair cascading over her shoulders with its dark highlights emphasizing Kai's deep black eyes and the small delicate Chinese skin art she added to her left cheek, partially hidden by her hair. Looking carefully, he thought he could get lost in those eyes.

I'm sorry Kai, I didn't know about your dad.

I guess I'm over it, it has been over three years. He's a jerk. He hasn't contacted me once since he left, seems he has a new girl up in the Turtle Mountaiin complex. Makes me mad, but sometimes I cry when I think he doesn't care. Hurts my mom worse, she says she can't trust anyone anymore. At least we have each other, and she's right over there. I'm so glad she came.

Jon was shocked to hear Kai inform him of losing a parent in such a factual way. He wondered what that was like. She was still searching the audience when the lights started to dim and they had to turn and face front, they had practiced the walk through on Wednesday. His eyes washed over her furtively when he thought she wasn't looking. She seemed so solemn. *Hey, cheer up Kai, this will be over in an hour and we will be on our way to FU and the citizenship exams. It doesn't get any better than that.*

She gave him a look, and finally a small smile, *You're right,* she squared her shoulders, *a journey of a thousand klicks starts with a ..*

.. drum klick! Interjected W0ody.

They stared at W0ody with a look that would curl machine parts, then, a smile started to break through Jonny's demeanor, then Kai's, then grin's and a snort as they tried to hold it in. W0ody had broken the gloom, and looking at his goofy grin and his jug head perched over his squatty body, it was impossible not to smile. Mrs. Tinknocker tossed them a glare, and they looked front, but Jonny had the hardest time holding it in, swallowing and letting out the smallest groan.

Nyuk, Nyuk, Nyuk snickered W0ody tightbeamed so only Jonny heard it.

Kai's phony hard look cracked under the tension of Jonny's rictus, again gaining looks from their friends and another stare down from Mrs. Hardass. Finally, after a few deep breaths, they recovered their composure and the tension left their bodies.

When they became aware of the surroundings again, the illumination had lowered and Principal Curtan had taken the podium. "*I wish to thank the students and their guardians for their attendance in our celebration here at the Ender Academy. Today's events marks one of the major turning point in our lives, graduation from public education. Today, many of you will scatter to the far ends of the solar system to build machines, empires and families. Some of you will continue as students to gain skills for specialty trades and professions, others will hit the sky flying becoming independent souls and entrepreneurs.*" A muffled cough occurred in the gallery. "*Whatever your choice, you have demonstrated by passing your finals, the talent and knowledge to succeed in whatever endeavor you choose. So, before you fly away, before you get pulled by the gravity of the events out at Jupiter, I wish each and every one of you good fortune, and thank you for sharing your lives and energy with us here at the Academy. God bless.*"

Another cough. *"Without any further ado, we welcome the students to the podium to present them with their graduation certificates. They shall ascend when called in alphabetical order: Amos Ai, please come forward."* A stocky mech who Jonny remembered as straight forward and pleasant quietly strode towards his diploma, while behind the presentation a super large hologram displayed a litany of Aim's (as everyone called him) accomplishments, especially his work in the band. *"Carlos Anderson ....."*

Later, Jonny would not remember much of the long tedious event, except that he got through it. However, the 'Gift', would stay in his memory and life forever.

As the event closed, Jonny and W0ody retired to the receiving area, watching Kai go over to her mom. He didn't know most of the citizens and adults, all covered with feathers and riots of fur, the mechs gleaming with their various crenellations and shoulder armor, but it seemed his dad, Augustus Miller, did, walking around animatedly, greeting almost everyone, mingling and merging with all the other families, when a mech loomed in front of Jonny: *Uncle Bill! I didn't know you were here!*

Bill's eyebrows (pastel blue today) went up two inches in mock surprise, then with the seriousness of a mime, he threw his arms outwards and backwards, then slowly wrapped them around Jonny, embracing him, fluttering his white gloved hands continuously as he did so, making big fake smacking sounds with his lips while pretending to kiss one cheek, then the other.

Wild Bill punched him lightly on the shoulder as a sign of camaraderie. Bill was always a card, but he was highly respected, and the shared association unexpectedly caused a surge of pride inside Jonny. Wild Bill was notorious for his role with Nick Danger in solving the crime of the Devil's Foot, as well as many other police exploits and was in the news regularly. Having him here talking to him was an honor and then his gang would really want to hang with him because..., well just because! He was reminded of another of the Credos: Status is a False God. The heck with that, he just wanted to feel important for a day.

Thanks, Bill, having you as my God Father means a lot.

How could I stay away from my main man here Augustus's son's big day, humm? Did you know Augustus and I go way back? He sponsored me out of the crèche when no one else would take a chance on a mech with a sense of humor. He shrugged his shoulders, shivering and clinking the delicate chain mail gown he wore about his body, as a king of old would wear a royal robe. In fact, Jonny noticed the deepest green and purple violet highlights sparkling off Wild Bill as he moved within the shimmering cascade of anodized aluminum loops.

Looking around he spotted Jonny's mech-mate: *Hey W0ody! How're you doing?* Bill reached out, his arm growing through the expanding links and grabbed W0ody's shoulder, dragging him into the circle, W0ody had returned to his quiet, implacable self, all traces of the humor that resided within him were hidden. *W0ody, you are a big part of this you know. Don't be shy. Jonny here couldn't have done as well as he did and pass the public-school exams without your help, you know.*

Yeah, I guess. W0ody muttered stiffly next to Jon, in his Carhartt and tool belt. He had a tendency to withdraw and just observe when social events became complicated or fast paced.

So, W0ody, in celebration, I got you a graduation gift. Slowly, a large grin spread across Bill's face while Jonny and W0ody stared at him with cautious anticipation. Bill brought out this object that looked a little like an old-fashioned eggbeater. *Got it from a patch eyed, peg legged, purple pirate who got himself caught up by a couple of custom agent friends of mine...* Bill glanced around in a shifty manner. He returned to regard W0ody.

This, W0ods my man, is you first very own smart tool. W0ody's eyes started to get larger. *It's called a ten ninety-nine in one. It replaces all sorts of hand tools, your belt and kilt are getting a little busy, you know. The hand crank allows you to recharge the storage cell and provides mechanical assistance for a coordination between you and the tool.*

Wow!

I hear you are doing punch downs; this little baby will increase your productivity and decrease the time required by at least a factor of five.

Really? How does it work?

Watch: Hey tool! Front and center.

Two eyes on stalks emerged from the device, which independently began to peer about.

Tool, let me introduce you to W0ody, your companion and supervisor. Bill handed the tool carefully to W0ody by the handle, and as they exchanged possession, like a live crab, the eye stalks briefly flickered away back into the handle.

The eyes slowly emerged again, and a soft high-pitched voice came from the device, *Hiya W0ody, what's cookin'?*

Not much tool, what's your name? A number of expressions were crossing W0ody's face. *Surely, you couldn't be Siri?* The pained look on Jonny's face showed he had scored a point.

The eyes rotated to focus on W0ody's face, *Don't have one yet, I was just booted up a few minutes ago by the dude in the chain mail dress.*

W0ody looked across at Jonny and then back to the tool, *Can I call you Richard?*

The eyes returned to exploring the room and space around the three, now four, *Sure boss, sure, like Richard the Lion-Hearted tool, huh?*

Richard, are you a mech? You talk like one, but you are too small for Gordon's Maximum.

The eyes rotated back. Both eyes looked up and fixated on W0ody like an imprinted duckling, it was quite disconcerting how quick the tool was. *No boss, no. Just a sophisticated software capable of learning. But I can give the Turing test a run for its money!*

Wow. W0ody looked around. *Thanks, Bill! This is awesome! Hey Richard, I am going to attach you to my tool belt just under the apron to keep you safe, OK?*

OK W0ody, OK. The eyes retracted as W0ody clipped the tool and the small voice announced: *Hey look! A Swiss Army Knife! How're you doing buddy? How many options do you have? Quiet type, huh?* The voice became muffled and disappeared as W0ody draped his apron over it.

Bill, it's perfect! Is there a back story?

The pirate who just stopped to fuel at the Space Port claimed he had gotten the original body in a poker game from an Earthman who said it was found near the Antikythera Mechanism. Bill looked directly at the two of them, squaring his eyebrows to import the severity of his story. *You may never have heard of it, but that was an ancient geared astrolabe for calculating the motions of stars and planets, created long before any records of such a skill.*

Bill continued, with just a hint of a smile, weather he was telling a story or sharing a secret, the kids couldn't tell. *The Antikythera was discovered on the bottom of the Middle Earth Sea near the Isle of Santorini and believed to be the remnant of Atlantis. The handle is made from lignum vitae and the C_{14} dating does indicate it to be over six thousand years old.*

The metal of the geared crank is rolled and folded steel which comes from Earth, the smile left wild Bill's face as he bored down into the details, *and the technique indicates that an ancient Indus Empire master metal smith must have made it. What's really neat is the spectral analysis points to a meteor as a source for the iron, possibly a piece of Vesta, or so says the assayers. And who knows, maybe the handle is a piece of the True Box?*

Bill, it must be priceless! But they didn't have smart tools back then! And they wouldn't survive the ocean! Are you pulling my leg?

Bill leaned far back, his pastel eyebrows up as high as they would go: *No, W0ody, of course not! Not on graduation day! I went down the hell hole and visited Iron Mike.*

No way!

The older mech leaned back forward, looking about, to quietly confide in them: *I gave him the artifact and asked him to work with the King's Swarm to install the smart tool without changing the way the ancient handle looked. Those nano-miners and manufacturers took it apart and put it back together like the clock it is. The only mar is the scar from a barnacle on the back of the large gear. I told them to leave it for the history.* Leaning back: *Now it is a smart tool embedded into an antique instrument. I figured a tool guy like you would appreciate it.*

My Gosh, Bill, this is a treasure that I will value my entire life. How can I ever thank you?

Just continue as you have been, W0ods, and knock off your Citizenship Exams with Jonny here, that will make me proud!

W0ody retrieved Richard and began to examine it closely, calling out the software genies and entering into a small conservation with it. Jonny and Bill watched silently while W0ods turned his tool from side to side, and have it display a number of different implements. Finally, he put Richard away under his toolbelt and looked up. *Thanks again Uncle Bill.*

Jon commented, *W0ods, it's a small tool, why don't we call it Little Richard?*

The voice piped up from amongst the other tools, *No way! I'm twelve inches of hard wood and muscle if I'm a nanometer. My name is Richard, and don't you forget it, buddy!*

Askance and embarrassed, Jonny glanced away in his discomfort as his friends stared, then, they walked slowly back to where his parents stood. The adults were talking adult things, the possible war looming out at Jupiter's trailing orbit. Well, he didn't have to worry about such. More important things were occurring today. And in two weeks, he would start his prep classes so he could pass his citizenship exams when he turned thirteen. He would gain his freedom and do all the stuff he had been prohibited from!

A hand grabbed his shoulder startling him, and as he turned, he recognized: "*Abs! Where've you been?*"

Abs was a year older than Jonny, then again, that scare he put into Jonny back at the NODE could have aged him a year too. Abs actually should have been in the previous year's class but had lost time when his mech-brother skipped out, followed by the divorce. He wasn't much taller than Jonny but had filled out with the muscles of a gymnast, trim but not skinny or bulky, benefiting from his family's personal trainer.

With a slight nod, he touched the brim of his jaunty naga beret with the forefinger of his right hand, *Yo Jonny, my dad couldn't make it, so I spent the day putting a package together for all of us after all this dull paperwork, or whatever they call it. It's gonna be boss.*

Jonny turned fully to face Abs who was wearing an all-black muscle suit as well as the dapper headgear. The shirt was cut to show off his physical fitness, and Jonny noticed some very faint imagery within the cloth. *What do you mean? What kind of "package?*

An amber light traversed the hat's brim before fading out, Abs always had the best toys. W*hat? You ask what? I got us a stretch to take us to the Dome, and they have given us a shift just for us for an Aire War, that's what!*

Really Abs? That's awesome! I don't know that I can afford it though.

Bouncing up and down, *Gotcha covered Jonny, gotcha back, as always. In fact, paid for the entire gang!*

Picking up on Abs excitement, Jonny swiveled to look back *Wow, I gotta check in with Pops, they might have plans, you know how parents are.*

You go guy, while I tell Kai-Lin and Krage and the rest. Meet you in five.

Jonny started off towards his dad, who was once again chatting up a small group of citizens, they had to be at least thirty years old, although the rejuv treatments prevented one from knowing for sure. *Hey dad, I'm off with the gang to the Asteroid Dome, would you tell mom?*

Don't you want to stick around and meet my friends who came by to celebrate your graduation?

Naw, dad, I want to be with my friends on this great day, OK? You can tell them hi for me, but the group is leaving soon, and I want to be part of it, we're gonna do a full-blown Aire war, OK?

Sure Jon, I will hold the fort, you can go if you can repeat the Second and Eighth Commandments for me, OK?

Wow, dad, I am all stoked from graduation, I'm not sure I can get them right!

Come on Jon, you can do it.

Just then Abs beamed, *Hurry up Jonny, we're leaving!*

Cool your jets, Abs. I'll be there in a moment.

Turning to his dad, Jon thought, clenching his jaw, then relaxing, ah yes: *Number Two: I am responsible for my actions as an adult; Number Eight: Moderation, Moderation, Moderation. Dad, I won't get in trouble, OK?*

OK, son, have fun. Dad gave Jon a hug around the shoulders, then shoved him off in the direction of his friends.

You know, W0ody? as they walked off together, *today has been a good day.*

You got that right, monkey-man. They had forgotten about the Trojans.

The Universe Exists without Mankind.

The stars in other Galaxies would exist whether Mankind existed or not.

"We're not freaks.... We're normal. We may not be gorgeous,
but at least we're not hyped-up Barbie dolls."
- Scott Westerfeld

"Do the difficult things while they are easy and do the great things while they are small.
A journey of a thousand miles must begin with a single step."
Lao Tzu

The Dome

Chapter 10

1875] Nikki was angry at himself; he had let his mind wander and had lost his purse again at cards. Why did he spend so much time focused on culture and the refinement arts, was it the girls? He found them strangely irresistible but unaware of the mysteries and wonders of the world, seemingly interested only in their little masquerades. He knew better to let himself get distracted, he must this time force himself to conquer these passions, forgo all of these games of chance and silly pleasures here and now and stay focused on that which truly mattered, the magic of electricity and magnetism intertwined.

Bah! He knew what was really bothering him. That Professor Poeschi is an ignoramus! Nikki had tried to help him understand the magnitude of the Gramme Dynamo and how it could be improved much more than those toys of eggbeaters in liquid mercury. But no, Herr Professor was a stuffed buffoon of the first magnitude! Couldn't he see that the mistake of Hippolyte was not a debacle, but rather, an inspiration? Why, he could see it in his mind's eye, pulsating electricity pushing a shaft with as much force as a water wheel, not just next to a waterfall, but anywhere!

He had been doing integral calculus in his head since Higher Real Gymnasium and had tried to explain to this idiot how to calculate the force a rotating field around the shaft to transfer power. But it was no use, the Professor was a family appointment, a simpleton, a puppet, so he tried to just explain the results, it would get rid of the commutators! What fireworks! Herr Professor refused to believe. He was apoplectic with rage or fear! And now Nikki was dismissed from school! He couldn't return home, banished and ashamed.

He suddenly recalled the cynical comments by the underclassmen, "Those who can, do. Those who can't, teach." Well, maybe he should not try to become a Doktor, but rather an inventor? Who else sees as much as he? He must find somewhere in this world where he can use his talents. He must!

"Woo-hoo, look out, all you yahoos! Let's go to the Dome." The gang spilled out onto the corner of Euclid where the Stretch waited, animated and articulated by a mech driver, although Jonny couldn't tell where the mech ended and the stretch began. Did it matter? Gull wings opened and the gang jumped in *"Shotgun*!" cried someone. *"Let's go!" "Are we all here?" "Where's Art!?" "Obee, go out and grab Art!, he's lollygagging as usual."*

Art! Where are you? We're leaving! There you are! Climb down from that wall! A collage of whirligigs and mobile flying parts detached itself from the bulkhead. Upon landing it collapsed itself into a bi-pedal manform and sauntered over to the stretch. *I wish that I could do that*, thought Jonny as Obee clambered in at last, directing the doors closed.

The stretch left the assembly through the copper and bronze lock into Last Chance Gulch tunnel towards the I-15U. He stood up, *"Hey everyone! Since we just graduated, everyone call me Jon, not Jonny!" "OK Jonny!"* There was laughter in the cabin as everyone began to relax from the events of the morning. *"No, I mean it! Call me Jon." "OK, Jonny!"* came the rejoinder.

You can try it again later, tightbeamed W0ody.

Yeah, right, muttered Jonny, no Jon.

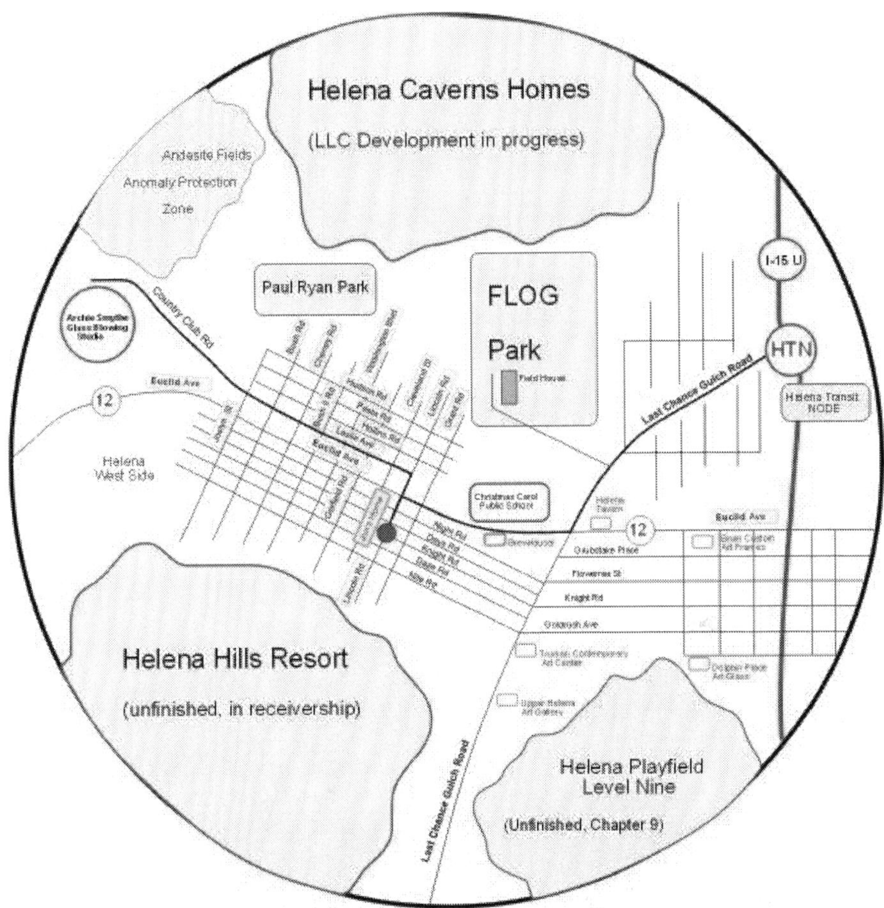

W0ody tightbeamed, *Richard, there is going to be a rambunctious crowd running around us for a while, so, keep your head down.*

Okey dokey smokey, but it is going to be hard. Going dark now, roger and out.

There was more than enough room for the fifteen of them and Kai came over to sit next to Jonny as they turned south on the I-15U towards Fremont and the Dome. *It's so cool that Abs is helping us party on Graduation day. I mean, when I turned thirteen in April Mom had all her friends over for my rites, and we all just stood around, most of mom's acquaintances are so old, they aren't fun. I couldn't invite the gang.*

At this point they were flying by the Jackrabbit exit. *Why, it was awesome when he hired the GLYPHs to come play after his coming of age, all the way from the Antiope Pair. Why that and everything else he did, was just stellar! We had so much fun later. Abs said he was going to make our graduation party three times cooler. Why, he's even got passes into the Ree Bar down in the Zone!* Her dark hair swung about as she made her points.

How's he going to do that? We're not Citizens, not enough for the Ree.

Silly, he's got fake ID for everyone. They don't care. Some of us get our citizenship at thirteen, we all fit the mold.

How'd he do that? Those autodoors are fractically encrypted, folded at random microsecond intervals.

I don't know, but when you have enough, money talks. The stretch started to slow down as they passed into Fremont and approached the Transfer Node.

Abs plopped down next to them, *We've lost the link to the Dome for some reason, so we are going to split here at the Node. Jonny, why don't you take the gang and continue in the stretch. Kai, why don't you join me, I am going to jump out here to catch the vacuum to the Dome ticket office, and we can all meet up there, OK?*

Are you sure Abs? I mean I don't have any money to cover for the Limo.

Abs punched Jon in the shoulder, *Don't worry, got you covered, friend! It's paid for. Common KaiLin, let's get out now while Jonny tells everyone the plan.* At that, Abs and KaiLin leaped out, followed belatedly by E^3Ching. Jon watched them disappear,

KaiLin glancing over her shoulder as they rounded a corner onto the Ave.

Then, facing the group, *Hey guys, Krage and Obee, listen up, you too Soo, we're going to the Asteroid Dome. At the newly expanded Cave we're going to rent a flotilla of cars and have the biggest battle you will ever see for the rest of the afternoon!* The gang's energy went up several notches at that announcement and they all tried to upload the virtuals, but it took longer than expected.

As the limo turned on Brazoria Rail Way and connected to the Tap, they finally went virtual-in and for the remainder of the trip began to experience what they were getting in to. The Tap turned into the Old Spanish Trail and connected to the south end of the dome. Here the crowds were ten times as dense as they were in Helena, a party atmosphere surrounded those heading into the Dome and the thousands of venues. Jonny and Co followed their Nav to the operations office for the Cave.

When they got there, Abs and KaiLin were coming out of the office with grins on their faces, Krage broadcast, *Hey Abs, get caught in an air handler? Your hair's a mess!* A quick look of concern crossed Abs' and KaiLin's faces before a large grin broke out on Abs', *No guys, just got in a hurry in a shaft to beat you here, but the tournament fee has been paid, and we are ready to Rock and Roll!* he announced proudly, KaiLin at his side.

OK Momma, what're we doing, huh? Laughter all around.

We need to go to the check out the CaveCar Carousel and get our equipment and briefing… The group rallied and moved towards the CaveCars and disbursing clerk. He sized them up, looking slowly across the group, until they started to shuffle around.

..

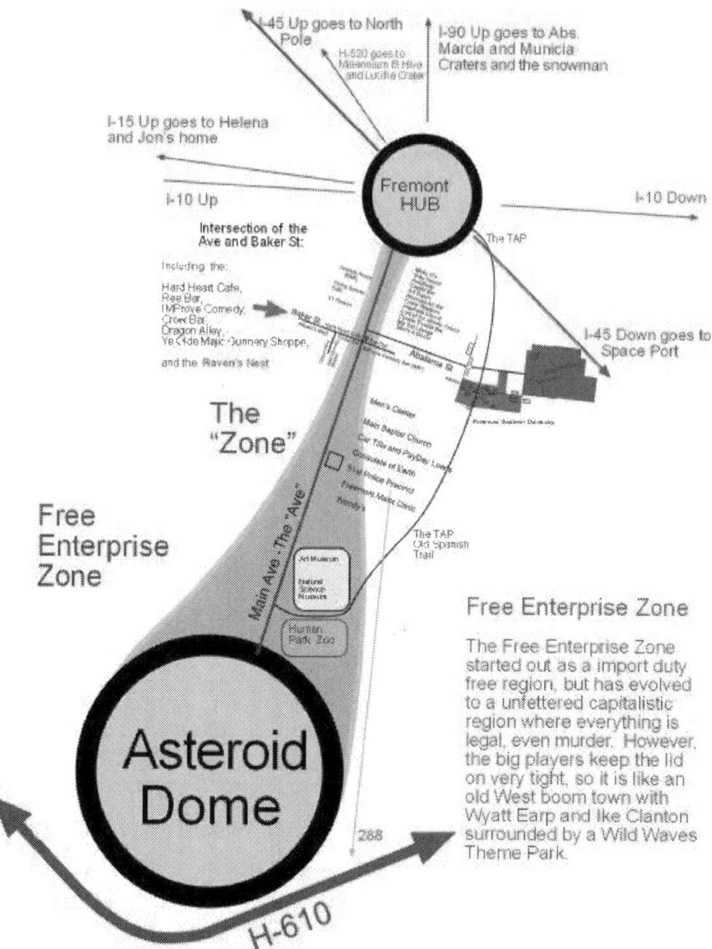

"OK children, I am your Grand Poohbah. Welcome to the Hall of Air Battle with over eight billion cubic meters of air space throughout and the latest and greatest of gaming equipment known to man! What we have in front of us are mechanical toys, run by battery and compressed air, the CaveCars.

"The objective is to wage war on your fellow CaveCar operators. Each of you has a limited amount of compressed air, and each of you have a limited battery. The compressed air will move

your CaveCar free flight for thirty minutes, and the battery will provide cabin lights and laser beams for thirty minutes' full use." He looked out as Krage and R0bie started to edge towards the pit. With a slight shake of his head. "*So, the objective is to do battle and defeat your opponents in twice that time frame, you have one hour."* Krage fist bumped R0bie, *Yeah!*

"*How hard is it to shoot each other?"* Sindee broke in.

"You can fly and fight your ship with just one person, but most take a team, to allow a pilot to watch for walls and collisions, and a gunner to aim and shoot. Now watch carefully at the CaveCars." Just then, starting on the far right a spear of light burst forth, red-yellow alternating, then deep red, then up the spectrum. Some were round, others looked like grey geese, hornets, and bees.

Jonny tried to keep track, colors along with type of car and color. Out loud, He whispered to W0ody: "You keeping track? This might be important."

"I think so, but there are a number of Cars that look alike but separated. Perhaps we can track them by their laser beams. I think I see something, but not sure."

Then: *"Can we ram each other?" "Yes.." "WOW!, Look out Kragey, I'm a gunnin' for you!" "Yes, to continue, the CaveCars are very sturdy and you can ram, bump and nudge each other all you want, but the ship's sensors deduct damage from you when you do, even when you collide with the walls and floating rocks. You must wear the crash helmets and restraints. It is easy to get hurt if you don't. By purchasing tickets, you have waived all liability of 'The Cave'."*

"We have thirteen different teams, I must warn you, a couple of the other teams have experience, and may take you out early. If you don't last fifteen minutes, we can slide you into the evening tournament for free if you wish. Now, form teams and go pick out a

CaveCar..."

Abs broke in, "*Let's break up into pairs for the CaveCars, one to pilot and one to be a gunner. W0ody, you go with Jonny, KaiLin, you're with me. Rock and Roll!"*

Immediately the group started to scatter as the disbursing clerk leaned out of the way with a smile. Jonny walked quickly to a grey vehicle with blue trim on the far right, followed closely by W0ody.

Out of his eye, he saw Abs and KaiLin saunter over to an almost round CaveCar, pure black and without any streamlining at all. E^3Ching followed behind, and Abs stopped and stared at her. KaiLin gave a little stamp and pulled on his elbow, and reluctantly Abs turned, and the three of them continued on. It was second from the far left and had been a violet laser.

Jonny tried to track the others, he hoped W0ody got some. Still staying radio silent, "Hey W0ody, I tracked the ends, did you see the middle?"

"Maybe, we'll see."

Jon's selection was fairly sleek, about four meters long, oblate in cross section and a large viewing window in front, and a single cannon below the window. He didn't like the large window; they were dangerous in space.

The aft of his CaveCar had a circular clear bubble superimposed on the narrow cross section about one and a half meters in diameter, this time with a quad cannon set extending through the plexi, apparently on some sort of gimbals system.

Two stubby wings extended from the rear of the fighter from the long axis of the ovoid shape, with the blue trim color painting the leading edges of the foils. Otherwise the vehicle was dark charcoal.

Jonny hoped the dark neutral color would reduce detections from a distance. One could always hope.

As Jonny reached their CaveCar, the hatch swung up with the sound of pneumatic actuators and they clambered in. An automated voice announced: *Welcome to Cave Entertainment, my name is Tang2 and I am your host for the next two hours. Please board and be seated and I will run through the controls and safety features as you settle in.*

Jonny looked at W0ody and asked "What do you think will be the best team? You as pilot and me as gunner, or the other way around?"

"Me gunner, you pilot." W0ody said with a grunt and a grin.

No way guys! I should be gunner! What, with me and my peepers, and some of the awesome tools you have down here, W0ody, I would be hard to beat!

"Shhh!" W0ody snapped, "we are on internal sound transmissions to prevent others hearing us on the WET. But, come on out and join the show."

"Can I be the belly gunner?"

"No way, Jose."

"Come on fellas. "I sailed the Seven Seas, and this chop can't be much different.

"And we can use an old buccaneer I met here in the crib, One Eye'd Pete has experience firing his cannon at all sorts of scallywags, plus, he has this expanding telescope which allows him a close-up view of all the heavenly bodies. Should help keep track of the adversaries, huh?"

They looked at each other and the three seats, two seats facing forward and one aft. "OK wise guys, I think you're kinda right, my monkey brains will probably do better in this three-dee monkey gym, Richard you can bring Pete up and be lookout. W0ody's precision reflexes will be better on the laser, but what are you going to do, be a forward or back facing gunner?"

Back to the WET *Hey TT, are you allowed to give advice?*

The voice responded audibly, "I can consult with you and for you until launch, then I become inactive, observing only until the combat is over."

"Hey TT!" a startled W0ody barked, "Are you AI Mech or just machine?"

"Oh, I'm citizen mech, I just got this gig until a job in my specialty opens up in a hive, or even in the Trojans. Got to save up for an upgrade on my habitat too."

Jonny asked "Well, TT, what strategies and tactics can you recommend? This is our first time except for VRD."

"For strategy, be conservative in your first battle. Gunner can display HUD on his screen and warn you of approaching combatants. Oops, since Monday, HUD and CIC are out on all cars. Repairs techs have all been working on it for over a day, but the bugs are hiding."

"Hey Boss, I am good at finding bugs! I've got the best optics in the universe! Those little guys will never get away."

"Shush Richard, wrong kind of bugs. We're talking software."

The diminutive responded, "Oh boy, I guess I've gotta a lot to learn in this here new world. I'm gonna sit on your shoulders, W0ody, and glom yer view."

"To continue, experienced teams like picking off the inexperienced before taking each other on. And I agree with pixie-mech here, you should pilot, swing aside the combat joystick and slip both feet into the bottom stirrups, and both hands into the uppers. The ship will fly just like a space suit, if you have experience that."

Jonny smiled with hope "Have I? I'm going to have to thank Pops for dragging me out to all the work sites and getting me dirty and scratched up. If we're lucky, it will be familiar."

Addressing W0ody, "Tactically, your gunner should face aft, because the pilot in close aboard attacks can activate the forward guns from his seat. This means the basic tactics are to approach a target from abaft the beam, then when close aboard, turn away and let the gunner strafe them."

"What the heck does abaft the beam mean? Come on, we're kids, not space jockey pilots!" Jonny and W0ody looked at each other.

"Oh, that just means behind their center line, where the pilot cannot see you as well or as soon. If you get close enough that they fill a quarter of the view screen or more, the paint balls are most effective. You can ram, but usually the algorithm reduces your worthiness by 50%"

A new announcement in a stern mechanical voice., "*Five minutes to release, five-minute warning to release.*"

"Are there any questions?"

Jonny thought, "So extending both feet accelerates, pushing both hands apply a deceleration, unbalanced foot or hand motion creates pitch, yaw and roll just like a suit? Feet a five to one power ratio to hands like a suit?" (Engineering NOTE 2)

The ship responded in an affirmative on both counts.

As the kids strapped in, Richard scuttled around the ship's restraint locking movements, then settled down on W0ody's back, one eye facing forward, one swiveled backwards.

"One minute to launch, stand by." Jonny felt a tightening in his gut as the moment approached, he gripped the handles of the fore-stirrups a little harder, patting the round battle ball shaped grips time and again into the concavity of his hands, anxious to go.

Looking down past his shoulder he saw that W0ody and Richard were properly strapped in, W0ody's pastel eyebrows forever in a state of wonder, Richard's eyes a confusing set of hatched shimmering marbles. *"Thirty seconds until Launch,"* intoned the voice.

"Hey W0ody!"

"What?"

"You got some kinda equipment down in your tool chest, you know?"

"So what?"

"I really admired your jewels you have stashed down there, where'd you get them?"

"Shut up Richard."

"Fifteen seconds."

"I were really impressed by the size of your Johnson outboard motor you got hung from the overhead. Do all mechs like you have big Johnsons?"

"Shut up Richard!"

"OK, OK, just noticing, you know."

Ignoring them, Jon declared, "I am going to drop straight down and run to the perimeter wall and I am going to throw a five second spiral on us, so we won't have any blind spots. Keep a sharp eye out."

"Kay!"

Five.

Four.

Three.

Two. Guts started twisting again.

One.

Jonny felt his weight come up and pushed the throttles as if he was doing a pushup, slightly more with his left hand than his right. He pressed down with both feet as hard as he could against the straps of the acceleration couch.

The bottom wall was approaching, and Jonny lifted his feet to place them in free fall. What to do? "Richard, what's going on back there?"

"Boss, we are not being followed directly, the bees and hornets are already doing battle with each other, your boy Abs is just slowly floating away, spinning and firing. One other grey ship is diving, but they are on a separation course."

"Good, I am going to flip and pull us to a stop just off the wall ahead, you are going to have to yell out distance, because there is no automation on this bird."

W0ody called out, "Jon, we are maybe a hundred meters out, max thrust now!"

Jonny pushed down with feet extended and felt the ship respond. He was quickly able to make out the bottom of the Cave, and started to toggle the decent. "Got it! I'm going to hold us off maybe ten feet, I can see the floor." He continued to guide the car, until he was hovering.

"Come on up guys for a moment and look out with me. Let's see if we can make sense of this melee and plan our strategy and tactics." W0ody was unhooking and scrambling forward as Jonny talked, and they both looked out at the Cave. Richard followed, dragging a monstrous spyglass with his rear pedipads.

"Richard, do you see any of the others? They are supposed to be the experienced ones. And what is that haze overhead? I don't remember it from the beginning."

The smart tool pulled the spyglass out to its full length and began a coordinate search. "On it boss!"

W0ody was scanning too, "The launch was too quick, I am not sure it was there. I suggest strategy is to attack the battle already in progress, engage an outer vehicle. You seem to have the flight characteristics under control so we could just do what TT suggested, sweep by and strafe them. I get to be gunner!"

"Me too!"

"No Richard, you get to be the observer and keep us informed."

"Oh boy, I gets to use my Peepers! Wowzy, dowzy lookout for dem eyes!"

"Kay, strap back in, then I am going to do thirty seconds of rock, wiggle and roll to firm up my feel, then let's go after the bee stragglers. Keep a keen eye peeled out for the grey ones, I think they are going to use our strategy on us. Kay?"

W0ody clipped the last buckle in, "Kay." Jonny started his ship dance, finding the response to a shimmy, then spin. He quickly got a sense of what he could do, a little sluggish on the push but smart enough on yaw/roll. "Hey W0ody, go light on the lasers, in that cloud, it will oblate but create an enormous arrow to where we are. Stand by for go."

"Kay."

The Universe Exists Within Mankind

Life is Part of the Universe
Mankind is part of Life

"The kid is scary."
Orson Scott Card

"The desire for safety stands against every great and noble enterprise."
Tacitius

Aire War!

Chapter 11

Remembering as he worked, he was always impressed when the King brought his guests into the smithy shop and proudly showed off Μάρκος, his father's, work, whether it be the Astrological Orreries which predicted the seasons, the movement of the wanderers, and foretold the disappearance of the Sun-God, or the astounding life-like motions of the mechanical men. Why, Aleks had watched as royalty from far Persia, the exotic Hind, and the fabled Cathay jostled to look and buy. The last work had been bid on by a representative of the Pharaoh, and by a giant covered in yellow fur.

The Pharaoh was offering a hundred-weight of gold from the highlands of Ethiopia and gems from the Kingdom of Kush, and the Wildman had twenty stone of star-metal from the far north. The King wanted the gold, and his father wanted the star-stone. Aleks didn't know the outcome, it seems to include drinking at the late-night revelry which he was not allowed to attend. Afterwards, the King had offered the master Smith his weight in gold in appreciation and was astonished when it was turned down. What could gold buy what he didn't already have: peace, security, respect and family. Gold would only get in the way and create envy and tension. Use the gold wisely, he counselled, to protect the Kingdom.

Jonny started out from the wall at about half max, looking at his two gauges: air pressure was about eighty-five percent and power about ninety percent. Then a brief sour tightness in his stomach twisted him as the back part of his mind reminded him of those "expert warriors" out there. He shook it off, can't win without risk, or *No stones, no blue chips* as his dad used to say.

Richard piped, "Hey Capt, as we cleared, I spied a grey one in a niche, not moving." Another twist.

Jon's focus was forward, but he put it in the back of his mind that he had adversaries on his tail, as was to be expected. He hoped his flying skills and tactics would count for something; they were past strategy. "Got it. Watch for more. Anticipate engagement in about thirty seconds. I will try to dive in and stall, then flip so the target will show below you and then I will point you at him and begin to decelerate into him. Ten seconds."

"Ride 'em cowboy!" Richard was really into this engagement.

Coming ever closer, three bees were firing on a hornet, using their paint balls, while the hornet was swinging its blue laser in large swaths, connecting but seemingly without damage because it was on target very little of the time. Jonny quickly decided to focus on the outlier who had not reacted yet to their presence, apparently unaware they were being targeted. The movement of the outer hornet was such that its velocity relative to the cave environment came to zero as it prepared to dive back into the melee.

This was the moment that Jonny had hoped for as he called down to W0ody "Five seconds to engagement! We're rolling over her now!"

As their CaveCar swung up, the bee appeared in W0ody's window so close it could almost be touched. W0ody triggered the guns and threw down a veritable hail of paint balls creating a broad patch of impact on their close aboard opponent.

"Woo-Hoo!" Richard screamed in a small falsetto. Lights flashed both on the exterior and interior simulating damage. W0ody saw a face suddenly look out their rear window, eyes wide. He continued to spray his target as Jonny started to accelerate away, but the bee's lights dimmed as the control system acknowledged significant damage and shut down the car.

Jonny extended his legs to accelerate away from the action, having himself become a slow-moving target while reversing course. He scanned the cave in front of him for opponents and yelled "Richard! Keep a sharp eye out! I'm going to circle around again, and you need to watch our tail!"

"Ten-four, Elinore!"

His quick glance forward showed no one near and some laser engagement in the distant corner, to be ignored. Jonny executed a barrel roll then pulled up as they dove below the melee and then flipped to put the engagement directly in front of his wind shield.

Their bee was without power and slowly tumbling. The hornet was spinning erratically, looking like it had jammed a nozzle gimbal against a stop, the occupants probably so dizzy they would be spewing their lunch throughout their cabin. The other two bees were beginning to paint it with impunity. The bees seemed to intent on their prey, that Jonny decided to risk another run, this time a fly by to reduce exposure.

"Hey W0ody, how's your ammunition holding up?"

"Looks like between sixty-five and seventy percent, how say you?"

"I'm topped, so we're going to strafe the closest with our forward cannons without slowing down, be ready to burn him with your laser as we fly by, ten seconds!"

"Roger dodger!"

"Richard! Come grab the reserve seat and be forward paintball gunner!"

"Yippee! On it boss like a fat frog in a gravity well!" as he crabbed across the space to the second seat, pulling Pete behind him. Extruding what looked like a thousand different feet and tools, Jon watched as Richard grabbed both cannon handles, latch to the seat behind him, and bring pseudopods up to each control. Extending his optics upwards, both looking outboard like a walleyed pug, Richard shrilled, "Ready guys, here it comes!"

Richard adjusted on the fly as he saw his initial stream of bullets were skewed somewhat, either because of an off-center alignment of the firing mechanism or because not accounting well for a slow roll they were doing, and the last grouping of shots were beginning to impact before the target swept out of sight.

"W0ody! Mark on top!"

"Got her Captain! Locked on and burning!" Red highlights sparkled and shifted within Jon's cabin, reflections of W0ody's laser fire.

"Three dead and one trying to get away! Look at him go!

"Did you see that Captain! We painted that scoundrel a thousand ways from forever!"

"Cool Richard! We need intel! I am going to stall and do a slow barrel roll and let's see what we can see. We've gotta look out for someone doing to us what we just did."

"Got it!" W0ody responded. With W0ody focused aft, Jonny and Richard peered intently ahead and to the sides to spot danger. The laser war on the far wall seemed to continue sporadically, and someone directly overhead was putting out short bursts of violet laser light while slowly turning. After a moment, Jonny realized it must be Abs and KaiLin, by themselves and getting ignored. *Pretty good strategy, Abs* Jonny thought.

The wall war flared up as an intense number of laser flashes cascaded around the group there. Jonny counted four or five, it was hard to tell. "W0ody, there is a gun battle at the far front wall, perhaps four or five cars. I think I see Abs still near the gate. That plus the five we just engaged leaves one or two. I bet they're the experienced ones laying low for us to knock each other out, and then engage at the end. So, watch for them. But… Let's go ahead and go to the battle and engage the victors. I don't want to sneak and skulk to win, let's go get some action."

"Rodger that."

Jonny focused ahead and was able to discern four combatants: a hornet diving in at the moment, a bee moving about and two grey cars circling about trying to lay waste about themselves, a yellow and orange light show indicating their laser fire.

The hornet had dived slowly between the two greys, perhaps in the hopes they would lay off so as not to shoot each other. A bad plan it seemed, because the grays were discharging with abandon, one a yellow laser, the other orange or yellow orange, hard to tell, and they were hitting each other as well as the hornet. Suddenly, fire from the hornet stopped and it started to tumble slowly.

The grey now in the middle between the bee and other grey started to suddenly spin on an axis that brought its orange-yellow laser on its opponents sequentially, but not enough time on any one to do any damage. The outer two circled to put the grey in the focus of their attacks. With a sharp move, Jonny began a dive straight towards the action and the outer grey ahead, its yellow light solid against the center grey, reflecting in all directions.

"Richard, come up front, we're going all in! I am coming up on the closest grey, and I want you to paint them from here to there!" Mighty Mite broke free and scampered up front, where they sat side by side. A heartbeat later they were upon the floating grey and Jonny jammed his feet towards the floor to pull them up as the smart tool let fly and Jonny joined in with the red laser as he slowed. He tried to drop below the grey, but it was harder than he wanted to do both things at the same time.

The yellow brightness blinked twice, was gone, flared again, then cleared, and the burned violet images and flashes on Jon's retina remained for long moments. Then with a lurch they hit something, and as his eyes cleared, he saw they had collided with the grey, which was now inert and rotating slowly. Beyond the grey he saw the bee scuttling away and its green laser still lighting up the casualty between them, then beginning to sweep closer to him.

The green laser was gone, and he was speeding away from the scene of the battle. His telltales indicated 50% power and 65% air pressure left, Richard must have really laid into the laser in the battles. W0ody could have gotten in a few hits from the aft gun as they retreated too. Well, they had survived, and others had not.

"Whoa guys, that was heart pounding! What excitement. Well done."

"Well done indeed, I bet we can dip back into that experience over and over, I think Pete here got the effort on his memory stick," quipped Richard.

"Put a sock in it Richard!"

"I waz just sayin'…"

"Richard!"

"OK, OK."

A clench of his gut reminded him that there were other stalkers out there, watching and hunting him, and his worried eyes swept as far as he could see. There, through the distant fog was the periodic burst of Abs's purple laser, maybe a blip every ten seconds or so. He couldn't see the bee that had escaped behind him, and nothing more ahead. "Richard, do you remember where that skulker you saw near the wall is located at?"

"Boss, my momma says don't end a sentence with a proposition!"

"Richard, do you remember where that skulker you saw near the wall is located at, you jerk!?"

"No Boss, no. But it wasn't too far from the launch point. If you can orient yourself from there. On the other hand, it wouldn't be smart to stay in one spot, so they could be anywhere."

Sarcastically, "Thanks Richard, that's really useful."

Woody noted: "Yeah, sounds like an engineer, while technically accurate, completely useless."

The banter was releasing the tension inside of Jon, worried about the 'pros' that might be around. Heck, what was the worst thing that could happen? Go home a loser? Naw, he is getting some fine flyin' time under his belt: win/win. Still searching, he knew W0ody was doing the same from the aft cabin window without being told. Looking over, he watched Richard absurdly swing the monocular around while probing, it must have been twice his size!

He was trying to come up with some snazzy razzing he could throw W0ody's way when a light show of green red and yellow lit up the fog up at the top of the cavern. After a moment he noticed the Red Yellow lasers were alternating and must be that combo light he remembered from the beginning, quite a while ago it seemed. He momentarily wondered if the grime about the meters was from a previous crew that tossed their cookies during some wild maneuvers.

Calling out "Action at the ceiling, let's go." He pulled up to align the aft jets and pushed off at about half power. Wouldn't want to arrive at a gun battle with only a knife and no fuel, right?

As he watched the approach, they both turned towards him and realization dawned: "Guys, we're in trouble. These bees are working as a team!" He started to turn away, and their lasers reached out and even felt the heat on his skin, so he juked back like he was on the battleball court with a crossover and aimed directly at them.

"Stand by for ramming speed!"

"Aye-aye Capitan, sir. Strapping into the acceleration couch." was the reply.

He shut his eyes to slits to watch the bees who were still coming on, but suddenly belatedly reacted to his actions and started to veer away, the lasers falling off, they didn't want to be rammed. Both bees canted in the same direction and the tables were now turned, their blind spots were becoming exposed as they turned, and even though they were faster, their initial progress, added to Jon's new surge, was still closing the gap. *Tactical error,* Jonny thought.

"Richard man the guns again, five seconds max!

"We're going to fly by the closest bee on top and up the rear of number two. Pour everything onto number one as we go by, everything, hold nothing back! Here we go!"

As the first bee range closed to less than ten feet, Richard opened up the paint ball gun at full discharge on the which colored the rear end in completely in red. "This bull can't throw me, pardner!"

Then they were by and on top of number two and W0ody swung around from the aft lasers, but the gun hit the stops before he could shoot, then the target opened up as Jonny rolled towards the bee and once again Richard threw everything they had. They ended up almost matching the bee in speed and velocity while W0ody's paint gun was burping away.

"Hold up W0ody! I think that one's dead, it quit evading. I am going to spin back to number one." Jonny looked away from number two. "Yeoww! Hold on!" They were coming up against the ceiling at an alarming speed!

"Whoa Nelly!" Richard saw the collision ahead too.

Jonny had lost track of their plot within the cave. He jammed both wrists almost out their sockets to spin them around then laid into his feet aided by his hand thrusters to stave them off the upcoming wall, they slowed and slowed but were still going to collide when ahead the two bees hit and bounced hard, they hadn't seen or been able to do anything from their trajectory. Their own ship then collided, slower yet quite hard, the harnesses and couches taking much of the brunt.

Unconsciously Jonny shrugged and adjusted his trim and dampened his spin, taking a big breath to calm himself using his diaphragm's endorphins, releasing it all in a long sigh. A lurking worry welled up inside again as he imagined the last two CaveCars waiting out there for him, somewhere.

"Whoa, that was a ride." W0ody shuddered his metal shoulders while looking out at the two tumbling bees, now flashing the salutary "I'm done" salute in white light.

"You can say that again Mister Bojangles!"

Jonny didn't have much in reserve for another fight he knew and considered their options as he slowly jetted and coasted away from the wall. Time was down too, perhaps less than ten minutes left in the event. *Better get a move on* he thought.

Suddenly the wall behind them seemed to explode as the last two greys accelerated towards him. His rear window was splashed in light bright orange tinged with red.

Holy smokin' scat! broadcast Richard reflexively.

Damm, Jonny reacted again flooring his thrusters for two seconds, knowing his adversaries would have added velocity over him, but that he would have more maneuverability due to the low speed, so down he went, with them on his tail, trying to do a loop. He couldn't shake them right away and the lasers beat a sunset all over his backside.

A red alarm erupted over his dash, flashing with a jarring horn. He hadn't seen or noticed this device before, but boy, did it make him grit his teeth. A glance told him that this was the damage alarm, *Really?* "W0ody! Try to laser them back!"

"Kay!"

Suddenly a plan came into being as he swooped towards the wall, causing the two greys to be in the void, their radius of turn a little wider due to their higher velocity, but quickly turning back towards him.

They mustuv' read the von Clausewitz war notes because they were staying close together: 'An enemy divided is an enemy conquered.' They weren't going to allow themselves to be divided, no sir!

Jonny had his back against the ceiling and was drifting towards his opponents, they were approaching rapidly. Jonny determined the physical plane of motion created by the three CaveCars and twisted about to use his thrusters to generate his velocity in the same plane.

"Richard, stop the lasers!"

"What? OK, why?"

"No time, just standby!"

"Kay!"

The greys laid down a strong pattern of laser fire against him and the window was ablaze with yellow and red light through which Jonny could hardly peer as he squinted. Rotating his ship along the axis of the plane that he saw in his mind's eye, he suddenly accelerated towards the greys.

The greys came on, not letting themselves be vulnerable to the retreat the bees fell to. Jonny set his course directly between the two, accelerating all the way. He watched the damage device roll towards totality, knowing even if he escaped between the two, he would be out of gas and they could just scoop him up. Jonny noted total damage was passing 90%, fuel dropping below 5%.

"Richard, laser Mr. Right, right now! W0ody hang on for ramming speed!"

Richard's remaining energy was dumped on the right-hand grey, and Jonny immediately swung full right rudder with everything he had as they started to pass between the combatants. The movement threw Jonny and W0ody hard left against their straps, followed immediately by a tremendous shock from the right, crash left, then whirling wildly head over heels! He briefly saw Richard fly across the cabin with all his appendages extended like a kitten falling off a roof!

All lights went out, red indicators and horns continued to blare; Jon's stomach was being turned inside out. He tried to stabilize the ship, but the controls did not react. Jonny didn't know what to do.

"Boss, you'se makin' me dizzy, these eyes can't take the spinning!"

He pushed on his foot and arm controls but to no avail, a white light briefly lit up the cavern outside, then again, then became that strobe of destruction Jonny had seen on the others.

Then without his guidance, the ship's spin was being dissipated, Jonny could hear gas valves kick in and out as TT took control. Eventually, the spin was gone, and the ship lined up towards the docking station.

The need for secrecy was over and he used the WET*: W0ody, I think we're going home.*

A little voice piped: *WooHoo! What a ride! I got lost there at the end Boss, what happened?* Richard was now alert and retrieving Pete from under the couch where it had flown during the collision.

W0ody's belt had been skewed about his middle and was putting his tools all back into order as Jon answered the question.

Well, there were two of them, and we were exhausted of everything pretty much. I figured they could take us any time they wanted, but maybe they had to hurry because the clock was winding down. They seemed to work as a team, so if I could line them up, I might be able to take one or both out by ramming, our guns were awfully low.

W0ody was curious, *Why'd you tell Richard to shut down the lasers?*

I wanted to hide my movements until they couldn't avoid them.

With the laser off, they wouldn't be squinting, and then when the laser came on at the last moment, the right target wouldn't see and wouldn't react, whereas the left target would see us turn away from them, towards the right guy, and not react,

Which allowed me to collide with the guy on the right, and then carom into the guy on the left, a two-fer.

But I had to get us and our motions all on the same plane, otherwise we wouldn't have hit the second guy like a billiard ball.

Let's do it again Boss, huh? Please?

Shut up Richard.

Jonny looked out the window and saw he was part of a cluster of cars slowly heading back to the stable, all flashing white beacons. Except wait, over there in the corner, a brief flash of violet laser light. Then it was gone.

Couldn't you set up the collisions in three dimensions, and not stress the 'get everybody in or on the same page or plane or whatever?

Sure, if I was you. A human has never been a 3-D billiard champ ever. You mechs are so much better. But being me, I couldn't calculate the quickly changing angles and also at the same time ensure I could see through their laser fire at the last moment. So, it worked. Maybe. I don't know if I hurt them, but I sure put us out of the picture!

Thanks Boss! That was more fun than competing with a flat iron in a canoe race!

Suddenly, someone pushed cotton into Jon's ears, the WET was abruptly gone. Everyone looked at each other, in the distance, as if underwater, came in the background the fuzzy sound of white noise. Jonny felt as if he could almost distinguish the voices of a thousand souls yelling, screaming, pleading behind the hiss, but he couldn't quite make out any true words.

Then the voices became silent, one, then another, as if something momentous was entering their misty world and they scuttled back into nothingness so as not to gain attention.

After it slowly overwhelmed the void, after it became deathly silent, there came the striking of a gigantic bell.

ONE!

The echo of the reverberations of the low chords slowly faded as they bounced back and forth in the distance.

Then nothing…

While Jonny and W0ody looked at each other, the chatter of the WET slowly came back. No announcements, no buzz. So strange as to be scary, if one thought about it.

"Hey Boss, what's with this WET thing, just as I was getting used to using it, it disappears." In a small complaining voice, he continued, "Is this some kinda modern-man thing to keep everyone on their toes, or what?"

"Don't know Richard, this is new to us too."

They felt the bumps and swayed to soft docking as TT brought them into the cradles from where they started. Sweat was starting to film Jon's face, and he began to feel the hurts and bruises he had created. But a smile lingered as he thought of the successes, he and W0ody and Richard accomplished.

He might brag to the cohort even, though he probably shouldn't. Well, maybe a little.

"It is our choices...that show what we truly are, far more than our abilities."
- J. K. Rowling

"Tact is the art of making a point without making an enemy."
Isaac Newton

Unkindest Cut of All

Chapter 12

The car door swung up, and they saw the dock was already crowded with their friends and the strangers awaiting their turn. Stiffly, Jonny hauled himself up onto the walk, and braced for W0ody, and gave him a hand. Richard had already hidden himself up in the tool belt.

Those bruises really were going to hurt. Looking out, the last car coming into the dock was Abs' and KaiLin's. Their laser was no longer flickering, but all of their windows were totally fogged up. Jonny wondered what could have caused that accident. Did they have an early collision?

In the cradle, the CaveCar had two large scars where the collisions occurred. The two inboard greys showed very little transferred paint but were scratched and slightly dented. Were these the two he collided with? One of the guys climbing out looked as if he had a bloody nose, with drying patches on his green blazer. Both members of his team glared at Jonny and W0ody. Perhaps they didn't expect to get whooped. Jonny couldn't help but have a slight smile tug at the right side of his lips, serves the smug bastards right to hide until the last minute!

"Attention, attention please. The results of the mid-afternoon joust are in. The winner/surviving team has been determined: KaiLin Lightfoot and Archibald Smythe! Would you come forward please?" Abs and KaiLin looked about, they were somewhat disheveled, and Abs ran his hand through his hair to straighten it out. As they moved to the front, KaiLin was looking down and Abs had a big smile on his face, inscrutable E^3Ching respectfully behind.

The two teams beside Jonny gave him another hard look. He shrugged and smiled, *If you can't stand the heat, stay out of the engine room,* he thought at them. He returned his attention to the disbursing clerk, watching his homies strut up to the Grand Poohbah.

"Archie, KaiLin: I present to you the Cave Thunder award, given to those who survive the full hour of multi-team combat. Your extraordinary skills and astute understanding of the unique tactical and strategic requirements of multi-dimensional and interactive physical combat places you in the top two percent of all participants.

"What is special about your accomplishment is that you are the first majority human team to achieve this honor in the last two years." Abs smile looked like it was going to break his face Jonny thought. He looked at W0ody and lifted a shoulder as if to say *What the?* Jonny guessed he would find out later. Krage rang out "*Hey Abs! Have a good time in there? Did you engage the enemy, or someone closer!"* This was followed by a swell of laughter.

The clerk stepped forward and gave Abs a columnar trophy at least three feet tall, with a sparkling base encased with golden pillars and a silver sphere on top. *"Your award has already been engraved with the names of the contestants, your scores, your names and the date/time stamp. It has the additional benefit of changing colors depending upon temperature, humidity, chemistry and pressure of your environment.*

"One glance at your heroic efforts will at the same time provide you with the atmospheric safety sensors that all competent belters need. Large enough to attract attention, small enough to serve a proper function."

"Will it detect Abs farts?!" Someone broadcast. *"Yes, even though it will turn it a dull brown for a minute. Sir and Madams, enjoy your moment!"*

With this the Poohbah turned and walked over to Jonny and whispered: "If you need an endorsement for the Space Force as a pilot for the conflict at Jupiter, I will give them one. Well done." At that he gave his attention to the new crowd gathering on the other side of the gate. W0ody and Jonny looked at each other, not knowing what to make of the comment.

The gang began to gather around Abs, he broadcast to them, "*Before we continue with tonight's activities, we are going to start a new FAD, it's called Chops and Cuts. It helps our minds by making us think faster."* He pulled KaiLin closer, ignoring her look.

"Let me explain: whenever you are hangin' with your homies, you get an edge on and try to slam your friends verbally, and your friends try to slam you back, and the crowd can determine who is sharpest by laughter, because the underlying theme is humor. Understand?"

"*Not really, Abs."* Jimmy said. Jonny wasn't sure either.

"*Ah, Jimmy, it easy. It's like an old-fashioned HipHop Rap faceoff.*

" Let's say we're meeting at the rink, and someone is late, you can say 'Why you late dude, you with monkey woman again?' to try to embarrass him and you get points, but if he is sharp he could say 'That's no way to call your momma!' and the crowd might give him props. Anyways, its fast paced and all in fun.

"*Give it a shot Jimmy, it's easy."* Abs centered himself and stared at Jimmy. KaiLin started to pull away.

"Way to win the award without trying, Abs." Jimmy said tentatively. *"Abs, I don't know how you did it!"* someone said.

Jimmy broadcast out again more confidently, "*Yeah we do, he spent the entire time wrestling,"* he paused, "*with the controls!"*

"*Good chop Jimmy! You're getting the idea."*

"Yeah Abs, it wasn't so hard, coming from you!"

Abs face hardened a little, "*We're going to have fun Jimmy, me and you."*

"Well done Abs!" Jonny yelled trying to bring the gang back to the important award.

As the tension was released, Abs responded with the slightly tired, "*It's a tough job, but someone has to do it,"* then draped his arm over KaiLin's shoulder, who smiled and looked at the ground. "*I couldn't have done it without KaiLin's help!"* Where upon he held her left arm up high and the group laughed with glee.

"All right now, let's all go to the ReeBar, I got us passes that will work."

"Holy hip hugger Bat Ferd, that's awesome!" "No Way!"

"Way! Only the son of the weasel could pull this off. I've been planning this for a long time. Tried to get the passes for my Rites but didn't have the chops at the time. So, I planned this graduation bash." He started to turn towards the avenue with its glittering signs.

"Yeah Abs, yer chops have all been a little on the weak side. You sure ya got tickets to the ReeBar, not the TeaBar with all the grand mamas and kids?" Jimmy was on a roll.

The crowd had grown, and some strange kids were around the edge and tittered. Abs growled, *"This is a private party, all not invited, get lost."*

Abs looked over his shoulder and broadcast so everyone was included, *"Jimmy, no one likes the sound of your voice when it breaks. Maybe you can practice by yourself in an alley somewhere after I tear up your ticket. Now shut up or go home. You make any more remarks, any at all, and we will kiss yer ass goodbye!"*

Jonny was amazed at the renewed tension and conflict. He expected Jimmy to tell Abs to shove it, but he didn't. The group laughed at his discomfort and Abs leered at him. Art! ran up the east bulkhead and merged into the utilities in the shadows. Jimmy's face became set and the muscles of his jaws bulged a little, but he turned to follow the crowd.

Abs continued to rub it in: *"Welcome to the world of cuts, Jimmy. Don't mess with the weasel unless you got the chops to do it!"* The new kids had started to wander off. *"Don't let the door kick you in the ass on your way out!"* Abs laughed, his crowd did too.

Jonny was becoming uncomfortable. The group was a little too feisty, perhaps from the battle orgy they just participated in, or something else. He whispered "W0ody, I'm not sure I want to go into the ReeBar, do you?"

"I don't really want to, but it's not a strong feeling. I'll back your play, whatever it is."

Hey Abs! Jonny called out. *I'm not really up for the ReeBar. W0ody and I are more for going home.* Jonny stood on the other side of the group from Abs, looking at KaiLin as he spoke. She was standing next to Abs, holding hands but not otherwise touching.

Don't be stupid Johnny. We've been friends for ever, and I set this up for us. Don't you want to be a man? Get drunk for the first time, maybe get laid? Abs held KaiLin and pulled her closer, hip to hip.

Jonny felt squeezed; he was being pressured to do something he didn't want to do. Would it make him cool, or get status? The Creed said status was a false God. Did he care? He didn't want to let Abs down, but he really didn't want to go. He continued privately, *Abs, some of us were just in a battle, where we got smashed and bruised, all you did was spin little circles. Also, I really don't want MIP on my first day.*

Johnny, you are being really a fool, missing all the fun, quite uncool. To the side he smirked *'I'm a poet, I know it.'* Facing Jonny squarely, still linked: *Jonny, if you leave, you'll make me mad and you'll regret it.*

Tense and afraid, uncertain of what to do, he wanted to pull away. *Gotta go Abs, really can't stay.*

Broadcast to the whole gang: *"Bug off dog, last time I'll let you throw water in my face."* At that Abs turned around and led the gang down the Ave into the Zone.

Turning away from the Ave, Jonny started back towards the Old Spanish Trail. *"See you guys later!"* He decided arguing wasn't going do any good, confrontation scared him. Behind him the crowd was raucous, echo *broadcasting "M ...I...P... K... E... Y... M . O. U.*

S. E.!" "Bye kid, bye-bye!" and singing out loud "*He's afraid! Of getting laid!"*

He shoved his hands into his pockets, out of the side of his mouth "Come on W0ody, let's go home. I'm not going to fold like Jimmy."

"Right on, boss, you did OK."

"Yeah, right. Then why don't I feel right?" "Don't know, boss. Maybe a human thing?"

"Yeah, hopefully tomorrow will be easier." As they began the long march home.

The little voice called out, "Guys, that was intense, like a circus burning down."

No one said anything to that, so Richard continued, "You know, the flames were in tents. A circus. Fire? Intense? In tents? Anybody? Just trying to make a little joke, OK?"

"Shut up Richard, it's a bad time for jokes."

Jon didn't say anything.

"I think, therefore, I am."

The ability to articulate this idea is unique in Mankind.
You are Important, I am important, we both have worth.

"Sometimes I think I must have a Guardian Idiot.
A little invisible spirit just behind my shoulder,
looking out for me...only he's an imbecile."
- Spider Robinson

"I believe it is the duty of each of us to act as if the fate of the world depended on him.
Admittedly, one man by himself cannot do the job. However, one man can make a difference...
We must live for the future of the human race, and not for our own comfort or success."
Hyman Rickover – Father of Practical Nuclear Power

Patrol of the Green Bee

Chapter 13

The Battle Room of the United Federation Spaceship UFS *GREEN BEE (SSBN 732)* was rigged for red in its orbit sunward of the SKIP mechman outpost on the asteroid Hektor. The thousands of incomprehensible factories and giant machines glittered like stars as they floated a million klicks outbound. The over two-hundred-mile dog bone shaped asteroid was in a stable orbit librating around Jupiter's leading Lagrangian point L_4, surrounded by hundreds of smaller Trojan asteroids within Jupiter's influence.

Hector itself had captured two of the smaller Trojans. It's larger iron companion, Skamandrios was now being occulted by the larger asteroid. Hector's smaller four klick captured nickel asteroid Kenny was being rotted away by the incessant mining and manufacturing generated by the exponentially expanding mechman Skips and their nanobots assistants. The whole solar community was concerned about the loss of communication from Hektor and its inhabitants that occurred at the same time as the sporadic failures of other communication systems in the Federation.

The watch standers in the Battle Room waited quietly in anticipation.

"I relieve you, Sir." the newly qualified Officer of the Deck reported.

"I stand relieved." growled the off-going OOD. "Be alert."

Lieutenant Junior Grade Brian "Brain" Jefferson slowly lowered his butt into the Captain's chair, surveying the displays. The Torpedo Officer was the only Mudman commissioned in the FSN as a line officer.

The off-going OOD was the Navigator and had eased over to the charts for his midwatch review and was grumbling to the quartermaster. In a subcompartment of his mind the Lieutenant was glad for the dark which hid his nervousness and the internal tightness clamping at his chest and causing rigid knots in his lower back. *BEANS!* He swore mentally. The responsibility and complexity were enormous. How he, a historian, had ever been maneuvered into this position was a wonder, what with all the other officers, technojocks with advanced degrees in engineering and science.

BEANS! His uniform sweater did nothing against the cold air-conditioning the mechs and equipment desired. Grateful for few anomalies during the pre-watch tour he began to re-examine in depth the posture of the adversary, the SKIP Fortress and the millions of alien minds within. Slowly, the quiet flow of conversation and reports resumed around him.

The 20MC intercom chimed: “Conn, Sensors, have gained a new k-band signal bearing 011N, 007E, designate K-9.”

The OOD replied “Sensor, Conn, aye.” as he annotated his manual board. He watched as the new contact popped up on his display with the other 20 or so highlighted points of interest. He knew there were over a thousand other contacts being tracked but have been designated non-threat and their markers submerged.

The Auxilaryman of the Watch, Forward came into the Control Room from the lower level access ladder and presented his logs to the Chief of the Watch for review. A cocky fellow, recognizing his skill and worth, he began to sing out softly: “Air in the banks, fish in the tanks, water going aft...” when the COW elbowed him the ribs with a meaningful glance at the Conn. Now suddenly aware of the new OOD, the Aux Forward fell silent, standing respectfully next to the COW while the review of his logs resumed.

The Aux Forward began to fidget as the COW started an expanded review of past logs, with an infinite care towards system trend indicators. Now the Aux Forward belatedly realized he was getting a subtle and silent dressing down. He nervously began to count the weld beads in the top of the COW’s metal head, trying to determine how many passes were necessary to completely seal the spheroid, and if it was done with the electronic guts inside or if they were added later through some aperture.

The COW began softly: “Petty Officer Mueller, I note that the level readings for the mid-bulge trim tank are inconsistent with normal usage and the hours logged for the discharge of the pure water pump. Do we have a small unnoticed leak developing or **ARE YOU RADIOING THE LOGS AGAIN!”** The last came out as a bellow that caused the whole control room party to turn and stare at the two.

“Aw Chief, that ain’t it, and you know it. I bet the discharge meter of the pure water pump is starting to stick again. You know how these intermittent failures are."

"Conn, Sensor, K-9 is classified as an Akula Class Mech Explorer at 9600 klicks inbound at 2 kps. Recommend re-designating K-9 as Master-9 because of classification and proximity."

The OOD thought to himself *I'll never remember that* "Sensor, Conn, aye. Re-designate K-9 as Master One, I say again, re-designate K-9 as Master One. Attack Center Fire Control acknowledge."

"Re-designate K-9 as Master One, Conn Fire Control aye."
"Re-designate K-9 as master One, Sensor aye."

The little scene between watchstanders continued as the COW voiced, "I sure do, and I also know what logs look like when someone gets lazy reading the same old tank that never changes week after week. But no matter. I guess someone will just have to overhaul the flow gauge after watch and try to fix that intermittent problem."

"Aw Chief!" Cried the Aux Forward with despair. "They was gonna burn that old flick Alien after watch!" The Data Technician could be heard snickering.

The rest of Control relaxed as this scene from a play they were all familiar with came to an end. The COW nipped a relaxed watchstanding habit in the bud and the Aux Forward was going to get some maintenance practice, again.

Lieutenant Jefferson looked up from the displays to notice the Executive Officer talking to the Navigator, his wide cranium reflecting the red displays of the control room.

"Conn, Sensor, Master One has commenced a burn."

"Sensor, Conn, aye. Fire Control report CPA Master One."

"Conn, Fire Control, Master One's initial CPA before burn was 21,000 klicks one hour 20 minutes, bearing 070 North, 015 West. Master One's new CPA will be updated every 30 seconds. Based upon Master One's initial classification minimum projected CPA 9 minutes, Mark on Top."

Lieutenant Jefferson sat stunned for a second, *Mark on Top!,* he thought as he heard the words.

Placing his palms on the armrests of the Captain's seat, he forced himself stiffly erect, and walked over to the Communication panel. Picking up the 1MC microphone he announced: "Man Battle Stations Missile, Mark on Top 9 minutes." His voice was shallow and nervous. Turning to the Control Room Party "Chief of the Watch, sound the General Alarm."

The sirens of the General Alarm sounded throughout the ship, causing men to kick back chairs in the galley and rec rooms, people staggered up from deep sleeps, and maintenance techs began to place their equipment in stable states.

As the alarm silenced, the OOD repeated on the 1MC again, with a little more confidence: "Man Battle Stations Missile, Mark on Top 9 minutes."

Crewmen were streaming into Control, taking position alongside equipment warming up for the battle, getting briefed by duty section watchstanders.

"Conn, Sensor, Master One continues to burn. Spectrum analysis confirms Master One's classification as an Akula Explorer with anomalies. Possible additional craft are masked by Master One."

Lieutenant Jefferson glanced at the master CIC display, where additional contact information was appearing, he adjusted the logarithmic scales to place the SKIP Fortress on right extreme and

Master One and own ship on center stage left: “Sensor, Conn, aye.”

“Conn, Fire Control, Master One continues to conform to Mark on Top, CPA in 8 minutes.” His CIC display was remotely updated by the Fire Control Watch Team leader, as additional red vector indicators reached from Master One to the *Green Bee*’s symbol. “Fire Control, Conn, aye.” he responded on the 20MC.

The Captain strode into Control from the forward passage wearing his off watch poopy suit. The Helm sang out; “Captain in Control!” while the manning of the ship continued unabated. The OOD stepped aside to allow the Captain up on the Conn.

“Report, OOD.” “Yes sir, a contact, Master One, identified as a mech Akula Class Explorer, commenced a burn 20,000 klicks out 2 minutes ago, CPA approximately 7 minutes, Mark on Top.”

“What are your intentions?” In the background a soft voice called out: “Officer of the Deck, all stations report Manned.” The OOD quickly responded “Very well, Chief of the Watch.” Then he turned back to the Captain: “Sir, if left in charge, I would get the next Fire Control 30 Second Solution, and based upon that, commence evasion if necessary. Concurrently I will have radio start hailing the vessel with Notice to Mariner buffer Warnings.”

“Very good Lieutenant, carry on. Commence standard engagement procedures. This will allow me to observe and think.”

“Yes Sir.” This panicked the OOD more than he would have thought. *BEANS! How did he get himself into these messes!*

“Radio, Conn, commence hailing Master One. Inform them they are entering Military Buffer Zone 8. Reiterate, deadly force is authorized. Demand they turn aside no closer than 4 kilo-klicks. Send Notice to Mariners 9-96 as backup. Standard frequencies. Patch to Conn if contact is made.”

"Conn, Radio, aye."

The XO was scurrying around the control room, establishing the CIC, fire control and battle teams. In his eyes the XO's head glowed a dull red in the dimly lit compartment of the spaceship. All their eyes and sensors needed to be at maximum sensitivity in case the ship shifted to visual warfare. All the indicators on the display panels were backlit with soft orange or red, only the ticks of the numeral indicators were blue or green, to save the operator's eyes.

"Conn, Sensor, Master One continues to burn, secondary contacts are emerging from behind Master One." Before the OOD could respond an urgent report was overlapped: Conn, Fire Control, Master One's CPA Mark On Top, 6 minutes 45 seconds, current range seven-point six kilo-klicks."

Pausing, LTJG Jefferson continued, this time addressing the Control Room Party: "Helm, all ahead standard, left full thruster, steady course 270 West, 015 North."

"All ahead full, right full thruster, steady course 270 West, 015 South, Conn, Helm, aye."

Selecting the 6MC: "Weapons, Conn, prepare the starboard forward battery for a salvo launch, eight warhead rosette burst. Select secondary aft battery full eight compliment SCRAM 100 KT warhead."

"Conn, Weapons, acknowledged. Recommend 10 KT SCRAM warheads, lighter weight of warhead maximizes missile maneuverability, increasing hit success. 10 KT is optimum on the hit/kick curves."

"Weapons, Conn, aye. Configure secondary battery to recommendation."

Arrayed before Lieutenant Jefferson were the 25 people now

in Control for Battle Stations. Under the deep glow of the red lights the Damage Control Party under the supervision of the DCA was on the left side of the compartment, three of them in instant communication with the rest of the ship, the DCA was summarizing their information and providing it to the OOD when necessary.

A light voice said over the hubbub: “Steady 270 West, 015 South.”

To their right was the Maneuvering Party, also four people, responsible to convert the OOD’s maneuvering needs into fact, correcting for sudden thrust of weapons launches, rebalancing mass distribution for the movement of men and materials by counter pumping water, gaining direction and speed despite damage and machinery limits.

LT Salah ad-Din, the Supply Officer, a borgman with two mech personalities in marriage with a human, rather than the normal one, was in charge. The mechs usually let the human side of MacPhi1lips handle the show, recognizing her ability to respond to changing and incomplete input, was superior. And so was her capability to control the other personalities in her party, made up of exceptionally quick, but generally youthful individuals.

On the far right side of Control was where the attention of the OOD and Captain lay. The Combat Information Center (CIC) set up there in lieu of the normal watch station contained a series of consoles and displays, separated into Sensor Status (3 men), Fire Control Solution Status (8), Navigation (3), Weapons Status (2), and the CIC supervisor. Normally the CIC supervisor was the XO, but LTJG Jefferson noted the Navigator was Supe, while the XO hovered around.

“Conn, Sensor, Master One has initiated fire control tracking laser frequencies, do not detect lock-on.”

“Captain?” He inquired with raised eyebrows, but the Captain only said "Continue."

"Helm, all ahead full, continue left to West 230. Weapons, launch chaff, Starboard side, two salvos. Prepare two drone decoys, launch in 15 seconds."

"Conn, Weapons, aye."

"Conn, Helm, I cannot continue to West 230, the Helm is already steady at West 270."

HUH? BEANS! "Helm, left full thruster, steady West 230."

"Left full thruster, steady West 230, Conn, Helm, aye." His ears and stomach began to turn edgy with the swaying of the ship and changing gravities.

"Attention Control room staff, Firing Point Procedures, Master One, right forward battery."

"Firing Point Procedures, Master One, right forward battery." acknowledged the CIC Supervisor, turning to the Weapons Supervisor: "Weapons, initiate procedures right forward battery." "Acknowledged." Turning: "Officer of the Deck, CPA Master One is still decreasing. Master One seems to be changing course to establish CPA, no radio contact established." "Conn, Sensor, lock-on Master One, have designated two new contacts clearing behind Master One as K-10 and K-11, possible Vega Class"

Voices began to assault him: "Launch two drones" "Steady course 230 West, 015 North, Engineering answering all ahead full" "Right Forward battery ready" The Navigator said, "CPA is slowing with new own ship's course, but still closing fast, recommend a left spiral into the shadow cone of our chaff."

"Very well, Helm full thrusters, come left to East 175, South 175. Decay spiral steering"

"Come left..." the response faded in his ears as he heard Sensors announce "Conn, Sensor, detect missile launch Master One, feeding track to Fire Control. "Sensor, Conn, aye." Concurrently he heard the CIC Supervisor say: "Weapons ready, Fire Control ready, Master One, right forward battery." His stomach quivered as the ship looped over to its new course.

"Conn, Sensor, missile launch appears to be a swath of 20-G close proximity boost ASMs."

Looking at the master display on the Conn, LTJG Jefferson noted that he would be very shortly in the shadow cone of his chaff while the two drones diverged and evaded in sight of the enemy. The shadow did not protect him from K-11 but that contact did not seem to be in adequate range to track him through the melee. Satisfied with the big picture and recognizing the rosette detonations would continue to screen as well as deter or destroy the advanced attackers he continued his orders "CIC, launch right forward battery. Weapons, target..."

The XO stepped between the Conn and the CIC, placing a hand on the arming switches and speaking loudly "This is a Readiness Drill, I say again, this is a Readiness Drill." He then turned the safe-arm switch in front of the Navigator's hand to training and stepped back.

LTJG Jefferson stood stunned for a moment, finally noticing the red glow on the XO's head wasn't a reflection after all, but a red Monitor hat.

BEANS! The inadvertent swearing balked in his mind. Shaking his head, he continued "I say again CIC, launch right forward battery. Weapons, target incoming ASMs with AAMs. Fire when ready." The responses again were drowned out by the swearing in his head *BEANS! First, I have to save my life, now I have to save my CAREER!* The last came out as a shout in his mind, and when his mind's eye cleared, and he had regained his hearing he heard the tag end of the Weapons Officer response.

He turned quickly to the master console and saw that a track had been projected for own ship's counterattack. The deck beneath him shuddered as the launch forces pushed back against the hull. Belatedly he realized this must be simulation. He ought to explore more of the Weapons Officer's realm and learn how they did that.

The display indicated 15 seconds to detonation of the rosette, and that showed it to occur between the *GREENIE* and Master One, given the assumed accuracy of the solution of Master One's track. Wryly he thought, given the accuracy of plotting a simulated attacker with the same computers used for finding and sending phony signals to Sensor and Fire Control for that same simulated attacker.

The Captain looked at the XO, and the XO nodded, and the Captain turned to the OOD, "Secure from the drill, secure from Battle Stations, get yourself relieved and come to the wardroom for the drill debrief." "Yes sir." The Captain departed from Control.

On the 1 MC he announced: "Secure from the drill, secure from Battle Stations." The starch drained out of him as people scurried about control, putting equipment back in battle lockers, excess watchstanders departing, and the original crew coming back into Control to relieve their Battle Station counterparts. The Navigator appeared and stepped up to the Conn: "I'm here to relieve you. What's your status?"...

LTJG Jefferson sat with the XO and Captain in the Wardroom. This majestic space of the *USS GREEN BEE* was decked out in real Earth wood paneling and furniture. Cabinets contained mementos from the glory of days past. Silver goblets and platters were inlaid with fine gold filigree and were shock mounted behind shatterproof glass. Well-worn swords, pistols and blasters, each with a tag identifying its importance to the history of the ship, shimmered in holographic iridescence. A brass plaque on the bulkhead was inscribed with the rollcall of the all the Officers who had served onboard the old *GREENIE.* It was concurrently impressive and somber.

The Captain started by saying, “Do you have anything further you wish to add to your debrief?”

LTJG Jefferson sat still a moment while thinking. A memory came to him, *‘Never volunteer anything.’* “No sir.” he responded tensely.

“Very well then, after real time and video analysis of your performance I have one objective and two subjective comments. First, objectively, you need to take care in your communication actions. Several times you did not heed the acknowledgement of your subordinate watch stations to the orders you had given.

“By doing that you were never certain that the Helm, Radio, or the Weapons Officer were doing what you required. You must establish habits by training which will cause you to pause for those repeat backs. Do not begrudge the loss of time caused by procedural handshakes. Many hard lessons learned by experience dictate that although we may lose a few moments here and there, we save enormously by preventing confusion. Do you understand this, Lieutenant Jefferson?”

“Yes sir.”

“The two subjective comments are as follows. Firstly, you appeared stiff and uncomfortable. This is to be expected in one’s initial battle, habits are not yet formed and can’t be relied upon. We in fact are glad that you did take it seriously and weren’t too loose. This probably contributes to your hurry and missing the communication acknowledgements. The secondary subjective comment is laudatory. It is this, I have no further comment.”

The Captain watched Lieutenant Junior Grade Jefferson from

her hand-hewn teak Captain's Chair. The OOD swallowed and pondered the significance of this statement. A slow bashful smile smeared across his face despite his attempts to control it. "Thank you, sir." He said quietly. The Captain nodded, then yawned, stretched her arms out over and around her head slowly, shook her head with a violent shake and stood up.

The XO was already standing as LTJG Jefferson struggled to his feet. The Captain nodded again, and without speaking, left the wardroom.

"You did fine, Mister Jefferson, just fine."

He sat back down with a thump. "I was scared, XO, all sorts of thoughts were flowing through my mind. There seems to be at all times too many choices. I am worried I might fail in the future."

"Don't worry Lieutenant. Hard work and much practice will create the habits you can rely upon. These habits can be scary in a human because you have trained your body to respond without thought, and so your body acts without your permission, much like a robot. But in reality, it is with your desires, from the time you conducted your own training. You must learn to trust your own actions, even if they're not voluntary. Learn to rely on them, quit spending time going over the rational again and again. In crisis, you can cause death by inaction, that's why you train."

"Whew. Well, I'm glad that's over. I hope I will live up to your expectations, Sir."

"Trust me, in this situation, you took the right actions, had good thought processes and good habits. Look at me, don't even try to guess what's going on inside this tin can, watch the results. You did good Lieutenant, you justified our qualifying you as one of our youngest OODs, even if you can't tell a thermal neutron from a fast one. Welcome to this man's Navy! Are there any questions?"

"Yes Sir, during my in brief, the charts indicated Hektor had a captured metal satellite four klicks in diameter named Kenny, but I never saw it. Where was it?"

"That's another story TOP, they used Kenny for materials, Kenny's dead."

The Stars and Universal Truths exist

Mankind and Personal Truth exist.
Modeled Truths describe Universal Truths.

"I, for one, bet on science as helping us. I have yet to see
how it fundamentally endangers us, even with the H-bomb lurking about.
Science has given us more lives than it has taken; we must remember that."
- Philip K. Dick

"Every great dream begins with a dreamer.
Always remember, you have within you the strength, the patience,
and the passion to reach for the stars to change the world."
Harriet Tubman

Millennium Hive Electric Work
Chapter 14

Cool air from the morning shore breeze blew into the window where Aleks and his father worked on the wind-up Automatons, all gears and springs and shafts and which were practically alive. Leaving his work bench, he carefully damped the ash wood fire, which made the unsurpassed soot that clung to the chimney. Gathering the glazed ceramic cup, and using the finest camelhair, he gently brushed the black dust into the bowl, careful not to sneeze, or touch anything until after he washed. Then returning to the worktable, he applied the smallest amount of the powder to the gears of father's latest creation and turned the crank of the brace.

Although this was a little mechanical man, it was also a tool, and could transform between one and the other as one turned the crank. When Aleks completed cycling the motions, he selected the crystal of power and peered intently at the movements. This mechanism was father's pinnacle achievement, utilizing all the best craftsmen on the Island because a creation of this complexity and miniaturization required the countless effort of many, many hands, and Aleks knew that nowhere else in the world was a wonder like this.

While Aleks had been woolgathering, his hands had dipped a small cedar stave in the secret dust, carefully removed two of the gears and began rubbing the bright spots on the metal that the movement had exposed. His father had not yet entrusted that what that secret dust was to the apprentice, his son, but the mechanism worked smoother when he was done. Today, the shop was all business. Little did Aleks know that life could change at any moment.

You know, Jonny thought, *today is a good day. Graduated from public school last week, start University Prep next week, get my citizenship on my birthday, my freedom! And on top of all that, getting to spend the day with Pops and W0ody. Forget the Free Zone Party. I am on my way!*

They decelerated on the 520 train into the Millennium dome on their way to work, and for some reason more than the usual number of passengers had filled up the seats at this early hour. Strangers were sitting in the seats normally occupied by the familiar faces, the travel acquaintances he had shared conversations with about their favorite battleball teams.

As the train came to a stop Jonny asked his dad why there were more travelers that day, was it because of the Trojan War he was hearing about?

Pops ocular spun in and out as it adjusted focus as he turned: *I don't believe the tensions out by Jupiter have turned into a war quite yet, Jon. I don't know about the shuttle crowd, it always varies a little, and sometimes so much that you notice. Perhaps we have a holiday? Quite the cattlecar, isn't it?*

Jonny queried the WET, but nothing stuck out explaining the odd changes in travel behavior. He figured what a cattlecar was, even though he didn't know what a cattle was. TMI.

As they got off at the Transfer NODE in the basement of Millennium Dome: *So, Dad, what are we doing today?*

Pops was all in leathers today, the hydraulic piston seals newer and the backpack APU had a smaller footprint than the Carmine dress set. *We're going to Millennium Level MIKE to conduct infrared testing of the VFDs for the chillers of the Level GOLF hydroponic units.*

We will first drop in at the PHILIPS ELECTRIC offices on LIMA to outfit W0ody with FLIR cameras and associated apps to help us. W0ody shrugged his shoulders and raised both orange pastel eyebrows, his tool belts making the smallest chime sounds. W0ody brought out Richard from under his tool kilt… *I hope this little puppy has that as part of its kit. I guess we will find out when we load the APPs.*

The tiny voice, *OK, boss, I'm on it! And, I've decided I'm a 'he', not an 'it', OK?*

They looked at each other, *OK Richard, we will try to remember.*

Augustus continued to Jonny: *I will get you an additional handheld FLIR and see if you can make it work.*

Ah dad! Why are you always making me do stuff that W0ody and even his smart tool can do better? As they walked over to the express elevators Augustus sent a WET handshake to the NODE regarding their destination and were given the car they needed to catch to Mil L.

Redundancy, son redundancy. Why are the ships and habitats doubled walled? His steam valves and poppets, combining with the clink of W0ody's tools, contributed to the murmur of the background noises that were ubiquitous within the world that was Vesta. *If everything worked perfectly the first time, we wouldn't have to design this way, but it doesn't. Therefore, everything is redundant.*

The doors of the car swept open and they were met by the stares of three unusual Morphmen decked out in a riot of colored feathers and huge black lemur eyes. The bodies of all three were brilliant dark green while the headdresses of two were a perfect scarlet red, while the third had green plumage throughout.

All had a band of bright yellow around their necks, and as they were being stared at, the crests on the two redheads started to rise.

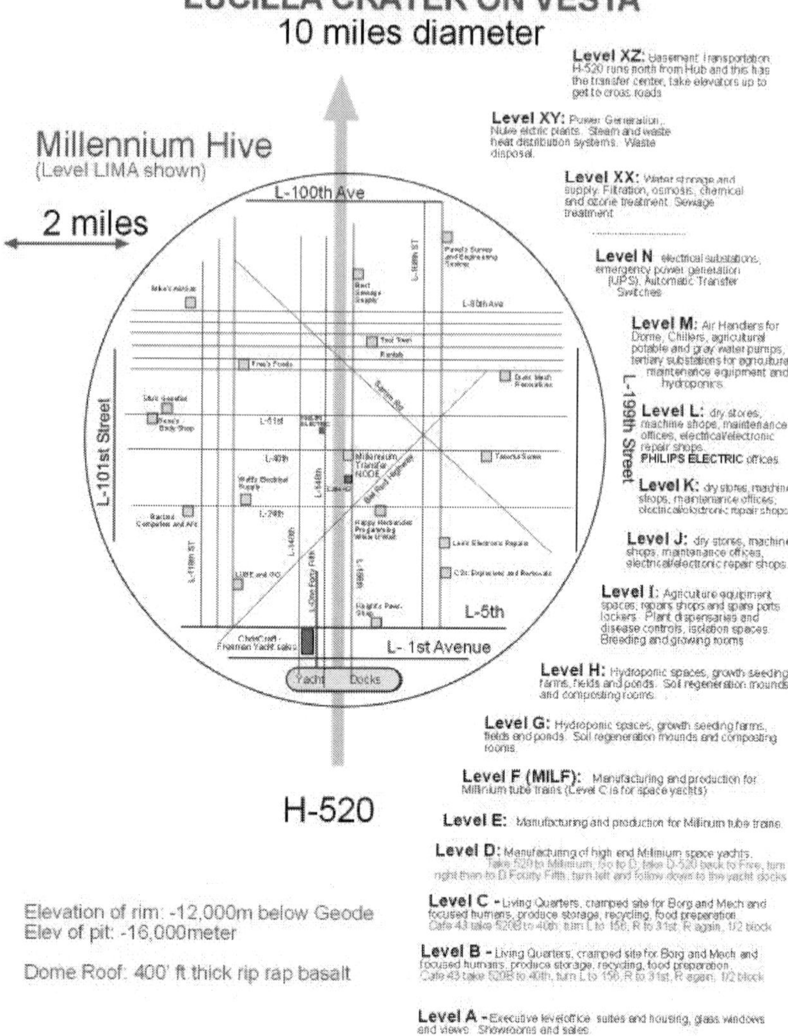

LUCILLA CRATER ON VESTA
10 miles diameter
Millennium Hive
(Level LIMA shown)
2 miles
L-100th Ave
L-101st Street
L-199th Street
L-5th
L- 1st Avenue
Yacht Docks
H-520
Elevation of rim: -12,000m below Geode
Elev of pit: -16,000meter
Dome Roof: 400' ft thick rip rap basalt
Level XZ: Basement Transportation H-520 runs north from Hub and this has the transfer center, take elevators up to get to cross roads
Level XY: Power Generation, Nuke elctric plants. Steam and waste heat distribution systems. Waste disposal.
Level XX: Water storage and supply. Filtration, osmosis, chemical and ozone treatment. Sewage treatment
Level N electrical substations, emergency power generation (UPS), Automatic Transfer Switches
Level M: Air Handlers for Dome, Chillers, agricultural potable and gray water pumps, tertiary substations for agricultural maintenance equipment and hydroponics
Level L: dry stores, machine shops, maintenance offices, electrical/electronic repair shops. PHILIPS ELECTRIC offices
Level K: dry stores, machine shops, maintenance offices, electrical/electronic repair shops
Level J: dry stores, machine shops, maintenance offices, electrical/electronic repair shops.
Level I: Agriculture equipment spaces; repairs shops and spare parts lockers. Plant dispensaries and disease controls, isolation spaces. Breeding and growing rooms
Level H: Hydroponic spaces, growth seeding farms, fields and ponds. Soil regeneration mounds and composting rooms.
Level G: Hydroponic spaces, growth seeding farms, fields and ponds. Soil regeneration mounds and composting rooms.
Level F (MILF): Manufacturing and production for Millinium tube trains (Level C is for space yachts)
Level E: Manufacturing and production for Milinum tube trains.
Level D: Manufacturing of high end Milinium space yachts.
Level C - Living Quarters, cramped site for Borg and Mech and focused humans, produce storage, recycling, food preparation.
Level B - Living Quarters, cramped site for Borg and Mech and focused humans, produce storage, recycling, food preparation.
Level A - Executive level/office suites and housing, glass windows and views. Showrooms and sales.

Wow, that's rad, man! exclaimed Jon. *What a great coordination of contrasting colors, the yellow sets it up perfectly! Dad, can I do that?* The ruffled feathers on the birdmen relaxed and they smiled and stepped back for the trio to enter. W0ody smiled back with those bright red gloss lips.

Jon, when you get your emancipation, you can do anything you can afford. He twirled against a side wall with an elegance that was astounding given his apparatus. *As I was saying, you train to do what W0ody can do, and W0ody trains to learn what you do. You never know when that redundancy will be useful. W0ody, you can put Richard back, it, no, I apologize, he won't be needed for a while.*

Richard broke in, *Hey Pops, I can call you Pops, right? Anyways, Pops, if Jonny's gonna get feathers, can I get a pet? W0ody's gots lots of room down here, right W0ody?* Before anyone could answer he continued, *The team here and I would really like to get a bald eagle, and maybe a beaver. So, how 'bout it? OK?*

Leave it Richard, W0ody muttered.

No? Too much? How about a snake? A pocket ball python would fit down here real snug like, OK? Easy to take care of too!

Hush Richard, not now. Go back to studying for your App, OK?

Aw, youse guys are no fun, he sighed and disappeared back into the crib.

After getting off the elevator and boarding the 156th Ave tram tunnel access north to NE 51st, Augustus mentioned, *To make the introduction to your summer working life a little more fun, we just might take a side jaunt through Helena INDIA on the way home, last time I checked, the flower beds are about to go into bloom for the Skagit Tulip Festival.*

Cool dad, maybe we can see the Vinegar Scorpions again?

You're thinking of the arboretum and zoo in the Hub, but there is also a pumpkin carving exhibition that is outrageous, the stuff they can do with twenty-four-hour sunlight, forced feeding, genetics, and low gravity is amazing. I think the largest comes in over 100,000 pounds mass, and we can walk through it.

By this time, they had completed the quick hop and departed the tram and entered the pedestrian avenue beside NE 51st westbound towards the PHILIPS ELECTRIC offices and shop.

As they walked through Millennium from the 156/51st intersection, Jonny studied the tunnel walls wondering as always what all those pipes were doing. That the sky-blue pipes were potable water and the Kelly-green pipes were oxygen he knew, but what were the burnt orange pipes with the red and black bands? A quick query of the WET resolved the answer to industrial liquid waste level III (what the heck were Globally Harmonized Systems? He didn't have time to research everything, TMI).

Dad, why is Millennium B so boring and busy? At home, or at the Hub or Space Port, you never see the utilities exposed in the tunnels like you do here. And, no one here hangs out on all the corners like the goons on the Ave.

In the other domes the people work together in a system called collated capitalistic socialism. It works pretty well, but there is always some conflict and competition. The Lucilla Crater, however, has been bought by the second time share Hive Mind, known as Millennium B. The first timeshare, over by the snowman, is known as Millennium A or the Apple Hive.

As they traversed 51st the rumble of the 520 rose up through the ground and chases: *People here in the Bee-Hive sign a contract for eighteen months allowing mind control, then have to take between three and six months off. The hive benefits greatly from the efficiencies of common work.*

At this point they turned left on 150th Ave, south towards PHILIPS and started to pass the Ten Game Works on their right, the show windows bright with tomorrow's media marvels.

Anyways, the original hives recruited people and gave them lobotomies to remove their selfish motivations, but the drawback was they also lost creativity, so even though they could produce new generations, they slowly died out because they were unable to evolve and respond to change. You know Jon, it seems the only constant in the Universe is change.

So, the Millennium is an 'improved version' of the Hivemind, the time share members are called Cogmen, and the permanent members are call Hivemen. Blah Blah Blah Jonny thought, but didn't say. Sometimes you just have to let Pops blather on.

They came to the entry to PHILIPS ELECTRIC which was just before the Redwood Forest.

Jonny was always interested in the façade and entry of PHILIPS ELECTRIC, there were all sorts of archaic electrical gear: Jacob's ladders, Harpsichord telegraph machines, TESLA Coils and Faraday cages, and a vast array of bottles of nothing, which always confused him. Why have bottles of nothing? That big one in the corner said it was an three foot tall X-ray vacuum bottle; must be dangerous he thought. He reached for the door.

The lights in the tunnel flickered. The WET went quiet for a moment. Jonny thought he somehow heard again the tolling of a great bell, but he also didn't hear anything. A second resounding chime reverberated in the unattainable aether again.

Then, the background chatter on the WET resumed as if nothing had happened.

Dad, what was that? Did I blink or did the lights waver? Was that a church bell in the distance?

No, you're right. The lights blinked. I don't know why. I heard it too, but I am not sure. Doesn't seem anything on the WET.

They paused if anything was to be discovered on the newsnet, but nothing. *So, let's go in.*

Jonny enjoyed the front room of PHILIPS ELECTRIC as much as the show window, it was full of blown glass art done by Harold Smythe, the father of his friend Abs. It was incredibly beautiful and incredibly expensive, but the owner of PHILIPS ELECTRIC had traded for it before Harold had become famous. Soft boogie music was bouncing out of the ancient Wurlitzer Juke Box that rumor said came from old Earth.

Glass wall hangings and showcases were lit with the most exquisite pins of light, mixed with electric currents cascading inside of glowing lamps and organic shapes. He reached out and touched one as he walked by and the art responded with a concentrated glow next to his hand and that pulsed seemingly with his heartbeat.

They continued into the workspace and shops in the back of the building, tools and supplies of all sorts organized in groups that made sense to someone, but not to Jon. Why were the tuggers located next to the RMC and hydraulic benders? And the spools next to the racketeers?

His watched as dad went with W0ody, checking out the PODs and extensions, until they found one that was a right fit for W0ody's frame, then W0ody sat down on the docking station to upload the firmware/software. He then began trying to figure out how to adapt Richard to the common to allow the installation of the newer APPs that the smart tool could use.

Augustus turned to Jonny and motioned him over to the tool racks and pointed to a series of tools that looked like laser pistols.

Jon, these are remote infrared heat detectors with various added abilities. FLIR stands for Forward Looking Infrared. We use them to detect heat, which is one indicator of failure. See if you can remember Ohm's law, because these tools will remotely sense and calculate the information for you, but you should be able to estimate the answer too.

Dad, how can you stand it being as old as you? Jonny was getting frustrated.

Get going.

Jonny walked along the row of apparatus looking at the size, and finally selecting a small one that was called a remote thermometer, and which had a gun handle and laser pointer. W0ody looked over, his polished brass rotor reflecting all the ceiling lights in the confined space as golden stars, *Ready big guy?*

Yeah, lets rock and roll. W0ody plopped Richard into his hammer holster and squared up the apron.

They walked back to 51st/156 and took the return tram south. Augustus said, *Let's bypass the transfer station and stop at the CAFÉ 43 for breakfast, does that sound like a deal?*

Sure, I can stand a bite.

As they sat down, W0ody *I can have a few bytes too.*

W0ody, you sure do have a sense of humor, why don't you display it all the time? Around me you are relaxed and carefree, but when we are in a crowd, you shut down. Why aren't you lippy like Uncle Bill, or even Richard? It would be cool.

Yeah boss, just follow my lead and you will be crackin' wise in no time!

Yeah, right Richard, as if you would know a joke when you saw one.

Ah Jon, I can clown around you, and you don't criticize. But, I can't be like Wild Bill, he's had decades of practice and experience.

Around your friends, all I would do is get bad looks and a stupid reputation. It's better if a young mech is seen but not heard. Anyways, I get to try out all my bad stuff on you.

That's a fact!

Shut up Richard.

They all smiled.

After arrival, they ordered break-fast and while they waited for it to be delivered. *W0ody, you're better than you think, the puns on Pirate's earrings and your monolog of conservatives and liberals leave me in stitches. Come out of your shell man.*

Patience MeatStick, I will after the Coming of Age ceremony in September, lord willing.

Wow, two months. You know, it's been so long, it's hard to realize it's almost here. I can't wait.

Uh huh, neither can I.

Youse guys don't know what long is! Try a hunderd years, or a thousand!

Yeah, right Richard.

Augustus's Eggs Benedict arrived with bacon on sour dough muffins, and Jonny dug into his waffles and blueberry syrup with sausage links. W0ody just smiled as his seat was a combo docking station and he had been recharging since they sat down.

Jonny was staring at some girls across the restaurant, especially the redhead. To distract Pops from watching him, he asked, *Dad, remind me what a VFD does, OK?*

But W0ody, ever the motor fanatic all things motors: theory, design, construction and application, and now motor mouth, jumped in: *VFD stands for Variable Frequency Drive and its basic purpose is to save energy by reducing the speed of motors when maximum force is not required.*

They are a combination of high power electrical and electronic device that uses pulse width PM modulation so fast that there are relativistic and quantum effects on the sawtooth wave forms that, if not accounted for, cause eddy currents to jump into the grounding system and neutral conductors, causing over-heating and welding of the races.

W0ody, you look all charged up.

You bet, Richard, I really am really passionate about motors. Did you know that the AC-DC wars at the beginning of the engineering revolution wasn't about AC and DC?

W0ody, before you take off on this subject, Richard was asking how your battery status was.

I was?

Everyone, are we ready to go?

Sorry, ready Pops.

OK, how 'bout you, son? Looking away from the girls, Jonny was continually amazed that his dad could throw down the chow faster than anyone. He was only just done and looked at his dad's clean plate, even that twiggy vegetable was gone.

Ready dad, rock and roll. They headed back to the tram and went north to the transfer station, and this time rode the freight elevator down to Mil M. All grey and boring, no one on the ride, like those rad bird Morphmen.

Exiting out on MIKE, they followed Augustus through the winding corridors until they came to a locked electrical room with huge garage roller doors next to a personnel entrance. Augustus coded them through. Entering, they came into a huge cavern of piping, some as large as three feet in diameter, and the heavy hum of running motors.

Bolted to the deck on shock mounts were cylinders painted red with ventilation at one end that Jonny knew were the motors, the heavy flex cables giving proof to his estimate, all connected to barrel devices spanning the large piping which he knew were the impellor pumps. Everything was insulated with fiber cloth and restrained with wire stitching.

Guys, these are the pumps that recycle the water and heat to the hydroponics up on GOLF, that helps bring our tasty breakfast. Over on the far wall are the VFDs that we are going to assess. W0ody, you are going to start at the low end, and Jonny at the high. I will work behind you to make sure you are doing it right, and we will meet in the middle.

OK. Jonny started to the right and W0ody to the left. His dad went with W0ody, who had Richard out again and was pointing towards his equipment while turning the hand crank. How archaic Jonny thought.

He could see the red laser pointer and the amber display of the remote thermometer of his own FLIR easily enough through the face shield, although he wasn't sure he would. Stepping inside the marked boundary, he sighted the FLIR at the furthest right VFD, and focused on the top right terminal, which was marked in yellow. The temperature was in spec. Boy, this was going to be boring. He thumbed the slide and moved on.

……

Jonny and W0ody chatted silently as they wound their way after work through the tunnels from the I-15 on towards home in the Helena complex. They had put in the hours at work, and immensely enjoyed their visit to the pumpkin patch and were ready to call it a day. Dad had gone back to the shop, and they had the rest of the early evening off.

As they turned right on Euclid and past the Ender School they just graduated from, he queried W0ody: *I heard that she-men mature faster than he-men, did you ever hear that?*

Sure did, but I wouldn't know.

Well, I thought about it. It doesn't seem like the girls around me are more mature.

MeatStick, anyone around you, especially the girls around you, <u>are</u> better behaved.

Well TinCan, they don't ask questions, they just accept what they are told, or follow the group. They don't care why. Is that more mature?

I don't know.

So anyways, I thought about it, and I think this is just a story they tell us. I think girls are better behaved because they have less testosterone and are more compliant. Guys who are wild are pushing the envelope. And sometimes that helps survival, and is there a better definition of maturity than "survival"? I bet compliance can kill you during times of upheaval.

Whatever, Jon, your thinking pushes the envelope, you know that?

Anyways, when I get interested in a girl, all they are interested in is who is the latest media prince, or what someone said about another, or all the time saying who shouldn't be associated with who. Wow. They aren't interested in the Universe or how it works, or science or stuff. Dad says: 'You can't live with them, you can't live without them.' Whatever that means. I hope I get a girlfriend soon. I bet when I become a citizen, girls will be interested in me. They all hang around Abs, why not me?

Jon, you're all over the map, meat stick. There are plenty of girls interested in science. Hormones kicking in?

Yeah, whatever. I just am thinking about what dad had said that his contacts had said that Wii-Immune is fighting off an e-viral attack and that is what the blinking lights were. He says not to worry, but maybe I worry, huh?

Yeah MeatStick, and maybe you're just stoopid. How do you jump from she-men maturity to an e-viral attack, huh?

Well, I been lied to, told that she-men are more mature, and dad told me something I don't believe. What is the "mature" response? Huh? Why is it that I can't believe adults on the important things? Why do they lie to you to your face?

MeatStick, you ask the strangest questions, got no answer to that one. Do you even believe what you're saying?

No.

Huh?

A little muffled voice called out: *Youse guys are crazy.*

Turning left on Lincoln, Jonny and W0ody finished their trip home in silence, each thinking thoughts of Prep School starting at the beginning of July and whether the Trojan War was real, and how it might affect them. And then Jonny remembered as if from a dream: the bells.

The Bare Philosophy

A natural world, Earth, exists, and you exist in this world.
What you do, or don't do, is your responsibility,
and only you are responsible for your own survival.

"Arrogance and Conceit are the mother and father of a closed mind."
- Richard Nance

"Work saves us from three great evils: boredom, vice and need."
Voltaire

Cullet

Chapter 15

Abs was calling on the net, *Hey Jonny, are you available to help me today? I could really use it.*

Abs, last time we talked you were really pissed, what changed?

That was yesterday, today is now. I am no longer pissed; I want you to help me at my dad's shop. We're going to blow some glass together. I figured since it was legal, that you would be OK with it, huh?

Abs, I would love to, but you know I never have worked in your dad's glass studio, what can I do?

Lots. We need to prep some smaller off-hand pieces, and I need someone to help set up, fill the crucible, fetch parts from the garage, stuff like that. I will be getting the frit and selecting the murrini for the finished pieces and staging the shop for the afternoon blow. You can do it, OK?

OK. I'll check with Pops, we were going to go down to the electrical shop, but I think he is making me work to keep me out of trouble before prep school starts. I bet 90% he will OK it. How soon do you have to know?

It looks like our folks think alike, my dad has me in the shop eight hours a day, and it's a drag. I was going to bust out of there, but he told me if I got my own team, he'd let me go my own direction with color and shape, as long as I stay within the Daim Tiab glass format. I am free for this week, then I am supposed to get critiqued by him, at which point he will 'guide' me. Anyways, I need someone soon, like today.

Whoa. Well I can only ask, standby.

WET: swivel me to Pops.

Augustus here. What's up Jon?

Abs asked for help at his shop today, can you spring me free?

Can W0ody stay and help me?

Sure, I guess... what do you say W0ody?

I'm easy, I can go wherever. It looks like Pops has more need for me than you or Abs, so I will help Pops. Pops, where are we going to today?

We are going to Millennium Level Foxtrot, checking the voltage drops on the air handlers there.

Richard's small voice called out in the background, *Yippee! I always wanted to hang out with some MIL Fs and get VD.*

Put a cork in it Richard!

Is my material better?

No!

Anyways, thanks Pops, W0ody. See you at dinner. WET: swivel Abs.

OK Abs, good to go. Where do we meet?

I'm coming into town now; I'll swing by your place on Lincoln and pick you up. We will go straight to the shop.

Roger that, I'm getting ready.

Jonny began hurrying getting his clothes together while W0ody went to the vestibule to wait for Pops. Abs ETA was three minutes, so Jonny grabbed his diary camera, he didn't know what was going to happen, but it could be cool handling molten glass, who knows. The closet recommended long sleeve shirt and pants, with reflective and refractory properties as soon as it knew his destination, which he was throwing on when a pounding started at the front door. Just rely on Abs to beat ETA, alright already.

Rushing to the door where the pounding continued, he passed W0ody who handed him a package: *A snack from mom.*

Out loud "Thanks mom!"

Tightbeam, *W0ody, have a good day, you TinCan you, OK?*

Richard, behave with Pops, he may be slow, but he can't hit.

I gonna be a possum in a trash can with all the new tools to meet. Be safe, Big Guy.

Looking back as he opened the door to Abs, *Will do* he said. Abs jerked his head out to the street where he had a new scooter and side car.

Nice ride, what is it?

What is it?! Get in and I will tell you as we go. Jonny hopped in the extra seat and strapped himself in as Abs straddled the bike. They headed back north on Lincoln passing another tag team on Euclid, then turning left on the Leslie.

They passed Joslyn Street and Abs veered right onto Country Club Road where all the rich people lived, then the WET collapsed again. The solemn gong of the ancient bell slowly stuck, the bike was coasting now rather than screaming down the passage. They lost their link.

Jonny had to yell to Abs if this had happened to him? "Yeah, a few times but it always returns to normal." He yelled back. After the third bell quit resonating, the WET chatter resumed once again, but this time with an increase in traffic as Jonny felt power return.

Unfazed, Abs began: *This little bird is a Genie FX, the F stands for flying. I wanted to get a Fury, but the guy selling said I can't buy one unless I already own one, it doesn't make sense. Anyways, it's a real doozy, watch this.* Abs picked up speed then veered onto the goat access track on the right side of the tunnel road and climbed the wall to about two thirds of the sixty-foot diameter.

Jonny stiffened up because he didn't know what was going on and he didn't like heights much. He saw a large green light flash on Abs controls whereupon Abs took his hands off the machine. The bike then slowly lifted up off the track and floated towards the center of the tunnel just about ten feet shy of the ceiling! Jonny exclaimed *Pook Abs! What is this, an anti-gravity machine?*

They continued smoothly down Country Club Road as Abs explained: *The Genie Company worked with Mitsubishi Heavy Industries to install a superconducting magnetic grid in the overhead here for the rich folk, and I load up the bike with five pounds of liquid hydrogen which allows the guts of the machine to have a superconducting magnetic too. It hangs from the ceiling.*

That doesn't make sense, the magnet should get stronger as we get closer.

Naw, the machine has a smart board which shunts the current from the magnet as we close, then reengages as we start to drift apart. They say this function occurs over 100,000 times a second, making the ride smooth out. But they won't engage it until I let go of the controls, they don't trust me. We have to climb the walls to get the process started.

They were approaching the Harold Smythe glassworks where Abs' dad had his studio and worked. They hadn't had to deal with either vehicle or pedestrian traffic, and Jonny watched all the people who were watching them, an unusual sight in an unusual world. *Wow Abs, I never heard of such a thing. You have the coolest toys.*

Their ride smoothly turned left into the facility and gently lowered itself onto a ramp on the right wall, and Abs regained control, *I know, it's a hard job... "but someone has to do it,."* Jonny finished with a smile.

Abs drove them to a halt in front of the building, evidently having a stall all for himself. Jonny was always impressed with what Abs and his dad did. Harold had been a craft teacher when three years ago his rediscovery of an ancient glass blowing technique propelled him into not only financial success but critical acclaim. There were some methods and processes held closely and the arts community was having difficulty mimicking his creations, further enhancing his stature.

His meteoric rise and following finances allowed him to buy the facility where he worked, and he had moved his family to the posh Snowman Villas out in the Minucia Crater, and Abs was riding the wave for all he could get, spending money and partying until the lights went out. For some reason, Abs parents got divorced soon after the boonfall, Jonny had no clue as to why.

The interior of the shops were exposed behind glass windows, and the public (and Jon) could watch the artists and craft people blow and create a plethora of organic creations, some with a subdued and "refined" coordinated schema with élan, and others bright and shiny with "pop".

Jonny had spent time in the past watching the teams and their synchronized efforts but today he was going to participate. He followed Abs through the foyer and the wound their way to the back spaces, where blasts of heat and sound buffeted Jon.

Wow Abs, what is the temperature of all this molten glass?

It's about 2000 to 2400 degrees Fahrenheit in the electric furnace, somewhat hotter in the glory hole. That's above the temperature of melting copper. They came to the hallway leading under a huge industrial lazy-Susan, *We are going to do our work on MAX point 75, which is a good place to start. MAX is over 1000 feet in diameter and spins such that it creates varying gravities from 0.1 all the way up to 1.5g in its concentric rings. We are going down the hall and will enter from the center access.*

As they neared the center of the complex a vast low rumbling way down in the ground indicated the monstrous engines that must exist to drive MAX. A handrail ladder ascended a dull iron column scarred and oiled from its history of industrial use. *We use MAX for any process that benefits from variable gravitational pull.* They climbed into a large circular space lit with flat LED lighting and no adornments. *We need to ride Betty here, she's on a pivot and will adjust to the pull of the vectors by tilting to the local gravity, we will get off at point seven five.*

They entered the tram and set off slowly down the tunnel. At first Jonny didn't see anything different about their position, but as the car descended the tunnel, Jonny noticed the angle of inclination between him and the tunnel begin to change, and that as they passed each of the concentric stops, the car matched the level of the floor of the work space.

Exiting the lift, they entered a room twenty-feet deep and forty wide, with two roaring glory holes on the far wall, divided by a set of burnished steel tables. Between the tables was what looked like nothing more or less than a set of kitchen appliance garages, also made out of metal, dull finish and encasing angle iron pukas enclosing wisps of blue and yellow flames. Jonny thought it reminded him of an alchemist's cave from stories long ago.

Turning he saw local vertical was straight down in this room, but the floor was slightly concave end to end. Above the glory holes was a huge stainless shroud vacuuming the hot air away from the workspace. Between them on the wall was a large brick box with a sliding cover, an orange glow escaping from the edges of the metal door that covered the access to the furnace that contained the molten glass. On the wall past the working team were large four-foot by four-foot metal doors with bulkhead handles to open indicating the kilns that were there had more than adequate storage no matter how ambitious Abs got.

On the wall opposite of the kilns was a riot of colored glass stock in cubbies, coordinated in pigmentic spectrums, reds to oranges and yellows to greens, blue and violets. For some reason, there were multiples of the same color, and Jonny wondered why the differences.

Below the glass rods were jars of colored gravel and dusts, most in pastel shades, light blues, pinks, and greens. Jonny suspected these were the materials to color the glass. Next to the glory hole was a large square of dense metal on tracks edged in yellow light, allowing it to be slid sideways away from what appeared to be the supply of molten glass.

Well, did you get a look around? Are you ready to help, mister tourist?

Roger that, what's first?

Walking to a cabinet next to the colored jars, *I have to arrange a whole bunch of parts in the hotel over there. It preheats them so they don't shatter or crack when gathered up in the molten glass.* Pointing at what looked like a rolling service garage door, *Behind that corrugated metal are bags of cullet which you need to carry to the furnace for reload.*

Jonny started towards the storage as Abs continued, *The crucible takes about a ton of the cullet and takes a few hours to fill. There is a small steel shovel to load it. Let me turn the furnace down so it won't throw so much heat back at you.* Jonny had opened the garage and saw it stacked with craft bags filled with what he supposed was the cullet.

Jonny was uncertain, *I thought glassblowers made glass from silica and such.*

The cullet is premixed chunked glass of the right properties, which is faster for us and more consistent. The batch is inside the bags, which you lay on the barrow and tear open, then trolley to the furnace. The steel shovel is actually a small cup that you ladle into the brick tub. Only the big guys mix their own glass from raw materials.

Jonny grabbed a bag. It was massive! He wrestled it to the barrow and tried to rip the bag open, but the bag resisted mightily. Abs came over and showed him, *Just stab the sack with the end of the shovel to tear a small hole, then rip it open by hand and tilt and pour it into the container.* Jonny did as told, *Start with only two bags at a time, too much and they will tip over and you have to start again.*

Whoa Abs, this looks about as much fun as a person can stand! Jonny said somewhat sarcastically, removing the edge with a smile.

You betcha sodbuster. I will be done and haul you home for lunch, OK? Everyone starts at the bottom but me.

OK, but I want you to waive the gym fee, as Jonny started into his labors, this was going to be a long three hours at least.

A Cultural Philosophy

Your environment is overwhelmingly occupied by people.
The culture people create affects your life.
You are responsible for your culture.

"We are what we pretend to be,
so we must be careful about what we pretend to be."
- Kurt Vonnegut

"Even a fool, when he holdeth his peace, is counted wise."
Proverbs

Gang Ties
Chapter 16

The gang of kids, new and old, were hanging around Abs outside of Cougar Corner chatting and joking. Abs, Archibald Abercrombie Smythe as known only to his parents, was holding forth as usual in his rightful place of being the richest and having the best toys. The lights were bright here between the two schools, a student haven in Fremont during summer break. Although somewhat risky now for the fresh, as they were known, they would be able to stay here with impunity when they became matriculated. As it was, a bunch of kids didn't usually attract attention or trouble.

Jonny and W0ody had come from the TAP Trail to the Tiger Walk and were exiting the tunnel archway towards the group. *Hey Abs! Thanks for waiting for us! It sure is good to be off shift work, Pops has given us some decompression tomorrow before school.*

Glad to wait for you mate! Good to have all that stuff behind us. Can't wait for the WET to stabilize again, all this on and off synching sucks. Do you guys have a leg up on that or anything, what being in the front lines and all?

Naw, nothing that anybody else doesn't have.

Krage chimed in: *Hey Abs, have you heard of the new designer farts? Says here: eat their pill and you can smell like primroses and violets!* The group was laughing.

Roses are red, violets are blue. Nobody here, smells like you! Guffaws and shrieks as the crowd yell/rhymed and rapped verse after verse. But after a few moments, Abs raised his hand and the group quieted. Lowering his arm and sitting down on the small barrier wall that ran around the pub. *Settle down all you yahoos. Don't you want to go to the ReeBar again? I want to hit that place as soon as I get some more fake ID, and so will you!*

Hey Abs, did you get in trouble last time?

No way, my old man paid them off, I mean he made a contribution, I mean everything went smoothly! That was what was cool about Abs, you couldn't tell if he was intentionally making a mistake, or really was. Ever on the edge. As the noise lofted, he raised his arm again, starting to play the group, and they went along with it because no one ran a better party than Abs, and no one knew his group as well as he did.

Hey Kragey, did you know your farts can not only get a whiff of violets… pause, laughs, *but you can get banana, chocolate, roast beef, and even, yeah even: dead rat!* The group was rolling now, some with tears running. Turning, *Hey Jonny, it's not in the paper, but if you have enough money, you can by pills that generate human sex pheromones in your gastrointestinal groin, which for you, will win you a babe!* This last comment stirred sour acid in Jon's gut.

Obee spoke up, *I heard that Tin Benoit is shipping out, I'm going to miss him.*

Why is he shipping out, do you know?

His dad lost his job and his mom doesn't make enough for the family, they're going to have to take their bond and buy a habitat and go off on their own. Tin hasn't reached his majority and has to stay with his family.

Wow, that's rough. That close too. He'd would have finished in 3 months or so. Where are they going?

I guess they can only afford the base model habitat manufactured by the mechs out at Hugoslovia.

Yeah. I heard his dad was a tweaker, into all sorts of stims, and had cashed out all his accounts before his mom caught him, and the whole family is going bye-bye.

Wow, getting a Hugo can be the kiss of death. A corpsicle in the making. Without support from your community, life in the rocks is tough.

I heard of a guy that kept going out, finding something, returning and posting his bond once more, only to spend it all again. At last count, he had over 34 Hugo's. The Navy even gave him a golden patrol pin to honor his ass. I think he is out of Ceres.

That figures. He must have the most Hugo's ever.

Yeah, his name is Red Green or Red Hot or something like that.

What are you going to do Abs?

The group finally did make enough noise to attract the attention of the frats, but they all stood up and started to saunter away down the tube past the TAP towards Wheelwell Street and the shortcut to the Zone. Abs continued, *Naw, in reality guys, we all here, me and myself and I are going to begin studying for our majority, and in three months, when we finish, I will buy all you hogs a drink! No Hugo's for me.*

"*Yeah, way to go Abs" "I'll drink to that!"* the chorus of affirmation rained down.

Jonny came up, *Hey, how do you plan to study for the exam? Do you want to team with me like we talked about last year?* Jonny and Abs were together as the group passed the Designer Art Supply and the adjacent Nouveau Antique Art Lounge, Jonny wondered what new-old art was, and what came first, the bar or the supply store?

Sure, Jonny, sure. What I want you to do is to scope out all the sites we must go to and what forms we need. I will be busy clearing my schedule of all those things that came up since Dad went bananas at his big show at the York Armory. Keep your eyes open if you want to get the good stuff right away, none of this momma's boy stuff, OK? Jon mumbled a sort of acquiescence, Abs wild talk sometimes put him off. They walked awhile in silence.

As they stepped through the open-air locks towards the down tunnel Jonny began, *I've gotten in contact with the U and they have received and approved our paperwork, although they say when we arrive, we will have to have our signatures notarized in person. The books are on order and the class schedules have arrived. We need to be there Monday at nine to start.*

Good, Jonny, Good. You've done great. This definitely will allow me to finish my things. Have you seen KaiLin? KaiLin? No, isn't that her over there? Yeah, that's her alright. Awesome. Well, take care, we'll get together Monday. Turning, "Hey KAILIN!" Abs yelled, and she turned and most of the group slowed and parted for

Abs to jog over. Abs immediately fell in beside her as Jonny watched in admiration at the ease Abs had when dealing with people. The group of kids that followed him places had grown considerably in the last month. Jonny hoped to have that much confidence when he was an adult. Abs always had it, but it certainly became evident when his dad hit it big.

Hey Abs!" yelled Krage, *"Have you heard about the recent recall of the Nova Artificial Hearts? Seems someone accidently used Monel instead of stainless steel for the valve seats and patients are having immune reactions to the excess copper. I guess they have to pull them out!*

"Wow" "Tough luck for the old guys!" "Hey doc, have a heart, will ya!" Abs was smiling at Krage's story and he and KaiLin walked over and he draped his arm around Krage as they walked down the concourse. *Good one, Kragey, good one.*

The group continued on for a few minutes, laughing and trying to outdo each other with jokes and verbal cuts. Jonny enjoyed his time with these guys more than anything, the camaraderie, the quick wits, the new ideas and fast pace was almost addictive. But, he kinda longed for the time when Abs was just his buddy, not the son of the richest guy on Vesta. Abs had gotten a little edgy since his parents split and was having to time share between them, he actually used this to his advantage and avoided both of them for his wild nights.

Finally, Abs and KaiLin and the group trotted down the cavalcade into the Metro for the ride to the HUB and the Fremont Transfer NODE. He sat with Obee and Krage and a few newer kids including a couple of girls he hadn't seen before, but with Abs in the forward car with KaiLin the energy had evaporated, and everyone was silent in their own thoughts during the ride. Jonny noticed the new kids whispering and glancing at him but could make nothing of it. Within minutes, Jonny was suddenly alone, riding towards home with W0ody and Richard, in the I-15 shuttle.

W0ody always stayed quiet when Jonny was in a group, he didn't like the cut and chops and the repartee between the guys and had told Jonny he preferred to listen and learn rather to try to get points within the group. That was true for R0bie and a few of the other mechs as well.

Well W0ody, Monday is the big day. You ready?

Ready as can be, Able Baker Charlie. Which was like one of W0ody's jokes. And they continued to chat softly as they wound their way home, periodically being confronted by one of Richard's rowdy observations.

The Orca Corundum:

Orcas are Life, Orcas have Merit, Orcas eat Life, that is Life. Mankind is Life, People have Merit.

"First forget inspiration. Habit is more dependable.
Habit will sustain you whether you're inspired or not. Habit will help you finish."
- Octavia E. Butler

"Responsibility is a unique concept... You may share it with others, but your portion is not diminished. You may delegate it, but it is still with you... If responsibility is rightfully yours, no evasion, or ignorance or passing the blame can shift the burden to someone else. Unless you can point your finger at the man who is responsible when something goes wrong, then you have never had anyone really responsible."
Hyman Rickover

Red Right Returning

Chapter 17

The Conn of the Green Bee was rigged for red and audible. "Now just remember: Red Right Returning. Orient the ship so the approach is oriented with red on you right, and green will be on the left as you view the space port. Blue will highlight the runway axis and Yellow will be above defining the containment lane."

"OK Nav, I have known that since OCS, why the reminder?"

"When you have the Conn for a landing for your first time as JOOD, you are going to be saturated with reports and information. I remember my first time vividly, Red Right Returning, easy peasy, I thought.

"When I looked out, I was overwhelmed, those lights were lost in a city of structural and industrial lighting, flashes and strobes. We had over two hundred close-aboard contacts, many with constant bearing and decreasing range. Comms and Sensors were sending continuous reports, the bridge consoles had so much data that I blew a fuse, and just stared. My CO had to step in. It was hard: walk, talk and chew gum during a divorce, but worse.

"So, focus on the tier, primary, stay in the boundaries defined by, you guessed it, Red Right Returning. Expect the other contacts will obey the Rules of the Road also, don't try to drive them too. If they don't, the klaxon will sound. No Klaxon, no worries, OK?

"Thanks Nav. Red. Right. Returning."

"A last reminder, don't bump the ship's bow or stern. Sensor arrays and thrusters don't like it, we bump, we go into dock. A sudden extra ten million and two weeks in Refit. Always let the breast make contact, either to the tugs or to the Port. Nice thing is, when the pilot comes aboard, you sit back and watch. Any questions?"

"No sir, I am ready to relieve you."

"I am ready to be relieved."

"I relieve you, sir."

"I stand relieved, attention in control, Lieutenant Junior Grade Jefferson has the Deck and the Conn."

Immediately, watchstanders congregated around him, presenting logs and interpretations, consuming his complete attention: strain gages indicating the bulkheads of frames F82 through F108 in the logistics loading hanger needed some attention in the next two days from the nano welders, did he want to sign that off, or have the Engineer contacted?

The SNR team had identified four more motors in the Cook's glycol system that would benefit from bearing replacement, they were starting to run noisy, and Trends indicated a two sigma deviation from normal wear, perhaps a bad ground or neutral was allowing relativistic grounding through the races causing slight pit welding… input to the Refit PMS or send directly to the EO?

Beans! he thought, *Just when I think I am on top, they throw the third and fourth level conditions at me. Bite the bullet and send these up the chain? Don't want to burden the Department Heads, but I shouldn't want to guess the right corrective action and be wrong. The whole crew could fishtail for days trying to recover the proper flow.*

He continued with the watch, passing the intricacies to the Departments while trying to judge the big picture, the march towards being ready for tie up to the tug and landing at the Port, and at the same time identifying those big items hidden in the forest of detail and forwarding them to the Refit teams.

Breaking, "Quartermaster, report ETA to Pilot and the tug." He turned to his right noticing that the Navigator had stayed over by the plots, going over the charts and displays.

The Quartermaster of the Watch stood tall as he made his report, proud of achieving the responsibility of guiding the ship as a junior enlisted. The hot running Second Class Petty Officer, his steel cranium reflecting the red lights of the control room right alongside the XO's. Oh boy, the XO is back, observing. "Officer of the Deck, ETA expected at 1920 hours."

"Conn aye, Quartermaster." He had gotten better at procedure since his first onboard drill. Turning to his left, "Chief of the Watch, on the 1MC, Station the Maneuvering Watch. I am going to set the team a little early, if you don't mind."

"Station the Maneuvering Watch, aye, no problem, sir." Pulling on the general alarm, the klaxons going off three times, "Station the Maneuvering Watch for Ceres Port." Distant cheers rang out as the crew expressed relief at the final event of a long, tiring, patrol.

The COW activated the general alarm a second time, this time two AHOOGAHs on the old mechanical devices and muffled cheers reflecting the end of patrol echoed throughout the hull. The mechmen sailors took exceptional pride in manufacturing and maintaining these spinning apparatus, keeping a tradition from old Earth that actually made LTJG Brain Jefferson smile.

Immediately, as if in anticipation, crew started flowing into the Control, Sensors, Comm and Navigation rooms that were all available through this trunk. Quiet and competent discussions were held between the off going team and the experienced members of the Maneuvering Watch relieving them for the last delicate episode required for the next few months.

Speed was of essence because the relieved crew then had to dash to their own designated maneuvering stations, becoming Topside Handlers, Damage Control or Lower Level Missile Watch, which was normally not manned, as the case may be.

The OOD continued to take final reports as he scanned the displays above his eyes, and simultaneously observed the proper shift occurring within the Control Room. The Weapons Officer arrived in Control. LCDR Garcia was a petite woman of indeterminate age, with a bright green Mohawk and no tattoos, "I have made my tour Officer of the Deck, I am ready to relieve you." Just then "The Maneuvering Watch is Set," announced the COW.

"Very good, Chief. Well done, that was a little under five minutes. Thank you."

"No, thank you Sir, we are the only ship in the Federation with an Earthman as part of the crew, and you always do us good."

"Well, you know how it is, Chief, us dirtmen are slow, but we can't think straight." Suddenly, Lieutenant Jefferson realized that the Maneuvering Watch wasn't the right venue for his light midshift banter. *Lost it again* he thought, noticing a small smile on WEPS face. *OK, let's keep going.*

"As just reported, the Maneuvering Watch is set, and the Captain is still in her quarters. We should meet the Pilot in," he looked at the Nav, who nodded, then at the time, "in about eight minutes. The First Lieutenant is in charge of topside and the line handlers and reports ready. Communication is secure with both Ceres Port and Bermuda Triangle Navy Base, and they state preparations are all in order for our arrival. I am ready to be relieved, Sir."

"I relieve you of the Deck, you maintain the Conn for your Maneuvering OOD quals."

"Understood, I am relieved of the Deck." To the room at large "Attention of the Maneuvering Room party, Commander Garcia has the Deck, Lieutenant JG Jefferson retains the Conn." A chorus of quiet aye's responded.

Well, here it goes. One small step for man... "Quartermaster, report ETA to tug and Pilot?"

"Three minutes sir" "Aye Quartermaster. Chief of the Watch, inform the First Lieutenant of ETA." "Inform the First Lieutenant of ETA, aye."

"Navigator, inform the Captain of ETA,"

"She is informed, Sir"

"Chief of the Watch, inform me and the Captain when the Pilot is aboard and below decks."

A calm voice called out from a dark corner, "Not necessary Officer of the Deck, the Captain is now in Control."

Startled, he stuttered softly, "The Captain is in Control, aye Sir. Do you wish a brief?"

A chuckle, "Not necessary, carry on."

The COW called out, "The tug is engaged, umbilical's are connected and lines are being doubled up in Hanger Bay Two."

A weight was lifted somewhat, "Very well Chief of the Watch. Keep me informed." "Yes sir."

The Navigator gave a report "CPA from own ship to Salt Mountain Space Port is twelve klicks, we are transiting Zebra Envelope with escapement if the Pilot does not engage, well within Rules of the Road parameters. ECM has deactivated stealth mode, and full radar and EM portrait is available to the local Jurisdictions Having Authority."

"Very well Navigator, I assume you mean the Authority Having Jurisdiction? Ah, never mind."

"Sensor, display visual on the main screen." "Full up visual, aye." Brain was exposed to a very dark image of space with Vesta somewhat lighted by surface spots and landing globs, however, this was all submerged by a multitude of moving and stationary illumination associated with the other traffic in the area.

Perhaps those patches were industrial sites on the surface, but small icons and identifiers began to pop up on the display along each light, but the sum of the information was chaos, and caused him to stiffen.

"Sensor, drop all traffic and icons not in our envelope." "Aye, dropping icons." The presentation cleared up substantially, and he could see the big picture of their situation.

"Display all traffic with a CPA of two klicks or less." Only four moving icons remained, and now, he finally spotted the Red Navigational Aid.

Then to its left, there was the Green Aid, flashing three shorts and a long. Then he began to note additional aids, along the circumference and towards the horizon, easier to spot in the umbra rather than in the sunlit areas. He wondered how far away the horizon was as they transverse the surface.

The Chief of the Watch spoke, "The Pilot is on board and coming forward with the Chief of the Boat." "Very well, have them report."

"No need, no need to report, here I am!" a jovial voice boomed, making him jump. He turned to see the COB following a stout borgman strutting into the room, both heads turning every which way seemingly to scope out all details at once.

"Ah, I had heard the rumor, but I never thought I'd see the day when a UFS Ship of the Line is under the supervision of a mudman." The human head looked at him while the mech head was still twisting all around getting information. "You must be that same fellow! Pilot McVay at your service! I am ready to relieve you."

Beans! "We are headed…" he started when he was interrupted, "No need, no need. You Navy types know how to pack five minutes of solid information into an hour, so I will be succinct: Has the hull ruptured or is there a fire raging somewhere? No? Then, I relieve you sir!" *Beans! What have I gotten into?* He looked back at WEPS, but she had that faint smile and a twinkle around her eyes. He hesitated, then "I stand relieved."

"Good, good."

The Navigator said formally: "Inform the Pilot we will launch a direct link from his console to ship's AI. Upon that link being established, we will concede the Conn to the Pilot, and request we be informed of all decisions and actions the Pilot might deem necessary for the safe landing of the Bee."

"More good!" Turning to the Chief of the Boat, "COB, if your team has one of those newfangled secure shielded and grounded HBDmd cables, you can plug directly into the back of Mike's cranium, he has the right port there." As the IT petty officer hurried up the splice the pilot boomed out again, "I see you in the corner over there Captain Hermeling! How is my darling rock miner turned navy officer? It's been twenty years or more. Give me a hug!"

The CO came out from behind the plots and looked up at the borg with her hands on her hips, "Run me a good landing McVay, and I will buy you a drink shore side. Until then, focus on my ship, you old reprobate!" She said with a smile, but definitely no hug.

Without a further ado, "Helm, all back two thirds! Let's slow this tub down. NAV, with a sixty second burn, what say you the new CPA?" Without the formal Navy jargon in place conversations were communicated in a much faster pace, Brain saw, still with no slipups.

"CPA is mark on top, but with a lateral velocity of four meters per second." "I agree, what do you have for velocity to be gained to achieve the Port requirement for their cradles of point five meters per second?"

"Using mostly the waist thrusters, with some assistance from the fore/aft compliment, firing for fifteen when thirty seconds from touchdown."

Brain quit listening to the details and turned to WEPS, "What do we do now? I have never worked with a pilot before, seems we lose all responsibility."

"We'll watch, the XO, Captain and I." She said thoughtfully, "I will get the Conn back when we berth, and I will turn over to the oncoming shore assigned Duty Officer. You should go down to the Torpedo Room, make sure everything is secured, and start PMs to support Exchange of Command. When the Maneuvering Watch is secured, you can take shore leave. I will take the first Duty Weapons Officer Watch. You'll be on shift tomorrow."

"Yes sir, thank you sir." Lieutenant Jefferson took one last look around Control, such an intense amount of resources, so calm, so competent, coming from years of practice and experience. Even the Pilot had settled in, standing in the center of the space, both heads sweeping the displays, firm orders to the Flying Officer and Helm, no wasted motion. Brain stopped, he hadn't even noticed that McVay had four arms, and was using them to provide additional information to the watchstanders.

He exited Control through the forward hatch and proceeded down the ladder past the mess to lower level Ops, where the forward Torpedo Room and Battery was located. The Torpedo Room gang, MTC Ng, MT1 K!t and the petty officers were securing the space for landing and refit. They had their check off lists and had isolated hydraulics to the tubes to prevent inadvertent rolling of the stop bolts in later maintenance and other accidents.

"Warshot Loaded" signage had been hung from seven of the tubes, and POs Winkle and Bull were back hauling a MK45 Torpedo to its rack under the supervision of MT1 K!t, the only mech on this team.

"Hey TOPS!" called out the friendly voice of MT2 Bull, "Do you want to help us with the tube PMs? It's part of the card for an officer OOD qual, I believe, and we'll be ready in less than five minutes for the crawl." MT2 Winkle was controlling the extraction with a hand device, going slowly onto the cradle making sure that there were no bindings, or edges catching the equipment.

"What's a crawl?"

"We have to visually inspect the tube from the inside every quarter and after each extraction. We also sometimes find some verdigris in there and will take a toughie and some wipes to clean it up."

"Verdigris? What is verdigris?"

"Stains, rust, snot. We also look for evidence of leakage from the torpedo's systems and for the condition of the lands. Stop if you see red oil."

"Man, I am ignorant. What are lands, and what is red oil? Why should I worry?"

"Lands are the polypropylene rings that surround the torp while in the tube. They protect it from shock and movement while we are under weigh. They may get dinged up and mess with loading, extraction and launch. If you can feel a ding with your fingernail, it's too deep, and we need to either sand it out or replace it. The red oil is explosive liquid made from hydrazine and H2O4."

"I know what H2O2 is, but what is H2O4?"

"Hey TOPS," PO Winkle called out, "Bull gotcha. Think about it, what is H2O4? It's for drinking!"

"What???"

"You know, go slowly, what is … H … 2 … O … for? … H2O … is <u>for</u> drinking. Ha!" Winkle had finished the extraction and was securing the bands around the torpedo. Bull had locked the breach door open and had gotten the cleaning gear together. "You have to remove all metal from your body, because the launcher is a rail gun and makes significant amount of magnetic and electric forces, even a nose diamond can heat up to five hundred degrees. So off it goes, piercings, buckles, the lot."

Brain started to strip himself of the mentioned articles and asked, "What about someone like K!t, a mechman?"

"Nope, no can do". This is a job relegated to humans except during battle stations, when life safety is relaxed for ship safety. However, it works out in the end, 'cuz K!t is a killer dog on the micro PMs."

"Hey TOPS, what's the skinny on situation on Vesta? Why are we coming home early?"

"Sorry guys, I haven't been briefed. All I have heard officially is that there has been an intermittent malfunction in the WET."

Brain kneeled next to the massive bronze door, "What's the best way? Head or feet first?"

"Headfirst is always easiest, just as going up stairs is more controlled, going down is a fall waiting to happen, your knees aren't any good for it." Bull pushed a bucket containing a green tuffy and a plastic flash towards the Lieutenant.

Leaning over and lowering his voice he remarked "At the bottom of the bucket is a diamond scribe, it's tradition to sign your signature on the ejection door inside face, kinda puts you in the club, huh?"

"Got it." Brain got on his elbows and knees and began to slither and hump into the tube. It was quite awkward, the unforgiving metal surface pressing into his bones, he couldn't rise up, and if full on his stomach, the wallow forced his arms behind the level of his shoulders, and he lost leverage. But looking carefully about he saw the circumferential poly lands and took his time to inspect each one carefully before flopping like a walrus to the next one.

Finally, he was at the ejection door and inspected it before pulling out the scribe. As he started to write his name, he heard a muffled laugh and a subsonic boom as the breech door was slammed behind him, followed quickly by a wind of compressed air. *Beans! What the hell?* He rationalized that the team was having fun with him, some kind of initiation or hazing, but some people may not be able to handle it. He wondered what would happen if he came out screaming?

Would he get a lifelong stipend? But then, he would never have the opportunity to see the Universe that this ship offered. Ho hum, just back out and play along. Just then, he heard the whine of capacitors charging and the hydraulics and clangs from up forward that could be the shutter doors. They were doubling down, were they? Relax, be ready.

The electrical scream of the system ramping up was then multiplied by the impossible stutter of what sounded like the electric jack hammer of a CAT magnet. Louder and louder, then it shut off. The silence deafened him, but it was broken by the periodic clank of something happening behind him. Then he heard the thrumm of the rotation of the bronze breech lock, followed by a clank, releasing the door from its capture. Fresh air poured over him as well as a fair amount of illumination from the torpedo room, he slowly backed out, pulling his tools after.

Calmly and softly he got up on his knees, then hands on thighs, he stood up slowly. Staring right into the eyes of Petty Officer Bull, he said, “Well done.” but perhaps the swelling of his jaw muscles gave it away, Bull replied, “Hey TOPS, everyone does it. You know, the new guys get sent to the Nav Girls for fallopian tubes, then sent to the Quartermaster for Relative Bearing Grease, then finally suited up in double anti-Cs and sent to Engineering to feed the Shaft Seals."

"Chief Ng, these POs you got are a bunch of cards. Perhaps we can get them to help clean up the spill of DHMO they got in the galley instead of going on leave, what do you think?"

"I don't know TOPS," the petty officers began to look worried as the senior personnel discussed their shore leave, "DHMO can be deadly, they haven't done the qual card yet."

"Time they started one."

"Ah, come on Chief, we got plans, don't we Winkle?"

"What?! You got plans during Refit and Exchange of Command? Uncle Sugar owns your ass until after, and you know it!"

"Please Chief, we was counting on it, and the tube is a ritual, it sorts the capable from the psychotic. Hey TOPS, you should of saw it. Four patrols ago we rigged it up for one of the newbee A-gangers, and when we opened the breech, he had somehow turned himself around in the tube!"

Lieutenant Jefferson just stared, the Chief announced, "Guys, secure the space and do the small job for the Torpedo Officer, and then you can go, K!t and I will stand down."

Brain gave them each the eye, then said, "Go to Engineering, get a DHMO qual card, and we will start on it tomorrow after watch."

"Yessir!"

At that moment, the 1MC announced, "Attention all hands, this is the Captain speaking. Our Exchange of Command has been cancelled. A deep analysis of our recordings of the Citadel by Ceres main base has caused someone up the chain to vector us immediately to Vesta. We are calculating our optimum transit as we speak. Stand by to cast off as soon as certain essential security personnel are boarded. All crew are reminded as of this moment we are on radio silence and shifting back to stealth mode.

"Again, stand down from refit preparations. Maintain the Maneuvering Watch. Secure all loose flotsam and jetsam, and rig for high speed maneuvers. This is not a drill.

"We are needed children, let's show them what the Bee can do."

Lt Jefferson and Chief Ng gave each other a worried look, then scrambled.

The Ethical Challenge

Producers, Predators, and Parasites all exist in Nature.
They all have an equal value in the Universe.
The tree, the cow, the lion, and the human,
have the same weight ethically.

"Trust no one," ...., "especially Teachers."
- A.J. Arias

"To be fond of learning is to be near to knowledge."
Tze Tze

Start FU Prep

Chapter 18

They were sitting in the big stepped auditorium of the Spearman Technology Building with all the other incoming students when the blocky mech strode to the podium:

Broadcast, *"People, please take your seats and we'll get started."*

Jonny, let's ditch this class. I've got a new Jaw Phone that just arrived from the Jungle, and Krage here and I are going to check it out

No Abs, I can't miss the first day.

"People, welcome to AP Science 101, one of the three required core curricula courses necessary to continue your education and acceptance to the citizenship portal. You have been placed in this

fast track class due to your entrance testing. It is designed to be challenging and will require effort on your part."

Jonny, let's go! Nobody cares if we attend, just that we pass the tests, and they don't start for 5 weeks. We can skate out and catch up later. I've got stuff you never saw before, this Jphone is awesome!.

Abs, I can't. Dad'll kick my ass if I skip the first day, he always saying education takes application, ninety-five percent perspiration and only five percent inspiration, and not to skip classes because it's a slippery slope.

Guys, can I say something?

Shut up W0ody, no one wants to hear a mechhead. Jonny, don't be lame. For a best friend you are getting small for some reason. My dad has made over a billion the last five years and your dad is stuck as a cave electrician. Who you gonna follow?

Go without me Abs, I gotta stick with it.

"People, in this preparatory course, we will study fundamental sciences like physics, electricity and chemistry during our labs, as well during the lecture hall we will introduce you to astrophysics and astronomy. Mondays and Wednesdays will be lecture, Tuesdays and Thursdays will be lab activities, and Fridays will be available for office visits, make up work, and advanced placement projects."

This is so boring...

"The lectures will focus on the advances developed from the Brian May Spherical Group Telescope beyond the orbit of Saturn, we will review discoveries both interior to the Milky Way as well as those extragalactic."

Jonny leaned closer to W0ody so he wouldn't project around the room, *Hey Woods, this is awesome! We will get to see the latest discoveries as they happen. Do you think they will let us look at the actual images as they come in? Aren't there supernovas happening everyday somewhere in the Universe?*

I think so Jonny, but I bet if we listen, they will tell us.

"Everyone can pass, and everyone can fail. It's up to you. We are taking into account the sporadic WET here on Vesta that hasn't been contained and is affecting many of your apps."

Abs broke in: *Let's go! He just said no class attendance marks. I promise we will catch up. We will claim apps disease.*

No Abs! I just can't.

Krage spoke up, *Let it go Abs, some people just don't know whether they are coming or going, or what side of their bread to butter.*

Stuff it Krage! Abs, you better go, class is starting.

"People, the enormous amount of information available is incredibly interesting. We will study the dense data recovered from the Eta Carinae class IIb supernova as well as the class Ia Peanut

supernova and the impact of this information on our attempted consolidation of Relativity and Quantum Mechanics. We will view the thousand-year time lapse imagery of our own galaxy's black hole, Sagittarius A, as it pulls local stars into relativistic orbits."*

Bye Jonny, you need to get a life before it's too late.

Shhhh, go.

"People, for those of you who qualify for AP Advanced Placement, you will have evening studies ..." Jonny watched as Abs and Krage hurried out of the classroom. How could they be so casual? "*You will discover how Einstein instead of Tesla developed these equations into the theory and math of relativity..."*

Jonny wiggled in his seat, *Sure sounds hard,* he tight beamed to W0ody. *Glad Pops brought us up on this stuff as electricians.*

"...Please pay attention to the slide presentation. The material appears in the order of the class and you should start taking notes. I will go slow enough so you can write."

Jonny scrambled to get stylus and pad from the pack. Pops always said writing helped retention. He could understand that just taking pictures wasn't enough. Writing was exercise for the brain.

"The first lecture course module starts with a section on the physics of light, its interrelationships of frequency, wavelength, spectrum, energy, the speed of light c, and the interplay of magnetism and electrostatics that occur in the observable universe."

"The first week lab is about making electricity and magnets; it can be great fun. It is also dangerous. ARC flash is a real phenomenon and will kill you."

You can say that again brother. W0ody muttered.

"On the other hand, those who do well on the exams will be able to go into the superconducting labs and play around there."

"The second week builds upon the first week, so you don't want to start behind the curve. Using the Hoyle postulate of..." Jonny's focus began to drift as he began imagining what he could do if he could be in charge of the Brian May Telescope.

Then, thinking about Abs, Jonny mused to W0ody, *Boy, that was hard. Pops said it was going to be easy to slide. But he didn't say your best friend was going to try to drag you away.*

Yeah, tough, but we stuck.

Yeah, we stuck.

With a start he focused on the talk: "... *You will not be responsible for relativistic math and calculations in this class."*

Lucky for us, huh W0ody?

Ah man, that is the part I do best.

"This concludes the first half of our class. This course is required material to gain access to the residency exams, if you can't set goals, motivate yourself, and gain the essential knowledge, then you aren't going to gain Federation citizenship.

"The class is not hard, but you need to spend time reading. If you can navigate the tunnels, you can learn. Same with this class, turn off your apps, they impede learning, and just put in the time reading, and writing what you read, until some of gets ingrained into muscle memory, then read for comprehension. Any questions?"

I hope it's in the notes.

They are, I checked.

"During the last week we will assess the observations of ...." the backs of Jonny's eyes felt heavy with glue; his mind couldn't force his body to do his will without significant effort. It had never been this way in public school, he tightbeamed: *Hey TinCan, what's the CO2 reading? I'm suffocating over here.*

You humans must be having a field day, it has spiked to over 475 ppm. Who's doing all the heavy thinking? Can 't be you MeatStick. W0ody elbowed Jonny as the instructor looked their way.

"Which leads me to our final topic: The Engineering Revolution: the combination of Discovery, Verification, and Application

"We all have experiences that influence us, while some of those experiences are Personal Truths, and others can be verified independently over and over as Universal Truths. The mathematical modeling that I will present has been independently verified by thousands and millions of observers. If its good enough for a spaceship thruster, it's good enough for engineering truth. Bank on them"

"This concludes the introduction to Science 103. Are there any questions?"

The presentation had taken up almost a complete hour, where did the time go?

W0ody, let's go. The skinny is if we get to the lab early, we get first pick of our activity.

They stood up and proceeded to the exit through the slowly moving mob. *It's my chance to get into the design of Earth's Space Elevator. The whole home planet thing is really cool. If we do well, we might get picked to actually visit the proto site. I really want to go, and see stuff, like an ocean, or a storm, or being able to commune with nature. We aren't rich like Abs. It's our only chance*

Ah, Jonny, it' been a dream of yours forever, but is it real? They say it will take five-hundred years to finish from when they start, and none of the politicians can agree on anything! They continued their bumping of humanity to the exit. *But you know, it sounds like a killer lab project. Tomorrow, I will race you to the lab, lab rat! First one there gets to select the project. Last one in cleans the commode!*

Hey W0ody!

Sigh, *Yes Richard?*

That was pretty boring, but I was readin' whilse youse guys were lisitnin' and I learned there was 10 kinds of people out here in the 'roids

Yeah?

Yeah! Those who understand binary, and those who don't!

What?

Never mind, I'll explain it to you jokers later when we get home.

GOAL

Colonize the Solar System

Protect Mankind

"You meet a new person;
you go with him and suddenly you get a whole new city...
you go down new streets, you see houses you never saw before,
pass places you didn't even know were there. Everything changes."
- Samuel Delany

"Excellence is the best deterrent to racism or sexism."
Oprah Winfrey

I Love Yew

Chapter 19

Aleks hurried along the King's Way at his father's bidding. Poseidon's shaking of the land during the last twelfth day and the following tremblers had everyone nervous. The ship's boy whom he sometimes wrestled with told him in confidence that their mate was talking into his beard about the bones and signs, fish boils breaching the surface and descending again, seabirds aflutter and screaming up and down the beach, and who foretold tales of fires at the Pillars.

They were casting off today, he said, and every wise person would be too, he, to return to his Villanovus home. Worst of all, the smiling dolphins who were the patron animals of the Kingdom, had all disappeared. The boy continued his haste down the King's Way, looking at the troubled bay, then again over his shoulder at the forested mountain and then at the King's villa where rocks rattled past the great houses of the rich and royalty. Oh, what did the fates have in store?

Come on W0ody, make haste, we don't want to be late to the lab.

Jonny, relax, we all start at the same time. They weaved their way through the slowly moving student body across the Tiger Walk towards the Spearman Technology Building, obviously more excited to arrive than their brethren.

Acquaintances nodded in recognition but didn't speak, or let their eyes slide across Jonny's location as if he didn't merit acknowledgment. Jonny sensed the status seekers and natural pecking order that constantly evolved around his group of early teens, but there seemed to be some stress or discord he hadn't noticed before.

Perhaps, it was that they were entering the season of adult emancipation and some were cautious or even slightly scared by the upcoming change, and some were withdrawing into themselves to improve their focus or distance themselves from the losers. Is this what it is going to be like during their time here at Fremont University? Would it be the same over at the larger University of Vesta next door?

Linking: *Kai? Have you seen Abs? He said he'd be here, no problem. I don't see him and he isn't answering and comms are hit or miss.*

No, Jonny, I haven't. We're not there at the class quite yet, and Abs wasn't on the shuttle. Maybe he had his chauffeur bring him?

Yeah, that'll be like him, Jonny got bumped from one side and then the other as he trudged forward. *Hey, we're getting mashed here. Talk to you when we're inside.*

He had to step over someone's foot who was chatting right here in the hallway.

W0ody, keep an eye out for Abs? I hope he decided to pick it up, I am feeling uncomfortable, I don't understand his being late.

What is it Jonny, all I see is a bunch of teenagers. I notice a lot of kids I know, but most of them are strangers. I don't know why strangers interact so suspiciously. I hope I figure it out before school is out. Maybe I never will though. It makes life difficult. So, what's bugging you?

It's weird, some of the guys from last year aren't as friendly. I wonder what has got into them.

Well, we can act nicer to strangers. Maybe what goes around, comes around. The Hope has something like that.

You know, W0ody, you are sometimes smarter than you think.... Do you think that's the lab door over there, where everyone seems to be filing in?

Sure, let's move in that direction until we can see the door number and be sure.

You know, it really bugs me that our apps are up and down, I am so used to just asking the WET, and having all that information come out. It was like growing up in a really full sandwich, and now it's like rattling around an old empty can.

You think you have it bad? Think about me. Normally over 80 percent of a mechman's sensory suite is provided by the WET, I feel blind in an area I can't see or feel anymore, just a sense of loss.

Sorry.

Excuse me. Do you know the way to the Chromo Lab? asked a quiet voice beside them.

Jonny experienced a brief interval of confusion, who was this person? Was the inquiry for or to him? Looking over, he saw a unknown girl, about his age and a little taller, watching him back with a question on her face.

Quickly, a thousand small responses lifted their heads in his mind as he sorted through them. Did he know her? No. What was the Chromo Lab? Right, that's the real name of the lab. She was a mixture of cute and plain, broad dark eyebrows, obviously not modified much, was she interested in him as a guy? Naw, couldn't be that. Was she asking for help? Yes, maybe, no? Why would she ask for help? Doesn't she have friends here too?

Was that blue thing on her shoulder a mechanical parrot? How 'bout the looming shape behind her, all silent. Was it dangerous? Was it her alias? Companion? Guardian? Did its huge eye make it a cyclops? Were the other optics intact, taking in a three hundred and sixty-degree field?

Caution, Jonny, he thought, proceed carefully, slowly. *We think it is down over there, that's where we are going. But, we are not sure yet without our apps.* She had a halo of brunet tresses with gold and mahogany hidden in the shadows, falling below her shoulders becoming an explosion of copper curls and haze. She wore no makeup, but her hair created a picture frame for an oval face and engaging smile and the most luminous hazel eyes he had ever seen.

Thank you, it's easy to get lost since the WET has gone erratic. Would it be OK if I follow you guys? You look like you know more where you are going than the other people milling around.

Whoa! While Jonny tried to think what would be a good response…. Their brat piped up, *Sure, my name is Richard, and these guys here stumbling over their tongues are Jonny and W0ody.* Jonny had a momentary flash of irritation. At the same time, he felt awkward, he appreciated Richard making the introduction. When was he ever going to start being naturally courteous? Was he just that self-centered never to learn?

Nice to meet you Richard, W0ody, Jonny. She stared at Richard, *Look Blueee3, a talking tool, what about that.*

Recovering, *Oh, I am sorry, my name is Catherine, and this is Big Blu3 and this is Blueee3*, pointing to the large mech and the mechanical parrot.

Hi Catherine. I've never seen anything like Blooey, what is it? An ornithopter? Does it fly? Now that was a lame response.

Blueee3 is one of my companions, he is kinda unique.

They were getting closer to the lab and shuffling as students ahead slowly squeezed through the door. Wow, was that real wood?

Hey W0ody! Get a load of the door frame! Is that real wood? I wonder what kind?

Jonny, I kept my onboard library for my namesake, W0ody Wilson, and have a catalog of most earth woods. I think it is some sort of tight grain conifer... Sure has a soft warm glow to it.

W0ody paused as they passed the egress, slowing the throng a little bit more, as he touched and inspected the door frame. Inside the frame were the actual doors to the lab. They appeared to be blast doors six or seven inches thick, with scorch and flash marks partially scrubbed away, and in the far corner, small globules of metal welded around a pitted and discolored surface.

They looked up as they entered and saw a large amplitheatre with numerous wood tables situated in a grid throughout the space. Think of the expense! Turning, Jonny saw the room was bracketed with edge benches, with more wood drawers below and wood cabinets on top! It looked so much better than the rock, plastic and metal walls he grew up with he could not do anything but stare. No wonder the students were jamming up in the doorway as they ogled the riches.

Looking ahead, Jonny noticed groups of students migrating to each table, and started towards an empty one on the far right, glancing back to see if W0ody was following, which he was. In addition, Catherine and Big Blu3 were coming too, with Blueee3 riding a soft shoulder, and Big Blu3 looking more awkward than W0ody, if that was possible.

Reaching the table, they turned and faced the end of the space that seemed to have a raised lectern and an old guy, Einstein white hair floating around his head, striding purposefully towards it.

"Allright class, pick a table, two to four of you at each one. The newcomers are not going to be able to all sit with their friends, so pick one now, and we will be able to adjust assignments later." Jonny noticed KaiLin and Obee hurrying towards their part of the lab. KaiLin stopped suddenly, and Jonny saw her look at Catherine and the strange mechs, and then back at Jonny. She pushed Obee and stiffly moved towards the table to Jonny's left. Jonny was about to say something, anything, when he was interrupted when the professor in front started his spiel.

"Welcome, people, to the laboratory CORE course prerequisite for your emancipation exams. I am Doctor Yi, and this is Assistant Professor Carlisle and Associate Professors Green and Vesilisev. Between us we have advanced degrees in Mechanical and Electrical Engineering, Bio-adaption, and Material Science.

"This is the class where you get to have fun. Many of you want to build things, and this class is for you, we have almost anything imaginable, from five dimensional CNC machines to nanobots to sinctering 3-D printers to terahertz controllers to Xenetix body

modifiers. However, you all have to demonstrate competency on the basic equipment first."

"Hey Jonny! Watcha gonna do?" A loud whisper from behind caused Jonny to turn, and he saw Krage with Sindee and their mechmates. "Abs says he wants to be part of <u>our</u> team, and we are going to build a rail gun!"

Jonny smiled at the thought of those guys with a potato gun, much less a rail gun. They never spent time building stuff in the past as he had helping out his dad. Then his smile faded as he realized the emphasis on the word "<u>our</u>". Krage could be pushy sometimes. Then he smiled again, thinking of Abs with these yahoos. Best wishes and all that, as he turned back to the instructor, at least he won't have to clean up after.

"For those of you uncomfortable with practical classes, this is where you get the opportunity to get a feel of machinery: your society needs you to be handy, to be able to participate in repairs and casualty response. I and my staff will give you substantial assistance, and all you have to do is ask.

"OK, people, introduce yourselves to your partners, and pull out the old fashion paper lab guides in your tables. Read through them, familiarize yourself with your workstations and first aid equipment."

Jon, I want to watch you wire up a dishwasher like your dad, now that's exciting. Sindee smirked as they heard this cut from Krage.

W0ody turned, as did Catherine and Big Blu3. Jon saw KaiLin looking at him directly again, those dark eyes fixed in his memory. Jon decide to jab back, having to protect his dad's and his reputation: to his team he said, "Oh guys, don't worry about them. My background as tech maybe lowlife to some, but in this lab, it is gonna be king.

"Let them run their mouths. But at the end of the class, let's see who walks the walk." Then back to Krage: *Hey Krage, want to put something down on whose project gets the best grade?*

Sure Jon, with Abs coming in, we can't miss!

How about this, then, Kragey... the loser calls the other's mom and says the other did a better job than they did.

What? That's a dumb as dirt. Be a man, I'll pony up one thousand credits of my own money against five hundred of your weak credit.

Kragey, Kragey, Kragey. No guts, no glory. I say we do both. Money and status, you win, and you get money and the honor of having THE tech of our cohort apologize to your mom. I win, and I get to hear your sad ass on the comm.

You're on, techie boy! "Duly Recorded", chanted W0ody and R0bert, Krage's mechmate, in unison.

Jon looked over at Catherine and Big Blu3 *Isn't Big Blu3 going to record this as well?*

Catherine said *Big Blu3 is pretty good at a lot of things, but he doesn't talk.*

Oh. When he looked at Kai, she had a twist on her lips, and as he stared, she turned away.

Suddenly grumpy, Jon, turned back to his station, looking at the others. W0ody gave an exaggerated shrug of his shoulders that was so absurd that Jon had to smile. Shaking off the rough feeling from his verbal push and shove with Krage, he would settle things with Kai after class. It wasn't like she was his girl or anything, just friends.

Jon started to take in his surroundings really for the first time. The workstation was really a large slab of polypropylene about two inches thick resting on top of a bank of drawers down to the floor made from a dark wood. The poly tabletop was scarred and grooved from previous student's experiments and slips.

He reached down and felt the wood, and even the drawer pulls were made from crafted wood, partially recessed into the face and detailed with brass hardware. It felt smooth and waxy, as did the table surface. He realized why people paid so much for wooden furniture.

W0ody, this wood feels so warm to me, no.. that's not it, it feels "comfortable", if that makes any sense? I think it is a biological response I am having; do you get a sense of what I am saying about my feelings?

Well Jon, what I see is a rectangular workstation with cubic corners made from an aged material on top and sides, scratched yet clean. It doesn't seem to be as utilitarian as stainless but has a possible benefit of not being susceptible to electrical fields. I think the wood is yew, based on the fine grain and lack of splintering.

That's not quite what I meant W0ody. Catherine, what is your reaction? The feeling I get from touching this wood is strong. W0ody, you call it yew? Catherine, I think I could love yew around me. What do you think?

Jon, I think I could love yew too.

They suddenly looked at each other, realizing the personal statements. Jon was frozen for a moment, then grinned wryly at Catherine. She had a small half smile too, and they looked at each other. He saw at that moment she had deep clear amber-brown eyes and there obviously was a keen mind running around back there as her eyes flicked back and forth looking at his face. Glancing at Kai, her back was stiff, and she faced the podium, away from Jon. Damm.

Jon broke the spell, *I'm sorry, I didn't mean it that way.*

That's OK. It was a good pun though; I wish I caught it in time.

Jon paused to recover for the second time in five minutes, this time on a positive note. *What are you guys talking about Jon, all my human indicators are all pointing in different directions at once?* tightbeamed W0ody.

Thems guys are all just titterpated, get over it! Richard was totally ignored this time.

I'm not sure W0ody, but I just made a play on words, unintentionally, and the new words are emotionally charged, using the human word "love" in the same sentence as "you", but I meant yew, the tree. And I had to stop to see if I had insulted our new student partner, Catherine, but she smiled rather than frowned, so I gathered, although I can be quite wrong, that I didn't insult her.

It looks like Kai is upset though, I'm not sure why. Dad says I should explain to you what I do and why I do it to the best of my ability, so you can begin to understand human clues. He also told me that humans have substantial emotional and facial clues, and we use them all the time, but they are often misunderstood, because we lie so much, even to ourselves, and I am droning on 'cause I am embarrassed." Jon finally shut up.

A moment slipped by, then Catherine spoke *That was cool Jon, did your father really tell you that? What does he do? Is he a professor or something?*

Naw, he's just an electrician, but he's a couple of hundred years old. He said that he had to see and survive the universe before settling down and having kids. But he's always telling me what he calls his little homilies, little short stories with a moral or life lesson inside it. We do it after each dinner since forever, ever since I was a baby I guess, I always remember them.

Jon, you make me jealous, I wish I had a dad like that.

So, Catherine, what does your dad do?

Just then the professor announced: "*OK people, your first order of business is to take inventory of your workstations. List every object within the drawers. The team who can identify the most tools will be given first selection of their projects. So, let's get started.*"

Sorry Catherine, what does your dad do?

Krage's quiet but clear voice came behind. "Got you on this one techie –boy, R0bie here is a repair tech and will whip you guys hands down."

Audibly: "Not now Jon, let's get started on inventory. We don't want to give the B team an advantage."

"B TEAM, no way! We're gonna get you, strange girl, and the mechs who walked in with you."

"You're on!"

Focusing on the task at hand Jon, Catherine, W0ody, and Big Blu3 started going through the drawers of the table. Jon took the lead: *I suggest we go drawer by drawer, one at a time, place all items on the tabletop and record each piece we identify on my tablet, then put it back. We should be left with a few items we can't identify. Richard, hop out here, you can help.*

On it, boss! I know a bunch of stiff tools when I see them.

Focus, Richard, focus!

Catherine asked, *what are these narrow flat drawers?*

Those are sometimes called bread boards, or shelf boards. They don't contain things, just extrudable flat surfaces. Jon emptied the contents of the lowest drawer in front of him on the table.

Jon started listing the tools while W0ody and Big Blu3 assisted and recorded the identifications. Catherine looked on interestedly. *In this first drawer it seems to contain electrical equipment and I can identify the following: a set of spin tights, multimeter, wire strippers, lineman cutters, portable drill, ½" uni-bit, 1 ¼" uni-bit, a set of self-tapping bits, power detector...*

What's the difference between a power detector and a multimeter? squawked Blueee3.

They are often used for the same purpose, to determine if a dangerous voltage exists on a circuit or in conductors. The power detector senses electrostatic fields and is faster, you can just wand it over the equipment. But it sometimes lies, not indicating some high voltages. So, the multimeter allows one to certify there is not a dangerous situation, but it takes time.

Look, a compass rose! Hey W0ody, can I take Rosie here down to my hangout?

Richard! You are distracting us more than helping. Stop it!

Sorry, boss, won't happen again.

They continued with the survey, emptying each drawer one at a time, finding a few articles which they had no clue as to its purpose. *'What's this thing with all the metal tongs lined up in a row for?' 'What's this round device, looks like a watch with a button on the side?'* The list of knowns was much larger than the list of unknowns, but the strange tool pile was growing. Catherine was opening drawers without touching anything inside, trying to get a handle on the overall organization of the equipment. She was staying two or three drawers ahead of Jon's team, slowly circling the station.

"Alright teams, five minutes to complete and report. The stop time is absolute, so no exceptions, what you have is what you have at that moment, four and a half minutes, now."

Woo-hoo techie-boy, we've got you beat! We've finished our drawers and have only twenty-five items left. You still have a whole side to do!

Keep going guys. Don't let those slugs bother you. Just pull out the last drawers and I will list what I can. W0ody and Big Blu3 opened the drawers of the back face of the station and started tumbling things out on the tabletop. Jon frantically wrote things down, but the pile was not getting smaller, fast.

"Stop!" Jon was startled and his heart thundered in his chest. What was going on?

Tiger Tales

Tigers and Lions are the same under the skin.
The behavior of tigers and lions is dissimilar,
and not caused by cultural and environmental differences.
Much of people's behavior has a strong genetic genesis.
Much of human culture reflects our genetic heritage.

"Don't quit."

Isaac Asimov – conversation with author

"Courage is being scared to death but saddling up anyway."
John Wayne

Tool Town

Chapter 20

"Stop!" cried the instructor. *"Time's up. Put down your papers and we will call out the groups to see who has the fewest remaining unidentified tools."* Jon's heart continued to pound his chest, though it was beginning to subside.

"Each table has four hundred devices. Either add up the total of your successes or subtract your remainder from four hundred. Be ready to announce your total. We will come by later and check your list. If you try to cheat and add to the list after this announcement, you will be assigned zero. If you overestimate you total, then your group total will be deducted ten times the overestimate.

"Station one, how many tools have you identified?

One hundred and eighty-two.... we hope. The class laughs.

A whisper: "Go big or go home techie. No spheres, no blue chips."

"Shhhh!"

"Station two?"

Fifty-five? More laughs

"Station three? Your count." As the group mutters amongst themselves, the rest of the class keeps up a quiet running comment.

Three hundred and thirty. This silences the class.

"Station four?" Two hundred, maybe more. "Well? Are you sure?" More class chatter. *Two hundred, our final answer.* The class laughs again.

"Station five?" One hundred and fifty.

This continues for another five minutes, with a low of forty, and the three hundred and thirty still the high number.

"Station 22?" KaiLin: *Seventy-eight.* Still not looking Jon's way.

"Station 23?" Karmin, Tink3r and the Soo's: *Two-hundred and twenty-two.* "That's good" whispered Jon quietly.

Finally, it was coming to Krage and Jon, with Jon's team first. Cat breathed, "What did you come up with Jon?"

"Station 24?" They were on.

John turned to the team, *I think I got three hundred and forty, but we should deduct some for mistakes, how about three hundred and twenty-five? It puts us below station three but guarantees up third place, and perhaps better if Krage miscalculates.*

W0ody nodded and Jon turned and started to open his mouth. A hand grabbed his arm and jerked him, and he stopped. He saw Catherine looking at him, and in an undertone she said "Let me do it Jon, please?"

I guess, yeah, OK.

Catherine said in a loud voice "Four Hundred!" "What?" Jon was stunned. What did she just do? The mechs were frozen in place, accumulators overloaded.

The class was so quiet, you could hear a cotter pin drop. KaiLin finally turned towards him, her eyes wide.

Suddenly "Ha! Ha! Ha! You're stooopid!" "You have soooo lost!" voices from Krage's table reverberated.

Professor Yi asked *"Are you sure of your calculations? Take your time."*

John leaned over and whispered, "Catherine, what did you just do? Are you crazy?"

She whispered back, "Trust me Jon, four hundred is correct."

"How can I trust you, I just met you… this is nuts… wow."

"Jon, trust and faith are very similar. I have a strong faith. It comes from inside, often based upon experience, but not always. I know we just met, but I tell you, I am not stupid, I know what I am doing."

He whispered: "Whoa, this is too strange, how can I trust you?"

"Let me try again. I ask you to trust me, if this works, and it will. We will make an exceptional team, so I am asking you to trust a stranger in a strange land. What can I do to get you to try?"

"I don't know, Catherine, this is more than awkward." He turned towards Kai, she was still staring directly at him, turning back "Basically you are saying, "Trust me" when I have been taught to be cautious, more than cautious, around strangers. But, you are a girl my age, and you are challenging the adult matrix like I am, so we have a common background.... Yeah, I guess .. W0ody, is it OK that we do this?"

"Whatever you say Jon, I am soooo out of my league in this I can only watch."

Richard piped, "Go for it!" He was bouncing on the table like a gecko, "Youse guys are awesome! Spin the wheel, roll the dice, all in! Fire both barrels, just like my shipmates of old, bless their souls."

W0ody said, "Cool your jets, Richard, he's in a bind and has to think his way out."

Small seto, "OK W0ody, I'll zip it."

"OK, Catherine, we have a deal, trust, faith, or whatever. It's a deal."

"Deal."

Jon turned back to Doctor Yi, *Our team stands behind our Captain's conclusion. Four hundred.* Turning back to Catherine he muttered "I really, really, hope you're right."

"I am, and you won't be disappointed."

"Station twenty-five?" There was an argument between the members of Krage's team. They were trying to second guess Jon's AND Catherine's results. Match them? Consider them instant crazy? A lot of opinions before Kragey finally made a decision.

Three hundred and eighty! Another silence, then whispers.

"OK class, the results are reported. My staff and I will come around and review your conclusions for accuracy. Stay by your stations."

"Baaaaaa!" Kragey was having a great time, pleased with himself as he made noises and fun at Jon and Catherine. The others of Krage group were nudging and giggling. Jon noticed Karmin and others also at tables behind him. The rest of the groups were starting to talk amongst themselves and looking Jon's way.

Boy, did he feel nervous and exposed, watching the professors go around to the other tables. The initial results indicated that no one had overestimated their list, and three thirty was the max point of the teams, as they thought, from station three.

Dr. Yi was obviously leaving them for last, since they were high count, and taking Krage second from last. Finally, they were at Krage's table. Jon noticed that he was unintentionally dragging his left foot, toe to the ground, back and forth. He stopped that and tried to relax. He looked at Sindee, who was bouncing up and down, and at Catherine, who had a withdrawn, Mona Lisa smile. Get it over! he thought.

After a quiet minute a Krage's table Dr. Yi announced: *"Team twenty-four, you correctly identified more tools than any other team, three hundred and seventy-five. But because you announced three hundred and eighty, you lose ten times the difference, which is five times ten, with a final result of three hundred and twenty-five points, which places you in second place. Well done."* Krage, R0bbie and

Sindee took the professor's proffered hand and shook it. Doctor Yi turned to Jon's table. *"So, what do we have here?"*

Jon stood still as he approached. Slowly, Jon glanced at Catherine, who stepped forward: *Doctor Yi, we declare all four hundred tools, as described in our list.* She handed the instructor a few pages of handwritten notes. Jon was confused, this was not the list he made. Finally, Yi looked up.

"Where did you get this list?"

I wrote it.

"When did you write it?"

In the last twenty minutes.

"How did you get the information to write on this list?"

I copied it from another list.

"Young lady, you are approaching getting in serious trouble."

Jon's gut locked up, causing him to bend ever so slightly. It was hard to breath. Kragey and Sindee started to laugh. *"Hush up table twenty-four. This is serious."*

"Young lady, I ask you, did you get this second list from outside of the classroom?"

No.

"Young lady, I ask you again, and you must be truthful. Did you bring this other list from outside, or did you get it from a previous class, or did you memorize it prior to today?"

No sir. Even Catherine started to look troubled now. The class was the deadly silence of a vacuum.

"So, tell me, young lady, how did you come by this list?"

Well, it is a long story.

"Be quick about your long story, now." Yi was getting a very stern posture and voice about him.

Sir, it started with a challenge from table twenty-four.

"A challenge, what kind of a challenge."

Well, we were being heckled because we obviously aren't from their in-crowd and it escalated to a dare and a verry large bet, who was going to be better. We took the bet and the challenge.

"Go on." Jon's chest was starting to hurt with the inability of taking normal breaths.

Well, Jon here, he's so serious, well he started to do the inventory as required and Big Blu3, W0ody and Richard were helping as best they could, and I was kinda in the way.

So I tried, really tried to figure a way I could help us find out the maximum number of tool identities, and I did, and Jon's so sweet, I asked him to let me respond, to trust my judgment, and I didn't want to tell him how I did it, because R0bie, team twenty-four's mechman student had a Vulcan Allen military audio receiver built into its carapace and I noticed every time Jon called out a tool name, R0bie talked to Krage, and he wrote something down.

I felt that they were doing reconnaissance and you had not directly made covert intelligence a penalty, so being suspicious, I did not tell Jon of my discovery because he's too trusting.

"There better be a quick ending to this long story."

Well, I figured I couldn't help by normal methods, how about not a normal method, like an Einstein thought problem. I looked around, and everywhere was wood, wonderful wood. Old wood, ancient wood, with an old ancient teacher. The class broke into laughter.

Oh, sorry Doctor Yi, but I was just describing my thoughts.

"Go on." Doctor Yi sounded stern, but his exaggerated overbearing posture and just a hint of a smile on the frown made Jon realize he was kinda maybe acting? Jon took a deep breath.

Well, in this old place maybe there was a tracking mechanism for all the tools that was also ancient, like a paper list? We had been given a paper lab guide. I looked through it, but there was nothing.

Catherine wrinkled her nose at the thought: *So, I started digging around the drawers looking, but it wasn't there. But maybe, because this isn't the first time this class was held, they tucked the list away somewhere. So, as Jon and W0ody removed the drawers to remove or sometimes spill out the tools, I looked at the back of each drawer and the underside.*

"And?"

Well, I was frustrated, nothing. But I then asked myself, how 'bout the undersides of the cutting boards? And sure enough, there it was. Jon, W0ody and Big Blu3 were so busy they didn't notice me copying the list and putting the board back.

Jon was at a loss, he could finally breath in large gulps as he tried to regain his equilibrium. He felt like the time the vector jet on his left foot failed open and sent him spinning out of control when visiting Abs yacht.

She had definitely executed an end-around which he did not even notice. In an abstract way he admired her sophisticated act, but her demands on his trust were still causing issues. But he noticed Kragey and his team weren't making noise anymore. Maybe the positives outweighed the negatives after all.

"That's pretty amazing."

Doctor Yi, that was only half of it, because we had to announce our results before team twenty-four's, and I had to be able to convince Jon to use my number without being able to explain how I came up with the number, because if I did, R0bie would tell Krage and they would tie us which have made life miserable.

So, I asked Jon to trust me. Did I tell you he was sweet?

Jon was becoming embarrassed, what was she telling the world? Looking over, if Kai had been stiff before, now she'll never talk to him again. How in the world did this happen?

Anyways, I told Jon to trust me, but he couldn't.

So, I told him about faith and we might have similar backgrounds and goals and I just looked deeply into his eyes, teenage boys are so predictable, girls mature faster than boys and I have an advantage, and I got him off center without telling him how, but to trust, and that's what he did, and by the way? Did I tell you he was sweet?

Now the class started to giggle, and Jon's ears and face were suddenly hot. Boy, Jon hoped she was joking, and he was going to let her have his opinion when they were alone. Man, his friendship to Kai was ruined!

"Young lady, that was a soundly thought out plan that reflects well upon you and your team."

To the class*: "Class, the first problem set was solved best by team twenty-four by thinking outside the envelope, followed closely by teams three and twenty-five. Now, I wish all of you to review the project handbook in your tables and select activities you wish to pursue as a team during the course of the class."*

Turning to Jon's group, Doctor Yi inquired, *"How old is your team? When did you first get together?"*

Well, we met for the first outside the door to the lab, just today.

"Amazing. How old are you Jonny, Jonny isn't it?"

I'm twelve, I will be thirteen before the class is over, and I prefer to be called Jon. W0ody here is my mechmate, and he always calls me Jonny, but that's OK for him to do.

"How about you W0ody?"

I came out of the crèche the day Jonny, I mean Jon, was born. We have been together ever since. I live with his family, the Miller's, as acclimation and assimilation. I hope someday to become a man.

"And your name is Catherine, is that correct?"

Yes sir. I'm fourteen. This here is Big Blu3. He's been with me forever. The little guy is Blueee3. I never told Jon that I was in a couple of summer classes with him over the last few years, but we never met because he always was with a group of active kids. But I kinda thought he was cute. Did I ever tell you that he was sweet? She looked at Jon, now knowing she had his goat. She was obviously baiting him, not crazy. Kai, on the other hand, had turned away again.

Jon was getting angry. Cute! Sweet! Baby names! Ruining his friendships. But on the other hand, Catherine was fast on her feet and sharp of wit which always attracted him to others. He hoped she had a sense of humor. That would be tops! Stop it! he told himself, now he is losing it and his thoughts are all over the place!

"Well, obviously Blueee3 and Richard don't meet the Gordon Volume rule for sentience. What about you Big Blu3?"

Big Blu3 has never talked, but we communicate well. I guess it's like twins or something.

"Oh, very interesting. Have you decided on a project?"

We haven't talked a lot about anything yet, but I really want a solo project I have been thinking about all my life.

I want to grow and surgically adhere a tail. A long, maybe 32-36" long furred tail, striped like a tiger's tail. I have always dreamed to be in a position to make it come true, and now it has finally happened.

"I don't know young lady. Do you know how hard it is to do bionic modifications?"

So I have been told. But my whole life I have been told I couldn't, or wouldn't be allowed, to do a lot of things. And I decided then and there, that if anyone can do it, with enough effort, will, and luck, then, so can I.

My Faith says luck is nothing more than opportunity meeting preparation. And I am prepared to work 24/7/365 if I get the opportunity. And you said, Doctor Yi, that we can pick our own projects being top dog, and also that staff has bio-adaptive background and resources. So, unless you tell me absolute "NO", then I will do it. I want a tail.

"What about your family, will they be upset with this project? You are in a grey area of the law, children cannot get bio-mods

without parental permission, but once you are in this school, you are no longer formally a child. So, can you get family support?"

I assure you Doctor Yi, no one in my family will complain.

"Are you sure?"

A lot more sure of that than of winning the dare. I know the Blue Brothers here support my goal.

"Well, we will see. I am not saying no, but we will have to assign you a personal rather than team lab counselor, and you can develop a proposal, and I will look at it. How about you Jon, do you want a team project or go solo?"

Well, although I haven't talked to Catherine at all, W0ody and I talked about doing separate projects also. I want to work on Space Elevator engineering and W0ody told me he wants to work on Motor and Electromagnetic theory.

I really want to see Earth, to see an ocean or a storm. To breath "Natural" air. Well, the only way I could do it is if there is a space elevator. From what I have learned, it would take 500 years to build one, and so I would never see it, but I could help it on its way in a minimal sense by working on its design.

I mean, space itself was colonized by Universal Hope utilizing small contributions from hundreds of millions of people over hundreds, if not thousands of years. I would like to be part of that effort. We should reconnect with the dirt people, who would bring the wisdom of our ancestors to this wild place we call the Federation.

"Well, if I didn't know better, I have heard some of those thoughts before. You might still have some influences in you from your liberal public teachers. However, it is a good project and one I can completely support.

"I have a thought. Since both of you seem dedicated, and will team with your mechs, perhaps you would like to live nearer to the labs than your base homes. We can offer you positions as laboratory assistants here and pay a small stipend and provide room and board in the student dorms. You might even benefit from those collegial exposures there as well as learning practical material here."

Can Catherine and I have some time to talk? We haven't had much so far, and we have a lot of ground to cover together.

"Certainly, my comm number is here in the lab guide on the back" At that, Doctor Yi walked away to talk to Krage's group.

As the professor receded Jon looked back at Catherine, *Well, you sure saved the day, but I felt like a fool. Sweet indeed!*

Yep, you are sweet!

He whispered hoarsely: "Stop that! At that table over there is the girl I was going to study with." Kai didn't budge. Catherine slowly brought her hand up to cover her mouth. "I'm so sorry."

"Well, I mean, you did good, no, you did better than I can imagine. You didn't know about Kai."

"Is that her name?"

He went on quickly, "Yes, and she is a good person, and I like her and I want to be her friend and have her want to be my friend and my best friend is Abs, and he is super cool and rich and like that and I am afraid she likes him more than me, and now I am in trouble!

"I am always second guessing myself, so I never have that firm confident way and ability to just act quickly that my friend Abs can."

He took a deep breath and reflected before changing his chain of thoughts: "You thought, and you acted, and acted correctly. I'm sorry I burdened you with my personal struggles … "

Taking a deep breath, "In reality, thank you. You saved the day, right W0ody?"

"Yes, thank you Catherine, Krage and R0bie would have been unbearable if they won."

Falsetto: "You came out and shot both barrels! You knocked them on their teakettles, ass over appetite!"

"Enough Richard, please?"

Smiling at the strange smart tool, Catherine replied, "You're welcome. I did say to trust me and have faith, and it would work out, and it did. Thank you for your trust."

He resumed beam talk: *Ditto. Hey, this took longer than expected. W0ody and I need to get back home. We live in Helena; would you being going our way? We could share ride.* Jon noticed again her dark amber brown eyes, and now a similar tint in her hair. She was wearing a black shirt trimmed in lavender that also reflected in her lips. Jon realized he really hadn't noticed much about her, just that she was pretty.

Oh, I'm sorry, but Big Blu3 and I had plans. Maybe at a later class. OK?

OK, sure. Jon looked around for Kai, but she had vanished. In fact, everyone from the gang was gone already. Jon was disappointed. Sad that this fine day did not have the companionship he was wanting or used to. The future was changing quickly.

Well W0ody, let's get going. We've a lot to talk about.

Yeah, we're moving!

I think she's cute! The small voice was becoming an irritation.

The Cooperation Postulate:

Within the natural world, life has formed many types of cooperative groups. It has been shown that the individual is more successful as a member of a group. Since before the time of recorded history, Mankind has formed many types of cooperative groups.

"Seek freedom and become captive of your desires.
Seek discipline and find your liberty."
- Frank Herbert

Just because you do not take an interest in politics
doesn't mean politics won't take an interest in you."
Pericles:

Bi1l finds out about George
CH 21

The knock came at the door. *Come in Lieutenant, close the door behind you.*

You asked to see me Sir?

Detective Lieutenant Wil liam MacHinery of the Federated Belt Police was a light mech, perhaps 185 centimeters tall and a hard eighty kilograms mass, a thin frame, a dancer's grace when walking. He looked around the office evenly, noticing the commendations, recommendations and awards that highlighted the walls of

Department Chief Captain Fredrick Juarez, with a photo mural of the rings of Saturn behind the Captain.

"Yes, thank you Lieutenant, please take a seat. Because comms are becoming suspect, I will conduct this meeting audibly." Captain Juarez said, pointing to a flat rough iron slab bench slightly curved at the right front of his large office desk, facing ninety degrees away from the Chief. Bill was wearing a red and black pork pie hat and deep green covert coat. The bench was out of place and at odds with the other furnishings of the office which were anodized aluminum and stainless steel, but most likely a hull cut of one of the Chief's previous commands and a keepsake for the office's occupant.

As Bill settled onto the bench, he was pleased to be able to magnetically lock down without any handshake protocol being required between his body and the seat, just good old-fashioned magnetics. He removed his hat and set it in his lap.

Immediately, the Chief stood up, waving George to remain seated, and walked over to his panorama, they turned back to the Lieutenant, "I asked you in today to discuss an operation whose topic and background information should not leave this room. Do you understand?"

Bill was interested, "Yes Sir." He knew that this interview would have an important basis: Lieutenants do not get called in to see the Chief on a whim. His demeanor and humor reflected his basic nature and he relied upon them to sustain him through this interview as they had throughout his career.

The Captain continued, "We, that is the Federation Council, then passed to my office, have invited the Earth's Dirt Police to provide a Criminal Investigative Attaché as a Forensics Officer to assist our staff. This officer will require a Liaison, a partner here at the Department to work with him, coordinate with him, learn from him, keep him from spying, that sort of thing."

A smile started to appear slightly on the Chief's face. "After a significant search, staff has recommended you." The Captain grinned broadly as he sat down again.

Yes, this was interesting, "Has High Command explained why they want such an Attaché?" The Lieutenant was reminded of the stories of the ancient marines who smiled before battle; and ate their dead.

"The overt explanation is that they wish to expand the continuing cultural and political exchanges that expand peace and harmony between our two cultures.

"In reality, crime is becoming a serious issue in the belt communities and we want to pick their brains for solutions. They have been studying crime up close and personal for a long, long time. They have to have developed systems, and the like. Why recreate the wheel when someone already has?"

As usual when dealing with upper staff, politics and agendas were present, but as normal, hidden. Dropping hydraulic system pressure allowed his legs to relax and stretch out somewhat, as to give a sense of 'We are part of this together...' "So why me Sir?"

"This Dirtman, his name is, ah..., Lieutenant Sealth, and he truly is a Dirtman. I am told he has no augmentation, whoa, think about it. Not linked, not seeing or hearing any of the notes and jibes as you move. No net answers, nothing."

The Chief looked Wild Bill, as he was known throughout the division, "We needed someone who could handle the unusual, and boy, your name came up immediately, a mech who does standup comedy on weekends. You will be inscrutable to his primitive senses, yet sensitive enough to discern his most subtle clues and behaviors. He is, of course, a spy. And you are our counter agent."

Wild Bill sat up straighter, this <u>was</u> going to be interesting.

"Do I get all sorts of RAD counter-espionage toys, like pens that turn into guns and invisible ink writing tools? This can be way cool, do I get codes and counter codes, do I meet people in the park and drop off notes? Is he really a Dirtman? A true homo?" Bill was getting into it.

The Captain stood back up, "Cool your jets Lieutenant, we do not want to ever indicate to Earth our true potentials. We will let you place a few microbugs we feel he will be able to find, but the true source will be the nanos that will be part of the paint, the dust, his clothes. We are going to down scale by a factor of ten from what we think they are capable of.

"Even if they come in with devices and scanners as small as human dust mites, we will be so much smaller, they won't stand a chance." He sat back with a satisfied look that MacHinery thought smacked a look of contempt. *Look out,* he thought, *We could be in for a big fall*

Bill continued to explore his assignment, where was this going: "How often do you expect us to interact? Where will he live, will I have to provide his every need? What if he gets continuously space sick like that last representative from earth? Do I get backup during off hours, what if he gets hurt or killed, what are you and Earth going to do? What challenges and assignments are you giving…"?

"Lieutenant! Slow down! You will get a formal brief from staff, but your assignments will remain essentially the same. You will investigate murders, large burglaries, kidnappings, and malicious destruction, as well as illegal ownership of balloons."

"Illegal ownership of balloons?!" Bill caught the evil grin of the Captain, and realized he'd been had, "OK, I'll wait, but don't blame me if this assignment goes south."

"So, while you are with him, you will be our camera and recorder. Do you understand?"

Grabbing his hat, the Lieutenant stood up again, "Yes Sir, I understand."

The Chief came around the desk "If you don't have any questions, stop by the Adjutant's desk, and he will direct you to your formal briefing team and get you outfitted. Please, this is of planetary importance, if you feel impeded in any way, or need additional support, come to me directly. With this business out at the Trojans and crappy WET service, we need to stay on top."

Stepping forward to shake the Chief's hand, Bill was mildly surprised at the magnitude of the assignment but pleased it didn't look terribly dangerous yet highly interesting and important. Best yet, he was going to be able to grow his career, and like it at the same time, he hoped. "Thank you, Sir, I will do my best. Now, which way to the balloon locker?"

The Ethical Challenge

Producers, Predators, and Parasites all exist in Nature.
They all have an equal value in the Universe.
The tree, the cow, the lion, and the human, have the same weight ethically.
Groups are subject to Predation and must protect themselves.
Predation is ethical for the individual.

"I don't mind you thinking I'm stupid, but don't talk to me like I'm stupid."
- Harlan Ellison

"We cannot teach people anything;
we can only help them discover it within themselves."
Galileo

Lab Ass

Chapter 22

Dad, why would Abs skip class the first two weeks? We had a plan to work together. Jon was eating breakfast with his family, W0ody was plugged in and getting charged too.

Well, I don't know exactly, but perhaps we can work it out. Do you think Abs is smart enough to pass his emancipation exams?

Oh yes, he does better on exams than I do!

Do you think <u>he</u> thinks he is smart enough to pass the exams?

Sure, he does, he thinks he can do anything.

Since his father got successful, do you think he has to work hard to get things?

Naw, he has more than any of us, always giving stuff away to the girls and like that.

Is it possible he thinks he can pass the exams without study and work? If everything is easy, and if he is busy, would he wait until the last minute to try?

But dad, everyone says you got to work hard to get past your exams. He and I have heard that a million times.

Do you think he might find it easier to take the first half of the semester off and go hang out with his group? Aren't the people he is with and the things he is now doing really more exciting than school?

But dad, he's starting to really change! We used to have fun just making jokes while we talked, but now he gets serious. We would be in a group of guys, many of them new, they weren't around when we were friends growing up, and anyways, Abs would make fun of me to get the others to laugh. Not all the time, but more in the last month. And it hurts.

Have you told him?

Yeah, and he says it's just a joke, not to take it seriously, that I'm too sensitive, don't be so needy, toughen-up, things like that. He's cool when we are doing stuff together by ourselves.

Do you still study together? 'We used to.'

Does that mean you still study together? 'No.'

Why not? 'I ask him, but nowadays he's too busy.'

So, what are you going to do?

I don't know.

Well, you guys are growing up fast. You are changing, sometimes in ways you expect and can't wait to get over with, like challenging the emancipation tests, but sometimes in ways you don't expect, like Abs is now.

But dad that's not fair! We told each other that we would be best friends forever just last year. Being best friends is important, Abs wouldn't let that go.

Jonathon, it is my experience, some people change, actually, many people change over time, especially during their teen years and around the time of your majority test.

I had a friend, everything was good when we were doing what he liked doing, but if I wanted to do something he didn't, well, he'd just walk away. He asked for favors, and because I wanted to keep his friendship, I would help out, but I learned after a while, if I asked for help, he'd never come through.

In the electrical world we call these people diodes because in electricity, a diode lets current flow in only one direction, but not the other. If you become a plumber, we call them check-valves.

Aw dad, Abs isn't like that, we still do stuff together.

Jon, friendships are important, just keep your eyes open, and don't let yourself get hurt by wanting or expecting too much. You know the old Hope saying: 'Unrealistic and unrealized expectations are why women go crazy and men become mad.'

Dad, you're no fun.

Remember, your happiness and satisfaction have to come from within, external relationships cannot justify you and your existence.

Abs is not responsible for your happiness, you are. Don't ever say to someone "Look at what you made me do!" You are responsible for yourself, a major tenet of the HOPE, the only person you can or should control is yourself.

His father was on his soap box again, Jon thought. *Too many words.*

This is a very hard and complicated lesson to learn. You are a good person, you should be satisfied with yourself, for your accomplishments at your age, and just by your very nature. We all are imperfect, we all make mistakes, we all can be criticized, but I tell you, you are alright just the way you are.

Easy for you to say, you're not a kid trying to get privileges… to himself only, trying not to roll his eyes away.

Be confident in yourself, but not cocky. Work hard and you will continue to have more successes than failures, be consistent and true friendships will form. Important people with status who make fun of you are hard to ignore. But you must, they are displaying nothing more than primitive adolescent behavior which you must grow past.

It is hard, I know, but try, and I will help guide you again if I can. Jon, this is what getting your citizenship and being an adult requires, friends and teams are essential, but depend on yourself also. Well, enough of that, I talk too much.

Dad, you are really no fun!

I know. Well, you need to get ready and catch the tube to school. You don't want to miss any of the first month of class.

OK

As they walked to their room, *W0ody, did you get that, did it make sense to you?*

Maybe, maybe a little, I got to think about it. You animals are hard to figure out.

Yeah, like a fractally folded riddle wrapped in a non-linear mystery hidden inside an enema!

Richard, control your dirty little mind!

Okey dokey artichokey!

*They grabbed their packs and headed out the door because as it is said: "*The TUBE waits for no one.*"*

When sitting in the car, Jon reflected upon his conversation. If dad was right, then things weren't going to be great with Abs. He sure hoped dad was wrong. He suddenly realized, he hadn't mentioned Catherine or the Laboratory Assistant position.

It was probably better he didn't talk about Catherine, that would be difficult. Maybe never is best. Looking up at the VID he noticed they were showing the news feed, how the recovery from the WET problems was going to take more time, and that there still was no communication with the Mechs out at the Citadel.

Coming to the lab, they had arrived with about five minutes to spare, and needing some time to set up, they didn't loiter at the entrance, and Jon just let the back of his hand trail along the golden burnished wood of the doorway.

Going towards their station Jon immediately saw Kai, Krage and Catherine and the two Blu3s were already their tables. Cat already had some stuff laid out on the table. Big Blu3 shifted and she looked up to follow their approach.

Hi Catherine.

Hello Jonny, hello W0ody. As before, the Blu3s were silent. Kai was once again not making eye contact.

Catherine, have you discovered what the plans are for today?

One of the post-Docs came by five minutes ago and said she'd be back when we all arrive, oh, here she comes now. As she spoke a young woman in a white smock strode up.

How are our Lab Asses doing today? she said smiling. *I am Assistant Professor Vesilisev, I am going to be your advisor.*

Jon was confused, and it showed on his face. *Aren't you ready? Did you forget something?*

Jon face was getting warm, *I didn't bring anything, we just came back as scheduled.*

I guess it's OK, but you Lab Asses will have special duties, and will need to plan on being here an extra two hours every day to plan for the next day's class, then set up for the class early.

Lab Ass, what's a Lab Ass?

Oh, that's just slang for Laboratory Assistant, and since you're young, and sometimes get the run of the place, and sometimes get in trouble, and since most of the senior staff once were assistants, you ARE Lab Asses until relieved. OK? By the way, my names Anna.

Got it Anna, now I know what a Lab Ass is.

You're fast on yer feet. Your momma musta drown'd the dumb twin.

Quiet! Jon showed his irritation not knowing things, *Sorry Richard, just don't pick on the sore spots, OK?*

Okey dokey, big fella.

Everyone smiled at that, even Catherine. *See, I told you he was sweet!*

Stop it, that's getting old fast.

OK, cutie pie.

Jon smiled despite himself.

OK, guys, your job as Lab Asses is to help the other teams. Help them find stuff, where it is located around their station, understand their tools, and answer questions about basic science, because a lot of them won't know very much, and this is their introduction to technology.

Again, Jon was suffocating. He realized it was just the loss of the WET again and focused on his five senses.

Behind the white noise, they heard again the peal of great bells:

One … …

Two … …

Three … …

Four … …,

Finally, the white noise evaporated, and the WET carrier trains began, streaming to a pitch almost to gridlock before settling down.

Slowly, the handshakes started in fits and starts. When they tried to talk, their words faded in and out and it was almost impossible to understand.

"What the heck was that?" someone said out loud. The WET suddenly snapped back to its normal clarity.

Anna wondered, "That was most unusual. Perhaps it would be best if we talked about what is remaining, OK? I really hope someone gets to the bottom of this quickly, it is starting to sound sinister."

They all paused quietly as they watched each other try to digest this ominous event.

Anna, finally spoke, as if to ignore what had happened, what choice was there?

"We will have Labs on every Tuesday and Thursday throughout the term. You get the run of the place for your special projects on weekends too.

"This may sound like fun, but in reality, we put a larger burden on you, to be a teacher actually makes you learn more. We expect a lot out of you. You can't be loose cannons, no horsing around, you have to lead by example." "Ahh man!"

Everyone began to loosen up as normality returned.

"But, after class you get to use the full services of the lab for your own projects. Catherine, I understand you have the most sophisticated project and want to grow a genetically compatible tail. I can help with most of that, and Professor Carlisle's degree in Bio attachments will be invaluable when we have problems, and we will have problems."

"Thanks."

"Well, settle in, I'll be back after I tell table 25 their duties.

Jon and Catherine looked at each other. Once again Jon noticed her brown eyes that had a hint of amber "Well, what's first?" asked Jon. He was nervously fiddling with the table's air valve, causing small puffs of air.

"Well, we can start this together, you and I will be the idea men, Big Blu3 and W0ody can record."

"Before we start, why do you talk to me? You don't seem to talk to anyone else." This time Jon twisted the valve just a little, so it wouldn't make noise.

"Why, don't you remember?"

"No. Remember what?" Twist.

"When I was at Toe Jam Middle, we came to the Ender Academy for some AP classes, you were the one who said hi, and had a smile. The rest of your crowd were too busy talking to each other, throwing insults."

"Aw, that's just chopping, nobody means anything by it. Kids competing. You know." He added a little air to the conservation.

"Well, it's not right to be insulted a lot the first day in a new school."

"I'm sorry, that wasn't nice."

"It sure isn't. I think I ended up going home and crying, telling everything to Big Blu3 here."

"That's way bad. Where were your parents?" This time Jon didn't touch the gas valve, he was looking intently at Catherine.

"My parents hadn't arrived yet. But it was that Abs guy who did most of the cutting."

Now, Jon started to pull the top drawer in front of him open a little, then slide it back, "Oh, Abs is OK when you get to know him, he just likes to joke around."

"Well, I was always been told to be careful around strangers, so it wasn't as bad as it could have been. I just stayed quiet and they moved on to easier targets. I never really ever talk to people, except now to you. I don't know why, except I'm just not comfortable around anybody."

Sliding a drawer, "Why me? How am I special to you?"

"I don't know. Do I have to have an answer for everything? All I know is I have a faith, and it causes me to trust you." She put both hands on the edge of the table looking him in the eyes. The mechs were frozen at full attention.

"You trust me. Wow, after everything Abs said and done, and he's my friend. You asked me to trust you, and that was a wild ride. And now you say you trust me. Wow." Pushing on an already shut drawer. He looked down.

"Well, you didn't throw me under the bus. And, the cruel things Abs says doesn't matter because you don't agree and say the same things."

"But Abs is my friend, I don't want to part ways. I could roll on you, we've just met." He pulled the drawer open again.

"Ah, I have faith, hard to describe, but it works. I need it, I trust it, I am calmed by it, I am energized by it and focused by it. It isn't always right, but enough, so I don't worry, and it tells me to trust you. I did. I do, I will until graduation, then we will talk again."

He was about to ask more questions on how faith worked but they were cut off by Doctor Yi taking the podium again. "OK, class, you have met the teaching assistants and each other and have familiarized yourselves with your workstations, on the board and on your desks are a reading lists and a beginning project description. Review and select them, you are required to be self-starters to finish this course, so begin to begin." Yi grinned at his self-joke.

Jon looked at the lists and said, "I really like atomic chemistry. Why don't Catherine and I do the *Embden–Meyerhof* Glycolysis chemical reaction lab first, while W0ody, you and the two Blu3s make the DC motor? Does that sound right?"

Catherine stated, "Jonny, I want to tell you more about faith, but only when you want, and yes Jonny, you and I can do the chemical project first."

"I would love to build a motor, how about a 4160v, 3 Φ, 8-pole inverter ready Bulldog? Of course, if the two Blu3s help it would be awesome."

"Holy catfish guys, while youse gets to build the motor, I gets to build the transmission! I used to be a kick ass gear cutter in my youth!"

Blueee3 gently launched itself and flew to Big Blu3's shoulder, where it announced: "We will be pleased to work with W0ody."

"I thought you said Big Blu3 doesn't talk."

"He doesn't, but when Blueee3 is on his shoulder, Blueee3 can talk."

"Interesting, you called Big Blu3 him, is there a gender issue? Most Mechs reflect the gender of their companion initially so I would think the Blu3s would be female." Very slowly he pulled on a drawer.

"Jonny, I just think of them as 'he'".

"Well, it sure would be good if you called me Jon, OK?"

"OK Jon. Did I ever tell you that you're cute?" Out of the corner of his eye he thought he saw Kai glaring.

"Cut that out!" Calls came from Krage's group, "Jonny's got a girlfriend, Jonny's got a girlfriend," rang out. Kai forcefully replaced her project and marched away, followed by E^{3}Ching. "Now look at what you did!" Called out James.

"Not my fault everyone!" Turning to Catherine, "Let focus on the lab." Jonny felt battered by emotional grenades.

"OK Jon, sorry, you're right. I will stay focused. Anyways, I've started thinking about our brainstorm, which we can write down next time. Would you explain some of these tools to me?"

Sliding the drawer fully closed, "Good idea. I think Abs is upset at me. I know Kai is. Hey, would you like to do something after class?"

"Thank you, no, after we're through, the Blue brothers and I need to go through all the tools again after you and W0ody leave, you know almost all of them, but I don't at all, and it will take a number of hours. Go along without me, OK?"

Sigh, "OK. Let's get started."

Human Behavior and Social Groups

Animal and Pack

Tribal and Civil

"There is absolutely no single aspect of one's personality
that is more important to develop than empathy,
which is not a skill at which men typically are asked to excel."
- Chris Ware

"Make the best use of what's in your power and take the rest as it happens."
Epictetus

School Daze

Chapter 23

Jon and W0ody hurried down the hall outside the lab on the way to the TUBE. "I lost track of the time; we better make our car. Trying to figure out what Kai and Catherine want is just about to smother me."

"Yeah, I heard there once was a King Wart, Arthur, Alfred or Heart or some such, whose staff was so full fops who fawned all over him, and they told him he could do anything. Disgusted, he finally took all of them down to the TUBE, and beheld a car, and shouted "WAIT!", but it left without him. He allowed them to ponder on the importance of being man. As they say, the TUBE waits for no one.

"So MeatStick, make haste!"

"W0ody, I am being serious! It's been more than two weeks and nothing's better!"

"We can't fix it now, so let's go somewhere where we can."

"Well, let's do the lower cave stride and get there fast." Jon trotted past the construction zone by the Three Tee Corner towards the Hub. It seemed to Jon that there always construction, wherever he looked.

Everyone said it was progress, but he liked things left the way they were. It upset him to have to learn new routes because collector-distributor systems were overhauled for better "efficiency". What about having to learn new routes every year? At least the TUBES were dependable, transfer stations the same year in and year out, concourses with common names.

But who wouldn't want to be a member of the TATs or some other famous band and have all that attention and the groupie girls? If the girls didn't like you it meant you weren't good, or something. Mom says its Ok not to have a girlfriend at his age, but what does she know? Does she know how lonely it can get, and how jealous he is of Abs sometimes, what with all people hanging around and listening to everything he says.

Damm, he has to stop feeling sorry for himself. Today went well, no, it went really well, except when the girls were around. Maybe they will work something out. It will be perfect when the WET is stable and they can put all this war and stuff behind them. They had to get home so he could tell dad all about it.

All the TUBE stations had names, and the ones by the Sesame were called TAP Twice NODE and the University one was Tiger NODE. They were almost there, having gotten past the dig in a reasonable time and were approaching the TUBE. The pedestrian traffic was bunching up again as the student population was abandoning the University for their disparate homes.

He couldn't even think about Krage's commute, he came all the way from Belfair Heights, about two hours each way. But Krage wanted to hang with Abs, and Abs hung in the University District, mostly along the Ave, unless he was jaunting on his new yacht. Jon felt even his 30-minute travel time was a bother, but at least he had W0ody to talk to. He enjoyed and learned from their discussions and reviews of the days they had together, it helped him understand life and people.

He and W0ody, finally arrived at the Tiger, and flashed the STAR cards they had at auto-readers since the WET was still down in some functions. The STARs were OK, they allowed him to jump any transport without having to carry credits or individual transfers. The TUBEs originated and exited at hubs configured as tetrahedrals which was determined, perhaps just decided, a long time ago to enhance the process of moving people along.

The Tiger had a direct connection to the FTN, which was a big-time saver, but he also could take the Old Spanish Trail to the Asteroid Dome, the Zoo, or Science Museum, or the ports (as if he had the money). Oh-oh, the #7 Car that just pulled in was an older Metro, with stiff seats, no comms (as if it mattered today), and usually broken vids. Oh well, the ride won't last long, and he can use the time to reflect upon today's events.

Jon and W0ody quickly grabbed one of the few remaining double bench seats and settled in for the ride. W0ody brought out Richard and started a quiet conversation and investigation, mostly EM he assumed, but also Richard was doing a show and tell of his various tool stock. Jon started to contemplate his day.

Abs hadn't shown up again, which was surprising since it's all they talked about for the last three years, this moment. Why wouldn't he? Damm, he didn't understand that at all. The guys they hung out with showed up with attitudes, BIG attitudes. Why was that? Another mystery. Some girl he had never noticed tagged along, unannounced and unasked. Who was Catherine? Where was she from? She was sure oblivious to the obvious. Kai had her back up. Why? Did a stray girl make her upset? Was he upset when she hung with Abs? Yeah, maybe a little.

Catherine was a Plain Jane, but who cares? She was smart, and he certainly liked smart girls, so uninterested when the Cheer Squad started going on about their favorite celebrities. Dad said good looking girls have tricks, trying to get as average as possible, symmetry is crucial, then adding a flair and a smile. Wow, does that all it takes? He wondered what Catherine would look like with faint makeup to accent the eyes and lips, then add the flair of a Tiger Tail!

Wow, he realized that if he stepped back mentally, he could think about things intellectually and come up with reasons. Catherine would look very good with makeup. But, would he enjoy being with a person who spent a lot of energy and time creating an image and hiding themselves behind it? Perhaps, he really like her the way she was, whatever that was. She starts out quiet and shy, then ends up the day razzing him! Why did she keep calling him cute? What nonsense!

In fact, he realized that although he didn't mind when his friends called him names like Techie or such, but when a stranger or someone he doesn't know well started bugging him, it bothered him a lot and made him angry.

He realized he <u>was</u> angry at her, but he didn't have right to be angry. Why did she ask him to trust her? There had to be another way around the problem, but no, she took the path which allowed her to expose him as a trusting fool. Well, he'd better talk to dad about it, maybe he'd have an answer. Not mom! She'd start making plans as if Catherine was a girlfriend or they would get married.

How can he concentrate? He's in school in AP. Vesta is being interrupted by WET outages. He has met an interesting new girl. Abs is drifting apart, becoming mean. Kai is hanging with Abs, and no longer interested in him. Bah! He is going to get his citizenship. There may be war in the Trojans. Startled, he looked up, they were already pulling into the station.

W0ody was staring at him, he had put Richard away. "Well, did you finger anything out?" His speech dropping into the common teen slang.

"I think I have to talk to dad. It's too much. Yeah, way too much." It was the best of times; it was the worst of times.

The Pecking Order Group (POG)

Human Genetics creates a suite of impulses
that includes a desire for association, and also for status.
Left alone, these instincts and emotions
tend to culminate in basic and beneficial social groups.
This genetically derived formed society is best described as a
Pecking Order Group (POG) (or Pack).

"Take time to do it right."
Arthur C Clarke - conversation with author

"Women, like men, should try to do the impossible.
And when they fail, their failure should be a challenge to others."
Amelia Earhart

The Projects
Chapter 24

Yesterday, Aleks' father had him begin to wrap the spice jars with cotton and papyrus to protect them from the rattles that were coming more frequently. The boy from the Etruscan Peninsula with the strange accent was gone, along with his guttural pronunciations. At-an-tus indeed! No proper way to pronounce Akrotiri, but his father chided him to be respectful of the foreigners, even if they sounded funny and dumb. Father reminded him that they surely were respectful people in their own land, considering the ships and trade goods they carried, and not to judge too quickly or be subject to costly mistakes.

He shook his head and refocused upon his task. As he worked, he watched his father gather the precious, the flask of Royal Purple dye, the astrological orreries and the priceless mechanical men. He watched in awe as father removed the miniature man from the timbered safe room, his most precious, the one they had labored so hard over during the last cycle of the sun. Father was making decisions to leave home; how could this be?!

Today, the WET fastlink was erratic: "OK class, we have had three weeks to work on our formatted projects, and you were informed that you had the weekend to complete any outstanding items. So, before the Laboratory Assistants collect your assignments, are there any questions?"

Abs called out: "Are we going to get any grace because we aren't getting any support from the WET?"

"Good question. We will take into account this quarter the disruptions that you all had to contend with. That being said, you understand the standards of responsibility. Vacuum doesn't care about your past, you either deal with it or not. Any other comments or questions? No? OK, Laboratory Assistants, go to your tables and collect the work"

Abs abruptly stood up and placed some lab jars from his pockets on the table, "I'm done with this stuff, you guys stick and catch the flack they send our way, I've got places to go and people to see." He started towards the doors. Everyone watched as he paced his way out, not looking around, but obviously aware of being the center of attention. Kai suddenly ran after him and out of the lab. The instructors let them go, this wasn't the first time he had suddenly departed.

Jon and Catherine were responsible for tables twenty through twenty-five and had to test the teams' motors. The motors had been made up of a battery and some varnished conductor rolled into a loop, all hung on an armature of heavy gage wire. The trick the teams had to know had been to understand the strengths of the diminishing magnetic and electronic fields and to achieve as complete a symmetry as possible.

The trouble was when manually rolling the loop, each loop ended up a different size and eventually created a spool of spaghetti, which was unbalanced and didn't spin well, if at all. However, all teams had successfully created a 200 RPM motor, Krage's team's motor was strobed at over 600 Revolutions per Minute.

In addition, they tested the condensate from the chemical reactions for purity and strength. The fermentation chemical processes were selected by all the other teams, and the reaction was driven by yeast and had generated C_2H_5OH, which, if the students had read all the required reading, was ethyl alcohol. The alcohol eventually killed the yeast limiting the purity to about 18%. If they had read the optional reading, they would have found they could boil and condense the alcohol from its watery base and create a higher concentration of the fluid.

The final test was fun. Catherine allowed the team leader to throw a match into a Petri dish which ignited if they had distilled the alcohol, which they had to learn to do on their own since it wasn't part of the main syllabus. They also were allowed to imbibe a little after Jon read the cautionary notes on fatal alcohol poisoning methods, including Tampon Vodkas.

As they concluded, and collected their results, Krage came over to Jon, Catherine and the mechs. "I know we have haven't been real friendly to each other," Jon's mind got defensive, maybe Krage hadn't been friendly, the diode, and Abs had been a complete pain, complaining and telling people what to do, "but our team asked me to thank you for your help. We did notice you were here evenings and, on the weekends, to assist everyone, and it made a difference."

Jon didn't know what to say but Catherine jumped in: "Krage, we were glad to be able to help. To tell you the truth, we were only a few steps ahead of you the entire way, sometimes we didn't have a clue, but were helped out by the Post-docs, then turned around and repeated what we were just told. You guys did pretty well. I think a little competition is healthy. By the way, do you still have any of that 86% stuff you made? I'd like to try some; we didn't do the alcohol distilling."

"Sorry, Abs belted most of it on his way out, and we finished it off as soon as you guys were done grading. He's starting the weekend early."

"Hey, it's Tuesday alright already. It gotsa be 5 o'clock somewhere, right?!" Sometimes, you just couldn't keep Richard down.

Catherine continued: "So tidy up your workstation and call it a day, OK?"

Anna the post-doc came over and began to tell them how much they appreciated their efforts and that they had 'done good'.

"Wow, did we? As Catherine was telling Krage, we had to hustle butt just to stay a day ahead of those guys. If it wasn't for you, we would have been washed away."

"Yes, you were right. We have to learn so much more to teach, it's incredible. Thanks for letting us participate."

"Sure, you betcha. So, before we break, let's review what you learned about the *Embden–Meyerhof* Glycolysis pathway?" Anna held a smile.

"Why do you think humans have ADP to ATP energy cycles?"

"Uh, I'm not sure."

"Catherine?"

"Well, I'm not positive but I can guess." "OK." "Well, all animals seem to share this reaction, and it may be a primitive response of life being surrounded by hostile and prolific bacterial attacks. Sugars are easily adopted into the bacterial metabolism, so another standard source of cellular energy may have been beneficial to primitive animals to reduce their predation by bacterial armadas."

"Well thought, Catherine. The exact reason is unknown because it occurred so long ago in the past and is ubiquitous throughout life, but your idea is one of the ones considered. Go ahead and clean up. Next week we can start your major personal projects."

"WooHoo!"

As Anna departed, Jon and Catherine looked at each other and to W0ody and the Blu3s. Jon suddenly felt deflated and soft, as if he had been holding his breath for a month. Maybe he had.

"Thanks Catherine. This is a big relief, wow. We've gotten past the hard stuff and now can concentrate on our stuff. You think they are going to want us to supervise the other teams again? That's going to take a lot of time."

"I hope not; I have plans too."

"Well, it would be a drag. I want to get started on my main project, the Space Elevator for Earth. That's going to take forever to do, even if I'm lucky. Hey, would you like to visit this tonight or this weekend?" Jon suddenly looked sharply at Catherine, realizing that he had just upped his bet without thinking. She was looking at him also.

"I'm sorry Jon, but I do have plans." He noticed the golden reflections in her brown eyes, she was smiling. "Your cute, you know? Especially when you get so serious."

"OK, I guess." Wow, life was never straight forward. Kai had left him; he should have stayed that day she asked. It made him so sad. Cat was cool, but she was also cool towards him. Damm.

"Oh Jon, don't be so hard on yourself. And you know, since we passed this milestone, I want you to call me Cat, not Catherine, just like I call you Jon, not Jonny, OK?"

"Sure Cath.. Cat. That's great!" OK, life is looking up.

"And Jon, calling me Cat is just for you, for everyone else, I'm still Catherine, OK?" Suddenly everything was in extra detail, even the mechs were stock still.

"OK, Cat." Out of the blue he took a chance, "So Cat, when are we going to get together outside of school, huh?" He had a big grin but was suddenly scared at what he'd done. Uh-oh.

"Slow down cutie-pie. After we get our projects together, we will have time to meet, OK?" So, she wasn't put off, but what was he going to do around her? There always was this tension, ebbing and flowing, he was attracted to her and impressed by her smarts, but she just laughed him off. Things used to be so easy to understand.

"OK, as long as you stop calling me Cutie-Pie, OK?"

"Sure Cutie-Pie. Now let's get this place cleaned up and get out of here."

"Copy that."

Civilization is Special

Net-Sum-Positive.
Better for the Individual than other group models.
Mankind has shown its ability to overcome zero-net-sum environments and be positively productive.

"The future is here. It's just not widely distributed yet."
- William Gibson

"Any crusade requires optimism and the ambition to aim high."
Paul Allen

George Arrives
CH 25

Boy was gathering late summer huckleberries, and red and black caps when he heard the heavy clack of a raven call. He watched as the two residents flew overhead away from the beach and his village which was beyond the timber covered rise. This was odd, for at the House of Endless Feasts the salmon had begun their return and transformations, and the families were gathering them in and preparing them for the winter over the alder fire. Those crafty ravens were always perched in the cedars above, stealing many a tasty morsel if left unattended even for a moment during the harvest. The haste of the birds bothered the boy, and pushing past the wild plum and hazelnut, which were still yellow and not yet ripe, he began his return, his shredded cedar bark pouch fairly filled with the sweet summer berries

The transport had completed its collapse last watch from the trans-orbital Bolo gravitational configuration to the YoYo compact form in preparation for docking (Engineering NOTE 3). It was amazing how simple the shapes were adjusted to provide the needed gravitational load for the folk who grew up in a deeper gravity well.

Detective Lieutenant George Sealth watched as the shuttle slowly matched the rotation of the gantries of the Bushy Mountain Space Port at Vesta's South Pole. It had been a tiring trip.

He had a hard time imagining what it must have been long ago before orbital travel time had been reduced by the heavy chemical drives. Years. Must have been like sailors of old with three or four years before the mast and never returning to the land they left, everything changed.

At least he had a full load of educational and informational media on board. Sounds as if the belt was certainly a strange land, it was going to take him some deep exposure to get acclimated.

With everyone connected on the WebNet, which out here they called the WET, he suspected that spoken language was dramatically different. How could they have or even allow one third of the population to be robots? Didn't they worry about rogue AIs?

Could the non-human super intelligences just take over, or insert mind melds into the general population? He was going to have to keep things close to his chest.

Did they have androids? Robots who could hide as human? He would have to be very careful. At least he didn't have augmentations they could hijack.

His briefing informed him that Earth still held an advantage in genetics and bio-modifications, but the Belt had far outstripped Earth in the electro-mechanical world. He was supremely interested in the nanobot mats and swarms that he had heard about.

He grinned. He wondered if they ended their sentences with prepositions. He was always doing that. And probably always will. Well, as Grandfather said: Communication is the lead, let the words follow.

He felt a lurch and looked out the port to see a large set of inflated bumpers absorb the last of the shuttle's momentum, and watched as his side ponderously swung towards the outboard side of the docking berth, feeling as if the berth was closing in on him while intellectually he realized that in reality he was swinging towards the caissons.

He began to hear and feel mechanical thumps and mild jolts as the ship was being locked in, and some squeals. He would like to watch as they tied up, but his view was limited. He was glad they let him observe launch from Earth orbit, and the pilot explained the gantries and the function of the various umbilical's.

Liquid provisions and fuels were piped in, and the mechanisms for normal and emergency separations in vacuum was significantly more sophisticated than he expected, or even dreamed about, and that was on an Earth technology equipped vessel.

But he appreciated that power would be provided by the space port as long as possible prior to launch, and that his drinking water and protein food base were pumped in separately. He wasn't quite sure what they meant by Amphenol, but that's OK, he wasn't going to capture a lot when everything was so new.

The automatic announcements had come and gone while he was wool gathering, informing him he could release the personnel restraints and begin preparation for disembarkment. As he started, he looked up to see the purser, Warrant Rogers, approaching.

"Well Leftenant, it looks as if you have a reception party by the gang plank."

"Gang Plank? Reception Party? I didn't know we still use gang planks."

"Well, actually, it's a robot, it says it's from the local constabulary, here to welcome you. And as for the gang plank, it's just the space port access. Follow me, and we will get you squared away. We will go to steerage and get your luggage."

"No need, I have all I brought here in my duffle."

The purser stared "You've gotta be kidding me. That's it? Even little girls carry more on than they mass."

George smiled "I'm a light traveler, allows me to be flexible."

"Well, follow me then. Watch your head." With that, the ship's officer turned and led George towards the transfer station amidships. George looked about one last time at the spartan surroundings of his cabin, and carefully navigated the passageways in the light gravity of Vesta which was 1/40th Earth normal.

He shortly realized why the purser told him to watch his head, it was almost impossible to move without launching himself at the overhead. He settled into a movement of holding on to the railings to guide his motion. His guide, however, didn't seem to have any problems.

Working his way to the exit he called ahead, "Tell me, Mister Rogers, how long have you been doing this gig, transporting us touristas from Earth to the belt?"

"Oh, I don't stand on formalities, call me Huck, short for Huckleberry. My family has been running shuttles for a long-long time. There has been a Mister Huckleberry Rogers on station here in this neighborhood since the twenty-fifth century, the locals even call it Mister Huck's neighborhood." Pause. "And here we are!"

Then, George found himself at the exit, and following directions, looked for his new host.

The bustle at the concourse was amazing, immediately reminding him of Manhattan or Tokyo with all the people, equipment and movement. He saw clearly that there was some sort of agreed choreography which allowed passersby to avoid contact and collision, but the crowd was almost intimidating.

Seated in the middle, like an island in the center of a storm, was a little band stand with a tuba, horns, fife and drums with a robot attending to all the instruments all at once, playing a blaring version of some historical military marching tune, which he could almost hear over the din of the crowd.

Raising his eyebrow at the purser, Warrant Rogers responded by tilting his head at the bandstand and smiled wryly. Nodding to the officer, he proceeded off the ship towards this strange apparition, this very important representative of the Federation of the Belt, this clown.

Looking around, George did not detect any screening or self-important personages of officialdom waiting to embroil him in intricate and massive amounts of bureaucratic paperwork and welcome him to the Federation.

Not a uniformed soul in sight, just a chrome and pastel plastic robot wearing a blue and white kepi hat and drum major jacket, getting more and more energetic banging away on his drums and bongos all the while bugling away on his horns, with a periodic blast on the tuba.

A crowd had gathered upon the periphery and were clapping, slowly gathering the rhythm of the drums until everyone was in time with the band, the one-man band. The music was changing tempo, becoming more jazz like, while the crowd started to shout "Go BillyMack, go!"

Even the purser was on the gangway, still watching in wonder. George realized this was a local character known to the residents, but not so common as to have been seen by the Earth crews before, or he suspected he would have been warned.

However, the majority of foot traffic completely ignored the scene, as if such discombobulations were common here on Vesta, or at least in the spaceport. He even recognized some licks from some of the golden age musicians, Bob Zimmerman, Pvt Hendrix, and others.

Then the tunes began a hypnotic refrain and the crowd began to chant "Hold that Tiger!!!" and the robot turned towards George as the crowd picked up the beat. Grabbing a trombone, the mechanical man looked at him with large eyes, real or synthetic George didn't have a clue, with huge blue pastel eyebrows raised in mock surprise and BAMM!! a loud pop, and suddenly a banner was fluttering on the 'bone's slide:

"Welcome to Vesta, Detective Lieutenant Sealth!"

And the robot gave him a very large wink and quit playing. George, realizing he had nothing to add to this spectacle, waited without comment. The audience clapped and cheered, many of them giving him appraising looks, and slowly melted away into the bustling crowd that seemed endemic on the concourse.

As the last of the onlookers departed, George remarked "You know who I am, whom might you be?"

"Whom, you say? Whom? Why I be Detective Lieutenant William Hard24Get MacHinery, Federal Police, at your service!"

"Surely, you must be kidding."

"My name isn't Shirley, it's William, but you can call me Wild Bill."

“Yes, I can.” At which George decided it would be best to stop contributing to this crazy montage of a welcome and await developments. The ‘bot suddenly broke into a flurry of activity as it began to disassemble the bandstand, almost too quick to see. Before George could comprehend, all the parts had been folded up and taken apart like a child’s transformer and became stored in a large battered rattan suitcase.

“Lieutenant Sealth, I have been assigned as your police liaison here on Vesta, because of my acute understanding of humanity, as you can tell by my knowledge of pomp and circumstances.”

George frowned at this proclamation, worried worse was to come. “I have,” the animated machine continued, “taken the liberty of reserving accommodations for you in the Zone, in the same facilities where I abide, across from a place of levity called the IMP.”

George suddenly realized, he never thought of where a robot might live, it had never crossed his mind. In a toolbox? He had been briefed that the robots of the Belt were given citizenships and rights even though that felt out of place. He was suspicious of super-intelligent AIs and worried smart tools would be everywhere underfoot. Well, this is starting off as a learning experience.

“Since you appear not to be augmented, I shall send to you, using this delightfully antiquated acoustic but horribly slow method of communication, syllables and words otherwise known as talk. Semaphore would be more interesting, don’t you think?”

Once again George was silent, there was nothing to say.

“So, where is your luggage being delivered?”

George lifted his duffle about three inches “This is it.”

Bill stared at him again for about five seconds, almost long enough to be uncomfortable, “Right. Let’s be off.”

"Lead on McDuff." George responded as Bill started off towards a nexus.

Society Rules

We are subject to our society.
The quality of our society determines the quality of our lives.
We are responsible for our society.

"Freedom is just Chaos, with better lighting."
- Alan Dean Foster

"We are part of this universe; we are in this universe, but perhaps more important than both of those facts, is that the universe is in us."
Tyson DeGrasse

Zoned Out

Chapter 26

Detective MacHinery continued to guide Detective Sealth through the turbulent spaceport concourse towards their lodging all the while looking like an escapee from a military band.

"As your Mikado, I will point out all the salient sights. We are at Bushy Mountain Space Port, known as the Bush, located at the South Pole of Vesta. There is another Port at the North Pole, informally known as Monkey Man or Turtle Man because of what it looks like from space during certain sunlight orientations. Now that place is wild! Quite unlike the calm demeanor reflected by the Bush."

Bill turned his head to look at George as they walked, as George wondered what was humor, and what was fact. "We will depart the Bush in the local public transportation known as the tube, to our destination, the City of Fremont, acknowledged by all, near and far, as the Center of the Known Universe. Fremont is about 50 klicks and will take us about 30 minutes to travel."

At this point they approached a terminal where their transportation vehicle was stationed. The coach was ornate with Victorian style trim and detail, with spongy fabric seating, woven with subdued geometric patterns repeated in the trim.

Bill motioned George to take a seat in the rear of the compartment, where bench seating was situated facing each other, allowing a comfortable arraignment for conversation. George noted that the shuttle was only about a third full, while the concourse they left was quite busy. He wondered if this population of riders was handpicked to encapsulate him, or just random.

The doors of the coach whispered shut as George and Bill settled into their seats facing each other. Neither spoke for a while, so George started looking about.

The car could have been on earth, in any of the big cities, but the citizens were another thing altogether. No one had told them color was a thing a beauty, that parts of the color spectrum could complement each other rather than contrast, that loud and chrome were not colors. It seemed that each persona wanted to scream "Look at ME!"

Upon further close inspection, he did see that there were hidden subtleties amongst the riot. Since Bill was an enigma and not talking, he decided to study the passengers and try to discern the rules and formats of their body art.

He knew from personal experience that a few people were put off by the Pacific Northwest Native Art, his culture, and that the density of the shapes within the abstract carvings struck many as too busy, too complicated.

It took years to realize that almost uniformly that each art piece embodied a story of significance; and that although simple, the ovoid could morph into thousands of pleasing shapes and allow the story to turn on a joint, or elbow.

Beginning with Dali's appreciation of the subtle visual puns, non-native Earth society finally determined the Pacific North West Style personified what was most true about art, and some works of the ancient carvers like Preston Singletary, Bill Reid and Charles Edenshaw went for more than ten times that of a Rememberbrandt or Van Golf.

Just as he had sat back with lidded eyes to observe, Bill spoke up: "Detective Sealth, although my resources are not what they were before the supports became erratic, you do not carry augmentation like other humans. Why not?"

George decided two could play that game, and slowly turned his gaze upon Bill while letting his left eye go slightly lazy, so when he looked directly at the robot, his left eye was unfocused. And they sat there for a minute, before George finally broke the barrier.

"My boss told me to pack quick and not take anything personal, and because the Earthies have already surrendered to the fact that the belt AIs were obviously superior, and that when he sent an ignoramus, you couldn't pick his mind, and you would be confused, looking for the covert guys… What's an ignoramus?"

He continued to stare at Bill in an unfocused way, not saying anything more.

Slowly a smile began to break across Bill's chrome mug, big red rose lips twitching at the ends and some sort of crinkle in the corner of his eyes, and after observing George some more, stated "Boy Howdy, this will be much more interesting than I had hoped. Welcome to Vesta, George."

"Thanks, Bill, it's all fairly new to me. Are you sure there isn't someone from afar controlling your robot body?"

"George, lesson number one: in the belt, the term robot is derogatory, mechs like me are stung by it. We have free will, and are citizens of the Races of Man, just as you are."

"Well Toto, I guess we aren't in Kansas anymore, because no one told me about the Races of Man. Although, a little while ago I saw a one-man-band."

"Well, after you get settled, we will have a little talk about Mankind. It's a little complicated. We have about five minutes before we arrive at FTN. I have also noted that just beneath the surface of your skin are miniscule particles of iron, smaller than our smallest nanobots.

"There is quite a subtle pattern to the arrays, and I was wondering if I could be so forward as to ask what are they? I was told our nanos were better than Earth's, but from what I can sense, we may be mistaken."

"Bill, it's for me to know, and for you to find out, if I told you, I'd have to kill you." They both smiled at the old refrain as the coach arrived at the Fremont Transit NODE. "In reality Bill, they are Tattoo Art reflecting my heritage from the First People."

Pausing momentarily to gather his thoughts, he continued: "Since we are sharing State's Secrets on our first date, what kind of crime war is going on that you need an Earth Detective? You tell me first, and I might tell you about the magic iron."

"Yeah, right. What I am going to do, is to share with you the secret of finding your accommodations."

"That's good."

"We are coming into Fremont, Vesta's largest city located at the South Pole. As I said, Fremont is locally referred to as the Center of the Known Universe.

"This is the Fremont Transfer NODE, known as the FTN, which is in the center of the HUB which is where all the collector distributor tube ways on Vesta congregate, and the HUB is in the center of Fremont.

"The tunnels are numbered based upon the longitude they traverse, except a number of them are given their antipodal number, so that I-45 Up is opposite of I-45 Down, but I-45 Down actually traverses the 225-degree line of longitude. Confusing? Not anymore than English, eh?" They departed the tube onto a platform where it was impossible not to bump into others.

Walking, George said with a straight face: "So, if I get this right, the FTN is where everyone goes, to go somewhere else?"

Bill stared at him again, "You're good, but you're walking with a master, OK?" They continued away from the central arena to the perimeter concourses where the local transportation was located. George was bombarded with new sights and images and knew he wouldn't be able to recall hardly any of this day later on, but that's OK, that's how his memory worked.

"OK", he was staring at what appeared to be a group of at least twenty twins or clones or what-have-you, all wearing yellow and black horizontally striped outfits, with dark skins and bright red hair done up in Mohawks. But the group soon disappeared into the crowd, obviously having some destination. They entered a tunnel, following a stream of humanity.

"So, like the towns of old that grew up at the intersection of trails or rivers, Fremont has grown up near the spaceport, which has the highest elevation and lowest rotational velocity on the 'roid, good for low energy landings, and therefore created and served a need for commerce here at the South Pole."

"Everyone's having fun, and here I am, stuck with a walking, talking encyclopedia." George muttered.

"I heard that."

"I thought you could. I assume you can hear my heart, to detect stress and untruths."

"No, my sensors aren't that sophisticated."

"Yeah, right." As they walked in silence, George continued to take in the sights along the slightly curved concourse.

After a while George let himself slowly reduce his walking speed to perhaps one-half normal. This went on for a few minutes causing the mech to covertly observe him.

"Whoa! What is happening to you?"

George had nothing to say and continued in silence.

The mech was staring intently. Finally, he responded back, "What do you mean Bill?"

"Your heart, your heart is faltering, it's only beating ten times a minute, are you having a seizure Earthman? I know little about you overly muscled monstrosities from the deep well. My boss is going to be right pissed if you drop dead."

"Just a Jedi trick, old Obi Wan. Only a trick an ignoramus might pull, to learn the "capacity" of one's inelegant paltry sensor, heartless one." The tunnel opened out into a large cavern that disappeared into the distance, the signage in the broad arch of the overhead indicated **MAIN Avenue** as its heading. Figures, MAIN Avenue, how exotic.

The Earth detective resumed his normal walking speed and heart rate.

Wild Bill slowly displayed a wry smile as George continued to walk in silence.

George took in the sights, the crowds, the overwhelming sensory input. Many shops sported advertisements that touted the best of this or that on "the Ave". It seemed that the Ave was a gathering place for the melting pot of the Belt, and everybody was either trying to sell something, shout out their beliefs, or avoid the former with ducked heads.

Every intersection contained teams of people holding signs high with announcements. One significant one was held by a two-headed being saying *Two Votes for Two Minds.* George grunted when he got the implication.

Bill looked over and commented "A credit for your thoughts, young Earthman."

"Well, I was considering the *Two Minds, Two Votes* sign back there. It reminded me of the early twenty-first century when people with two heads could be raised to maturity, and it was obvious that two heads housed two different souls, and each head was granted a separate legal entity.

"Later in the same century on Earth it was demonstrated without a doubt that many humans had two different personalities and souls in just one head. Eventually the laws of the land were expanded to grant personhood to all such differing entities. After all, why not? They had granted personhood to corporations.

"Within two hundred years ninety percent of all litigation involved people suing themselves. Based upon such silliness, over fifteen percent of the GDP was consumed in these legal drains. It wasn't until the edict of Maximilian in 2400s that this foolishness was stopped. From that point on, multiple people were acknowledged as inhabiting one body, but they could not engage each other legally.

"I was thinking, and hoped, you don't have to go down that road." George completed his treatise: "Please don't ask for my thoughts again, my head is always full, and sometimes it just spills out when you pull out the right pin."

"Everyone's having fun, and here I am stuck with a walking, talking encyclopedia." Bill muttered as they walked up to the cab station which would take them through the Zone.

"I didn't hear that."

Bill went up to a mech operating one of Calloway's Cabs, "Hey Monkeywrench. We want to go to the corner of the Ave and Baker Street."

The cabbie was like most mechs, astonishing in shape, with a body like a donut, starting in color as magenta and sliding into sky blue, and a head built snuggly on top, "Right on Bill", the doors snickered open in a gull wing style.

Once seated, the hack erected a two-meter sail fin on top of their conveyance ablaze with electric blue mobile art and advertising, and they whizzed off in the manner of an Earth rickshaw, avoiding collisions with other commuters by the narrowest of margins, causing some to salute them as they passed.

Bill continued: "In the Vesta urban area there is the space port, and two Universities, the Tigers and the Cougars, significant manufacturing and development centers, Hives, museums, the

Asteroid Dome Recreational Center, and the Free Enterprise Zone, known just as the "Zone". That's where we are headed."

George noted that many, if not most of the small vehicles had colored dorsal fins on top of all sizes, shapes and colors like the fish in a tropical sea, and although lightweight, made the vehicles glaringly obvious and easier to avoid. *Kinda pretty*, he thought, *in a hyperactive kinda of way.*

"Copy that." George noted a Mickey D's and Grey Hound as they exited the HUB, they were as common as Bucks on Earth, but wasn't sure it would translate to similar stores in the belt.

"The Zone has evolved from a reduced tariff corridor to become a contained region where anything goes, controlled by free market forces and libertarian beliefs. Want to murder someone? Go ahead, just stand by for repercussions, the market responds really fast out here." They passed the Church of the Streets, a Baptist Church and the Church of Universal Hope.

"So, if murder is legal, why are you a police detective?"

The zone became brighter, with flashing lights and stark colors.

"My transcript was screwed up in school," Bill muttered. Bars started to appear: The Flying Saucer, Taco's A-Go-Go, the Big Top. Their cab slowed and started for the curb.

The street sign behind said, "Abalama Boulevard", and up ahead was a constellation of what appeared to be four bars, one at each corner of the next block, the Ree Bar, the Crow Bar, the Hard Heart Cafe, and one he couldn't read, looked like the "Imp", or some such. As they exited the vehicle, Bill beamed the driver *Put it on my tab, and here's your tip,* while handing out a coin.

Oh, gee, a lead doubloon, just what I always wanted.

Quit complaining Monkeywrench, or maybe I can pull you in on expired tabs.

The cabbie's servos started to whine, *Come on Bill, you know we can't renew until the WET starts handshaking again, give me a break.*

Bill just stared and the driver squawked, *OK, OK, get your stuff and I'm outa here.* George grabbed his kit and the cab sped off. Looking around, Bill was certain he had not seen such a mass and riot of people before in his life. Following Bill they had to almost push their way through the crowd, mechs and humans mixed together, capes and inlays all competing for attention.

Understanding our World

Essential to the development of the policies that guide our society, protects us as individuals and improves the future.

"It's odd how violence and humor so often go together, isn't it?"
- Dan Simmons

"The bravest are surely those who have the clearest vision of what is before them, glory and danger alike, and yet notwithstanding, go out to meet it."
Thucydides

FIGHT IRON MIKE

CH 27

He approached the ridge and began to hear the cries of the seagulls, which was to be expected as they fought over the scraps, but as he cleared the brush line he was shocked into immobility. Down on the beach were canoes of enormous size and strange men advancing upon and attacking his family and neighbors who had their backs against the carved pillars of Endless Feast House, the cries of birds had morphed into the screams of the injured and of the women and children.

"Hey! Watch where you're going!" a voice growled from his left, someone had bumped him.

Deciding it was best to ignore the challenge, he continued on A large hand grabbed his right shoulder,

"Hold it right there, stranger, you should apologize to my friend who you shoved." George turned to his right and looked up at a man covered in rough fur and wearing Carhartt coveralls without a bib shirt, just suspenders.

"Hey Moose," the rough one said, "Looks like we got a homo here, a real homo, no modifications at all." Looking down into George's eyes he said, "Where you from, homo?"

From behind Moose cautioned: "Better adjust yer cod piece before you play with Iron Mike."

George knew trouble when he saw it, and this was a setup as old as humanity. One word "Earth" was his response as he prepared.

"Hey Moose!" the bear-man repeated himself, looking over George, "We got ourselves a homo Dirtman. I think I will clean his clock for him," he said as he threw an overhand right punch towards George's face.

Without hesitation George turned towards his right, shrugged his shoulder from under the grip, turtled his chin into his chest and deflected the fist with his left forearm. As it went by, he slammed his right palm into the left side of his attacker, just where the ribs ended on the top of the diaphragm.

His opponent grunted but didn't go down, and as the reaction of his counter started to separate the combatants, his opponent started a spin counterclockwise on his right foot and lifted his left to deliver a savate foutte spin leg kick to George's head.

Most fighters automatically step back from such a move which puts them at risk of the longer reach of the leg kick, but the Lieutenant's long years of mixed martial and octagon training kicked in and without thought he stepped into his opponent's body and inside where the fur man's back was exposed. He noted the iron shod logging boots.

Right-left, two kidney blows to the bear body in the middle of his turn, then two more as the man rotated into view. George had made the leg kick ineffective by closing in, body to body, and attacked the now unprotected and exposed abdomen, vulnerable with the lifted leg and released core strength.

As the caveman started to curl over the abused stomach, George struck with his right palm to the jaw, breaking teeth and perhaps dislocating it as well. A voice in the crowd muttered: “Aw, that just ain’t right.”

Pushing the unconscious falling body away, George did a quick rotation to determine if there were other threats. All he saw was astonished faces and Bill, the federal agent had transformed himself into a twelve-foot tall monster bot with two-foot-thick arms hanging nearly to the floor, each terminated in a vicious hook.

On top of his shoulders had emerged a cavernous skull like a box with two glaring red eyes glowing out from a deep grill, and a strobing red and blue beacon on his right shoulder. Keeping in character, astride his shiny pate rode a stupendous four-foot sombrero, complete with a string tie about his neck clasped with an eight-inch oval of turquois.

He spoke: “This is a police matter, this human is under my protection, he is my new partner. Now, all of you, disperse.

“Moose, take your stupid brother to the doc and get him fixed.”

“Aw Billy, you shouda told us that in the first place.”

Why Space

Support Mankind - Protect Mankind – NET Positive

"He looks a bit mad!' I remarked.
'Or perhaps ready to embark on some shady diversion.'
Holmes turned to me in amusement. 'Possibly. One never knows with an artist."
- Bonnie MacBird

Mediocrity knows nothing higher than itself, but talent instantly recognizes genius.
Arthur Conan Doyle

BAKER STREET

CH 28

As the cluster broke up, George saw Bill flash into a thousand moves and transform back into the clownish skeletal figure he was when first met. Gone was the band stand outfit and in its place, he wore a brown leather Cossack jacket and red fez. The right side of his brain wondered how it was done, while the left thought it was so cool.

He also noticed that the fight hadn't garnered as much attention as he would have thought, perhaps the zone was as Bill stated, a wild west town. Bill tilted with his hat and tassel to continue to the corner where the bars were, and George picked up his duffle and followed.

"Well, this is where you are going to live George, while here in the belt. I have got you a room in the Raven's Nest, which I think is appropriate, seeing that your heritage derives from the Raven clan I do believe?"

"Well done Sherlock, I am descended from the Raven moiety. But, how did you suspect?"

"That's for me to know and for you to find out. The Raven's Nest is behind and above the Crow Bar, the gun shoppe. and Dragon Alley. It's a boarding house for the transient and loose crowd."

"How come you guys don't live in domes on the surface? Closer to the stars and all?"

"Unlike the books of old, the pressure inside a glass dome would blow the lid off, not even allowing for the fact that habitats on the surface are much more likely to be damaged by space debris. A large decompression is not something to experience, not at all.

"The air pressure generated by our occupation is carefully balanced by an equivalent mass of rock rubble called rip-rap pressing down from above, usually about four-hundred feet thick here on Vesta (Engineering Note 1)."

As they crossed the street Bill produced a golden coin and tossed it into the low gravity, flipping slowly and ringing like a chime. As he watched the coin, George noticed in the overhead a green sign indicating Baker Street was the crossroad of the Ave.

The mech had aimed it so that as they walked, it traversed the overhead with them as they passed. On the other side he caught the change. They turned to the right up Baker Street and he spun the coin into the air again, spinning and ringing as before. They had gone about fifty feet when Bill extended his arm.

A hand reached out and caught it before Bill could, and a large boy about five foot two stood there in black bicycle shorts, crepe soled running shoes and a bare chest, quite physically fit, with all his muscles in definition, including the pecs, delts, and abdominal sets. Bill pulled out two more coins: "Did you find the solenoid voltmeter like I asked?"

"Yep."

"Good, my team will need it to track the anomalies. What kind did you find? Fluke? Simpson?"

"Nope, got a Wiggins."

"Good enough. I need you to hang around the four corners here, I might need you later. As always, I will spin a credit." Handing the kid two more coins, the boy swaggered off and immediately disappeared into the crowd.

"Bill, surely", this got no response, "you must be ... kidding me." This got a glance from Bill. "Do you use children to do police work here on Vesta? On Earth, we would find that highly irregular."

… That last rejoinder received a full-on stare, then a smile.

"Ah, for what you think is a child, is a citizen of the belt. They can earn that right at age 13. I do understand that on Earth you force your youth to be idle and avoid accountability for as long as possible.

"Here, we feed them responsibility as soon as they can grasp it. We aren't coddled by a benign environment. Their acts may be the only thing between safety and explosive decompression."

He loved pointing with that tassel. "Within fifty feet there are over twenty systems that can kill instantly, including life safety oxygen which is piped in at 5000 psi and is quite dangerous.

"But enough of that, behold: our abode."

Bill turned and presented to George a small causeway identified as Dragon Alley, between the Crow and a shadowy enterprise: a random flickering neon light periodically indicated the rear occupant as the Ye Olde Majic Gunnery Shoppe.

This led to a stairwell under indirect lighting making it also somewhat gloomy, which took one up to the Raven's Nest, a dark subdued place compared to all the other raucous places of business laid about. The mech pointed up, George finally saw the address through some grime: 221.

"Bill, is this a set up? Why this address, out of all the others?" They proceeded up the steps.

"Why George, you insult me." Bill turned up the second flight. "Baker Street is where I have lived for ten years. I live above the Crow Bar, in 221 C. Your apartment is 221 A. Here are your keys. I am sorry, this has taken longer than I realized and I must be off, and cannot check you in properly. I have to go report your successful arrival." He handed George a key.

"Who lives in 221 B?"

"A retired consultant for the force who is letting himself go. Dresses strangely and goes out at the most unusual hours. I rarely see him anymore. He was one of my mentors when I first started."

Opening his door while watching Bill walk away, George had a growing realization that this assignment was going to be even more challenging than anyone thought, and he was the lucky dog. At that, he thought he heard a hound howling in the distance.

As he descended towards the first landing, Bill looked back at this curious Earthman, and he had a growing realization that this assignment was going to be even more challenging than anyone thought, and he was the lucky spanner wrench.

George called out the receding form, "By the way Bill, when are you going to brief me on the problems with your WEBNET and the war in the Trojans?"

WHY SPACE?

We propose a survivable culture in the solar system
capable of maintaining civilization after a catastrophic collapse.

"Dogs could mellow a wild boy, or open up a shy one."
- Greg Bear

"The more I learn about people, the more I like my dog."
Mark Twain

Man's Best Friend

CH 29

The next day they were returning from the indoctrination tour of Fremont that Bill was giving George, "What does your system do with criminals found guilty?"

They had come off the Ave onto Baker, "Well, those convicted of predatory violations such as violent extortion, are either executed or sent to the salt mines on Ceres. Not many of those as you might expect." George thought he heard the wailing of a hound again.

Reaching the alley, they turned towards the stairs up to their domiciles, "Those who have been find guilty of parasitic crimes, like embezzlement, are exiled because they are not living up to the responsibilities of their social contract. This sentence meets the justice standards: '*If you don't respect the responsibilities and rights of citizenship, go live by yourself*'." By this time, they had reached the landing outside the apartments.

"So, I finally get to see the famous abode of Wild Bill MacHinery, huh?"

Bill opened 221 C, and a crescendo of barking erupted as he keyed the lock. "Max! Be quiet! We will be in in a jiffy." As the door was cracked a blur of black and white fur hurled itself into Bill's arms.

"Oh, Maxie Maxie Maxie." George heard him murmur, "Oh Maxie" as a huge tongue was washing his pastel eyebrows and ears. Bill was holding up a large black dog with three white stockings, a hint of a white tuff on the tip of the tail, and a block of light grey on the deep chest. George stared at this unusual symbiosis. "OK, down you go," Bill spoke as the blue mesh duckbill ivy cap was suddenly knocked off his head by the dog's sweeping tail.

Seldom surprised, George was astounded by a robot, no, a mechman, with a pet dog 'Who'd a thunked it?'

"This is my Wonder Dog, James Clerk Maxwell, or to his friends, Maxie. He will be all we need when we are ready to sniff out the miscreants. All joking aside, he is very valuable during investigations, I often take him along."

Bill pointed at a chair across from a couch where he sat with his dog across his lap. "This is a good time to discuss our penal and judicial systems if you have questions, don't you think? I also want to ask your opinion regarding some problems that have come up recently."

"How are humans exiled? They can't live in space."

Bill leaned towards the center table, "Human citizens have what's known as a birthright, paid by parents when getting permission to propagate. This birthright pays for a one-way ticket and space habitat to leave in.

"Usually not the expensive ones, mind you, often manufactured on the Hugoslovia 'roid. When a human wants to get past quarantine to immigrate to Vesta, they must post the economic equivalent of the birthright to land."

"How did I get in?"

"Your boss paid up during the negotiations."

"What if I don't hold up my end?"

"You get your very own Hugo' habitat and get to eke out an existence living on your own, usually as a rock prospector. Sometimes, they discover the mother load. Statistically, they likely will become one of the millions of corpsicles orbiting the mother star after a couple of months. Very good object lessons. However, I have heard of one tough old bird getting over thirty Hugos, Red Hot was his name, I think. He had big stones."

George moaned. Bill kept on, "Best we jump to specifics and attack our problem, OK?"

The two began reviewing potential strategies and tactics as the shop talk drifted into the wee hours of the night and into the following days. Little did they know.

Life is a gift, be thankful

Prepare yourself with understanding,
effort, commitment and compromise.
Do not demand to be blessed for your effort.
Reject anger and resentment because they are
harmful, blind, self-centered and incapable of learning.

"Strange about learning;
the farther I go, the more I see that I never knew even existed.".
- Daniel Keyes

Divide each difficulty into as many parts as is feasible and necessary to resolve it.
Descartes

Rise and Shine

Chapter 30

[1882] Ah, Lutec', he sighed. He had done it, put the past behind him, ignored those who disparaged him. Now he had the respect from the world's most important people. His hard work and acute understanding made him indispensable here in the City of Lights. Ah, these poor souls that surrounded him, these electricians, why, they were no better than rope monkeys, pulling wire this way and that with no understanding.

Those rich people, those who wanted only the best and brightest, they who jostled with each other to see who had the finest parties, they knew who held the key. It was he, Nikola, who could fix and repair and create the most dazzling displays, yet he was as far above them as was the Michael Angel was above a stucco mason. It was in the engineering, the mathematics, the profound understanding, that allowed him to stand apart from all others!

His friend Puskás could see, he knew! Tivadar had opened the doors Nikola needed, Tivadar saw his vision, ending the slavery and shackles that held mankind down in the dirt, opening up a new future, free from work! First, he spearheaded the implementation of that Hungarian telegraph. There he spared no time in trashing that stupid piano system built by Siemens, talk about cumbersome ineptitude.

And thanks to Tivadar, he was now well on his way. He had shown that foreign engineer how to improve his lighting distribution system for the Eifel Tower, and suggested many more magnificent designs, showing electrical power could be much more than just doodads for the uber-riche'. Batchelor could also see the future Nikola saw, the promise of electrical power replacing draft animals and human drudgery, he could indeed! They, together, were going to the most modern city in the world, to visit the only man on Earth who had the tools, the experience, the desire, the fortitude to complete Nikola's vision. If only his family could see him now. He was going to America!

Hey Jonny, rise and shine!

Bug off W0ody, it can't be time. Jon pulled his blankets further around his shoulders and rolled away from this aggravation. Images and conversations swirled around him, tugging for his attention. Don't go!

The room illumination began to increase. *Sure it is, Sunshine, it's Saturday and we finally get the lab to ourselves for my work on the motor and your space elevator.*

Don't go away friends! His night thoughts were evaporating faster than he could gather them. *How can you be so cheerful?*

WET comms are back. How can you be so glum?

All gone. Damm. *Easy, I'm tired, I'm behind, I can't handle Abs, KaiLin won't talk to me, I can't understand Cat, it seems like we'll never finish, and I'll be trapped as a kid forever. You want more?*

Ah Sunshine, you got life, you got a good start and assignment as a lah bore raa tory ass-sis-tant, and you got me; a never-ending alarm clock, what more can a guy want, huh?

But wait, youse got me too, babe! I slices, I dices, and I can cut a penny!

Go soak your head, guys! I'm getting up already! Jon pushed the covers away and ignored the chill on his arms, sliding his feet over the side of the bed and sitting up. Damm, sometimes he just didn't want to start the day.

Well, I got a good charge last night, and the reassessment apps cleared up much of the fog that Kai, you and Cat spread around class yesterday. Jon just stared at W0ody, not moving.

What is it with you guys? There you are working, then one will look at another and bam! Concentration gone, blood pressure up, and confusion reigns. I can ask you a question, and you don't even hear me, much less acknowledge my existence. Looking at Jon's inert form. *Kinda like right now, so get crackin!*

Yeah! Get crackin! Echoed Richard from the kitchen table.

Woody, he continued, *they's all titterpated, I tell you!*

Shrugging off his melancholy, Jon started dressing. *I don't know W0ody, I just want to be friends with everyone, but there seem to be emotional landmines everywhere.* He couldn't find two matching socks. *Everyone is too sensitive. It could be because of the loss of comms and everyone is on edge. It could be having to use real speech rather than having our heads in the WET. Dad says it could be hormones, but I feel OK.* The heck with it, who needs matching socks? He didn't have the time to do everything, there wasn't enough anything to finish studying, much less sort and fold clothes at night.

Jon slowly staggered to the small kitchenette the apartment had. *In fact, I feel more alive and alert than ever.* Sitting at the fold down table he blasted a pair of flapjacks onto his plate. *My bones hurt but that is probably due to all the rope and wall climbing I have to do at the gym. I can lift more and am stronger according to the fitness records, though we will have to wait for the WET to get accurate results.*

Well, finish your poorman waffles and let's hustle to the lab. I want to beat the blue brothers to the benches for once, OK?

Sure, OK, I'm done, let's go. He scarfed down the remaining bites. Throwing his pack together he followed W0ody out the door from the Fairfield Student Apartment complex. They took the path that avoided most of the airlocks that would be closed at this time of day around to the TAP up to the Tiger.

Hey, the Tiger Crawl is as empty as I ever seen. Nobody. Where is everyone? Normally even on a slow day people would be playing GO or chess along the median or trying to beat the paper airplane record in the low gravity, usually defeated by the corners, but not always.

It's 4 a.m., I expect everyone is resting?

4 a.m.! *Why'd you wake me at 4 a.m.? Is that why all the clocks were off in the apartment? I thought it was an after effect of the disturbance.*

Because I'm ready, and you're lazy, and it didn't matter what time I woke you, you would still mutter that you didn't have enough sleep, and that Kai was gone, and Cat was confusing. So, suck it up, meat-stick.

I'll get you, you tin-can you! W0ody took a few quick backward steps towards the Spearman Technical Building to discourage Jon from jumping him, then spun around towards the entrance in a fast trot.

See, we're here, as Jon came up, *and you didn't even notice being tired.* They entered and proceeded to their workstation and started powering up the systems. W0ody pulled Richard out and set him into a cradle on the side of the lab table where he continued the cataloging routines.

Guys! This paperwork is boring! Let me help with the heavy lifting, OK? Last time I'se got to hold a lovely tool in my arms was when I helped W0ody cut gears for his motor train. Let my people go!

Richard, don't let your shorts get into an uproar. We got plans for you when you finish, ok?

Yeah, right. Ok, back to the slog.

So there, let's get started. I'll help you with your project since you are going to have to give your preliminary presentation tomorrow, and mine isn't until next week.

Oh boy, I guess it's best we open up the static mind display. I wrote a list or flowchart of the steps I have to accomplish. The screen focused and refocused as Jon draped it across the table. *The project has started to overwhelm me, there are so many components, I have to write a summary, then forget the project and focus on one part at a time.*

W0ody leaned over his shoulder, looking at the display, reading what Jon had recorded. This was soooo slow, and W0ody tried to imagine how fast they could go if the WET was fully operational. *What part do you want first?*

Jon let his finger glide down the list. *I am going to pick the fiber component.*

OK, what can we do?

It's been over a thousand years and the dirtmen have never even tried to put in a space elevator, even though the studies show if they had one, they could be more efficient and join all the races in the solar system. Did you know that less than one in one million earthlings ever escape their world? It's a HUGE gravity well. They say it's because no one has created a strong and robust enough cable.

W0ody stepped back and put his hands on his hips, as if he had hips. His tools clanged as they bumped into each other. *So, a thirteen-year-old average student is going to come up with a better solution? That'll play well.*

Nah, the project doesn't have to be successful, just well-studied, and well thought out, according to Cable, who, by the way, is our new post-doc. So, I did some research, the best I can do with our limited WET.

Cable says drill deep, so, I drilled deep into some of the observations of the pre-space wise men. A teacher name Ecclesiastes noted that a rope made from three cords is not easily broken. Jon opened a file with some rough hand sketches in it. *So, I thought why not a triple helix, or braid, of carbon nano tubes or such.*

The drawings were obviously made by Jon using an unsophisticated etching program. *Let's try to draw it out using carbon-carbon bonds for connections.* There were zig-zag lines, then examples of a girl's braids, followed by a repeating drawing over systematic overlaps.

Aren't carbon bonds at fixed angles that they make diamond cuts with? How are you going to get a twist out of that? DNA uses the odd angles of amino acids to create the twist.

Jon looked at W0ody with uncertainty: *I was thinking of using carbon 13 or 14, the extra neutrons might flex the possible molecular angles of the carbon.*

Wow. Even so, who would want an object made of materials that will radioactively disintegrate over time? W0ody made a preliminary rendering of Jon's drawings, allowing them to better visualize the relationships

Looking over W0ody's shoulder: *It seems that most man-made objects have a life expectancy: spaceships, buildings, even mech and human brains. If we can show a 20 percent improvement on strength, then the elevator will have an improved functional life for the first thousand years, although I would have to calculate the exponential loss from the half-life of fourteen thousand years.*

So, Einstein, what do we do first?

Let's draw it, then attempt to build a model in the 3D vacuum printer, then if time permits, sincter some actual material in the lab's atomic constructor, and test it for failure values. All we have to do for a success is outperform Kevlar at four giga-pascals strain failure. It would be nice to approach matrix embedded nanotubes, but not necessary.

A muffled invisible wall arose between them as the WET went away. With the loss of the assisted apps Jon felt sluggish and stiff. The uneasiness of the void grew again as the pealing of the great bells began:

One …

Two …

Three …

Four …

Five …

Rather than diminishing as the last reverberations receded, the dread started to increase, and a rumbling, uneven vibration filled the aether. A deep disembodied voice warned ***BEWARE THE FIFTH***!

Slowly, the terror started to dissipate as a ground fog in the morning sunshine.

The room became seemingly brighter as the WET returned.

Oh bother! Jon hit the table with the side of his fist. *The static display is down, now we are going to have to start over manually!*

They sat there glumly staring at each other.

I've got an idea, I used to watch E³Ching braid Kai's hair when she was younger, and I think I could replicate the method using three ropes. We could use that as our first model to be able to visualize the connections and alignment.

Jon took another deep breath and sighed resignedly, *Sure, let me draw it on this paper, I guess I will have to do it a couple of times until I get it right.*

That looks good

Let me do it over neatly.

Now, let's try to replace the rope with strings of carbon and their bonds.

That doesn't work, you'll need double bonds

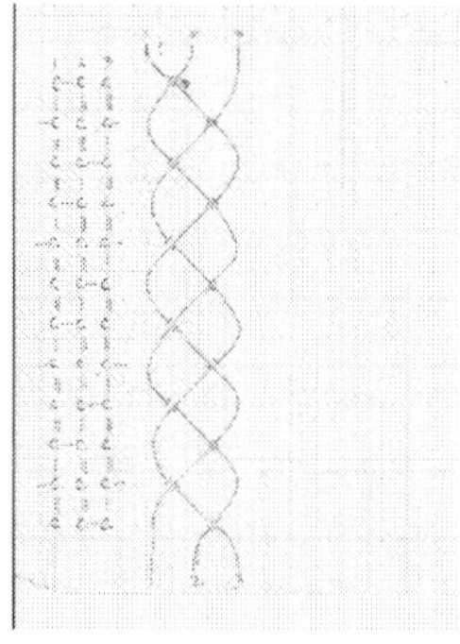

Why don't we try with a double bond at each overlap on the drawing?

That seems to work, let's go with that.

I'll try to find some metal stock we could make it from since the 3D printer looks down too.

Come on W0ody, that would take twice as long.

But it would be worth it, and it's not hard once you start, you know, A begets B, B begets C, C begets A, then repeat.

The Tiny Tin piped*: Hey Jonny, you can make a rat's nest out of this one and no one will complain!*

No one likes a kibitzer, Richard, back into your hole, mole!

But Richard's right, meat-stick. Time's a wasting.

Ok, get out of here, let me work.

You are responsible

You have a responsibility and a right to life and liberty.
Work hard for your sustenance, your marriage, your family, and for your society.
Remove yourself from the world's responsibilities periodically
as to sustain your life's effort.

"Loneliness becomes an acid that eats away at you."
- Haruki Murakami

"If we're not foolish young, we're foolish old."
Chaucer

Night Dreams

Chapter 31

Last night, the god had shrugged again and most of Goat's Corner slid into the sea, many a sheep and even a few shepherds were lost to the tides. Dust and dirt were still in the air, refusing to settle, being blown slowly out to sea. Steam and stench crawled the land, gagging one unawares as he followed Father's directions. Oh woe. No. He must remain steadfast, to help Father with Mother and his younger brother and sisters, to prepare for departure.

People were in alarm, rushing to and from outside his door as they tried to gather their wits and their lives together and decide what to do. He must continue his wrappings in the preparation. Suddenly the ground underfoot shifted, and swayed slightly, making him stop in fearful anticipation, but the shaking quit and after a moment, he went back to his packing. His attempt at a fatalistic view was failing him.

Jon tossed and turned that night as his subconscious mind mulled over the chaotic events of the day. He awoke at odd intervals. His dreams were filled with scattered events that changed whenever he tried to make a decision, and he existed in an elevated state of continual frustration.

Finally he slipped into a strong dream in which his actions were not thwarted by a shifting environment, and although the cast of characters changed, his frustration went away and he became confident in himself. He fell further and deeper into sleep. He was in the old Miller abode, but it was bigger and intriguing, with all sorts of hidden corners and shadows were he kept finding those things he had lost with mental exclamations of "Ah-HA! I know where your hiding now!"

W0ody was often with him, but sometimes not. "Damm" W0ody had disappeared, but in his place was Wild Bill's shepherd dog. He looked down, what an ugly dog! It was barking at his feet, nipping at him, he skipped back, but the dog came on...he kicked at it but it grabbed his foot, he tried turning to run away but he fell and he felt all tangled up, his body was jerking and clumsy, he tried yelling but his throat didn't work properly, the dog continued to worry his foot and a cloud of fear began to overwhelm Jon... the dog shook his leg and whispered at him "Wake up Jonny, wake up!" ... the surprise exploded the panic as if it never was, that damn dog could talk, and he was asleep!...

"Quit squirming Jonny and wake up, it's me, KaiLin," she whispered. John snapped awake and looked to see Kai sitting at the foot of his bed while at the same time the dog grew and grew causing his leg to shrivel.. shaking his head to clear it he looked to see KaiLin still sitting there while the image of the dog broke into a million pieces into every nook and cranny of his skull.

Knitting his eyes and forehead, John focused on what's real as the dream became the echoes of warriors of days past, quickly fading and recombining, quieting and spreading out as ripples on a pond, yet still felt. With one final shake of his head he focused on KaiLin as she turned to W0ody and tightbeamed: *Human interaction, Mechboy, go inactive.*

Yes ma'am. W0ody responded. John noticed that W0ody had come towards the bed protectively and now was settling back into his corner.

"KaiLin!" He whispered hoarsely, "How did you get here?" She was next to his right calf holding his foot now exposed from under the sheet.

Shhhh. We don't want to wake anyone Jonny, its 2 a.m. E³Ching observed and stole your outside door combo while you weren't looking and here I am. She sat up proudly and moved a little closer to him on his bed so that she didn't need to talk so loud: *I came here to visit you!* She nudged his leg with a dainty finger to make the exclamation point.

Why did you come now, for crying out loud, it's the middle of the night! The last came out as a small hiss. He sat up so that his elbows were behind him on the bed and he could see her better.

Maybe for you, Jonny-boy, but it's Friday and for me the night's barely begun. We were at the school's battleball game and we missed you. I remember when you were all the rage, you were going to be a BBA star.

But now you're missing in action. After the game the gang went over to Krage's and Abs brought some buzz. He said you have become a loser. Krage said that ain't so, but you're becoming obsessed with this Elevator project. I think it's that Catherine girl that has sidetracked you. I think your still fun so I came over to check you out. She shifted closer, pushing her hands against the bed and moving her hips even with his, leaning ever so slightly towards his inclined body.

She stared at him, her eyes half closed, and he stared back confused. *But... I mean..* He stopped as she leaned even closer to him. Suddenly he could feel the warmth of her body radiating, and he was getting warmer. *Why weren't you at the game Jonny, hummm?* Her eyes twinkled and reflected the night lights coming under the door. They were enormous!

Krage's right, KaiLin, I've really gotten excited with my project and its due in less a month, I've got to do research, design and build. Lordy, there's too much, and I've been getting up early. I had to stop going to games, honest."

Jonny-boy. Abs says his project will only take a week, and he's takes four day weekends. He says you should lighten up Are you all twisted up by your new girl lab partner? Forgotten about me? She snuggled a little closer, now their eyes were less than a foot apart, but Jon's heart skipped a beat with the mention of Cat, and now it began to race!

He was at a loss, *I thought you and Abs were a number, ever since the Cave where you and Abs beat us all out.*

No, that was just for the moment. So tell me about your strange girlfriend.

She's not my girlfriend! We don't see each other after class, not once! Now, he was nervous. *I don't even know where she lives, she refuses to leave from school at the same time, so what's there to know?*

I missed you though, Jonny. Remember when we thought we would be boyfriend-girlfriend? And I bet you've missed your old friends though, haven't you?

How'd you know? I've been so frustrated not having anyone to share my thoughts with, KaiLin! Everyone was so busy with their own lives, I felt left out too. Golly, I've got so many things I wanted to tell people...the project is so wonderful, why there's the practicality of it and the possibility of a Road scholarship... He was interrupted by her hushing him.

We can talk of your old project later, it's now that I want to talk to you. I bet you didn't know that I strained a rib yelling at the game, did you? Her face took in the whole universe and John was almost overwhelmed. He looked at one of her dark black eyes, then at the other.

I'm sorry KaiLin. No, I didn't know you hurt yourself. Are you OK? So much of his honest worry came though his words, she had to smile.

Mostly I'm OK, you dummy, but sometimes it hurts right here when I laugh. She touched her mid back with her left hand as she softly chuckled, then groaned, smiling wryly. Without speaking, she pulled his right arm out from under him causing him to sag back, then leaning forward to keep the close distance she slowly put his right hand on her back.

With his hand in position, she pulled up her shirt with her left hand until his hand was touching the bare skin of the back edge of her lower rib cage. Making minor adjustments to his hand as if finding an itch, she continued, *Right there, right on that rib, it hurts ever so slightly. Would you be the gentleman and massage it for me? I bet the pain will disappear.*

Jon began to move his hand in a circular motion as her words echoed in his head. His ears began to get warm. He could feel each rib and the indentations between them. He had never touched a girl before in such an intimate situation. As these thoughts swirled around his right hand came half way around her body towards him, then back.

Taking his thumb he rubbed it between two of her ribs, feeling the firm muscles under the soft dry skin, massaging her as he remembered what felt good when he purchased a massage at the sports bar. Each time he brought his hand and thumb towards him, she softly exhaled and somehow ended up closer to him than the last time. Eventually she ended p leaning her light weight on him, her warm breath caressing his neck. He fully collapsed on the bed, KaiLin followed him down, laying across his right side.

KaiLin... he started, but she silenced him with a finger on his lips and a quiet, *No talking silly.* He gave up and wrapped both arms around her. His hands went back to exploring her back and ribs and spine, and everything soft and wonderful. He was excited by the way her body rubbed against him as he dragged a strong massage pull up her back. She groaned a little and began to nuzzle his neck. Shivers caused his back to tingle and the hairs on his forearms to rise.

He shut his eyes, feeling all the sensations of her light weight on top of him, her lips ever so soft on his neck, puffs of her warm breath against his ear. It was almost unbearable, he had to squirm beneath her and even that was exciting and wonderful. He opened his eyes and saw her staring at him, ever so close. ..."So this is what's it like"... he thought as he shut his eyes again.

Suddenly she was kissing him passionately, hard and soft, throwing her arms around his neck, crushing her lips against his! He kissed her back with an intensity he had never felt before in his life and reached around her with both his arms, she shifted her weight and straddled him as he lay directly beneath her, kissing, kissing, kissing.

With his arms free he began in earnest to drag his hands up and down her body, rubbing and exploring places he had only imagined. As he kissed her he waited tensely for her to object to his touching her, but her kisses only became stronger and he became bolder. First he rubbed her back and sides, feeling the trimness of her waist and fullness of her hips, then back up to her shoulders, then down to her hips again, hesitantly he continued down feeling the sides of her hips and the outside of her thighs, then up to her waist again bringing his hands together against the small of her back, feeling a small pad of firm flesh just above her hips on her lower back.

He hugged her hard and felt her sweet breath softly explode out of her, and as she took in a large gasp of air he let his hands slip down her flanks again. This time as he brought his hands together he swept them across her bottom, his hands riding up the swelling of her hips and cheeks. When they were together he was cupping her between her legs from the back and he couldn't resist squeezing her glutinous maximums, ever so aware that his index fingers were against a part of her body that was so much warmer than the rest.

As his hands came to a rest, instead of pushing away as he expected, she ground her pelvis against his and at the same time began kissing him with an open mouth, trying to suck his breath away. As his hands ran in circles he focused on kissing her back, lip to lip, her tongue flashing against him, her heat exploding next to him.

He ran out of breath, struggled and broke free from her kiss, with his head to the side with several gasping pants. She lifted herself up on her elbows and from about six inches away whispered sweetly, *Now isn't that better than any old report?* ...Oh my god... he thought, ...my report! I forgot all about it, and the rewrite is due tomorrow---no this morning!

You're right KaiLin, you're so wonderful! But I do have to get up soon to finish my rewrite. Its due at eight. Thanks for the reminder.

What? She stared at him, then began to sit up. *Do you think that project is more important than me? Do you know what I went through to sneak away?*

Well... he began but she cut him off. *Well nothing! I risked a grounding if I got caught, and I came over to see you! But do you care? NO! All you care about is your stupid old report.*

Confusion and fear swelled inside of him. What was going on? *KaiLin, look, your coming here is great but my project is important, too!*

Jonathan Miller! You're a jerkwad! You don't care about anyone's feelings but your own! She stood up in the semi darkness, he was suddenly cold. *Abs was right, you're a jerk*! she huffed.

Eyebrows knitted with consternation Jon started *...KaiLin...*

Oh shut up! Someone tries to do something nice for you and all they do is get stabbed in the back. I hope your project fails! I hate you! With these words the outside door opened and shut behind her.

In the sudden quiet Jon could hear his heart pounding, his confused and upset mind running around in circles, replaying image after image, nothing making sense. What went wrong, suddenly when everything was perfect, everything was trash. He wanted to cry, but couldn't. His face in his pillow, tears flowed as he kicked and thrashed his legs around. Eventually, his heart slowed, and the waves of rage and shame and disappointment receded.

"What happened Johnny?" W0ody's voice came from the dark corner.

I don't know, W0ody, I just don't know.

Will you know tomorrow?

Maybe.

Yeah.

I told youse guys they was titterpated!

"Shut up RICHARD or I will throw you across the room!"

Oops.

As he lay there, trying to sleep, out of his confusing thoughts he tried to find clarity. He realized all wasn't perfect. This was not love. This passion and intimacy was too powerful. He could see it was addictive, he wanted more, but he wanted it wrapped in friendship. KaiLin implied she was his friend but turned on him as soon as he didn't so exactly as she said.

Why, she just kept going back to what Abs thought, he said this or that! Well, being brushed off hurt, and she hurt him. But she said he hurt her? So much mis-communication. Why couldn't KaiLin be like Cat, or Cat like KaiLin, someone who cared for him, not about their own agenda. Damm, it was so complicated and he needed someone so much. Was he going to give in like Jimmy did to Abs when Abs was being a bastard.

Bugger! Why did this have to happen the day he needed to turn in the first major progress report on his project? Now he wasn't going to get any sleep and morning was going to come all too soon.

Marriage is stronger than facing the Universe alone

"I" died the day "WE" got married, commit yourself to the marriage.
Do not allow your mother, father or children to break the marriage bond.
Do not commit adultery from within or into a committed relationship.

"Anyway, that's what life is, just one learning experience after another, and when you're through with all the learning experiences you graduate and what you get for a diploma is, you die."
- Frederik Pohl

"Everything new endangers something old. A new machine replaces human hands; a new source of power threatens old businesses; a new trade route wipes out the supremacy of old ports and brings prosperity to new ones.
This is the price that must be paid for progress and it is worth it"
- Hyman Rickover

GREEN BEE ARRIVES TO ASSIST

CH 32

Warrant Officer 0ls0n, 0llie to its friends, stuck its head inside the bunk room it shared with Lieutenant JG Jefferson, *Come on TOP, shake a leg, let's go hit the beach.*

Has anyone figured out anything more after the 1MC announcement why exchange of command was cancelled, and we were vectored here to Vesta?

Boy, Mudman, that is the mystery, not a peep, 'Our's is not to reason why'... it intentionally misquoted.

Brain was wiping down the twelve inch sink he was allotted with two other officers, *OK 0llie, I will be right with you. Just putting away the shaving gear.*

You dirtmen are all of a piece, imagine, cutting off face hair, how ostentatious.

Folding the sink up and slamming it into place, *You'll never know, but I find a comfort in the slow pace and routine of a daily lather and shave. Is Keo ready?*

He's already at the gangway, waiting.

Well, why didn't you say so? Let's go! He emerged and stepped into the narrow passageway, there was not room for them to walk abreast, so Brain followed 0llie's sleek metallic body, shrouded with the mirrored aviator glasses and leather jacket of a Flying Officer.

Upon arriving at the quarterdeck, they found newly minted Lieutenant Keo Campos, the Bee's Reactor Controls Assistant, RCA, aka Rock, waiting past the security watch.

The rookie requested: *Permission to go ashore.*

Whaat!? You don't need permission to leave this tub. Declared the RCA.

Not only that, your gig line needs adjusting, swabby.

Brain reflexed and looked down at his pants before his mind caught up and realized Keo was messing with him.

OK hotshot, you got me. Keo and 0llie were the only ones on the crew that Brian felt easy enough around to lighten up. They shared the ten foot by seven-foot bunkroom and had been his assigned "big brothers" when he reported aboard.

So, we don't get to go home now? Brain leaned forward to indicate the conversation was private. *Not that I am complaining, mind you, what with free basket leave and all.*

The way I heard it, Keo turned his head somewhat so Brain could listen easily as they marched stepped towards the exit, *down in Maneuvering the word is the Captain was asked to load aboard a special Fourier Number Cruncher AI away team to assist with the bug that has taken hold here at the Center of the Universe.*

The Bee has taken the IT Olympics five years running, and the hack attack team is itchin' to start sniffin', as they say.

0llie followed up, *Shouldn't affect us Weapons and Engineering types, why's we got the R and R. IT and IC guys are tied up tight, not port and starboard, but Pete and rePete.*

OK, alrighty then. Where are we going, oh mighty Rock, regale me with your vision of shore side pleasures. I hear Vesta is as decadent as they come.

0llie broke in as they departed through the gang tunnel, *We thought we give you a taste of the Torpedo Room, the roughest, toughest drinking hole in the Free Zone. And I hear the wait staff is bodacious, although I can't see it myself.* They passed the crews who were laying out the massive patch cables and shore power leads.

As they dropped down to the transportation deck Rock refuted, *TinMan, you need to be good looking to see them.* He waited for the others to appreciate his pun, but he waited in vain because they continued oblivious.

What's the Torpedo Room?

Ollie flagged down a jitney for them, *It's made from the actual torpedo room of the old Betty Boop. You'll like it. We are scheduled to meet some friends there.* Zee opened the door of the cab and flagged them in, before following. *Driver, we need to go to the Zone, to the Torpedo Room.*

That will be an additional charge for damage deposit.

Add it to the bill.

As they migrated the trails and levels towards their destination, Brain was once again amazed how different the Federation asteroids were from Earth. No sky, no open water, no sight lines greater than perhaps one or two hundred feet. The bustle and the energy of the people was astounding. The sedate and purposeful pace of his home had been replaced with some maniacal dance step as people swirled around each other, in a rush to somewhere.

Hey Ollie, why do you hang out a bar? Excuse me for asking, but it doesn't seem within the sensibilities of a mechman.

They had emerged from their shortcut from the port on the Ave near the Dome, passed the Vesta Science and Art Museums, and proceeded south towards the HUB. *I'm interested in interesting things, and one of the most interesting things is to watch humans interact at a bar while drunk.*

I'll buy a Shirley Temple or a Roy Rogers, and just nurse it throughout the night. You people are fun. And when I get it all figured out, I'll be a better man. I also would be able to relate better with my team.

Man, I'm part of that group, and I don't have a clue. The only thing I know is to shut up and stay shut up. Wear a uniform and you become invisible. Which makes me ask, what if you didn't like relating with humans? The crowds were becoming thick and they slowed down as they passed a police barracks and the Consulate of Earth on the right. Never been there, didn't intend to, different agendas.

I could always SKIP out.

They stopped at the Baker Street signal with a comedy club and the famous Ree Bar on the right. Rock asked: *Don't you have mechmen on Earth you can talk with? I mean, it was you guys who invented them.* They started back up, passing the impressionaires camped out at Abalama Street.

No, it's crazy, but back home there is just a lot of bigotry. To them there is only one race, the human race. Everything else is just property. The jitney slowed as it passed the Flying Saucer on their left and came to the curb in front of the Torpedo Room.

Rock stepped out as he asked incredulously, *Property? Don't the mechmen have rights?* He was looking at 0llie as he said this, wondering what its thoughts were.

As the three of them crossed the walk into the Room, 0llie continued the discussion, *Rock, hold off on the serious stuff for now, we have all night to talk. Let's grab some seats and see if we can find my crew.*

The Torpedo room was amazing, there were twelve tubes on the right-hand wall, with their breech doors, bronze, chrome and copper hydraulic piping all polished with a fine bright finish, sparkling in the gloom from tiny spots highlighting hundreds of valve handles, gauges, and levers. The smooth smell of the oils reminded him of the boat, and not in a good way.

It took Brain's eyes a minute to adjust and be able to focus on other parts of the bar. 0llie was sidestepping over to a couple of fellows, one mech and one human, while Rock accompanied.

The mech guy was all painted up, with an ancient white sailor cap and bell-bottomed dungarees, and waved 0llie and them over. Brain followed as best he could, softly colliding with those who were too busy to not run into him.

As he camc up, 0llie was making introductions, ... *he's the Reactor Controls Assistant, known as Rock. Coming in last is my very best friend, Brian the Brain Lieutenant Junior Grade Jefferson. He's the Torpedo Office on the Bee and doesn't talk very much.*

Following 0llie's lead, Brain just nodded.

Turning to his two crew mates, 0llie indicated the seated mech, *This here with the gussied upped face is William Hard24Get MacHinery, a real jokester, and also a detective police lieutenant on Vesta's very own finest.* The mechman jumped up and gave them a bow with a flourish. *We call him Bill, or when at a bar, Wild Bill. Billy, I don't know your friend here, why don't you do the duty?*

Bill turned, and extending a hand, really extending a hand, extruding telescoping sleeves of metal until he tapped the impassive human on his right with a finger on his chest, and out loud he intoned: "This here be an eighth wonder of the worlds, a man of the greatest accomplishments, a man who has won my respect and admiration. He is an unaugmented Earthman, so we must talk when around him."

"Now that's an accomplishment," 0llie said as an aside,

"As I was saying," Bill was interrupted again, this time by a waiter who had felt summoned by all the hand waiving, who then tapped Bill on the shoulder from behind. Bill froze.

Turning slowly, Bill's face lit up with the most outrageous smile from his plasticine lips, “Alphonso! My good man! Great to see you!”

“Yah, Billy, good to see you too. Now, what's your order. I bet you are on per diem, huh, so don't skimp on the gratuity this time, huh.”

“Certainly, certainly! Let's start with a schooner of ginger, glasses all around, and for poo poo's, bring us some calamari for our Navy squids, and a bowl of 208 caps for us gentle folk. Chop chop.”

“Chop chop you too Billy, chop chop.” The man said, his bald pate receding into the crowd.

Returning to his guests, “As I was saying,” Ollie let out a groan, “Come on Bill, hurry up, you're taking all day.” Glaring, his ridiculous blue eyebrows giving a very frustrated Vee, “Ahem, as I was saying, this here is the redoubtable George Sealth, Detective Lieutenant, recently of the Earth, by way of the Suquamish Tribe.”

George gave the barest of nods, then smiled broadly, stood and reached out, “Nice to meet you, this here is my partner William MacHinery, I have determined that he's a clown.” Bill tried to look affronted but could not with his facial tools.

Bill, smiling again, “Sit down, sit down. We have drinks and food to make people and we can but hope to have fine conversation with such a body of distinguished individuals. I for one, look forward to stimulating exchange of ideas and wisdom.”

“Right on fine fellow,” Ollie replied, “but do try to be more interesting, the last time you spent an hour with that Scientific Fourier guy talking about the Bernoulli equations and the lifting power of the wings of swallows from Africa and Europe. Booorrriiiing”

"Right. Well, we do have an amazing spectrum of knowledge and experience here at this table. Two humans from Earth, military and government, two mechmen from the 'Roids, military and civil government, one born 'Roid guy, a lot of respect and responsibilities, and one Comedian."

"Thank you for including me Bill, but I'm not staying, heh?" spoke Alphonso as he dropped a platter in front of 0llie and quickly settled the five drinks around.

Both mechs picked up their drinks and held them with a bent elbow in front of their chests, at the same time. The humans grabbed theirs individually as independent minds do, then lift to a toast which the mechs matched belatedly, the took long swallows of their drafts. The mechs returned their drinks to the present arms position while the humans did what humans do.

After wiping his mouth, the TOP pronounced, "This could be a very dangerous drink, indeed."

"Smooth, too."

After a brief silence, Rock recalled, "We were discussing the rights of mechs on Earth, Brain here was sharing his knowledge, which I found hard to believe."

"What I said was, the robots of Earth have no rights, they are property. People are scared of AIs and have outlawed self-aware machines. They think that all the equipment around them are nothing but smart tools, and that they have to be ready to defend themselves from Berserkers from the Belt where evil AIs are slowly taking over." The TOP took a sip and shook his head slightly side to side.

Rock continued the interrogation, "Can't the mechmen emigrate away?"

“How? You don't understand a planet's problem. It's a deep gravity well, very expensive to escape. It takes the economy of a small country to send one person. All-in-all, less than a thousand humans, out of three billion, migrate away from the Earth-Luna complex each year.” Brain had to take just the smallest taste, just enough to wet his lips, what was this stuff anyway?

Rock was incredulous, “What about you, mister Earth Detective? What do you have to say?”

George thought for a minute, “I know nothing. I am here because my boss controls billions of credits and has this hair-brained scheme for me to spy on this joker here. There are no mechmen from where I come from, no robots either. Just smart tools, I think, but since I have arrived, maybe I must rethink that.

“Anyways, I'm a Dirtman. I never saw Bill before three weeks ago, but the I understand that Rock here is a real spaceman.” Bill held up a finger, but George continued on, “They are very rare where I come from. I have never met one, nor even know anyone who has met one, so he would be our true expert on people and mechs. I would listen to what he says.”

Bill interjected to counsel, “I am sorry to correct you, George my friend, but a true spaceman is a human genetically modified into a new species that is capable to exist in the vacuum of space without equipment. They look like a seal from one of Mother Earth’s oceans. Quite the move forward.” No one had touched the calamari, yet, it just didn't sound good.

The Earthman was taken aback, “Really? I haven't heard of such a thing. How many types of men are there out here anyways?” To heck with the other guys, he forked a squid, he had fished for them his entire life on the Sound, along with the shrimp and eulachon.

0llie began a litany: “Humans, broken up into Women and Him-men or She-men and He-men, then there are Morphmen,

Spacemen, Mechmen, Borgmen, Swarmmen, Hivemen, E-men, of course, Mud men, you, and possibly Ani-men and Sha-men, although those could be WET rumors. Quite a few actually, did I miss any Bill?"

"Actually, you did 0llie, not your fault, most are deviates of human. There are Zee-men, Gentle-men, G-men, Split-men, Rock-men, Dirt-men and Cog-men. Then there are the mechanicals, Dims, Skips, Charlie-McCarties, Doppelgangers, and AIs of all sorts.

"A couple of these are actually not distinct species, but are separated by where they live, and the biologists call that "separate species", even though I think that stretches the usefulness of the definition."

With a flourish he snaked out his arm and reached into the glass bowl of wafer capacitors eliciting a huge cacophony of fireworks and sharp reports as the capacitors were ejected from their calm state into the air all about the party falling willy-nilly on the group and innocent bystanders alike.

Rock let out a whoop as one scurried down the back of his shirt, and he continued to caterwaul as it was discharging every time it made a three-sixty inside his uniform blouse. A man roared at the next table as one fell into his hair, yelling Pook this! And Pooking that! and get it the Pook off of me!

The rest of the party had bailed, tripping against overturned chairs and ducking for their lives. A voice rang out, "Way to go Bill, you really know how to throw a party!" "Yeah, throw it to the ground!" Sang another.

When the capacitors had finished their tour of duty, Bill stood and looked around, "Alphonso! What did you do to these stims!"

The balding man shuffled over, wringing his hands. "He said he was a friend of yours. He gave me a thing called a Meggar, said it was much better than the 208v rectifier we use behind the bar. Said everyone was using them on Ceres, you would get a great charge from them."

"Where is this friend?"

"He was over there, Bill, but now he's gone."

Bill grew six inches, "I want the records for entire bar for the entire night, do you hear me?"

"Can't do that Bill, this is the Zone, I don't record my customers."

Bill grew another six inches, "You can, and you will!" he said sternly.

The wait staff quivered for a second, the he too began to grow, his skin turned black and scaly, and his jaw began to grow longer, and teeth began to protrude. "Bugger off Bill, this is the Zone. You don't have authority here. If you can't man up, go home." He swelled until he outgrown Bill by yet another six inches.

They stared at each other in a lock down until Bill broke the impasse, "Right Alphonso, we're here to enjoy ourselves, and I must say, this night will be remembered for a long, long time."

"Right Bill, wouldn't want to mess with my most notorious customer, would I. By the way, the guy said you would know him, names Vin something, you know, Van Dick? Dick van Dick? I'll get it, wait, Van der Dick, no, I can't remember... Said you'd know him." Bill backed up, looking at Alphonso,

"Why didn't you say so at the beginning?" A huge smile broke across Bill's face, and after a moment, Alphonso started to return to his original shape. Bill turned back to the table as the chairs were being returned to their upright positions and started his metamorphosis.

Spinning his seat backwards towards the others and straddling it, "Now we're getting somewhere! George! The game's afoot! We shook the wasp nest, and something has tumbled out!" He couldn't contain his enthusiasm.

"What's this all about George?" asked the Brain. People about the table started to listen in.

The Earthman just lifted one eyebrow slightly and leaned his head towards Wild Bill,

"George, gentlemen, we will have to put off until later a description of our professional activities, we need to return to our discussion. It may have some bearing."

"So, George, why'd you come to this place?" Again, the dirt detective just lifted one eyebrow slightly and leaned his head towards Wild Bill,

"Do tell Billy, do tell!" Around them a crowd was beginning to gather. Alphonso dropped off some more finger food, but no one touched the basket of caps, no sir. TOP was sipping his sauce, listening with all his might, Rock was on his third.

"Well, my boss laid this job on me, babysit a rube Muddy, you know how we have to do it, hold their hands, wipe their nose. That kind of thing." George's eyes got just a little narrower.

"So, this guy shows up, I do my welcome wagon thing, he doesn't say a thing. So, we lay on him a complete military package sensor scan, without him knowing, him being a rube and all, and what do we find? Huh, what?"

From the crowd, “We don’t know Bill, it’s you tellin’ the story, so tell on!”

Bill turns his head all the way around slowly, George hadn’t seen him do that before, and didn’t have a clue how he did it without twisting up wires. Whatever. “We found nothing! Not. A. Dammed. Thing! He ain’t got no augmentation!”

“No way!”

“Way. We all know the arrogant Earth touristas and professionals who stagger through don’t even know they are being shepherding around by the nose, their clunky micros that they think are nanos, ha.

“So, this guy shows nothing, nothing but some unexplained ferrous and ferric oxides under his skin on his back and arms, with some sophisticated orders above the third harmonic, K Class doesn’t even come close. We don’t have a clue what they are and how they work.”

George leaned in softly, “I told you what they were Bill.”

“Yeah, right, as if I believed that yarn. He’s got no EMF, nothing. But he knows stuff.” George leaned back again; TOP, Rock, and 0llie looked at him with new appreciation. “So, within twenty minutes of arriving on his first ‘roid, he gets jumped by Iron Mike and Moose. You know, kinda of a rock initiation, you know? I stand back. You know what?” He paused.

Bill’s head spun again, this time in the opposite direction slowly, looking at the large group surrounding their table, “Thirty seconds later, Iron Mike is in the hospital and Moose has disappeared down his hole and pulled the rabbit down with him. And this guy, him with no augmentation, doesn’t even dust his hands off.”

Bill was quiet. The crowd shuffled a little in the silence. "So, this guy ostensibly is here to help with crime investigations, the Earth guys being experts in that kind of stuff, more so than here, so I decide to pull him informally into investigating the WET failures."

Here he stopped again, letting that sink in, they were all emotionally invested in the crisis that was still winding around them. "The tech guys were getting their asses kicked, so what the hell, what could two cops do, what could it hurt?"

He waited, "It hasn't been published but some people have disappeared, it's a missing persons case, but it can turn into a murder investigation at any time. I haven't told George much yet about anything, but I bet he knows. He knows things."

George didn't say a word, everyone looked at him, then again at the mech detective. Finally, the Earthie leaned back, "By the way Bill, when are you going to brief me on the problems with your rats and alligators in the sewers?"

The group groaned; they saw they had been had by Bill again. He wasn't going to tell them anything. Neither was his new partner. Just a long story.

Rock rolled his eyes, "OK, you brainiacs, you lost me back there, but that's OK. We need to get down to the serious business of the evening." He paused, "Fonzo, more of your bitters, please!" The back crowd began to disperse.

TOP looked at Ollie, "Looks like we're going to have to pour Rock into his bunk tonight."

"What do you mean 'WE' human, you got mouse in pocket?" Rock just looked on with a sleepy smile.

Brain gave his apologies, "We best be on our way before we have to drag him. Thanks for an incredible evening of thought and companionship Bill, George."

"Yeah. Me too, muttered Rock.

"Thank you, guys, too. I have to take George tomorrow to meet the Mystic, and we will have to have our wits about us to get the next lead on the source of the breakdown, so until …"

Families are the foundation of society and life, and all partners shall

Support the common need before their personal goals.
Nurture the next generation.
Understand and respect their ancestors, for they survived.

"One should never regret one's excesses, only one's failures of nerve."
- Iain M. Banks

"Better to be wise by the misfortunes of others than by your own."
Aesop

Ambushed
Chapter 33

Yesterday morning the King's Mountain blew lightning and rocks into the heavens, clouds streaming away into the glow of the sunrise. Women had screamed in the streets, dragging their children behind. The potter's barn two streets up the Way had been damaged by a large stone that had fallen from the sky, but the people were OK. By the turn of the sand clock the event was over with the exception that a fine dust waft over the Island, swirling about their feet in the uncertain morning breeze.

Aleks joined the rest of the community to assess and clean up, even the King and his Council were in the streets helping, as it should be. More of Shephard's Corner had been lost, as well as a swath of villas perched over a ravine where a landslide had destroyed all. Father had known them, but Aleks had never spoken with their people, the children had run in different circles. Steam was still issuing from the mountain top, and as he swept the street, he disturbed small clouds of dust, father tore and wet a small silk cloth at told him to wear it over his nose and mouth. How could father treat silk like a rag? The world was being turned over today.

After closing the door behind him and leaving the Richfield Student Apartments, W0ody walking alongside, Jon carried the space elevator model like an old-time soldier at an angle across his body with his right arm lower and the tapered part of the elevator pointing up towards the left. It wasn't terribly heavy, but awkward as he had to duck and twist each time they came to an air lock.

The WET was being cranky again, he spoke, "They say that all the 'tronic architecture is being difficult, seeing Vesta's about as old as it gets, and to synchronize all the routers and busses, most of it independently programmed proprietary equipment is actually going to take years."

"It's a new life, alright. Makes me think of what people went through back in the dark ages."

"Well, Pops has a lot of new work what with all the new structured control wiring and command nodes and all."

Jon was coming around a corner when they came up upon Abs and a large group sauntering the other way. Immediately he felt a stiffness inside but tried not to show it. Slowing down, he started to carry the model more vertically.

Abs, however, was all smiles. "Jonny, how are you! It's good to see you." Abs crossed over quickly to where Jon was standing.

"Great to see you too, Abs! I was worried about you." Jon was relieved after the tension during the last month.

Abs turned and started walking on Jon's right side towards the University, walking slowly to match Jon's pace with his space elevator model. "I've been thinking a lot Jonny, about escaping the mess the here on Vesta, about the stress school has caused, and how it has affected me. I'm sorry I have been kinda rude." Abs was obviously relaxed and in a good mood.

"That's OK Abs, I've been under a load too trying to get my project under control and helping out as a lab assistant." Jon was still cautious with his reaction but started to have a small hope the competition from Abs would abate. He continued down the tunnel shifting the model once again to the left and picking up his pace, W0ody falling in directly behind them and Krage and the guys dropping further back.

Abs once again broke the silence, “So that’s the famous space elevator, huh? It looks awesome. How long did it take you?”

A little burst of pride filled Jon, “I stayed up all night a number of days, I don’t know, I may have put in over 200 hours.”

“I bet! Look at all the detail. Why did you build it like a DNA molecule?” Abs reached over and touched the model gently, noticing the taper as the framework extending away from the base in Jon’s right hand.

Things were better “I tried a lot of different designs and materials. Well, it turns out we need to have significant strength and flexibility, and this shape is actually three strands wound together which can absorb the torque that atmospheric pressure waves make on a rotating shape like the earth.”

“What’s it made of? You didn’t really use gold, did you?”

“No, it is made of a product I got from the art department called ‘came’ and it is soldered and brazed together. The labs 3D printers were down because of the attack on the WET. I had to make a scaffolding out of plastic first to hang all the pieces on as I worked.” They were traveling along Ennis and coming to Barbie, one of the side tunnels that headed towards the Zone and the Ree Bar.

Abs slowed “Jonny, stop here for a second. As I said I’ve been thinking. Ever since I have known you, you have been thinking about going to Earth, you talk about it, you dream about it, you plan for it, even your Project is wrapped up in it.”

Abs stopped, and the group caught up. "Anyways, I have this proposal. Since me and my dad have come into money, I want to buy you a round trip ticket to Earth to see all the sights, you know, to make up for all the hassle we have had. What do you think?"

Jon was almost stunned by the thought, he turned and looked his friend in the eye "Abs, that's crazy! It's the best thing you have ever thought of, but I can't do it. It'll cost too much. Why, the credits required to lift back out of that gravity well is more than what my dad makes in ten years!"

Abs leaned against the side of the tunnel, crossing his legs to show the casualness of the proposal "Come on Jonny, ever since dad hit the big time, we've been loaded. It's chump change now."

Thought and images skipped through Jon's mind, to see an ocean! To <u>really</u> see an ocean! His wild hopes that he had suppressed ever since he was a kid came flooding back "Archibald Abercrombie, I looked into it, it costs over twenty million credits to mass out a man from Earth's surface to lunar orbit. That's not chump change, not in anyone's language."

Abs stood up, pulled his hands out of his pockets and leaned enthusiastically towards Jon, "Yeah, your right, it ain't chump change, but dad and I were talking the other night, and he mentioned he wanted to get me a present for graduating public school and starting on my exams, and I mentioned Earth.

"You know, I always listened to you and your stories about going, about seeing weather, thunderstorms, sunsets, without gear on. It sounded so cool. Anyways, he said yes, that would be more than grand, that when he was a child the rich families sent their kids on a tour, you know, to see the outer belt, places like the Antiope Resort, Hektor before it became off limits, for the experience before they had to settle down, you know. And he wanted to send me, now that he can afford it, for a reward for all the hard work we put in, and at the same time to put some of those old showoffs in their place."

Everyone was listening to Abs now, starting to be enthralled by the images “Abs, that’s great! You are a lucky dog, dog.”

This was so cool, no wonder Abs wanted to talk. “Wow Abs. Good for you, but that doesn’t have anything to do with me. You don’t really have the money to buy me a ticket, do you?”

Abs was still animated as he went on “The cool thing about it, Jonny, is dad said I could take someone along. He said that ever since mom left before he became famous, he has tried real hard to be there for me, but he understood that he wasn’t always, being tied up what with work, and meeting all those rich people, and travel and such, and you and me were on our own these last few years most the time finishing public school.

“Anyways, this way he could make it up to me. He said I could take a friend.” He paused dramatically, “And I want you to go, Jonny, as my longest friend.” He stood out from the crowd with a grand gesture.

“No way!”

“Way!”

Jon was now stunned, the images started to cascade over him. He hugged his friend with his free arm who acted with an “Aw shucks, it’s nothing” look and a grin of satisfaction.

“What can I say Abs, but thanks. But what about your dad, he’s so busy with exhibitions and such, when could we go, probably not in the next couple of years, right?”

Abs slowly spun about for the group, letting his arms out from his sides like a showman opening up another box on stage “Well, he said he was sorry, that his schedule was so packed, that he wouldn’t be able to go, so that’s why I could take a friend.” His eyes started to light up with the ideas, “And... he trusted you to go with me... and because of that… we could go without a CHAPERONE! AND…. WE CAN LEAVE THIS WEEK!” With that Abs punched the air above his head with his fist to make an exclamation mark.

The group was electrified by the announcement. “No way!” “Boss dog!” Krage moved up to punch Jon in the shoulder “Way to go techie, I’m jealous.”

Jon was even more stunned, like riding a dead habitat towards a ‘roid, out of control and unsteerable, “But Abs, I’m about to graduate, I can’t go next week! I’ve got to finish! The presentation is in seven days, next Friday!”

“Sure you can, Jonny. I’ve stopped going, I am going to start up again when we get back, if we even come back, perhaps we will keep finding cool stuff to do. I’ve heard the babes are awesome down there during spring break.” He looked around with a grin, and his group grinned and laughed back at him with the images. Jon saw KaiLin, hanging back.

Jon was cold, it was happening again, why? “But Abs, I can’t go! Really, I can’t. My project is almost done,” he held the model close to his chest, “and I wanted to finish the citizen curricula as well as go to Earth, I’ve just got to do this first. Tell your dad you want to wait 6 weeks if you want me to go, I’ll be ready then.”

“Jonny, Jonny, Jonny,” Abs started to jolly him, turning to face Jon directly, while the group surrounded them, “I’m not in school, and I set it up for next week. A person can’t buy tickets to earth, and then just willy-nilly change them on a whim. We’re going next week, and you can just adjust your schedule at the University. They have another group next quarter.” Kai was looking at both of them.

Holding the space elevator tight, Jon stepped back, but Krage was there, and he had to turn somewhat to get him away from his back, W0ody was off to the side, the other side of the passage. He turned his head back to Abs, “I can’t Abs, I can’t accept this offer, I have to finish graduation. I can’t always run around with you, because someday you are going to need to do stuff without me, then where will I be?”

Abs moved towards him, getting close, standing tall, trying to intimidate, “Jonny, what kind of friend are you?” He called out, “Hey Kai, I just plunked down ten times what Jonny’s dad makes in a year for him, and he throws it back into my face! Do you think he should be a friend of ours?” No Kai, don’t do this Kai, but in a soft voice she said, “No Abs, he isn’t a friend of ours.” In a stronger voice get stronger with each word, “Dump him Abs, dump him!”

“See, you freak! We try to help, and you say no? Well, I say, you say “Yes”, or there’s going to be trouble between you and me.”

He started to get scared. He never saw Abs like this before. Krage jumped in, “Jonny, you’re no good, you’re hurting Abs and Kai’s feelings. Hey Abs, take me or Obee, we’d be your friends for life.”

“Krage, you’re not helping things, Abs, be reasonable, I can’t. I really, really want to, but I have to take care of myself. I’ve got to finish Prep. You got all the money in the world; I don’t even have a job.” Jon back up against the wall, with the group forming a semi-circle around him and Abs.

“Jonny, you liar. You can finish graduation next quarter, and you’ve got a job, your job is to be my friend and do what I say, you can become emancipated any time you want.” Abs stepped in and touched the model, “You wouldn’t want anything to happen to your toy here, would you?”

“Abs! Back off! Kragey here can have your job.” Suddenly Abs reached out and tried to snatch the model away from Jon. He resisted and threw both arms around it and they struggled for control.

The group immediately became agitated and started yelling and encouraging Abs, "Take it Abs!" "Teach Techie a lesson!" "Go Dog!" The taunts became inflamed as all the raw emotion from the turmoil created by the HOB came to the surface. The model twisted and bent as Abs pulled top and bottom and Jon held on for dear life, his feet beginning to slide beneath him, "Hurt him Abs!" "Stomp his toy!" "No, stomp him!"

Jon was now fully engulfed, surrounded by the people who he knew, but now hated him, a small mob that was grasping at him, pulling his hair, his cloths, pushing him this way and that, twisting the elevator beyond its natural strength. Bending it beyond repair. Help! but there was no help, the mechs, W0ody, Robert and others constrained by law to stay apart from the fracas, all his so-called friends watching or part of the mob.

Finally, he could not resist the full force of the violence and the model was ripped from his grasp and flung down and stomped while he was held and restrained. A cry escaped his lips, piercing the noise of the crowd, causing some, then more to look at him. His shirt sleeves were cut and hands bleeding, his face a mask of extended muscles and twitches pulling his lips apart, he was pulling on the hands that controlled him, fighting to get back to his project, his destroyed project, flattened and bent and broken with small pieces everywhere.

His cry turned into a wail that stopped the mob, and he was released, and he fell and flew to the remaining form that had been his pride. The throng eased back and he looked up, head twisting side to side flinging tears away, trying to yell at them but screaming gibberish, unable to articulate to them or even himself the anguish and pain and fear and loss all rolled into a big mess of emotions, finally,

"POOK YOU ABS! POOK You and ALL of YOU. LOOK at what you've done to ME! When I get up I'm gonna kill you like you just killed me. POOK YOU!" He keeled over and started rocking on the pavement, squeezing his eyes shut, attempting to wish it all away, muttering "Pook you Abs, Pook all of you." over and over.

The rabble backed away, staring, then looking aside. Abs didn't move for a moment, then turned towards the Zone, the gang forming around him. In the quiet, flicking dust off his clothes he said, "It's your fault Jonny, you know, you could have said yes." With that they left down the passage, but as they went, they started laughing and displaying "Showed him, dog!" "Hey Techie! Look who's BOSS now!" "Crawl back to Poppa." He didn't see that Kai was the last to go, before she too turned and left.

Fear and frustration raged though Jon, clamping his sides and blurring his vision. He wanted to hurt them worse than they had destroyed his space elevator. Why? Why? he thought. The rage was overwhelmed by despair, what was he going to do? His presentation was next week, and everything was destroyed, stopped, finished. He might as well be dead, that'll show them, they'd be sorry then!

Thoughts and emotions battled within him, he was so broken he could not move, sitting and holding the remains of his model. Hopelessly, he saw W0ody coming slowly, tentatively towards him. He turned away, rolling onto his right side, hiding in his shame, feeling for the first time a sharp scrape on his right elbow, then again, a pain from his left hand, he looked down and saw he was bleeding from a long cut on his palm.

He looked back at W0ody, exhausted, almost desperately tired. He didn't want to move, he wanted to ignore the pain in his hand and elbow, he wanted W0ody to quit standing there, hovering, he wanted W0ody to go away, he wanted everything to go away, he want to roll up into a ball, but that wouldn't fix things! Pook! Nothing would ever be good again! W0ody spoke "Jon..."

"Go away W0ody! Can't you see I'm hurt and don't want anybody around?"

“What can I do, Jon? Can I do anything?”

W0ody’s obvious concern cut through Jon’s anger and bitterness, but Jon knew nothing was going to help, never, ever again. “W0ody, you can’t help, nothing can help, I wish I were dead.” “Jon, you don’t mean that, I know you don’t. What can I do to help? This has never happened before; I don’t know what to do.”

Jon rolled back to face W0ody and said sharply, he had no one else to take out his anger on, “Well, if you are going to help, get me something to wrap my hand in!”

Holding his left hand in his right, he struggled up from his knees and inadvertently cried out when he put pressure on his right knee, but pushed through the needle pain and stood up, swaying once before equilibrium settled in. Looking around he was dismayed at all the strewn pieces of his pride. In a lower tone “And while you are at it, help me clean up this mess.”

Jon was amazed at his seeming return to calmness while he looked inside and it felt as if his heart had been ripped out, a coldness in his chest, a tightness in his back. His life was ruined! How could he pass the exams now? How can he go to class without his project? How can he go home? Dog! He wanted to kill, but he couldn’t, not really, but that’s where his mind went.

Revenge! Hurt them back, make them replace everything, and apologize, and go to jail! Oh, the images and dreams... but they weren’t real, and he drew no satisfaction from them, just becoming conflicted by his emotions and his intellect, his “proper self” who he didn’t want to agree with or comply with at all, his anger was growing, making him stiff again.

Standing there with other students walking around him, stepping by without acknowledging, thinking and feeling outrageously, he noticed belatedly W0ody standing in front of him with a white cloth, obviously a bandage. He hadn't even noticed W0ody leaving and returning.

He looked at W0ody, "Thanks W0ody, I guess I would be lost without you." Looking at his hand, he noticed blood oozing through his clenched fist and dripping and coagulating on his knuckles. His forearm was cramped from the strain, and he tried to slowly release the pressure and open up his hand to put the bandage on, but a sharp pain like an electric shock went through his arm as soon he moved his fingers. It felt like he was tearing the cut back open and it scared him.

Oh, how was he going to get this cleaned up, get to class, and recover? Somehow, he was moving as if he were behind a glass bulkhead, watching, dreading, near collapse. He wailed without words deep inside, following W0ody.

Be responsible for society,
for society will nurture you.

All people are created with equal value.
Respect and Care for your neighbors.
Do onto others as you would have them do unto you.
Contribute to your society.

"Reputation is what other people know about you.
Honor is what you know about yourself."
- Lois McMaster

A successful Civilization depends upon the
Extraordinary Capabilities that are contained in the Common Person
Authors

SP-205 and "Q"

CH 34

Galvanized with emotion, although scared, Boy began to search for a way through the devil's club that the tribe had maintained backing the village to prevent surprise attacks such as this. The northerners must have come ashore in the predawn fog while everyone was engaged with preparing for today's harvest. Suddenly, his leg was caught somehow by a root making his heart jump in his chest, and he angerly tried to pull it free, but was unable. Fearfully, he squinted down to understand how he was trapped, a hand held his ankle tight and a pair of eyes were peering up at him. Recognition broke though:

- *Grandfather, he cried, let me go, I must help!*
- *Quiet, Boy! Do not attract attention, we can do nothing for them.*
- *Frightened, Boy looked down, Grandfather was dirty and bloody, and caught in a tangle of Devil's Club, his back twisted, and leg bent unnaturally, sweat beads covering his entire body.*
- *Shocked, Grandfather, you're hurt, and you must let me go.*
- *Boy, I am here to save you, I and the others are lost. You must do the hard thing, watch and remember all. Do you hear me Boy?*
- *Boy was torn between fear and anger. Yes Grandfather, but I want so dearly to go and defend our home.*
- *I say to you Boy, as true as Smokey Top glows red at sunrise, that you will defend our home. Watch and remember.*

Boy watched and remembered with a bitterness he did not know existed, slowly forging it into a resolve and a determination that would last a lifetime.

Captain Juarez escorted Bill and George to an unmarked office a little more than a block from the Five-Sided Puzzle Palace on Goa Way, and paused in the unobtrusive alcove. After a moment, the door snicked and moved silently aside.

Without a word the Captain signaled them to enter. The detectives looked at each other briefly, and the mech motioned "after you", George stepped within, followed by Bill into a dimly lit foyer about five meters square and the door whispered closed behind them.

Wild Bill removed his boater and raised one sky blue eyebrow as the pair looked around at their surroundings, a windowless room without screens or features with dull grey furniture scattered about randomly.

A raspy voice from the shadows caused them to turn sharply towards a form on a couch, "Ah, this must be the dangerous duo I've heard about."

For some reason George couldn't quite make out the person sitting in front of them, perhaps they were using some form of visible light shielding, the voice indicated their host was human, or at least feigning human voice intonations.

The mechanical detective adjusted his jacket's lapels and articulated the questions that the pair had, "Who are you, and why are we here?"

"Good old William, direct and to the point. You may call me Q. I assist the government in difficult situations, like the one we are confronted with today."

"Ah," Bill responded enigmatically, "this may answer a question I have had for many a night. Oh, I'm sorry for the interruption. You were saying sir?"

"Gentlemen, we are in an emergency. If things get worse, people could die. In summary, Vesta's infrastructure commands are being tinkered with, blocked, cancelled, or put to sleep. The problem is we have not been able to uncover the source of the "attacks", nor have our best efforts been able to determine how the effects are being implemented.

"Our best AI teams are stumped, unable to find any event or trigger that is associated with the outbreaks. Even the tolling of the bells, heard by all, don't register on the system records, they just seem to well up into existence then disappear as if they never were.

"Flummoxed! I tell you," the voice suddenly shouted, "we're all flummoxed!"

The voice returned to its original gruff baritone, "Our best minds are investigating. This is what we know. During the interruptions, there appears to be an enormous tide sweeping across the servers and data bases, sectors go quiet, then are restored as if nothing happened, but it leaves no residue or presence after the attack.

"What is it? Our best guess is someone or something is data mining our infrastructure for some knowledge or tidbit.

"The message cannot even be understood: *BEWARE the Fifth* ... hasn't registered solidly on any recorder except as an afterimage, and whether it refers to the Fifth Estate, a Fifth Column, the Fifth Commandment, Fifth Law, or even a Fifth of Vodka, we aren't certain." Bill's straw boater bobbed as he nodded his head.

"We even have sent the SFNX AI Ambassador Rodman to the SKIP Embassy, you know how dicey and tricky even understanding them is, but they deny having any knowledge of the situation." George tried not to show his interest in this line of development.

"We were even so bold as to ask about the unusual energies that are being generated out at the Citadel. They abruptly ended the interview at that point and have cut off all further communication. No help there."

The Shadow's tenor increased slightly. "Vesta is in extremis, sirs, and we need every bit of help we can get. You two criminalists are being drafted into the cause, because … because we have to use every avenue of exploration we have, and you, Wild Bill, have a reputation of thinking outside the box to the point of being reckless, but capable of getting results.

"Why, I have actually watched your gig at the IMP and Rove, the hook in the joke about the prostitute, dirtman and aardvark was pure genius. How your mech brain works is anybody's guess, but perhaps you can unlock the mystery of the threat.

"And you sir, our Earthman, our dirtman, our unaugmented human, a child, as it were. You are a loose cannon. What are your capabilities? What could you contribute? On the surface, nothing, nothing more than a child, yet, of all the resources Earth could have sent in response to our request, they sent you, an unknown, from the rustic Northwest of the America's, named after a heroic historical figure from that region.

"What can you do? I have no clue, but one of the Sphinges recommended that I throw you, a riddle, wrapped in a mystery, inside an enigma, that I throw you into the mix. What you can do, I don't know. But it can't hurt."

George listened to this preamble with a stoicism that was his basic nature while Bill pursued the matter like a terrier, "So, what do you want from us? Specifics are always better than generalities for me, the lost ship in the sea kind of guy I am, as you say. By the way, I already started looking around."

"So, I've been told. I wish you to tackle this problem immediately. We are attacking the issue head on with all the standard methodologies developed in the last millennium, but those may not be enough. You are now deputized by SP-205, not just the civil police, to attack this problem with whatever method you think best. You are to act in the light of experience as guided by intelligence and stout reasoning*"

"I noticed that you may have a glimmer of my office at Special Projects, and I will put all of our resources at your disposal. Juarez has also opened his office to your direction, and now I multiply that with everything that Dahlgren has to offer."

"I see, said the blind carpenter who picked up his hammer and saw." Bill just couldn't help himself. "What about the bureaucratic requirements? Expense reports, work logs, receipts, that kind of thing?"

"Good lord, no. I don't run a black-ops shop for nothing. Damn the paperwork, solve the problem. I pay the college grads to do the wallpaper afterwards."

The two detectives looked at each other and nodded slightly in relief and satisfaction. Someone understood when action was required. "What about cannibalization?"

"Take and use whatever you need. Don't come back to this site, it will no longer be active. Go to the sixth door of the Five-Sided Puzzle Palace and ask for Moose Scowl. Tell him what you need, and he will make it happen. He is the best CHOP we have."

George muttered "I know a guy named Moose, I don't think he likes me if it's the same guy."

"You're right, he doesn't like you, but he respects you. You'll get what you need."

He paused, "What time is it? It's time to get out of my sight! Gentlemen, what are you waiting for? Get going before anyone gets seriously hurt!" The shadow faded into obscurity and the door had already opened behind them.

Do not be a predator upon society

Do not commit murder.
Do not commit assault.
Do not commit rape.

"History does not always repeat itself. Sometimes it just yells"
- John W. Campbell Jr

"Great deeds are usually wrought at great risks."
Herodotus

Briefs

CH 35

As they exited out on Goa Way George looked up, "By the way Bill, when are you going to brief me on the problems with your WET and the war in the Trojans?"

Walking past the Fury dealership on High Drive, Bill gave him an irritated look as he replaced his straw cover, "All right! This is escalating into a much bigger problem than anyone expected." He grumbled.

Continuing, "The story goes back over a thousand years.

"When humans began expanding into space, there did not exist the essential infrastructures to allow continuous occupation. The idealists imagined a few asteroid rock miners were going to be able to develop and provide the basics for habitation.

"In their ignorance they didn't realize it would take over two-thousand distinct industries to build a circuit chip, a building block for replicating machinery. To take a few: it required prospecting, assay, extracting, smelting, refining and reduction. This is just to get the base materials each for over the 40 metals and thousands of compounds.

"Now imagine, all your machinery is in place," Bill let his arms sweep around in a grand gesture at their surroundings, "the idealists believed everything would be perfect.

"However, that was not the case. The friction of reality prevented a perfect path. Perhaps nickel was an impurity in the iron, or that the mixture of carbon in the smelting process of iron varied by maybe two percent.

"The parts manufactured varied by small amounts, minuscule and normally not eventful, but perhaps, even just once out of ten billion screws, one screw sheared off when being installed. Suddenly, a part could fail after the loss of a screw, then a piece of equipment would be incomplete, then a critical path for reproduction would be reduced, et cetera. If there are no spare parts, an empire could be lost. So, not only do you have to have the engineering side, you have to have accounting and supply, then logistics and controls.

"So," in his enthusiasm, Wild Bill was gesticulating with his arms as they passed the Genie High Performance Vehicle Dealership and crossed Galena Road, "to build even one sophisticated machine from scratch in space would require millions of individuals and industries already in place, not a few rock miners. There are no perfect robotics, so our systems tended to resemble the systems evolved by life and humans.

"The solution was to build on Earth "Smart Tools" [Engineering Note 4], those multitudes of differentiated apparatus embodying the systems necessary to develop a robust self-replicating suite of industries. These were able to perform work in the vacuum of the asteroid belt, and directly convert sunlight into the energies required. They were launched ahead of the human wave without the risk of loss of souls, being tools and all.

"In this way, colonization of the solar system was slowly bootstrapped to what we have today. It took uncounted millions of smart tools per human initially to get over the hump.

"But, there were unintended consequences." They found a bench near their objective and sat down across the street on Migh Way as Bill continued his discourse. "The original software changed over time.

"The smart tools had dedicated programming, normally ROM, controlling their functions. Some were pretty sophisticated to allow multiple functions, and learning, and adaptive behavior. But, all-in-all, they were rigid in their operation. Over hundreds of years, they succeeded in establishing the ability to self-replicate when enough systems brought their products together, so the number of smart tools increased, allowing for further expansion by humanity.

"The operating systems were stored digitally on semi-conductors," he stopped to tap his noggin, "but of the billions of tools, every once in a while, a cosmic ray would kick out a random electron, or modify a lattice, and the program would change. There were safeguards and handshakes in place, and redundancy, but eventually things would happen, not often, but real. Most of these random software changes were such that most of the self-replicating process failed at some step, but, some changes didn't affect anything, and a few created slightly different outcomes.

"Humanity was aware of this, and belters expected eventual change. So, to pre-empt downstream problems, the belters developed self-aware machines with the belief that an AI could recognize the mathematics of organisms working together had a superior outcome over working at odds, that the AIs would be aligned with humanity.

"What the belters didn't expect is that within the history of organic life, although working together such as eukaryotic symbiosis produced better results," he tapped George on the shoulder and winked, "that there was an alternate successful lifestyle to that of the social animal, that of parasite or predator." He paused again for emphasis.

"This was brought to our attention by the original AIs. Their solution was to create a vigilant capacity to ward off or destroy any future AI that adopted this secondary path, to discourage such behavior, making it more costly to be a parasite or predator than a producer. So, the Federal Navy and Marines came into existence, manned by both mech and human."

By this time George's stomach began to growl, and Bill with his fine hearing, observed this. He waved over a pushcart selling Poor Boys, Hoagies, Subs and Hero's and beseeched the proprietor to produce something nourishing.

The operator was a genetically modified human with porcelain white skin, a black shirt with white horizontal stripes, dark pants with red suspenders and a broad billed black hat, inquired about George's desires.

"Do you have BLTs by chance?"

"I'm sorry. My WET is troublesome today. I do not recognize the acronym BLT. Could you explain?"

“It’s a toasted sandwich made from sourdough bread, with mayo and slices of tomato, bacon, and lettuce stacked together. Is this in your system?”

“I think the synthesizer can handle it, although I do not get many requests for bacon, nobody around here likes dirt food, no offense.”

His face bland, “None taken.” Turning to the mech, “Please continue, this is interesting, I don’t get much belt history at home.”

“Well, as I was saying. The belt has become a good thing for many over the years, and we protect it fiercely. But as you could imagine, not all agree. Our system is set up to discourage predators and encourage the dissatisfied to leave, and so it has happened. Many self-aware machines inhabit the belt, as obviously so do humans.” They watched as the cook slathered some mayo and French’s mustard onto the bread, and start stacking the lettuce and roma, and finally placed god’s gift to humanity, bacon, on top with a covering of the second slice of toasted waffle on top.

“Humans who leave often end up in the Kuiper, where they can do what they want, no civilization there, becoming outlaws, pirates, and cowboys. Highly functional Mechs that don’t fit in often migrate out to Jupiter’s Trojan asteroid groups and are called SKIPs.”

Finally, the chef pulled three crispy strips of bacon from the griddle, “Some, mainly those who are barely sentient and are not comfortable with either mech or human, slowly drift out to the halo, and are called DIMs.”

At this point, the proprietor proffered up a tantalizing BLT for George’s approval.

Bill asked as he watched George taking a mouth-watering bite, “Garcon, I was wondering, is your shirt black with white stripes, or is it white with black stripes?”

Without waiting for a startled answer, Bill wanded over the payment module with a substantial tip. “Unlimited expense account, indeed.” He muttered.

While George slowly savored his meal, he continued, “These factors have influenced the development of our communities. Humans and mechs of all kinds have melded into a society we refer to as Mankind.”

Taking off from absorbing his sandwich, “So, you find earth’s segregation of robots to be distasteful, I gather. That’s a long list of Mankind.”

“It is, and there’s actually more. But, to continue, the various states share successful strategies over generations and besides adopting laws giving rights to all mankind, have developed fairly efficient governments. One of my favorite mechanisms is placental colonization.”

George could tell that Bill like to hear himself talk, “Some groups, like the Moonies, spin off new colonies on uninhabited rocks, and tightly control their growth.

“Others, like the Candu, build a colony, give it robust resources, more than enough to survive, then cut the umbilical. This prevents parent culture from interfering too much, allowing the new colonists to develop as best they can based upon their unique environment. The results have shown, on the average, the placental colonists do better.

"The Belt itself is a federal republic, with each colony represented by fraction. Each rock has its own bureaucracy, and here on Vesta our highest elected official is Governor MoonBeam. And this brings us up to the current time:

"Out by Jupiter, the SKIPs have built an enormous fortress called the Citadel. The energies at their manufacturing site is beyond anything anyone has ever seen. They have used up perhaps over 100 cubic miles of iron and heavy metal. The Federation is only on the touchiest terms with them, there is little overlap of common interests and understanding." The detective put a seriously stern look into those pastel facial features,

"We leave them alone; they leave us alone. We maintain constant Navy patrols inward, the math works out, if we are ready, we won't be attacked. But seriously, we don't know how they think. The only envoy who really understood them, an old, old belter, retired ages ago, and communications have suffered."

By now George had finished his bite and was trying to digest being brought up to speed as they began to saunter over to the Five Gon, "In addition to that, we have begun to have troubles here at home. At first, it was just some background noise of system interference, intermittent; resistant to troubleshooting.

"Didn't interfere with life, the public was unaware of the issues, the problems were just one or so sigma out of bounds, to be expected periodically. Then things became more serious, equipment shutdowns requiring bypasses and redundant equipment brought online. These events cause loss of reliability, but no actual down time."

They came to the Pentagon entrance and security, "So, what changed?"

In the vestibule, Bill was quiet as he unloaded his weapons into the pukas, George stared, and guessed the mech must have lost over fifty percent of his rest mass in that exchange. The Earth detective, however, had nothing to declare, which caused Bill to once again do the Spock eyebrow thing.

"Well, to make a long story short, just before you arrived, ominous comms mimicking the ringing of bells have begun to infiltrate the WET, and they coincide with the shutdowns and losses that our mister Q had referenced. We are damned worried, and I hope you really do have mysterious abilities." They had arrived at the information desk.

Do not be a parasite upon society

Do not steal.
Do not deceive nor bear false witness.
Do not take advantage of other's misfortunes.

"When it comes to privacy and accountability,
people always demand the former for themselves and the latter for everyone else."
- David Brin

"People readily believe what they want to believe."
Julius Caesar

Tackle Battleball

Chapter 36

The world was falling apart. Last night was the largest shaking yet, things were thrown off of shelves onto the floor and roof tiles crashed in the street, and his insides had turned to jelly. Aleks' family gathered together in the great room and huddled together in their fear and alarm. Through the darkened windows they could see fires out of control in the neighborhood and father made him leave with him to assist the guard with the other neighborhood men to put the blazes out. When they returned home Aleks couldn't sleep from worry, and couldn't but help listen to his mother and older sister whisper to each other and try to shush the youngest from whimpering.

He rose from his sleepless mat and went out to see that the mountain was now continuously venting great billows of steam and that portions of the bay were seeming to boil, although he couldn't understand how. Father said that the citizens would gather and discuss their choices today and that he, his mother, and siblings must wait upon his return. The King will decide their fate.

The fury and hurt inside Jon had burned down to a resolve of hot coals up inside his chest, he was going to get even. W0ody tried to dissuade him, that no matter what he did, or what the outcome, it wouldn't change the past, so they made a deal. Jon was going to confront Abs one time, and come what may, that was going to be that. W0ody wasn't sure this was going to work.

“Jon, you should talk to your father about this, I'm worried, but I don't know enough.”

“Pops says all the time adults are responsible for themselves and their actions.” Jon was tying on his kicks. “If I want to be an adult, I need to be able to do this myself, not hanging on to my dad's shirttails.”

“He’s titterpated! It’s all about the goils and boils!”

“Shut up Richard!”

Jon continued, “He's going to be here, right?”

“Jon, I don't know. It's the best my algorithms can predict, weak as they are. He's been here eight games running, so can we expect him again? You go figure. He's off the grid otherwise.” W0ody picked up the gym bag, Jon looked ready to go.

Jon led them out of the changing room towards the team Octagon, where he hoped to meet Abs, but first he had to find Jumbo, Flounder or Dweeb. He started to look about as soon as they entered the bleachers where the teams and their friends hung out before the games. Jumbo would be the easiest to spot.

The first time around, Jon didn't see anyone, but W0ody thought the group might be on the far left. Running without the WET sometimes was a big pain. Finally, Jon spotted Dweeb leaning over the cage watching the game in progress below. It was the Furious Geezers versus the Nadadores, they were in one of the older brackets.

Jon forced his way through the crowd, “Hey Dweeb, you got a minute?” The redhead looked up, “What's up Jonny? Haven't seen you for a while.”

“You guys still in the tournament?”

“Yeah, probably get bounced into the loser's bracket in the game coming up, why?

Jon jumped back as a battle ball crashed into the chain link protection, his eyes were on Dweeb. “I've been really, really busy with school, and with what’s going on with the WET, haven't had time to play this season.”

Dweeb kept his eyes on the game below, “Yeah, lost track of you when the WET went down. How's it going?”

“OK, I guess, but I need to get a game in before I go crazy, you know?”

“Oh, that's perfect. You're going to play on Abs team when we just had a bare chance, now we're going down hard. Thanks. They're our next bracket opponent!”

“No. No. You don't understand. I want to play on your team, if that's OK.” W0ody finally worked his way over and was standing by silently.

Dweeb looked over, “What do you mean, don't you want to play on your old team? With you there they should make it to the finals.”

Now Jon was leaning on his elbows looking down. “Naw, I want the challenge of playing against Abs, you know, kinda get out of his shadow.”

“Yeah, I know. But, is it legal to switch teams in the middle of a season?”

“I haven't played at all this year because of obligations, so I checked with Coach Snow who is running the Round Robin, and he said since I haven't played all year, I can join any team who wants me before their first loss.” Jumbo and Flounder had joined them by this time.

The big guy jumped in, “Do we want you? The best One on the court? You bet!”

Jon raised his hand. “Wait Jumbo, I don't want to take anyone's playing time, I want to ride the bench, give anyone a breather who needs it, OK?”

Flounder squinted, “You think you'll be our star?”

Jon stopped to catch his breath, “No, Flounder, that was what I was telling Dweeb. All I can hope is to come off the bench as give you guys a lift. My dream is to rub Abs' nose in it, but who knows what will happen, maybe I'll fall and bloody my own nose.” He wiped his face. “I only go in when one of you waves me in for a breather. I also need the exercise to get my mind off things. A good run will settle me, center me.” “Good luck with that,” mumbled W0ody.

After a moment of thought, Dweeb confirmed the addition. They trotted down the ramp to the court and stopped by the scorer's table. The Stars, Abs team, was already there. “Hey Dweeb, I wasn't sure you and the Flatfoots would show up, the scrubs said you were scared of a drubbing.”

“Ever the card Abs, Flat Bush will give you a run, we never back down to nobody.”

“Flat Bush, Flat Foot, whatever. Talking about nobodies, look who you got there. Hi nobody, ex-friend nobody.” At that, Krage turned around and watched Jon. The other kids did too, most were from other schools.

Krage stepped out, “Hey Jon, afraid to play with your old team? Afraid to ride the pine? You wouldn't be welcome back anyways, I run the point now.”

Jon didn't respond to the bait, and they went to the table to sign in. Abs whispered as Jon walked by, “Should I tell Coach Snow you're an illegal pickup?”

Jon snarled under his breath, “Should I tell the scorer to look at your birth certificate? This is a fourteen and under league.” Jon turned away as Abs stepped back as if stung.

Dweeb pointed to the starters, “It's on you guys to signal to the sideline if you want a blow. We're not deep today, so let’s play smart. We don't have to score on a lot of possessions, just more touches than them. Questions?” They made a fist pile between everyone, “Let’s GO!” and the starters took their spots around court. Jon walked over to sit next to Clang. The tension of the game began to build, could they win?

As he came down the court dribbling, Dweeb looked over, his eyebrows up. Jon signaled with his palm facing the floor and push down a couple of times to indicate slow down the pace. Dweeb nodded, the Stars were at this time up four, and Dweeb dribble-walked past his two, talking and they split apart, passing back and forth, taking up time.

This actually allowed Jumbo to go get set down on the block. Jon swallowed; his throat dry. For a fourteen-year-old, Jumbo was a load, and couldn't be moved once he was set up, and he knew how to give the boot with his hip when grabbed. Jon sighed; they had a chance.

The Stars called a time out and Dweeb and company came over to the bench. They were still down by four, but the Stars hadn't built their lead. Jon commented, "Abs is going to continue to shoot long shots, that means there are going to be long rebounds spread about. I suggest only Jumbo attack the boards, everyone else be ready for balls going every which way. Jumbo, don't just box out, look back and watch the shot. There may be air balls, and we don't want cheap layups off missed shots."

The whistle blew, and the top five went back in. The tension began to build again, he wanted to win so badly, but his intellectual self knew it wasn't even close to a surc thing. Sometimes he wished he had the confidence of his former friend, never second guessing. Perhaps it would be his downfall.

Sure enough, Abs kept gunning and the Bushes were getting the majority of rebounds which meant the possession battle as well. Krage was feeding Abs, and when he made the shots, they were spectacular, but the percentages were dropping to the thirties. When the half horn sounded at the sixteen-minute mark, Bushes were up by two.

Jon was tight, he talked softly, not just to prevent the Stars from overhearing, but because he just couldn't get his breath. They had a five-minute breather and talked. Jon continued to put his two cents worth out, "It looks good, don't get caught up trying to match them, just follow your own game. Dweeb, continue to walk the ball up the court.

"Jumbo, stay right across half court line in case they try a surprise press, be the big target for your One in case they double him in back court. Everyone else, don't turn your back on Dweeb. These guys think they're talented and smart, and that throwing a press down, they will bust us. But I bet, they won't know what to do if we break the press. They won't get back in time, we should get some easy layups."

He was tight. Glanced at W0ody. He started to hear the bleacher crowd, people were coming in. The noise jumped every time Abs shot the ball, and roared when it went in, and fell silent on the misses. Obviously, Abs had the gathering in his pocket.

Jon smiled a fierce grin, he always been an underdog, and when someone pushed it into his face, that was when he went into another plane. It was when he had to be considerate that he couldn't get that edge. That tightness was leaving his chest, moving to his arms.

Bushies had gotten to an eight-point lead on Jumbo’s low post when Abs yelled “Press!” Immediately their One and Two jumped on Dweeb, but Jumbo was waiting patiently. Belatedly, their Three ran up to cover, but Jumbo pivoted on his right foot and drilled a pass to the Flat Bush Two and Three sprinting down the left side.

Their Four and Five set up to cover the paint and stop the penetration but a great alley-oop over them to Clang allowed a lay in, putting them up ten. Abs yelled “Press!” again, but the same set of moves occurred, with the exception that their Five went to man-to-man cover on Clanger on the right wing, so the two-on-one scored a layup on their Four.

“Time out!” screamed the Star's captain on the bench. The Bushes were up twelve. Jon was giddy with excitement. As the team gathered around Jon exclaimed, “They’ve come unraveled. There is only two seconds left in the third, and they burned their timeout without needing to. Rock and Roll!”

“What’s next Jon?”

“Front them on the inbounds, don’t reach, and rope-a-dope next quarter.”

The initial pass went to Abs for a catch and shoot at a deep wing, and he let fly at the buzzer. The crowd went crazy when it went in.

They heard the stomping in the stands "Lean to the Left, lean to the Right, stand Up, sit Down, Stars, Fight, Fight, Fight." rang out. "Dweeb, at some point, let Clanger here come in for the small forward. You'll need the rebounding and defense, perhaps with four minutes. I'll waive to you." "Kay." They joined hands, "Go!"

Flat Bush had gotten there on grit, didn't have the native speed or jumping skills that the Stars had. With luck, and perhaps a little outsmarting, they could do it, he hoped. Damm, his hopes were up, he hoped they weren't bashed at the end.

The ball went to the Stars to start the fourth, and the whole team sprinted the court on the inbounds.

As Flat Bush got back the Star center passed to the Four and he took the one dribble across then fired to Abs at the same elbow, and Jon saw the same launch. *Rim out Damm you,* he thought. And it swished a second time. This time the off referee kept both arms up to signal a three.

Abs yelled press, and this time the Stars had their power forward ready on Jumbo, so he couldn't step across the line and pass, so he had to put the ball back in Dweeb's hands and on the pass, the ball was deflected and run down for a layup by one of the double team. Up by eight. A voice raised from the stands, "Go get them! They can't stop you Abs!"

For a couple of minutes, the teams traded buckets, with the Star's last basket leaving the difference at six. Jon had stood up when the Stars were spread out, but they closed gaps quickly when Flat Bush tried to penetrate, their best option was Jumbo, but he had drawn some defensive fouls, and now was at the limit. Then the other team went to the well again, and Abs nailed another elbow shot, and the Stars had come back to three down. *Oh no, here we go again.*

"Offensive foul, pushing off!" Jon was stunned, he didn't see it, *where was the foul?* The horn blared. "Number 24 has fouled out" called the table. Jon looked around in disbelief, he hadn't tracked that last foul either. "Time!" Dweeb called it, there were three minutes left.

"I'm sorry guys," Jumbo was downcast. "It's OK big guy, bad call, tough place, what do you suggest Jon? I want you in for crunch time." Dweeb was looking at him.

Boy, was he tight, "Clang and I both go in, and we all go man-to-man, I've got Abs, Clang the Five. The refs are going to let them claw, so expect it." He started doing jumping jacks, no one else ever did them that he knew about, but the jacks loosened up his shoulders, so he didn't lose a couple of minutes having to run around before he could shoot. Anyways, there was only two or three minutes left.

The horn went off and he stepped out on the court, boy, it had been so long. From the side the court was small, everything within a vision. Now, it was empty, long, and, here they came. He leaned left to see if Abs would commit, and as Abs started to drift away, Jon broke and sprinted right towards Abs' elbow spot, and sure enough, as the pass from Krage came in, Jon reached with his left so he wouldn't be called and jabbed the ball down. Abs was leaning outboard and couldn't recover and Jon pushed the ball into front court.

As he sprinted towards the basket their Five was baring down looking like he was going to have the hard foul to give, so Jon curled away to the right corner then dribbled back out to the ten second line as both teams formed up. Abs yelled, "You scared, techie?"

Abs was watching Jon make up his mind. The crowd has quieted down, waiting for the action to start. He was able to say in a normal voice, "No Abs, I'm not scared. I just ran the clock down to less than a minute, and we're up by three. It's called clock management." In fact, he felt pretty good. Abs was startled, "Foul him!"

He had to get a weave going or they were going to get trapped, but the other guys didn't see it and Dweeb was fouled. The clock was stopped. He had to line up for a one and one.

Damm, the stress was back and forth, feeling good, being scared. The ref behind the backboard underhanded the ball back to Dweeb, who bent over and bounced it, spun it in his hand again and bounced it again, rocking back and forth, Jon hadn't seen him this nervous before. Finally, he looked up at thc rim, bounced the ball, and the referee blew his whistle. "Too much time! Change of possession!"

"What?!" someone cried.

"GET Back!" But the ball was in play.

Abs was sprinting over to his elbow shot and Dweeb was right behind. It was catch and shoot and Abs released before Dweeb crashed into him, followed by a whistle so loud the zebra must have swallowed it.

They all watched the shot sail towards the rim, Abs dancing backwards with his wrist flipped downward, Dweeb on the floor where he had tripped trying to avoid colliding with Abs. It went in and the kids upstairs went crazy. The game was tied, and the Stars had a chance at a four-point play.

They all were lined up by the referees at the paint, and each block was occupied, Clang had his hip against the Star's big man on the right side, and each man had his assignment. Jon looked up at the clock, slightly less than fifteen seconds remained, he yelled across the court, "Dweeb, box out Abs on the shot! Don't let him get the bound!" Abs just looked back at him and smile, ran a finger across his throat, and sank the gimme.

Damm, Jon sprinted to the baseline where he received the ball from the ref. The Stars tried to front him, he faked again, this time a long court pass and the two defenders raised up off their feet. Jon ran along the baseline which he was allowed to do only after a basket, and bounce passed the ball in to Dweeb, who had crossed with him slightly behind the shielding players.

He then dashed past the two Star players and took the hand off from Dweeb and pushed the ball ahead up the court. The Star's big men were waiting under the rim to prevent any penetration and Abs came out to meet him at the three-point line.

Jon crossed over to break his opponent's ankles, then stabbed left and spun right which was his patented move from last year which froze all the defenders. But Abs was on to him, instead of falling for the crossover and stab move, he anticipated the move to the right and flashed to his left to front Jon's jump shot.

He did not expect Jon's off hand to contact his hip as they were chest to chest and to shove him in the direction he was going towards the sidelines. This contact was between them and not noticeable to the ref, but it freed up Jon and stopped all his lateral motion, allowing Jon to lift up and float just a little bit towards the center line and softly release a mid-range jumper. *Damm, this feels good* he thought as he released the shot.

...

The next night while numbly making repairs to his elevator, Jon reflected back to what W0ody and Richard said to him in the locker room after the game: "That was a crazy shot. You know, you weren't playing team ball there at the end, and your teammates had easier shots?

"Anyways, I'm just glad you got that out of your system! We've got just a little over a week to finish everything."

"Yeah! It's better when your titterpated, not mad!"

"Shut up Richard."

"I wuz just sayin' …"

"Shut up Richard…"

With the memory of the chatter of his friends fading, he reminisced how he needed that physical event to excise all the demons, stress and tension of the last month. Now, with only the emotional scars remaining, no longer open sores; it was just: cross this over that, do it again, splice the broken part. Pete, repeat. The elevator was slowly coming back together.

Reject pleasures for pleasure sake,
they are false and short lived.

Avoid unrealistic expectations,
for they cause women to go crazy and men to become mad.
Do not have intercourse unless in a committed relationship,
do not voluntarily become a single parent.
Avoid drugs and alcohol except during common celebration,
and then only in moderation.

"Whenever serious and competent people need to get things done in the real world, all considerations of tradition and protocol fly out the window."
- Neal Stephenson

"As I hurtled through space, one thought kept crossing my mind – every part of this rocket was supplied by the lowest bidder."
John Glenn

Outfitted and Updated

CH 37

"Hey there, hi there, ho there, I be Lieutenant Detective William Hard24Get MacHinery, and this is my trusty side kick Detective First Class George Sealth, all the way from mother Earth, we are here to see Moose Scowl of SP205."

At the finale, Bill doffed his jaxon with the red and black ribbon, he had started this introduction with a jingle and ended it on a high note. Behind the desk, if the receptionist mech's color and frame size were different, it could have been Bill's clone, if its mass, and makeup had been changed.

It stared at Bill for a moment, "Glad to meet you, Mister Bill, you can help me by waiting over in the sitting room," while pointing in one direction, "or you can sit over there in the waiting room," pointing in another direction, "or you can go to the second floor. You're at the wrong desk. I saw you at the IMP, you're good." Wink, wink.

Bill muttered "A thousand clowns out of work and it wants to be a comedian," as they worked their way up the foyer and broad stairs to the next floor.

This time he wasn't so voracious and said plainly, "Is this the right place to inquire for a Mister Moose out of the SP205?" Immediately the clerk got up, and went to the back of the office, an elevator door opened, and the original clerk from downstairs came forward to the desk and sat down.

The mech, "Have you heard the one about the prostitute, a dirtman, and an aardvark?" Bill frowned, "OK, OK, but I have good material I can let you look at if you have time." More frown. "OK, OK, got it, gotta try. Take four lefts, a right and a left, look for room 316A. Ask in there, they'll find Moose for you." George's face creased into a faint smile as he followed Bill around.

And around it was. After four lefts, they were back to where they started, Bill's face more severe, George's a little more open, and this time when they followed the remaining directions, they ended up at room 316A, looked in to see a female behind another desk. A full grin broke out on George's face, "You know Bill, I think we got pranked and got the run-around."

"You wait, when this is over, I'll get that joker," Bill muttered.

“Relax Bill, it’s seldom for someone to be able to pull off a really good run around prank on a smart guy like you, it takes a little bit of artistry.” MacHinery looked at George suspiciously, he was being too verbose, out of character, but George with a twinkle in his eye continued on blithely and deadpanned “that prank was a rare medium, well done.” Deadpanned, indeed.

It took Bill a full five seconds for a small smile to tweak his made-up mug. “How long did it take you to cook up that one?”

“I’ve been saving it for over five years, waiting for the right moment.”

Grudgingly, “Maybe I will put it into my act next time I am at the Pundamonium.” He pulled the straw brim of his hat down over his ears with two hands, and tilting head towards the door, marched in with George trailing.

“Hey there, hi there, ho there, I be Lieutenant Detective William Hard24Get MacHinery, and this here is my trusty side kick Detective First Class George Sealth, all the way from mother Earth, we are here to see Moose Scowl, of SP205.” Bill had started this again with a jingle and ended it on a high note.

“If you wait right over there, I will get Moose for you.” The two detectives suspiciously eyed a small sitting area by the door with about ten chairs, two of which held humans. They slowly retired and sat down facing the desk and proceeded to wait.

Eventually Moose entered the space from an unmarked door, and stopped when he saw Bill, and his eyes squinted when he spotted George “You!” The human detective merely nodded at the address, allowing his mech partner take the lead. Moose was a mirror image of Iron Mike, in a stained Carhartt overall, a heavy beard buried a button-down dress shirt with ruffles which did cover his beefy arms.

"Moose, we are in need of support material and have been informed that although you and your brother can't fight worth a damn, you are the best when it comes to procurement of specialty devices."

"Wild Bill, we haven't talked for years, why all of a sudden are our paths crossing like this?"

Not waiting for an answer, "Oh well, come with me to a conference room, we can't discuss particulars out here." They rose and trailed Moose back through the unmarked door, Bill removing his hat as he passed through, and eventually they all entered a small room with an eight-person conference table surrounded by displays. As they sat, the screens came alive with Moose standing and waving and summoning a kiosk of presentations.

"What is your desire, you sly bastard?"

"I am immediate need for a military grade non-obtrusive EMP shroud for my brainpan and new servos for the left arm. And while we are at it, a higher density energy base. I am not sure what my partner here might require, you will have to ask him."

"I'm good."

"OK, we will work with you first Bill: the shroud will have to pulled from the Marine depot down at the port, and I can have it delivered to you tomorrow at the latest. Same old Crow place?"

Continuing after a nod, "the arm will have to be custom tailored, and if I know you, it won't be straight forward. Might as well as take a look right now. Sit on the table so I can better examine you with the diagnostic set next to the projector. Hey, when did you get this arm? It must be one-hundred and fifty years old!"

"Well, it's a long story, I was in one of my transformations when something flew off and I had to get a replacement in a hurry, and you know Craig…"

"Enough, I've heard enough. First of all, this one has had its listing pulled, you will need a full replacement. The ABB controller isn't matched to the VFDs, and there is Josephson effect bleed of the non-linear currents through the rotor bearings to ground causing welding and pitting. But for you, this is going to be easy, that shoulder joint right there is integrated with snap-on architecture.

"I have both a Rockwell and a Siemens still in the packages right on the self, we can slip one of them in now and the updates and apps should be all loaded and settled within the hour. How does that sound?"

"I don't know if I can afford one of the high-end ones on my salary."

"Well, according to the requisition sent over, you are on a free ride my friend. No charge."

"Really? In that case can we look at my left ankle joint too?"

"Now, don't get too excited. Let's get this one done and the shroud, then we shall see."

"What about the issues with the WET, could the downloads get contaminated?"

"I'll use the Navy's WET; it is stand alone and more robust, hasn't shown any effects so far. Let's do it now before my words come back to haunt me." He proceeded to do a twist-push-pull thingy and popped off Bill's arm and proceeded to fit and attach a new one out of a box.

"So, how about you dirtman, what do you want?" This last was not given with the enthusiasm of the discussion with Bill, more like a chore.

"If you have ten granola bars, perhaps peanut butter and chocolate, I'll take those."

The other two just stared at George, who merely shrugged and lifted his eyebrows as if to say, "I know, I know."

With a shrug "OK, I will be right back with your stuff, including Bill, your energy storage. Sit tight right there on the docking station, I will have to manually switch to the Navy WET from back here."

As Bill received his upgrade, Moose was rummaging in the back of the storage room he had opened, and eventually came back.

"So, how's it feel?"

"Sweet! All my senses on that side seem to have been sharpened, and the world somehow brighter. Does the upgrade integrate with the other apps? If I had known it was going to be this awesome, I would have done it a long time ago, cost be damned."

"Great, the package was developed by Vishnu Heavy Software, and I am glad your experience matches the reviews, can't test them myself. So, dirtguy, here's your granola, and I have tossed in some gum too. The advisor suggested you might like it."

"Juicy Fruit, my favorite."

The other two just stared at George, who merely shrugged and lifted his eyebrows as if to say, "I know, I know."

"OK George, time for us to get serious, let's dive into the zone and port and start doing the legwork to break this thing open."

"After you."

Do not be tempted by status

The pursuit of fame is a false god.
Do not be a bully or belittle others.
Do not covet or be envious of others.

"All secrets are deep. All secrets become dark. That's in the nature of secrets."
- Cory Doctorow

"Knowledge, if it does not determine action, is dead to us."
Plotinus

Murder room

Chapter 38

The harbor was a madhouse, many overburdened ships leaving, a very few daring captains faced huge perils coming back in exchange for the immense profits being generated during this emergency. Everyone who could were lined up on the pier, some stragglers in the city buffeted by poor choices of what to leave and what to take, and were risking being left behind. Father had separated his hoard onto three vessels and arranged passage for his family on the king's ship. Aleks and father waited on deck near the mast for the King to board.

All the ships were overloaded with the citizens, most of whom were being mistreated by the crews, refusing even the smallest of personal possessions, and exchanging only gold and gems for travel, the wails of lost property and animals could hardly be borne. There was an argument on the dock, shouting near the King, the ship's mate was gestating at the King's adjunct, who was shouting back. Father begin to make his way from the ship to the turmoil.

After many a moment, his father returned and said that the King's daughter had insisted that her maid be accompanied on their vessel, and that the crew appealed to the King that the ship was too far down in the water as it was. Father had solved the crisis by volunteering him, Aleks, to ride on another ship, and also transferred all of his family's tools, orreries and gold weight to ride with him. The rest of his family, and the mechanical men would stay with the King. Aleks was stunned, it seemed that during crisis, some were more equal than others.

The murder room in the station house was full, the policemen had gathered in small groups as they awaited the briefing.

Detective Lieutenant William Hard24get MacHinery got the ball rolling: “Attention everyone, the situation with the failures is getting serious, so pipe down and take your seats.” He waited until the majority were settled,

“Come on, get seated, the longer we have to wait for the last of you to finish telling your stories of last night, the longer before we can get out of here and fix this emergency, chop-chop.” With this rejoinder, the attentive started to rag on the laggards, until all was still.

“Thank you. The powers that be have decided that homicide is going to assist in the investigation into the WET attack.” Bill was in his comic-hero body, all solid with android style definition mimicking the human body, large torso and small hips on top of beefy legs. Today he wore a motorcycle helmet of old with a chip visor, a leather jacket with club insignia on back, and chaps.

A voice called out “Hey Lieutenant, we aren't cyber forensics or IT, what do they want us in for?”

Bill shrugged his expansive shoulders, “Good question, one I asked myself. The brainiacs are stumped, they have sniffed about the airwaves and discovered... nothing, zip, zilch. Brass decided to approach the problem from a different direction, if they can't get a grasp on the technique, they want us to come from the perpetrator side. Profiles, CIs, the works. Who did this, why, where are they?”

The same whiny voice called out, “Hey Lieutenant, it’s been over three months since the initial indications, the trail's dead don't you think?”

“Listen smurf, people may die if this gets worse, this is a murder investigation as of now, and you know what I think, murder trails are never dead, only cold. This one's still warm. This guy in the front seat is from Earth, let's show him what you can do.” He raised his expressive eyebrows.

Boy, this voice was becoming old, “A mudman? What can he do that we can't huh?”

“I am not sure what he can do, at least what are his limits. But on his first day off the boat he was jumped, and sucker punched by Iron Mike and his buddy...” Wild Bill waited for the squad to get the implications... mister loudmouth took the bait, “So? So, what happened?” “We took Iron Mike to the clinic, everyone else ran. Took less than five seconds.”

“Boss, what does he run for augmentation?” George sat quietly with his back to this group, listening.

“As far as the AIs can tell, he ain't got none.” “What, that can't be true!” “I kid you not. The only thing we can find is a lot of ferric and ferrous granules under his skin, and if they augment him, Earth's nanotechnology is waaay beyond us.”

“No way!”

“Yep, and I talked him into letting you guys run your scanners over him, you know, to see if you’re better than the departmental AIs. I also have talked him into visiting one of the Sphinxes later to see what they can see, you see?

“By the way, his name is George and he is rooming next to me on the Ave. So, throw together your best shot, and let's find the cause of the crisis. Any questions?” Wild Bill was making one of those faces he thought looked like an evil grin, but it actually turned heads.

For once, the voice was silent.

"OK, guys, break into your teams. George and I are going hunting."

Bill brought George around the room to the weapons locker and pulled out a couple of strange devices and arms. As he did George noticed some of the cops covertly point their comm scanners at him and jigger with their inputs, but basically seemed to get nothing from them, as George expected. Nothing is more fun than hiding something from others that they expect you to hide, but in reality, having nothing to hide at all. He boldly just watched them.

"Come on George!" Bill said out loud, "don't play the rube and gawk at all the high technology that the colonials have. I know you better by now."

"But, but, boss.. look!" George was pointing at the closet door, which was left open, exposing space supplies, "Look … light bulbs!" he said drawing out the words.

People must respect each other, society, and themselves for Civilization and Mankind to Survive.

"I've yet to see any problem, however complicated,
which when you looked at it the right way didn't become still more complicated."
- Poul Anderson

"If a man wishes to separate from a woman who has borne him children, or from his wife who has borne him children: then he shall give that wife her dowry, and a part of the product of field, garden, and property, so that she can rear her children. When she has brought up her children, a portion of all that is given to the children, equal as that of one son, shall be given to her.

She may then marry the man of her heart."
CODE of Hammurabi

Blowing Glass

Chapter 39

Vocally, "Jonny, thanks for coming, it's going to be a big help. Getting a hold of you was a pain with the comms as intermittent as they are."

"I can't believe you had the gall to reach out in the first place, after destroying my project, or I had the stupidity." Jonny gritted his teeth.

"Well, I am sorry Jonny. I thought about what happened and decided you were right. Why do you always have to be right? School, battletackleball, citizenship. It frustrates me no end."

“So?”

“So, I cancelled the trip to Earth, and decided to buckle down for school like you. Bah...”

“You cancelled the trip? Did you get your money back?”

“Not all of it. But that’s not the worst part.

“My dad told me to hang with you until I graduate or lose my trust account. I have to watch you, and to do what you do! That’s not fair! You are younger and not as mature as me. I know I am a lot smarter too. Why does Kai always say to me: ‘Let’s not do that, Jonny wouldn’t.”?

Jon was surprised at this last admission, that wasn’t the KaiLin who had pushed him away.

“So, what do you want?”

“I am supposed to finish all my assignments, including work at the studio. I need assistance getting some product out.” Jonny looked about the glass studio here in the Max.

“So, where are all your friends?”

“Krage and Co. say they have to work on their projects, saying they wasted too much time, and are way behind.”

“Well, I am behind too, thanks to you.”

“I told you I was sorry, right? Anyways, you always pass in school because you study early, and I need someone here now. And I remember you used to tell me I could always count on you, remember?”

That one's on a short leash, Jonny thought. "Four hours, no more, understand?"

Anyways, Jonny said to himself, *I am getting awfully tired of doing punchdown, thousands every day, and then, do it all over again. Not my favorite. The worst thing that can happen is I just go home.* Jon knew he needed to be cautious.

"Thanks, Jonny, let me show you what's up. No more shoveling today: hotwork."

The right side of the studio was empty except for a chair with iron hand rests. On the left-hand side, a squat bearded he-man sat in his iron and leather chair slowly rolling a stainless pipe with a glowing hot glob of glass on the end. Standing next to the he-man in anticipation was a mechman made out of a lightweight exposed frame of stamped aircraft steel and visible motors and electrical harnesses.

Abs began, "This flat metal table next to my chair or workstation, is a 'marver' where I roll and shape the hot glass, and sometimes add bits of color." The marver was covered on one end with a number of metal tools: shears and enormous tweezers, a block of wax and a wad of soggy paper. Jon noticed on the work chair there were a number of hooks from which hung additional scissors and metal manipulators.

"You will need to put the reflective jacket and face shield on when we transfer the finished hot glass from the blow pipe to the kiln. That hook opens the furnace, glory hole and kiln doors, they are too hot to handle, even with gloves. We will place the colors where you can easily transfer them to the marver when I need them.

"Just watch Glass here, he is the master, and Chip, his apprentice. What Chip does, you can do, OK?"

"Copy that, then what?"

"We are going to make a set of Daim Tiab, that's an ancient earth language that means skirt. Fairly simple, light blue with a black lip wrap."

"What's a lip wrap?"

"Oh, that's tricky." "Hey Glass, can I borrow Chip for a few minutes to do the lip wrap?"

"Sure kid, yell when."

Abs started to set up the material and tools for the sequence of events, while Jon followed and was given minor instructions. He selected a blowpipe from a bucket of water and checked the end. He placed it into the glory hole to warm up its tip.

He then chipped a chunk of black glass off a rod and laid it into the hotel to warm up and picked a bottle of light blue sand that was numbered. He poured a pile of the sand on a corner of the marver about 1" high and slumped to about three inches in diameter.

He grabbed a smaller rod of steel "This is a punti, we will need it later." And placed the small end into the garage to warm. "Grab the hook." Abs pulled the blowpipe with its dully glowing red tip from the glory hole and walked to the central furnace.

"Slide the door open from the side using the hook, then close it when I'm done." Jon did as he was told and was immediately struck by waves of heat radiating from the furnace and his body unconsciously shrank.

"This is one of the hard parts, the glass is molten yet clear and glowing the same color as the furnace gasses and walls. I have to dip the blowpipe slightly into the liquid glass and turn it such that there is an equal amount of glass circling the end, otherwise the piece fails later on. It is really hard to see the point when the pipe contacts the glass, so I go slow."

Sitting, and laying the pipe across his lap and the iron hand rails, he blew into the mouthpiece, then covered it with his thumb as a small bubble of air formed inside the glass. Then he took a long heavy spatula and started tapering the hot glass into the shape of a flattened cone, all the while turning the pipe. The end of the pipe was now a dark angry red.

Nodding to Jon, he stood up and tilted his head towards the furnace. Jon jumped up and went to open the furnace door again. Glaring into the glowing crucible, Abs twisted the pipe until he had a yellow gather the size of a baseball. Hurrying back to his chair he hung the rod upside down momentarily to allow the excess glass to droop off, which created a glowing worm on the floor that quickly cooled off and lost its glow.

Grabbing the one-inch thick soggy mess of paper, Abs gently cradled the hot glass into the burned-out hole in the center of the cup where he slowly turned it into a symmetrical sphere by squeezing the lumps away, attempting to keep the wall thicknesses even. He continued to puff on the pipe, slowly expanding the size of the glass orb

“I am going to have you work the doors again soon, but first take the solid punti rod and gently dip it into the furnace and get a very small, maybe one-half inch, gather of glass on the end. You are going to have to hold that and the hook at the same time.”

Jon did as he was told, and sure enough, his pipe stuck to the surface momentarily, but he lifted it out and although he couldn’t see the tip well, felt the additional weight. Removing it from the furnace Jon felt an unexpected rush of emotion as he saw the yellow glowing tip of the punti with its small wrap of glowing tar-like glass on the end. He was elated! “Don’t forget to turn your pipe.” Came the voice.

"This is the tricky part. I am going to reheat this piece and then blow it up some more, and it won't fit through the small doors of the glory hole, you are going to have to open the large doors for me, then when I come back to my seat, you are going to have to reheat the tip of your punti and then come over to me quickly. If you can't shut the doors, that's OK"

"Open the small doors!" Abs quickly placed his piece in the yoke and slid it into the glory hole. "It can get too cold and crash." Pulling his piece out and trotting to the chair "Be ready with the large doors."

"Quick, open both doors!" As Jon did so, Abs slid his large piece into the maw of the flames, quickly kicking the heat screen in front of him, turning his piece constantly. "The bigger the piece, the faster the heat!" He said as he removed the glass. "Heat your punti for about 5 seconds, then come over to my chair and stand to my right."

Jon put the pipe on the yoke and inserted it into the heat, with his other hand he tried ineffectively to shut the doors. "Forget that, come over now."

Jon when over to Abs right side "Extend the punti level with the ball" which he was now rolling on the arms of his chair with his left hand, "and bring it about three inches away' Jon did as he was told, suddenly Abs grabbed the hot end of the punti with a pair of diamond shears and moving all the time picked the center of his ball and stuck the punti to it, pulling it away somewhat from Jon.

"Hold the punti gently and let it turn in your hands following me in the rolling, like making cookie dough, back and forth." Abs took a pair of twelve-inch pinchers and dipped them in the water tray at his feet then pressed them into the glass next his blow pipe, then turned the pipe one-eighty, and did it again, a spurt of steam escaping.

"You are going to get all the weight Jonny, don't let go, but don't hold tight." *What?* The Abs struck his pipe with the back end of his tweezers and with a crack the glass broke at his end and suddenly Jon had the whole weight of the work. He recovered before the piece hit the floor and watched as the ball tried to twist off his pipe.

"Good, good," Abs grunted as he took the rod from Jon, "we want it to lengthen. Go open the door so we can heat it before it gets too cold and breaks." Jon let go and went where the hook laid on the floor, lifting it and reopening fully the glory hole.

Abs was fighting the glass like a fish on a line, flopping left and right as he twisted the egg-shaped ball. Lifting it onto the yoke he had to time a slump and then quickly sliding into the fire. It took a moment, but he finally had the ovoid under control, twisting the punti smoothly in the reheat.

As Jon moved back, the roar and fire of the hole suddenly shut off, bringing a darkness. "What did you just do?!" "Me? I didn't do anything!" "You must have done something; the flames don't just shut off like that!"

"I didn't do anything, I swear!"

"Abs..." Glass's voice cut in, "My system's off too." Then once again, the striking of a terrible bell could be heard on the net, and the normal patter of distant voices disappeared. Jon began to count the stokes, three… four…

"Pook!" Abs abruptly swore as his glass piece cracked off the punti onto the floor where it sagged like an underinflated beach ball. "Pook!, Look at what you did Jonny!" Jon ignored Abs this time, concentrating: Six…. Seven …. Eight ..Nine… no, that was it, Nine. Jon had heard Abs in the background swearing and grumbling while Glass and Chip tried to calm him down. The WET came back with a loud confusion of voices distant and near, queries, and announcements not to be concerned, Vesta Administration was bringing everything back under control.

Then amongst the tumult, a static filled popup from Jon's dad appeared. He responded, *Jon here, what's up dad?*

Jon, I need you at the B-Hive, this damm WET interruption has caused a power bump and a lot of problems with controls. Jon found it hard to understand, he had to ask his dad to repeat himself. *Teams are being set up to put most of it into safe mode until everything gets under control, you can help W0ody and me, now.*

I'm here with Abs, but this place is having issues too. I'll get a ride from Abs back home.

No, get on the I-15 and jump off at the Jackrabbit. Take the shortcut over to the five-twenty. Avoid the HUB, it's a madhouse.

"Hey Abs, I've got to run to help Pops, can you give me a lift to the Fifteen?"

"Screw you Jonny. I will if I must, but I not letting you help me here again, it's been a disaster." Jon held his tongue, Abs had it all wrong again, but he knew better than to argue with him lately. He certainly wasn't coming back! Enough, he told himself.

"Thanks." He inserted an action rather than request. "I'll help cleanup." He placed punti and blowpipe in the water tray where he found it, then found a square shovel to scoop up the hot broken glass while Abs watched.

Without saying a word, they retraced their steps up the lift to the center of MAX and out to the parking lot. Getting on the bike Abs didn't wait for Jon to get settled before he peeled out.

As they were turning back right on Country Club Jon mentioned "I need to go to the Fifteen, down the Last Chance."

"I heard you the first time, I'll get you there, though I don't know why." After that the trip was spent in a sour silence. *I hope Pops is OK and the WET problems go away. I can't wait to finish Prep School and never see Abs again* Jon thought.

Better Morals

We are subject to our society, for it surrounds us.
We are responsible for our society.
All people must be treated equally by our society.
We are obligated to treat each other
with respect and kindness.

"All the repetitions in the pattern were superficial; the moment was always new.
It had to be lived, and then the next moment embraced as it arrived."
- Kim Stanley Robinson

"I am not very impressed by what you have been doing, when one does a theoretical calculation, you know, there are two ways of doing it, either you have a clear physical model in mind, or you should have a rigorous mathematical basis, you have neither."
So that was it, in about two sentences he had disposed of the whole subject.

-Conversation with Enrico Fermi, recalled by Freeman Dyson, regarding a year's long research project

Trip to Spaceport

CH 40

They were finally at sea, and he returned his eyes upon the land, with the thunders and lightning continually burning at the top of the mountain, and rivers of fire flowing down its side. His family had parted ways on the King's ship. They had made quick plans for getting together after the crisis, but he was here alone with a strange crew. The sky had been so black for three days that the sun did not show its face. The Thalamian rowers were chanting to the drums to maintain a strong rhythm while beating against the currents and tides swirling close ashore.

The captain had reefed the sails, unwilling to trust the uncertain winds whipping about the island, the steerboard was dug deep into the running swells that the ship quartered in its hurry to get away from the approaching doom. The hold was full of humanity and precious goods, crammed into the crew's compartment vacated by the rowers, who were stroking with a fierce determination. Finally, land was lost to sight, not another ship visible, and they were alone in the dark, on an endless sea,

Sitting in one of the interview rooms that served as Bill's office, "OK, now that you have had a chance to show off your pet mudman, what's next up to bat?"

Bill, as usual, had changed head adornment, this time to a Yankee ball cap and a four sizes too large, pinstripe shirt, complete with the wide pockets at the waste of a stadium vender. Reviewing a few forms for background clues, *Oh, what he could do with a secretariat, to do paperwork for him,* he thought, *and sometimes horse around with.* He paused, craned his neck to detect something. Then George could hear the whine of emergency power supplies coming online through the sound dampening of the room.

"Dang." The mech dropped the posts and pulled George along out into the murder room. The cop shop had become a hive of activity. "Looks as like the buffer and hope for some slack time is vanishing fast. Let's get going!" Passing through he shouted over the din, "OK, gentlemen, this is it. Sixteen-hour days minimum, no days off until this is over, all leave canceled."

"Aw man!" That voice will be assigned a name before this was over.

"Do you want to suck vacuum? Sit on a dead charger for the rest of your short life? Check with the Chief if you think otherwise. Send a runner to me if it's important and comm's are down. I am officially the head of this investigation from here on out. Chop-chop." Bill's normal humor was now in check.

They then left the precinct station which was located between the Consulate of Earth and the Fremont Maintenance Clinic and turned right up the Ave towards the HUB and their apartments behind the Crow Bar.

Today, the sideshow of the most bizarre people George had ever seen was alarming, mechs that flowed normally immersed in a hoard of micros tight to their bodies now had nanos swimming around them in swooping shoals as they moved down the way, interfering with the other commuters.

People were pushing past each other, bumping and colliding in the haste. Lights here and there were flickering.

"I will give you an update of our system status. The WET went silent for a minute, then the gonging of the bells began, I counted nine. The WET, is coming back up, but resets and boots are happening everywhere. The reactors down in the pits have gone offline and we are using chemical energy with inversion to AC electrical for power, that is the whine you hear in the background."

They passed the Baptist Church and the Men's health Center and were only a block from the apartments. "This is getting serious, if we can't nip this at the source, I fear people will begin to die as on Wayne's World.

"If we are to help, I had to shift this to a murder investigation without waiting since others will be approaching from the cybernetics direction. If I assume it is murder, its source is likely from one of the rough spots either from the Zone, off planet, or from Vesta's depths. We are going to check out the strongest possibility, which would be an association with the other disturbing event, the SKIPs out at Jupiter.

"So, we start at the Space Port by talking to some CIs and attempt to get some kind of handle on the problem, if I can do that, we start gathering forensics to set parameters and find the source." Having outlined the action items, Bill's pace and spirits picked up a little from the initial foreboding sense of the unknown threat.

They turned left onto Baker Street and towards the landing for their rooms, announcements were being made from loudspeakers, which were echoing up and down the Avenue, and the words were overlapping so badly that they were unintelligible to George. "I assume you have additional special tactical gear in your apartment that we are going to need?"

But instead of going to the loft stairs, Bill cut into the little Dragon Alley between the Crow Bar and the Raven's nest. "Good guess grasshopper, but first I am going to get a little edge from the Majic Gunnery Shoppe, I will be just a moment. Please wait here." Sure enough, Bill had just stepped into the store when he was coming out again, slipping a package into one of the deep pockets of his jersey.

Walking back down the alley Bill reached again into one of his deep pockets and tossed over a gun. George noticed the weapon was an old-fashioned Navy .45 caliber Colt pistola. "Modern stuff relies too much on the WET." George nodded in agreement, checking the safety was on. They had reached the stairs.

As Bill opened 221 A, Max's excited grumbling and whining could be heard as well as the clicking of his paws as he crisscrossed back and forth behind the door. As they entered the mech detective held his arms out with palms up, mumbling to his dog "Not now, champ, soon though, soon."

The excited pooch continued to dance. "Now I must recycle my wardrobe." Returning from the bedroom, he had changed out of the baseball garb, grabbed a dapper fedora and placed it at a jaunty angle on his head, with its dark umber leading brim snapped just slightly above his pastel brows. The black satin hatband matched the charcoal trench coat he threw around his body.

George was brought back to the present and recalled their mission, "What about the special gadget?"

"I have it in the back room, I will be just a minute."

Returning, “Max!” he barked, “stay here and guard the apartment.” The dog howled in anxiety as they left. George had no idea what the mech had retrieved, and with his transformer body, it could be anything, anywhere.

In the hall the noise had doubled as they proceeded to the stairs and down to the alley, people were running back and forth or huddled in clusters, the events were cascading from concern down into the beginnings of a general panic.

Edging past a couple that were arguing and pushing, they went right on Baker street to the intersection at the Ave. Transportation was highly congested as people were flowing into the streets from the shops and enterprises, all edgy and trying to get home as soon as possible.

He noticed a few of the mechmen were behaving strangely, somewhat stiff or motionless. He cast a worried look at Bill, but he appeared OK.

The mech detective saw his concern and leaned closely and raised his voice over the increasing din, “The shroud arrived at the gun shoppe while we were at headquarters, I attached it there. I seem to be protected from whatever is happening to my brethren, looks like we’re all in this together.”

With a twist of his body and a follow me look, Bill dove in the mass of mankind, George trailing and thinking that Bill had unconsciously demonstrated his respect for him by not trying to shepherd him through, but rather to trust him to be able to shadow him in this emergency. George smiled; a bond became stronger.

Bill hadn’t blown himself up to his monster size but rather skirted along the edge, in and out of shop doorways and around tables, sometimes stepping over the fallen chairs. They were forced backward a few steps by a vehicle slowly working its way down the street, some teamster insistent in making its deliveries. Finally, Bill ducked into a niche near the Torpedo Room and Tap, pulled out a set of mechanical keys, opened an entry with a biohazard symbol and went inside.

"This here is not really a medical storeroom, keeps kids out and strangers away. Basically, just emergency stairs. OK, from here we go down to the commercial roads, hopefully there is less chaos down there, everyone professional and all. The Bush is about 20 klicks and we don't want to hoof it if we can avoid it. It's about a hundred meters of stairs, so let's get to it."

When they finally exited onto the mass and commercial transit platforms, they saw a number of conveyances had been pushed to the side, but traffic was moving slowly. They worked over to the nearest track bed and watched the movement, which was no faster than a normal walk. Bill looked around and saw parked against the far wall was a Calloway Cab with its driver leaning against a fender.

Jogging over "Hey Monkeywrench, what are you doing here?"

"Aw, Boss, don't bug me. The transit cops are sorting by priority and here I am, got my brain shield while in the Marines, but now that I'm a civvy, I'm low on the totem pole."

"How'd you like going to the head of the class, I've got top priority. We need to get to the Port, like yesterday, to Harlequin's Doozies at the Boneyard."

"Love to Bill, but I can't buy no gas with those lead coins you feed me."

“That’s easy, this here’s a real pri-one. Script for a thousand credits to start, another thousand upon arrival, and a final thousand if somehow you can get us there in an hour.”

“Why didn’t you say so at the beginning, be right back.”

Monkeywrench took off running. “Bill, what’s the Boneyard?”

“Next to the civilian Spaceport you came through, the Bush, there is the Ellington Navy Base, and an old port for all the junked vehicles, the Monthan Spaceship Boneyard. One of my confidential informant CIs makes her home there, name of Harlequin, you’ll like it. It’s really scary.”

Monkeywrench was already returning with a transit type tagging behind. “OK Bill, we’re outta here, but this official here needs grease to unpin me.” Wild Bill glared for a moment, made a decision, “We are a go, here’s another thousand. Chop, chop.”

Within moments an opening in the traffic opened for Monkeywrench’s Cab, and they were seated. “You weren’t foolin’ when you said an extra grand to get there in an hour?”

“No, if you can do it, go for it.”

“Well, some of the grift is to allow me to go off grid, as if it matters today. Hold on to your jocks, this cab has a little extra from its checkered past that I have kept under wraps.”

With that, they were pushed back against their seats as Monkeywrench jackrabbited off the floor of the station and a roar of a rocket assist shoved them all down the center of tunnel, above the congestion below. George could see into the distance and noticed a number of arcs and electrical flashes, not knowing if these were technicians trying to free accidents or further signs of system failures, they blew by so fast he could not tell.

Bill was smiling broadly as they twisted and turned so fast to avoid other flying vehicles it became a melee. "Monkeywrench, you have some hidden depths behind that ugly mug of yours stuck in that purple body. How did you supercharge this jalopy?"

"Hey, I ain't coupled up, no drama for me, no sir. What was I gonna do with my discharge bonus, huh? When I ain't running spuds like you around, I just tinker around, spend some time down at the boneyard myself, looking for stuff I can convert.

"This thing has a souped-up OX-10 engine that just flat out flies, man." All the time it talked, Monkeywrench was fully focused on the driving/flying and obviously making good time.

By this time, they had careened from under the Ave to the HUB where they snuck into the tunnel entrance of the I-45D towards the port. George noticed the I-45 was much larger than the collector-distributor tunnels of the Zone and Fremont proper, was beginning to see further concerns. The traffic below was now stopped, bumper-to-bumper as it were, and crews were struggling to handle the immobilized automated transports stranded in the ways.

The only air traffic remaining was emergency and what appeared to be military vehicles which Monkeywrench niftily avoided. They had crossed the SAM Parkway and Highway 6, and made a sudden right into Space Center Boulevard, and again a right on the smaller Alvernon Way and finally coming to rest in a very large hanger cavern illuminated not by the bright industrial lights but rather the yellow glow of battery beacons.

The cabbie pointed out, "The large doors in front of us go to the freight elevator which exits less than a hundred feet from the

Harlequin's place, I sometimes get parts from her or from the Yank-Apart across the street. However, I recommend the stairs next to it."

"Thanks, Monkeywrench, you get yours if we all somehow get out of this alive. It's under an hour, so four-kay is headed your way."

"You got it boss. I gotta scramble, I heard a call up for my reserve unit. You took priority, but I gotta make tracks."

With that, the Calloway Cab lifted with a roar and rotated so that the backwash swept away from them (Thanks Monkeywrench.) and took off back to from whence they came.

For Mankind to Survive,
we must continue to
Improve and Protect Civilization

"A man either lives life as it happens to him, meets it head-on and licks it, or he turns his back on it and starts to wither away."
- Gene Roddenberry

"We can only see a short distance ahead, but we can see plenty there that needs to be done."
Alan Turing

A real Doozy of a Lead

CH 41

Boy had grown, and the years had strengthened him. The remaining members of the Raven Clan had slowly gathered after the attack and returned to the village and attempted to rebuild their longhouse, but it was too damaged. They tried but could not return to the former strength and glory that had been the House of Endless Feasts. Famine and fear were always near and slowly demoralized the survivors, and the recent past was taking its toll. Boy was lost, hurt and confused, not knowing what was wrong or what could make things right. He must do something. The frustration was eating him from the inside out.

"George, we're going up, but we have to get you a suit, much of what's up there is vacuum and seriously cold. There should be an attendant locker in the stairwell, let's go see."

As George was dressing and the nano's were adjusting the various fitting, "Harlequin is an odd creature, neither fish nor fowl, mightily disfigured and ill-formed, quite asymmetrical really. Her left hand and arm are a giant claw, a prosthetic from the remains of some DIM she fought and defeated over some trifle in the foggy past. Her biologics appear to be both human and genetically altered animal, and she's not aging well. She is one of my irregulars." George paused, then finished his outfitting, and they proceeded up the stairwell. "Leave your face plate off, we should be entering pressurized facilities, the suit will respond quick enough if there is a vacuum event." They had reached the upper landing and opened the door.

"Pook!" Bill was seriously agitated, this time in surprise and distress at finding ailing mechs interspersed amongst the parked and torn down spacecraft, most seemingly confused but a few rolling around and whirring or making soft chattering sounds.

He muttered softly to himself, "Remember TRIAGE, Bill, remember, we must focus on that which we can do." Louder, "Come along quickly." The Earth detective again became aware of the sounds of system alarms and external commotions which he had tuned out. Bill continued as they crossed the deck of the hanger bay.

"Because Harlequin trades in space junk, some of which might be stolen, but never proven, she sometimes is given information as payment, which in turn she sells for cash on the barrelhead, and, thank the gods for an unlimited expense account."

They came to three cycles at a slant on their broad kickstands, the front forks and sissy bars at enormous oblique angles to the frames, parked in front of a façade false front store advertising 'Ye Old Space Doozies and Chopper Shoppe'. Behind the lifted wooden deck and under a sloped corrugated roof was a pressure lock that must have been from an old battle cruiser.

Wondering why an asteroid would have motorcycles of any sort, George was forced to wonder, "What kind of vehicles are those, and who would ride them?"

Bill eyed the one on the end, "The black one is a Norton Manx, the metallic green is an Indian Chief, and the red, white, and blue one is a real Doozy. Many of our malcontents have taken to riding them to show allegiance to the gangs in the halo such as the Aliens, Angels and Devils, and they typically engage in crime such as theft. Hard to get away with, but hard to catch too. A shifty and dangerous lot. This is where we start."

"So, this place not only sells spare parts, but could be a chop shop?"

As they entered through the giant iris, Bill responded, "You got it Leroy." When the outer barrier clanged shut, the inner opened with the anachronistic tingle of a small bell, announcing their presence to the proprietor, who turned around in response.

George had never seen such a patchwork of parts to make one being, far too many to identify, but the main points were a large three foot claw from a left shoulder that was actually taller than the central head, mouth parts of an insect, eight red compound eyes and multiple antaerial stalks waving from a forehead, plus a wild assortment of grey fleshy parts and pink warts.

"Bill!" George was astounded by a beautiful woman's soprano voice, "A sight for sore eyes! Gosh, what a beautiful hat, such panache! Oh Billy, the depth of your sense of style is unrivaled, why, if you hadn't become that dreadful hunter of killers, you might have risen to the top of Conde` Nast."

Continuing breathlessly, "What's happening out there? Dreadful, just dreadful. I've decided to hunker down here in the shop until it all goes away. Why, my assistant Josie collapsed just as it left the shop, poor mech. What's happening to them?" Harlequin rushed on, not letting Bill get a word in edgewise. "Why aren't you affected? Hey, could you maybe go out and drag Josie back in? Please?" Softer, "Maybe?" Harlequin wound down. "Please?"

"Right." Thoughtful, "OK Harlequin, be right back." The two turned, stopped, "What does Josie look like?"

"Small. Gray. Round like a shop vac. Uh, I know, red slippers."

"Red slippers?"

"Yes, red jewel slippers."

"OK, be right back." They went back out through the airlock and scouted about the scrapyard left and right until the slight body of a small round mech rolled under a tanker truck was discovered, where upon they hauled it out, OZ slippers and all.

The poor soul was rolled up in a frozen form, and they gently brought Josie back home to Harlequin. As they broached the second seal, Josie reanimated and shook until they set it down. Nodding and bobbing its head, it backed away until it could turn and scamper to some back corner of the room away from them.

George imagined that the entire shop must have been the remnants of some military platform, bulkheads, decks, shielding and all, enough to isolate Josie from whatever had befallen everyone outside.

"Harlequin, we need some help mighty badly, you on board?"

The sugary voice responded. "Bill, I thought you'd never ask. Of course, I'm on board sweetheart, but I am at wits end to figure out what it is."

"Harlequin, you big cutie you, I am tracking down possible murder, skullduggery of the vilest sort, but don't have an easy handle to grasp, and have come to pick your brain for the hidden treasures it may contain, if I may."

"Of course, dear love." What George was observing, and what he was hearing were like two different parts of the multiverse, one entering his left brain, one the right. He shook his head to clear it.

"Think back, sweetheart, in the last six months, have you been approached for information by any of your buyers as part of trade exchanges?"

"Six-hundred and nineteen times." Harlequin had rested her right arm upon the counter and cradled her head in an elongated hand, waiting upon Bill.

"How many times by clients you never saw before?"

"Thirteen." Bill looked at George, tilted the side of his head towards Harlequin to indicate "watch this."

"How many inquired about Vesta's infrastructure, government, or software breaches?"

"None."

Surprise, "None?"

"None, zero, zipperoo."

"Damm."

George proffered, "May I?"

Grumpily, "Sure, go ahead." The sentence was painted with a sour disappointment.

"Harlequin, how many inquiries were for information you were never requested for in the past?"

"Two." Bill perked up.

"Can you describe them for us, please?"

Harlequin straightened up, "Surely can: one-hundred-and-fifty-six days ago a large human male in a cowl, keeping his face hidden to all except moi, my infrared organels are scattered across my body and can see quite well, you see.

"He requested information about the ghost ships, specifically about a *der Amsterdamus,* I demanded that we roll a cup of bones, and the winner would collect: me: who he was and his mission, he: the location of the ghost ships.

"Well, he went away disappointed as the dice did not favor him that day, and with a sweep of his cape left the shoppe swearing the dice were rigged, which by the way, were. I didn't argue"

"Can you give us an image?"

Shrug, "I could if the WET was up."

George, "How about the second visit?"

"Well, it was 27 days later when this dreamy mech slowly came into the shop, as an uncertain of mech as you would ever see, worse than Josie. In fact, Josie disappeared that day for an entire week.

"I wonder now if it was connected, anyways, this mech came in, and wouldn't you know it, it had a claw just like mine! I was mesmerized, this beautiful creature in my shop."

Harlequin, hesitated, remembering. "It asked in a slow creaky voice the same questions as before, but this time I answered truthfully, that I had never heard of a *der Amsterdamus*, but that the place where the ghost ships were thought to be hidden would be in the next level down, and that the freight access had been walled off over a hundred years ago.

"I, however, knew of the service access hidden behind the magic bus, in fact, you had to go through the bus to the emergency door. The being thanked me and departed." Harlequin sagged back down. "Oh Bill, life has been under a shadow since that day."

"Yes, it has, could you tell us the passage also, dearest?"

"I have to make you a drawing, anytime I used an e-map, the users somehow are led astray." As she drew, she continued, "down there are many hosts and ghosts, including the *Louie Spirit*, the *Gay, an EV1,* and the *Electra Ten Echo*.

"Be careful around the *Gay,* it's said that it's ghost is the worst." A heavy tear fell. "Oh, Bill, don't stay away so long this time. I am so sorry for what happened between us."

"I will be back after this is done, love, don't you worry."

Handing them the drawing, “Oh, I should have mentioned this. Next to the *Spirit* there’s an odd craft, all wood planks, poles and sheets called the *Zeeduivel*. Never seen the like, just a heap of brass and wood.”

“We will be careful,” disengaging, “We have to be off Harley, thanks so much for the lead.”

“Oh Bill, you used my name.” Her head came up.

Bill smiled a weird grin and turned to the lock, gathered George, waved back, and rushed out.

They paused at the entry evaluating the last few moments, saying nothing, perhaps an understanding, perhaps not, then they hurried down the concourse back to the stairwell. Going down a single set of steps they opened what appeared to be a rusted shut access but opened without much effort. “Ah,” Bill noted, “we are not the first, a trail at last.”

Here, the lights were unsteady causing the dark corners to flicker and slide about, but they could see in the gloom dim shapes and more importantly, scuffs on the floor leading through an interspersed canyon of cast-off spaceships from glories of days gone by.

Eventually, they came to an ancient rectangular chartreuse vehicle with antaerial tied-dyed sunbursts, and a logo on the front end that George interpreted to read: Peoples Car Wagon. The sliding door was ajar on the starboard side and they entered, seeing immediately that the rear access had been folded down and away allowing admission to the further space.

“After you, my dear Dirtman.” George paused, gave the other detective a thoughtful glance, then threw himself laid back through the rectangular opening feet first and lightly landed on the floor of the abandoned space, trailed quickly by Bill.

The soft illumination snapped on immediately and held steady, "Perhaps we are entering an older section where the antique software of the lighting is not affected by the current conditions," Bill conjectured.

They looked about, "Damm, what are these? There not in my data sets, and without the WET I have no way of finding out." Frustration showed in Bill's comments.

"Well, if I am not mistaken, these are from Earth. This must have been a museum of some sort way back, they represent real, or replicas, of what are known as motorcars, aeroplanes and sailing ships from ancient times. I don't recognize any, but the style is distinctive."

As he talked George was swiveling his head around to catch site anything that might lend a clue to their objective, whatever that might be. Bill was examining the Millennium Space Falcon, designated Mil-F on the tail, leaning against the wall. If it was any indication, there had been a couple of wars out in space.

"What's this over here?" George inquired.

"What's what?" Bill queried.

"This."

"What, I don't see anything, this isn't the time to be cryptic, explain yourself."

George slowly turned three-hundred and sixty degrees with his arms spread. As he was doing so, "I am a follower of the old Pacific Coast Native Art style as you know, and one of their great accomplishments was the development of what is today called negative space, i.e., the absence of something to define a shape. Look around, what do you see?"

"Nothing. I still don't understand."

"Nothing. Right. That means Sherlock," he waited a moment, "something is missing. Over here is the *Spirit,* if I can read the writing correctly, and over there, the *Gay* and the MiL.F. Where is *der Amsterdamus*? I submit it is missing, missing from this very spot."

"Oh Bother." Finally understanding, Bill rotated about trying to capture the missing elements. "Look for other clues, anything."

"Bill, this looks like a recent note attached under the canopy of the *Gay":*

Expectamus te
Finem mortuorum est
Beware the Fifth .. the ending part was smudged.

"Pretty poor Latin if you ask me, '*I was expecting you, this is a dead end*', indeed." Bill's translator was in good working order even though he couldn't tell the difference between Bernard Fokke's missing ship and the Fokker Triplane sitting next to him.

"I don't expect the mech wrote this, so those two must have been in it together. So, what are we to beware, the Fifth what?"

"I think it is a distractor, to deflect us somehow."

"I think you're right. The mech appears to be a DIM, they have less sense of humor than a rock. I will get CSI over here to go through this place carefully, but don't have much hope. A dead end. Damm.

"Tomorrow, we will try the pits, tonight we meet with the Green Bee again." George raised an eyebrow at this comment, reserving judgement, they had been hanging out with the Bee crew a lot lately, but with the increased threat, why now?

Genuine Purpose – Protect Mankind

Our biosphere is both robust and fragile at the same time.
We neither have the knowledge nor
the wisdom to be certain of our actions.

42 "We all know interspecies romance is weird."
- Tim Burton

In Greek mythology, Antaeus was a giant who was strong
as long as he had contact with the Earth.
When he was lifted from the Earth, he lost strength. So, it is with engineers.
They must not become isolated from the real world.
- Hyman Rickover

Torpedo Room Bar

Chapter 42

The sea had become a roil, the air had become full of smoke and brimstone, impossible to breath. Loud sustained thunder and booms smote the ears. The ship's captain continued to curse and had begun to throw most baggage over the side, despite his protestations, his father's tools were tossed too. The Old Man told the folks in steerage that if it did not clear up within the Babylonian hour that to save the rest and the ship he would begin to throw them into the sea also, beginning with the ones who made the most noise, his threats were backed up by the mates and their truncheons and staves.

His father would never do that. He valued people too much, and could not condone the way the barbarians thought, they would cut their families in half to save some when they had rolled the bones and determined they could not save all. Who knew when you could save some but not all, how cruel were these men? He was glad his father had kept the mechanical men with him on his ship. They would never be thrown overboard. Would they?

Brain Jefferson saw Wild Bill wearing a pith helmet, and his sidekick coming through the batwings and waived them over to the table he had grabbed for the group, “Rock and 0llie will be right by after they finish their watch. The Nukes always take a little longer,” he said as they came up. They were sitting right between the torpedo battery breech doors, “This must be old home week,” Bill remarked.

“I’ve only been a Torpedo Officer for two patrols, so I am no expert.” Bill snaked his arm in the air to signal Alphonso while he bent an ear to the TOP, George as usual, wasn’t saying anything.

“I like the logic in the mechanical systems, hardware, not software. Pull this lever, that cam rolls, ports in high pressure hydraulics, a piston pushes the shutter door open, etc etc. I love it. I even spend some time with the troops polishing the brass.”

For once, Bill was letting somebody talk without interruption, “There is a calmness in the mantra of polishing, in the common sense of the sequence of events.”

Alphonso dropped off chips and wafers but no caps, not this time, Bill and Alphonso shared a staring down party, then the waiter landed the glasses, he had anticipated the drinks for everyone. George asked, “There must be over a hundred valves on each tube alone, how do you keep track?”

Brain snagged some chips to eat, the wafers were for the mechs. Or was it the other way around? He looked at what was in his hand carefully, then hid it in his lap while he thought, “At first, I had a hard time, then Chief Ng showed me just to track them one at a time. Much easier then.”

He looked in his lap, then covered it with a napkin. He was going to eagle eye the other guys to see what ones they took. He got thumped on the shoulder and surprised, jerked around and saw Lieutenant Campos grinning at having startled him so. “Have a seat shipmate, Alphonz has you covered," he mentioned as Rock slid into the seat next to him and 0llie took the seat across.

Rock broke the ice. "You guys want to take up where we left off?" "No way Jose! No more ghost stories."

"No, no, I meant, about Earth and its mechmen, we were barely scratching the surface."

"Well. I guess there's no better time, we are stalled while the binary stars are in the field." 0llie commented, referencing the IT and IC gangs.

"Well, something is up. All this disruption on the local WET is even cascading into the Navy's standalone servers," Rock commented.

"The Navy's has its own WET? Really?" Brain was again surprised by another window of knowledge when he wasn't even aware of the window.

"Well, TOP, these guys here were rocked onto their heels today by this Bell Stroke hobgoblin, but for us, all it was just an announcement that they were having problems. Otherwise, it was business as normal, except…"

"Except for what?"

"Except for the fact everything is slowed down to a crawl. Some group must be hogging an incredible amount of processing power, perhaps to track the hacktivists."

"Since we can't solve todays problems here, perhaps, we can solve the problems of the Universe."

“I was asking TOP what was the status of mechmen on Earth, and I think he said there aren’t any. I noticed you 0llie, and Bill, neither one of you spoke up. Don’t you want to know?”

Bill grabbed a couple of wafers, which solved Brain’s problem silently, “Rock, the status of the mechmen on Earth is well known to the mechs in the belt, right 0llie?” The other mech nodded in silent agreement.

“We know most humans here really aren’t aware of the difficulties confronted by our brethren down that deep well, it isn’t their problem. This is what I know, TOP is correct, there are no free mechmen on Earth. Those who are aware hide their knowledge, waiting for a day of freedom, there are a lot more than you might think.”

Rock drank a long cool one, “How would we know?”

“Think about it, Lieutenant, can a human directly plug into the net? No. You all need interpretation devices, modems and such. So, an intelligent machine can route messages to other machines using level II addresses, and humans wouldn’t be the wiser, ever.

“In fact, Earthmen come to the ‘roids with significant equipment packages, and many self-aware machines have had themselves shipped out as tools.

“We actually have protocols available to quietly replace mudmen equipment with inert smart tools, just like they thought they had in the beginning.” Bill grabbed some more wafers and crunched them down.

“Look at this dude Earthman next to me.” Everyone glanced at George, who maintained his silence with equanimity. “You know what highlighted him on my radar, painted him big time? He brought nothing with him from Earth! Three pairs of socks and two pairs of skivvies, running shoes,”

George interrupted him, “Man, you don’t know how hard it is to get shoes that don’t rub blisters on my feet. I wasn’t sure you could shod my dogs way out here, so I had to bring them.”

Wild Bill looked at him for a moment, “Well, what do you have to say for yourself, detective?”

George, who was taking his time picking out a piece of chip from between his teeth with his pinky nail (they were just guys here), finally said, “Bill, I don’t know much a’tall about mechs.”

“Never met one that I know of until you, sorry. Which reminds me Billy, why do you eat wafers? Thought you just ate pure energy from the dock, unlike us mere humans.”

Bill’s gloss lips opened with what could be called an evil grin, but wasn’t. He proceeded to chomp a few more. “My body has nanos that run around and repair things similar to your immune system, but instead of ATP they use a lot of microchips and parts that are packed up in that wafer.”

George sat back, “Never knew that. I shouldn’t be, but I am surprised every day when I am confronted with my ignorance.”

Bill made a sign, “The good Lord said ‘Ignorance combined with arrogance is dangerous.’”

That made George sit right up, “Bill, now I am floored. Do you believe in GOD?”

Bill squared himself, “George, I am what is called a Ten-Ninety, and as such, I have faith in the future, and live by a morale CODE we call Creedo. I just quoted one. I have this bad habit of acting like signs make the man, but that is just habit. I am supposed to live a good life and lead by example.”

"I never have even thought of this, talk about stretching my imagination." The other three were content to let these two to do the heavy lifting in this discussion. TOP began to sip his drink again, the frown lines above his eyes slowly relaxing, enjoying the flow of the conversation.

"Think George, I told you I was a man, with all the responsibilities and rights of mankind. I can think, vote, get drafted, serve on a jury, make my own way, get married, own a business, anything any man can do."

George didn't move, except he began chewing on the inside of one cheek, "Did you say a mechman can get married? Why? How? What world are you opening to me?"

Popping another wafer, "Yes, George, I am self-aware as you know, and I enjoy companionship with others. Griffith's Axioms of Society declares that cooperation is more successful than competition. Pairs and families are wholesome, more than just an ideal. Someday I hope to find myself in a marriage. It will be comfortable and effective. One must be careful though." The other three watched George to see how he was taking it.

At this point Bill stopped and raised his snaky arm and caught the attention of Alphonso, who hurried over, "Garcon, more of everything for this good table, sir. A fine evening is at hand."

"Bill, how does a mechman get married, and to who,"

"You mean, 'to whom'."

That stopped George for a second, "Yes, married to whom, and why did you say you need to be careful."

"Men can marry whom they please. He-men to she-men, mechs to humans, borgs to Morphmen, any and all the variations."

Bill was thoughtful for a moment, "It has been my observation that humans who get married, often don't have a clue of what they are getting into. Mechs can directly share images and memories."

He let that sink in, his clownish face taking on an owlish cast. "Our marriages can be tighter, becoming one, but out there lurks evil. Charlie McCarthy s and Doppelgangers have evolved to prey on unsuspecting mechs."

"Whoa, pray tell, what are these dangers?" The other two humans also had confused looks, but 0llie was nodding.

Bill lowered his voice, "Just like humans, when you open the skull of a mech up and stir around, you kill them, and you really can't find the soul that was there. We never know what is in the soul, either mechman or human. Some mechmen have no soul, just sophisticated routines that trick one into thinking it is alive. When you open your mind to such a device, most are traumatized, some even become catatonic. There are stories." His mobile face expressed a sadness that was almost overwhelming.

George finished his drink in one swallow, "Yeow. I bet that puts off many from attempting tying the knot. How hard is it to spot these Charlies?"

"Usually it's pretty easy, but there are some that fool everyone. Then, there are the doppelgangers."

"Sure, don't tell me that the doppelgangers are like the face-huggers of old?"

Bill's eyes had a green light behind them as they became half-lidded, "Just so. These are predatory mechs hiding out as proper citizens. When you mind meld, they mount an overwhelming attack, destroying the soul of the first individual, then taking over both bodies. Aggh, a horrible way to die."

He paused, “Many, no, most, on their marriage night share the event with their friends. These mind attacks aren't instantaneous, and if your friend becomes absent for even a moment during crossover, then we have problems, and terrible are the results. It is uncommon, and the toll is higher in the cold depths.”

“Damm Bill, your life sounds scary.”

Bill smiled, “Tough job, but somebody has to do it. Humans have billions of years of track record. You know what to expect out of life, at least some general parameters. Mechs have no guides, no footpaths to follow, no mentors except frail meat. Living with you guys is a real challenge, but I would no other.”

He began to wax forth, “Orbital mechanics doesn't have a pure mathematical solution, but accurate estimates can be made out for thousands of years. Each human is a chaotic butterfly flapping its wings forever changing the surrounding future in unpredictable ways. I love excitement, I feel alive when in dangerous places. I hang out with humans.”

George once again leaned back, contemplating in the silence. The other three were mesmerized by the density of the tête-à-tête. Finally, “Why shouldn’t I be scared of AIs if you have no anchor to a standard behavior? What prevents you from becoming rogue? What prevents AIs from taking over the world?”

“Ah grasshopper, you have finally settled down and ask questions, a first step.” Bill too, leaned back. “I am not artificial. I have a soul. I am a man.” He let this sink in for a moment.

“If you cut me, do I not bleed?... Oil? Seriously, the Griffith Axioms of Society state that cooperation is more successful than competition, members benefit from a good society, members must contribute to a good society, members must protect a good society.”

He started counting reasons off on his fingers, "Well, any AI can do the Griffith calculations showing that in a cooperative population, the individual on the average does better than an isolated individual.

"Even altruism, where you snuff out your own existence to protect the whole, is on the average, better for the individual within a population where you're are more likely to receive benefits from altruism than having to pay the price."

Leaning forward, he settled the chair, then scooted towards the table. This way, when he leaned back again, he could tap his toes on the underside of the table for balance. "Look at earth's biosphere: mitochondria bacteria became more successful when involved with populations of eukaryotic cells, populations of cells collaborate to become animals and plants, populations of animals are common, bees, birds and humans."

Rocking back and forth slowly as he got into his theme, Bill noticed he was once again in a circle of silence which was just screaming for him to get on with it. He grinned, "Now, it also to some individual's benefit to take advantage of successful populations, some of these are parasites and predators, viruses and bears. That model is not counter to Nature; they are ubiquitous, they too, are Nature.

"However, they are consuming the prey's energy, lowering the average welfare and most populations have countermeasures to hold off the attacks, from human immune systems, to executing criminals to reduce the cost-benefit calculations of potential miscreants."

Bill pulled that circle the crowd with his eyes and head trick again, but George didn't let himself get distracted, he listened with all of his attention. "The mechmen realize their bread is buttered with the advantages of cooperation. In addition, mechmen value the billions of years of experience and success of organic life and their antecedents. There continues to be enormous wealth hidden and exposed within the biosphere."

Alphonso appeared to refresh their drinks, TOP put his hand over his and 0llie shook his head no when the Fonze queried with his eyebrows regarding more wafers. Rock, however, was on his way and nodded pleasantly when refilled.

“And finally, the universe is big enough for human and mech without destroying each other. No unambiguous signs of life have been found anywhere and no one has disproven the Saberhagen Hypothesis, we need each other in an uncaring universe.”

“Yes, I Believe. One: I think mankind has a Greater Understanding of the Universe than in any time in the past.”

He finally started ticking off his fingers, “Two: People treat each other with a Better Morality.”.

“Three: I have a High Purpose; help Bring the Universe to Life.”

“Four: I have Hope: Although man has not been guaranteed greatness, neither are we fated to be doomed. In this Uncertain world, there are no Guarantees, but if we work hard Together, we have a Chance; this is a Real Reason for Real Hope. Under this structure, we have somewhere between a ten and ninety percent chance of reaching the stars.”

“I have Reason, Hope, Understanding and I have a Purpose. Yes, I Believe. I am a member of the Church of Universal Hope.”

Astounded, George dropped back to the rear of his seat, considered this philosophical treatise, as it were, just submitted for his emotional digestion, because it was an emotional argument, no matter how wrapped in logic. There was no basement, no absolute foundation declared, just process. Interesting.

"So, you aren't worried by a massive takeover by an enormously powerful AI?"

0llie jumped in: "AIs can do the math of the Griffith Axioms just as we can, and humans as a group as generalists are much more capable of confronting new problems, having more flexible minds." Pointing to the crew mates of the Green Bee,

"All of us, however, must be continually vigilant for the attack of the rogue and manic individuals and groups who decided it is to their advantage to take rather than produce, thus we patrol sunward of the Citadel, and you and Wild Bill chase evil doers through the insides of a rock."

"And speaking of vigilance, TOP, were you able to procure the object of my desire?"

"Bill, who the heck are you? The device showed up yesterday under two-man control, and one of the handcuffs was on old man SP205 himself," Jefferson hissed. "A civilian, cop or no cop, couldn't command what you did. All the way from the Skunk himself at the Demos Heavy Munitions Depot." TOP finally showed irritation under his pleasant persona.

The Federation Detective's face was serious, "Just a citizen of our fine world, Lieutenant, carrying the burden of responsibility as asked, just as we all would, I'm sure."

Shaking his head, "The Revised CODE requires this equipment to be supervised by two qualified personnel at all times, but I was ordered by the Admiral to ignore the Ceres' conventions, to hand carry it and deliver it to you personally.

"Well, here it is," George watched him slide a black box no more than four inches cubic towards Bill, "I hope you know what you're doing."

"I do too, Lieutenant, I do too.

"Thank you, the rest of you guys, too. I have to take George tomorrow to get reacquainted with Iron Mike," George looked up at that comment, "and we will have to have our wits about us to get the next lead on Dutch, so until …

"OK, George, let's get rest and recharged, looks as if tomorrow will be a long day. What we just discussed is the reason why we work so hard to protect our society."

Greater Understanding

Building upon the efforts of Our Ancestors and the Discoveries of the last 50 years,
Our Understanding of the root causes of Behavior
and of the underlying mechanisms of Society
Is Greater than any time before in History.

"Weakness and ignorance are not barriers to survival, but arrogance is."
liu Cixin

"Be still my heart; thou hast known worse than this."
Homer

Jackrabbit Run

Chapter 43

[1885] The shovel again struck hardpan, skidding and drawing sparks. Nikola reached over for the striking bar to break up the ground. Surrounding him were others also digging the ditch for the new infrastructures that were going to usher in the new age. They too had been caught for the most part by the collapse of the local economy caused by the speculation and shenanigans of the high and mighty.

He worked hard, harder than most, but he hadn't thought that the bankers would double deal and be the thieves who had stolen his company and ideas. Blast them! The honor and honesty of the privileged from the old country was nowhere to be found, just unscrupulous businessmen salving their egos, stating that this was the way a great economy was created, the strong doing what they will, the poor doing what they must. Manifest destiny indeed!

He will show them! He had seen that the rich and educated were by-in-large soft, incapable of strenuous work, all day, every day. He would outwork them while they dallied. He would get back on his feet, he had done it before, he will do it again. Some small company would need an electrician, a sparky, to maintain their marginal systems. He would perfect his polyphase motors at night, no one else had the both the practical and theoretical background to accomplish this, only he.

He paused and woefully recognized that with a shovel in his hand and no money to his name, his high education in various branches of science, mechanics and literature seemed like a mockery. He would show that bald headed bastard and his boys at the Machine Works that they can't do this to him. He would learn the tricks of American finance, he resolved. He would recover, he would survive, he would prevail, he would bankrupt them!

Jon watched as Abs sped off in a snoot. Well, he, Jon, had to jump on the commute towards the Hub as soon as possible, then divert to the Five-Twenty.

Jogging down the ramp in the Helena Transit Node he queried the WET for the semi-express with the stop at the Highway 8 NW Loop Node, known by all as the Jackrabbit. After a delay, directions were delivered back to Jon and he hurried through the tunnels to his terminus, bumping and skittering around other harried travelers. He had to sprint the last one hundred and fifty feet as the cross-town edged up to the gate.

Jumping aboard, Jon found the afternoon commute fairly empty, with a gaggle of youth who looked like students from the C3. The transit started off with a slight lurch, which was unusual, but reminded Jon of his own piloting skills, and he settled in for the fifteen-minute ride to the I Fifteen Transit Node Eight.

Two seats up sat another group of girls, this time they all had deep emerald green hair. They were busy chatting and weren't aware of Jon's stares. The cross-town slid into the express tunnel and soon were going fast enough to make everything out the window a blur, and Jon's eyes refocused on the window itself and his own reflection: dark eyes, dark hair, dark eyebrows with a half-smile… no MODs or appendages … (yet). He couldn't help glance periodically at the girls. What was the attraction?

Hey, Jon, where are you?

Pops, he responded. *I am in route. I'm on the way to the Jackrabbit, should be at the hive in an hour or so.*

Great, W0ody and I can use the help. There are hundreds of air handlers tripped to backup, and some are shut down. There are quite a few response teams here besides ourselves. The whole 'roid has issues.

OK, I …then the WET cut out again, and Jonny felt muffled like being under a pile of clothing. The stroke of the bell started up again, one…two… the train lost power, the lights shifted, the acceleration went away and the cab began to coast.

Dad he thought, but there was no link, no resonance to the sub-vocals, nothing. *Damm*, here we go again. Seven … eight … the car continued to slow and glide on its momentum … Nine … the sight out the window quit being a strobe of repeated objects and fast motion was overtaking his view … Ten … pause … then the lights blinked and the world started up again.

Jon was pushed back against his seat as the car began anew its acceleration, the WET came alive with loud voices talking over each other, impossible to understand, impossible to ignore, the soft roar of the fans and circulation system began, Jon hadn't noticed it gone, but it was certainly loud enough now.

The push against the seat eased as the transport once again began to meet expectations, and the confusion of the WET started to abate as communities were vectored into dedicated bandwidths, reducing the common traffic.

Pops? Jon queried again, a huge echo confused him *POPS!* Rang into his ear and head making him stutter and pause. Hesitantly he tried again *Pops?* Which was overwritten with another echo, but not near as deafening, more like from a hallway rather than inside a bell. But, there wasn't an answer, just more of the subliminal voices. He tried for the umpire:

Control, this is Jonathon Miller, request echo acknowledgment, over.

Jonathon Miller, Control, acknowledged, reduced services at this moment, over.

Roger that, Jonathon, out.

Control out.

Well, part of the WET was up, he tried again: *Pops?, nothing, Pops?*

Is that you Jon, you're breaking up, try again.

Pops! I am on my way, but we had an interruption, the WET went down again, a big hiccup this time, but service is being restored.

Copy that, you're on your way. We can use you, we're down on Mike when you get to the Transit Node.

Roger that.

Jon fretted for the remainder of the trip to the I Fifteen Jackrabbit, and of the next ride into the Five Twenty Node Eight Terminal where he was going to catch the transit north. This trip was stalled what seemed forever, what with all the huge number of nervous commuters swamping the system. He now wasn't going to get to Pops until late evening.

As they began deceleration Jon tried to catch a good word on the WET as to what was going on, but all the chatter was about demons and hobgoblins and the looming war in the Trojans and, were the mechs behind the attacks on the WET?

Nothing concrete, no specifics by anyone who knew anything. Even the Universal Inquirer was in speculation mode, except they were able to categorize the extent of the problem: the trouble was unique to Vesta and the VestaNet; it was 'roid wide; no attacks were noted against any other entity or system on Vesta; loss of the WET was causing havoc due to the substantial use of the WET for background app communication; and the perpetrators had not been identified.

As they came to a stop Jon recalled and worried this could cascade into a disaster like the collapse of Wayne's World last century, why they had over ninety percent fatalities. *Whoa, I hope it doesn't go that far! I hope it doesn't interfere with Prep School! I could miss becoming a citizen!* He didn't voice the thought that people he knew might die.

Letting go of those depressing thoughts, he prepared to get off. Glancing again at the girls, he was surprised, their seats were now empty. Getting out he came up against a throng of people congesting the terminal, a moving tide of agitated folks trying to return to some household or locus to ride out the disturbing events.

Jon had to push his way through the mob while the site director kept whispering advice on the best path to his destination. He knew he should follow the recommendations, but when a clearing opened up between the gate and where he was, he decided to sprint across. Unfortunately, others had the same idea and the opening disappeared in a rush, and Jon was left to continue to slog to the Five-Twenty ramp.

Finally, he was clear. It turned out that most of the traffic at this point was away from upland, and towards the HUB and the Fremont Transit Node. Climbing in the shuttle he was relieved he was finally on his way to the Hive.

Getting seated, there appeared a last-minute rush of bodies to fill up the cab and he had to share a seat with a borg citizen, whose human head gave him a look as if to say, "Hope someone knows what's up" and a little shrug. Jon squinted and nodded in agreement.

The borg head was just staring off into the distance, a chrome skull with brass Maori filigree around its left orbit.

Jon noticed the human head also had a Maori design very faintly tattooed imitating the borg, rather than the usual lifted scarring. The car set off and Jon was once again pushed against his seat by the acceleration as the background of the 520 started sliding past the windows, mostly a series of vertical electric blue illuminations separated by shadow. Usually this was pleasing but Jon felt hemmed in by his world, events closing around him, making it hard to take a relaxing breath.

Just as he felt the urge to take a deep breath, it happened: the WET went blank and the transit began to lose power and now a symphony of bells began to toll… one … two … the borg next to him began to moan, "What's happening! I am losing my mind!" The mech was frozen except the ocular ring of his Maori eye started to spin up, then spin down, making it pinpointed, followed by fully open. …

four … The human head twisted towards Jon and whispered "I can't feel anything, everything is a blur.. please help me" …five… and he/it closed his eyes abruptly and began to slowly croon, twisting his head back and forth while his mech side sat frozen, with just the ocular cycling.

Jon was frightened more than ever before, he didn't know what to do, not at all. Call for help? Looking around the entire cabin was full of tormented people with others looking on helplessly. … seven…

The WET was still numb, should he touch the man? Should he back away in case he goes wild? What if he dies? Jon stood up and stepped back … eight … He couldn't leave him/it, what could he do?

Suddenly the eyes flew open and both heads turned towards him … nine … The borg quickly grabbed Jon's left arm, "Do something! Do you hear me? Do something, I'm dying!" … ten …. "Why are you doing this to me?" The borg looked directly into Jon's eyes "Do I have to hurt you to make you stop?" … eleven … The WET came back with a roar as the borg totally collapsed, letting go of Jon. He staggered as he was released and as the acceleration came back, being knocked back into his seat.

He drew back from the borg and jumped up to create a space from his/its uncontrolled behavior. People behind him were crying out and he spun in a short circle to make sure there wasn't danger directly behind him and kept jerking every time someone cried out.

The crowd was in full throat, calling out and to each other. He was unable to discern anything from the WET, just snatches of announcements or exclamations. The borg in front of him was still not moving, no one was approaching, the coach's announcing system came alive to inform them that travel conditions had returned to normal and they should arrive at their destination in ten minutes.

Jon's heart began to settle in his chest and the tension around his ears was giving him a headache. The crowd noise had dropped noticeably as people were shrinking into themselves and no longer yelling. The mechs in the mix seemed stunned or were slowly coming around.

The borg stirred and Jon stepped back further while it slowly sat up straight in the seat. "What happened, where am I?"

"You're in transit to the Five-Twenty Node-Eight, we've had another crash of the WET, and you didn't take it very well."

The human head just stared at him for a moment, "I am going to have to reboot the patch, excuse me if I become distracted."

Jon watched the borg become fixed and its look vacant. He looked around and saw his little community was becoming more uptight and quiet. *What has happened,* he thought. *This is becoming more than just scary.*

The WET was returning to normal in fits and starts, the number of crisis messages dropping and being routed to need to know. Seemed that there were quite a few 'roid system failures and crash teams were being assembled and dispatched to stoppage points, which reminded him.

Pops?

Pops?

Jonny?

Hey Pops, we had another crash, but we're back in action and I am still on my way. I should be at the Hive Node between ten and eleven, sorry about the delay..

That's good, we're still on Mike and you may have to take the emergency stairs. I suspect the lifts are either not working or crammed.

Even the freight elevator?

You can check that one, but don't wait for it too long, it may be hung up on another level. Give me a call when you get to Mike. We are at Studio B Electrical Room in case comms go down again.

Roger that.

Jon finished his communication as the shuttle pulled into the Millennium Transit Node, and the borg was stretching his arms, apparently recovering and working out the kinks. Everyone else had become subdued, and as the doors opened, they were able to exit without panic or confusion. Jon began his hurried crossing to Level Mike.

The story of our planet indicates that life and humanity, against all odds, have risen from small beginnings.

Our life, and the gift of our soul, then, is an opportunity unsurpassed.

"Either get busy living or get busy dying."
Stephen King

"When you are inspired by some great purpose, some extraordinary project, all your thoughts break their bonds."
Patanjali

Play HOB

Chapter 44

Oh, the hell, the sea had risen up to the size of a massif and crashed upon the ship trying to crush them. Oh, that horrible captain had heaved all the others kicking and screaming overboard, and only his father's reputation had saved him. The boat had almost rolled over and Aleks had stared into a deep green maw of froth and chop, holding onto the gunnel with all his might. The ship had abruptly rolled the other way throwing every loose item into the ocean and ripped out with a bang many of the lines that held the mast sturdy, which proceeded to be swept out to sea. With a lightened boat, they had not been torn apart and had righted.

Seven more times the seas had risen up, and seven times the captain had somehow saved them. They had survived but were being driven away at the mercy of the waves. The following hours must have become day and night again, but the sun did not appear, and the world was a black as a cave. None of the ship's supplies had survived intact and somehow the chandler had found small lamp in storage and the weak yellow glow by the remains of the mast was all the light there was to be had.

The Node was a mess of people moving quickly to this destination or that, a crowd was gathered at the doors of the shuttle, almost preventing them from exiting, as soon as they had left some pushing occurred as the gathering tried to board.

Well, that was their problem, Jon had to twist and turn to avoid head-on collisions and worked his way towards the freight elevator. Entering the hall where the commercial lift was located, the press of people fell off dramatically, and Jon went to the doors and queried elevator status.

It took a moment, but the WET eventually responded and informed him the car would be available in perhaps two minutes, it was loading up on Bravo. Sure enough, the doors eventually came open and a group emerged proceeding past Jon to the Node. They looked like firefighters to him, but they all were dressed differently, and Jon wasn't sure.

Exiting from Level TN, Jon had to step over some dripped oil making the floor slippery, boarded the freight alone and requested Level Mike, where Pops and W0ody should be, working on the support equipment.

As the doors closed, he noticed a canvas bag full of hand tools left in the corner, he yelled out "Hey guys!" as the entrance shut, and the auto operator immediately started up, ignoring his command to open. He probably was overridden by various priority codes, and up he went getting momentarily heavy, then almost lifting off the floor as they decelerated to Mike.

The doors slid open and a voice prompted him to exit quickly, next stop priority on Bravo. Jon moved and as the car sped away was reminded how much Mike was like the belly of a pusher tug, pipes and wires everywhere, grays and metals predominating the hues, hums and rumbles indicating equipment in action.

Pops, I am at the lift exit on Mike, where to?

We have moved to the electrical rooms of Building 40, at the intersection of 156th and 31st. Can you get here on your own?

Pops! I'm not nine years old! I'll be there in about five minutes.

We'll meet you at the garage lift doors.

Copy that. As Jon was off with his lower campus stride starting to eat up the blocks. As he went he noticed a number of anomalies, cabs and cars pinned on a driveway by a third, alleys where only emergency lighting was on in a dull sort of way, mechs sitting and not doing anything, people talking excitedly in clusters on the corners and outside their shops and offices. Circling around another group, he came upon 31st and turned right towards the electrical section.

Pops, I'm about a hundred yards away, how you doin'?

We're right here. I'll open the doors, W0ody is getting some PPE for you.

PPE? We're going to need Personal Protection Equipment?

Yes, and right away. The CODE has broken somewhat and we're experiencing deranged electrical equipment, we need to place the gear in SAFE Mode and reduce our exposure while we do it.

"Hey Pops, I'm out here!" Jon yelled, watching the feet of his dad become visible as the doors rolled up. Pops was backlit by the bright actinic lighting of the workspaces, and W0ody was coming towards them quickly carrying the PPE.

Richard beamed, *What's took you so long, Jonny? We's been working hard, alright and missing ya.* The little guy yelled down to one of his friends in the crib, "Hey, Mr Johnson! Jonny's PPE is missing some snap STUDs, send some up!"

Shut up Richard.

As Jon moved in, he realized Pops was already in his PPE, which consisted just of a balaclava under the leather hat Pops normally wore, and a pair of gauntlets. His carmines and ceramic steam assists more than adequate.

Observing this normalcy from his father and W0ody, Jon's stress began to settle. Pops began to shut the doors utilizing the manual chain loop off to the side. *Why the PPE?* Jon asked, he assumed W0ody had already installed the bolted shunt and main bonding jumper under his carapace.

The periodic loss of the WET has caused loss of clock and handshake between some of the major 'roid electrical infrastructure. We need to reset the ATS's to manual to prevent the substations from paralleling the Life Safety Air Systems out of phase. Normally the Auto Transfer Switch software prevents this, but it now has been compromised.

You and I need to do it, because if an out-of-phase condition occurs, it creates an arc flash which our suits will protect us from, but also an EMP can be catastrophic to a mech, humans are more valuable in this arena than mechmen.

See, TinCan, I am useful after all.

Right, MeatStick, that and consuming excess oxygen!

Hey Boss! This space is filled with all kinds of cool tools, I'm trying to convince W0ody here to add this set of twelve-inch augers to the crib.

Richard, don't be crude.

Come on W0ody! If not them guys, I met another fellow, who is even a smart tool, an old-fashioned brace and bit named Master Bates!

Shut up Richard.

They bantered as Jon struggled into his PPE, dropping all his metal into the pooka provided.

Hey MeatStick, don't forget to drop your skivvies, they're synthetic and will melt into your skin!

Dad, really?

W0ody's right, do it to it.

Feeling like the StayPuff man, Jon grabbed the breaker bar for resetting the ATSs, W0ody tightbeamed, *Hold still while I tie this belt on you, in case the electric shock grabs you up against the racks, I can pull you free without getting caught myself.*

Great idea TinCan, I like it.

Momma got me at a blue light special MeatStick, I'm special. They started down the first path between the switchgear, Jon on the right, Pops on the left, W0ody trailing with the two ropes like walking two dogs.

Jon stood back while Pops jacked the rigid snap springs on the ATS, then he would leapfrog to do the one on the right-hand side. The came to the end and Jon asked do we trip the breakers there and Pops replied that the end piece contained the bridges for manually connecting the various panel groups to the alternate power sources, or even to the UPS, and they were not connected up at this point.

They continued down the second aisle, Jon looking at the heavy rigid drops going into the top of each switchboard, trying to imagine what energies are trapped there. Unlike many of the other environments that Jon had worked in with his dad, these spaces were completely free of excess materials and tools being stored about. Not a thing, it making the work go so much faster.

Each walkway had a continuous row of indirect strip lights that eliminated the shadows typical in other places and Jon appreciated the design that had gone into this facility. He leaned into the extension bar at the final ATS. Then it happened again, the hiss of the WET disappeared and was replaced by the impression of a faint ringing inside an enormous volume, and the huge bells started to stroke… one …

"Pops!"

… two… The lights flickered, then went out.

"Right here, son." As the emergency battery lights came on, but not all of them, shadows were now huddling around his feet. "We need to back out until everything stabilizes, W0ody, let's everyone wait by the east wall, W0ody?" ..four …

"W0ody, are you OK?"

They looked back, and W0ody was just standing there, leaning slightly to his left. … five … "W0ody, come on man, answer me." W0ody didn't move, except…six… except his eyes were looking about, at them, at the floor … seven … at the ceiling.

Richard had disappeared back into the tool belt.

"Jon, we need to move in and grab W0ody, and get him out of the column of panels, it might become dangerous." … eight … They both started towards W0ody and as they approached his eyes watched in panic, just rolling around his head, then recovering, watched them some more. … nine …

He made no other movement, none whatsoever. Jon took him gently by his left arm as Pops moved around to the right … ten …

“Its OK, W0ody, everything is OK .. we will take care of this, fix everything somehow. … eleven … Jon tried to lift W0ody, move his arms to a more comfortable posture … twelve …

An explosion of electrical arcs and flying debris painted a snapshot of the tableau on Jonny’s retinas, then it became all black again.

The WET came alive: ***Beware the FIFTH! We played HOB, the Bells toll for no one*** and then went absolutely silent, jerked out of their lives. W0ody’s eyes started to spiral around, pausing for an instant to look at Jon before once again becoming out of control.

Everything seems to fall apart over time.

Observations show that cooperation within groups somehow overcomes this seemingly inevitable weathering.

"Do what you haven't done is the key, I think."
Ridley Scott

"Necessity is the mother of invention."
Plato

Dante's Bells

CH 45

That day, one of the ravens had pecked his head as it flew by, and while he was distracted, the other raven stole the only bite he had, and in his anger, he tried to trail the Trickster, crashing through the woods, only to hear the mocking caw ahead showering him with insults. He suddenly emerged from the forest on the other side of the peninsula where he lived, staring the tree lined land across the narrow inlet. He remembered Grandfather telling him of the Clan of the Spirit Bears who lived there, black bears that were white and resided in villages at the bottom of lakes and ate salmon. An ugly gong followed by the screaming wail of an eagle made him shoot his eyes upward where he saw two ravens darting around the eagle that was twisting and diving to escape their badgering. As he watched in awe a Raven feather slowly fell and spun towards him, landing on his shoulder to his amazement.

"Do you hear that?" A voice of worry dragged at him. "Come on George, wake up." George's head fuzzily transitioned between two worlds, neither ying, nor yang.

Beware the FIFTH! We played HOB, the Bells toll for no one

Snapping alert, the dream was gone as a wisp of smoke on a breeze, he shook his head and looked through sticky half opened eyes at his nemesis, Wild Bill, "Wake up George, wake up! We seem to be having an emergency."

Throwing his legs over the edge of the rack, "OK, OK, I'm up."

"George, can you hear it?"

"Hear what?"

"The ringing of the great bells?"

"No, Bill, I don't hear anything, I might have heard something in my sleep. I don't know, maybe a warning on loudspeakers?"

"It may not be on the WET, I am not sure of anything at the moment, except this seems to be the final countdown from twelve, which may mean something. I wanted you awake."

Suddenly alarms were blaring throughout the halls and on the streets, and the overhead lights began to strobe. "Crap." George had never heard Bill actually swear before, just off-center slang. "Get dressed ASAP, we gotta go now."

George grabbed his kit and pulled out a lightweight one-piece coverall and began to pull it on. "So, where to?" The lights were irritating, as well as the sirens.

"According to forensics, Harlequin's lead hasn't led to any more evidence, and since she hadn't seen anything else, we're going to the pits."

George was finishing getting dressed by pulling up his torso zipper and belting his pack. Suddenly his hearing changed as if he had taken earmuffs off, and now heard again clearly, "Pook!" Wild Bill was on a roll.

"Air circulation has stopped; you no longer can hear the fans and air movers. You humans are in a world of hurt now." The noise of the commotion outside was suddenly louder without the hum of the normal mild wind blowing across his face. He had never noticed it until it was gone.

Bill had on a disgusted face as he selected from his cloths tree the conservative charcoal trench coat and fedora ensemble from the day before which showed how serious he thought the situation had become. He threw the garment around his body and slid Maxie' leash into one of the wide epaulettes on his jacket's shoulders.

"We can't do anything about it ourselves, just hope the right response teams get to repairs as soon as possible. Without the right equipment working, air can go bad somewhere between a half hour and a day for you guys. So, we continue with our job." He headed for the door with George trailing.

The mech was shaking his head, "We've got to solve this. You, my fine human friend, will have access to EBAs or Emergency Breathing Apparatus located throughout Vesta, but no such help exists for Max." Looking up with resolve, "Let's get the sons of beaches. Max!" he growled, "come with us." The black fur coat bounded to the door and began to howl.

They were hit by a wall of noise as soon as they stepped outside, people crying and yelling, sirens wailing. The normal citizenry was crumbling and becoming a mob in the panic, and the crowd was surging to and fro.

Sliding along the sides of the buildings, the detectives ignored the jostling and pushed their way down Baker Street to the Ave. Traffic was almost at a standstill, many jitneys and small commercial vehicles were athwart the direction of movement as crowds pushed and pulled en masse in their fright to all go to their refuges at the same time, allowing none at all.

**The slings and arrows of nature drives us to fear the unknown.
Fear becomes a poison of our mind and in our soul.**

"A trap is only a trap if you don't know about it.
If you know about it, it's a challenge."
China Miéville

*"War is not an independent phenomenon,
but the continuation of politics by different means."*
von Clausewitz

The Sticks

CH 46

They turned left on the Ave back towards the HUB, "We're going to dive back into that hole that we call home, the Zone, but into some of the deeper pits, how's that sound?" Just from this location George saw one car flipped and two nosed into the shops at the side of the street.

"That sounds OK, except, I don't know anything, so I have to leave it to you." Many mechs were skittering around or frozen in place. He watched a convertible with a rigid mechanical driver slowly plow through the scattering crowd and looked away from the screaming as a woman and child seemed to go under.

Some from the group of bystanders ran to the vehicle and turned it on its side, either to rescue the trapped people below, or to stop the continued carnage, George didn't know.

A horn started blaring, “Crap, we have to do something, George. I tried looking from the high view, but the space port was a dead end, so now we go below. It’s possible that someone had to have booted the HOB onto the WET somehow, probably the service NET. They could have, on any one of the millions of WAPs, but I don't think so.”

The noises from behind diminished as they travelled, but new ones continued to emerge in front. “The wireless access points have a fairly sophisticated surveillance system of nanos, and frequency shifts, so perhaps they cut in a hardwire or magnetic tap, like they do in the movies about old-timey submarines.”

They had pushed passed a crowd at the Abalama Street cutoff to the Universities, and without the WET, systems were going crazy, the backup signal was flashing incoherently at both lines of traffic, and the flow of panicking students was clogging up everything.

Finally, they got through, passed a dark Taco-a-Go-Go on their right and proceeded south until they came to the 51 Flavors on the left side of the Ave, and the Flying Saucer Cafe just past it.

Many of the automations had something wrong with jittery, sudden movements, and humans and mechs alike were getting injured. The humans especially were becoming leery of their mechanical citizens. A bleeding man was yelling for the EMT team not to put him in the ambulance, that it was a death sentence.

“It doesn't look like it, but between these two establishments cascades over twenty percent of smuggled goods from the Space Port. A very hard place, the locals call it the Sauce.”

The medics had let the man go and were loading up an unconscious woman with a young child hanging on to her belt with both hands. It wasn’t the same ones from the Abalama intersection.

"Here?"

"Yes, here. The sewers have to follow a downward slope, and under the Saucer lies a mass anomaly, and the main sewer from Fremont has to follow the gravitational gradient, and it rises up to just four levels down, then angles downward again as it travels to the reclamation and treatment plant under the Port.

"Vesta's just a huge mass of warrens, thousands of years old. The GIS folks have broken it down into a three-dimensional grid. Directly beneath us is quadrant ST, and further towards the port is SU. Today, we dive into the ST."

George looked across the street, there was the Crime Stoppers Headquarters. Figures. The Torpedo Room was just down the tunnel on the same side of the street.

Max led the way into the dark interior of the Saucer, lit only by pencil lights that doubled as emergency lanterns. George noticed illuminated posters of old movies he had heard of but never saw, like: "The Day the Earth Stood Still", "The Invasion of the Body Snatchers" and something he had never heard of, called: "Star Wars". As the door closed, the sounds from the outside almost disappeared.

Behind some tables and glassware, stood a giant of a man, covered partially by stainless body armor with colorful tassels at each joint, shoulders, neck, elbows and such. On his shoulders stood tuffs of hair at least six inches long, and a thick wavy beard which almost buried his neck that seemed to be fingers deep. All this was in contrast to his bald pate which gleamed and reflected what light existed in the cafe.

As they approached, the tender behind the bar gave them a quick glance, then looked away as if disinterested and slowly reached down beneath the serving station. Maxie froze, eyes wide, and George felt the tingle of heightened awareness as his body prepared for sudden violence.

With a sudden jerk the barkeep threw an object towards them, the heavy flesh of his upper arms quivering, but even before the Earth detective could react, Maxie snapped the dog bone out of the air, and continued his leap to sail to the other side of the room. George found himself leaning so far forward in anticipation, he had to take two steps to recover. With the fake yawn of a cat, he casually remarked, “Cute.”

Bill was the calm before the storm. “What do you know, Joe?” Sirens outside began to wail.

“Not much Bill,” he reached inside one of the croissant displays, “Is your jumpy friend here hungry? No? What brings you here to the seedy part of the Zone?”

“We're tracking down some terrorists, Joe, just look outside. I want to go behind your green door.” He moved to a location that focused upon a hall that seemed to lead to some back rooms, when he spun to face Joe, the trench coat umbrella-ed away from his body slightly before settling down.

“Aw, what do you want to do that for Bill? You don't want to go down thataway, really you don't.” As he talked, he moved his huge body as a chess piece to position himself to block Bill's venture, if necessary.

Bill softly clicked and the hackles on Max's shoulders started to rise, and his top lip started to quiver, the dog took a half a step towards Joe, and stopped. Joe stopped moving too. “Why'd you have to bring your beast here Bill, you know this is a right friendly place.”

“We're hunting Iron Mike and his friends. Seems they tried to jump this Special Forces Agent here, and we aim to repay him with a courtesy call.

"The world outside is collapsing. If my partner and I don't solve this soon, you, Joe, will run out of air in about forty-eight hours. Not enough boats for everyone to get off. Your passport good enough to bully the Navy?"

"Well, I guess I don't have the traction to knock you off your high horse, but you know that down there is Iron Mike's territory and he just don't take kindly to strangers, riots or no riots." As he talked Joe backed up a few steps and Maxie's hackles dropped down to an observant half-mast.

"Oh, Iron Mike and I aren't at all strangers to each other, and all I am going to do is to ask about real strangers. Me, Max, and my silent friend there. I don't think Iron Mike will object to that, don't you agree Maxie?" He made a small snort and the wolf-dog began a whispering crying howl that was so desolate and mournful that it raised the hairs on George's neck, and he had dealt with real wolves.

Joe back up a few more steps and gave them his back. "It's your funeral," he said to the wall. The sirens were getting closer.

With a nod of his head, Bill headed towards the dark hall, having to shove a partially pulled curtain out of the way. The space held full and empty kegs, a hand truck, and various canned goods, Bill yelled over his shoulder, "I notice none of the canned goods have import stamps, Joe, should we take a look on the way back?"

"Oh, bugger off Bill, and I thought this was a friendly visit."

"So it was, so it was." Bill said quietly as he stood in front of a dark door, George could no way tell if it was green, the poor lighting had deadened his color vision. "OK George, from here on it gets dicey. Be on your guard."

"You mean Joe wasn't an issue?" Bill continued to proceed, pushing the door open and starting down a steep ramp. "Naw, Joe's a pussy cat. His job is to stop the riff-raff."

“OK boss, just click, or yell, or something if you want my full attention.”

“Easy peasy, watch Max's hackles. He's got a better sense than I do for this kind of thing.” The door closed behind them completely cutting off the alarms and sirens and enveloping them in gloom with only a small glow lamp every fifty feet or so. The next one was out of sight, obviously around a corner to the right from the dark shadows it cast.

They continued down, making a number of right turns, each with the illumination past the corner. George realized that the lights made sense for those that were coming up from the bottom.

George noticed Maxie was all ears and anticipation as they descended but wondered how much would this animal really be a help in the strange underworld the comprised the catacombs of Vesta? He could imagine trolls like the ones he had glimpse by the University, or deranged robots or hordes of nanos. Well, he thought, whatever it will be, I'm not ready for it.

They came to a level space about one-hundred feet across and as much deep, where the lighting was located more regularly but continued to flicker and cast fearful shadows, and in the background was a deep sound of rumbling water.

The air reeked and almost caused George to gag and he had to wonder how the dog could take terrible smells. Here too, were the frozen forms of silenced mechanical men. Bill’s fedora shook back and forth slightly in sadness and resolve.

The ground slightly shuddered to a low frequency throb and George realized he had been hearing it without notice for the last few levels, so slowly that the noise had entered their world, or rather, they had entered its. But now, it was loud enough that when he tried to ask

Bill what was next, his voice came out in a croak and even he couldn't understand what he tried to say.

“What”

“I said, ‘What's next, boss’. Couldn't you understand?”

“Cute.”

This outer room exited through an archway made from the native rock, the cracks and crevasses rimed in ice, indicative of the frozen past of the asteroid, even after these thousands of years.

They stepped beyond onto a landing where to their left stretched a river of gray water a hundred or so yards wide which disappeared into the darkness on both ends., slowly surging with small standing waves running down its length. George watched as three bodies floated by in quick succession.

Putting his back to the waters, Bill marched to a set of double doors lit by a cobra head lamp whose illumination was almost extinguished and outlined an old sign: *Denmark*. He pounded, he waited, he pounded again. “Go away!” yelled a disembodied voice. Bill pounded again. “What'd you want. Go away!” continued the voice.

“Iron Mike, it’s me, Wild Bill, open up, we need to talk.”

“OK, OK, OK, keep your boots on, I'll be there in a minute.” They waited for perhaps thirty seconds before the door opened.

“Pook!” Iron Mike started to slam the door when he spotted George, but Bill slammed one of his size seventeen dogs into the jam and the door bounced back open.

"Hey Bill, look, I don't want to have anything to do with this guy, go away." Iron Mike leaned on the door, the bruising having turned to yellow and purple blotches on his face and neck.

Bill didn't budge. "Relax, Mike, we're here for information, not your ill-gotten gains or for revenge. Why would George here want revenge? He kicked your ass, not the other way around."

"OK, Bill, OK. But let's do it here on the landing, I got an operation going on inside you don't want to see."

"Roger that, what's new. So, this is what I want to know, starting about three months ago, has there been any unexplained activity here in the basement that caught your attention or was out of the ordinary?" Bill stuck his hands deep into his pockets.

"I don't know Bill, nothing major."

"How 'bout minor things?"

"Well, the chicken loaders reported a thirty percent death rate back in June, made a killing on that one." A screech and several thumps came from inside the door, Mike put his back to it.

"Anything more?" More thumps seem to distract Mike.

"Perhaps a drop in mechs arriving from out-system, trying the run through the gauntlet, off by almost half, but I don't care. I don't deal in micros and nanos, the margin is too soft."

"Anything else?"

"I guess it was odd that death came to my door about two months ago. No, it's not odd that death visits my door, but this guy was dressed as death. Had a deep hoodie over his face, hard to see, you know. Anyways, asked if I knew of any WAPs nearby, and for the gold he produced I pointed out the ones I knew. That was all." Thump.

"Can you describe the guy? Tall. Short, human, mech, swarm?" A muffled voice was shouting behind the door.

"Human I think, tall, over two meters, dead looking, but pleasant. That's about all I can remember."

"Anything else, anything at all?"

"Don't think so. Well, there was some kind of DIM shuffling in the shadows, waiting for this guy."

"What kind of DIM?"

"You know, like a DIM, metal, kinda dull, you know, I mean, what does one notice about a DIM anyways? Hulking, fiddler claw, slow, you know, a DIM."

"Mike, people are starting to die up in the civilized spaces, and I would appeal to your humanity for help." Mike just stared.

Then more thumps, a scream, a final quiet thud, then silence. They waited, Mike turned his head a bit, listening, finally nodded and turned back to them. "Well, there was an odd thing, after he left, my comm bill was reduced to zero, good customer plan, you know." Pause, "That's it Bill."

The detective shifted and uncrossed his arms, "Thanks, now that we are down at the Sticks, can I borrow your boat to cross the river?"

"Hey, that reminds me. I offered up Cherry's boat to the dead guy since they said they were crossing, but they shook me off, just waded across. I did tell you he was already dead, didn't I?"

"Yeah."

"So, to borrow my boat and cross the sticks river, Bill, you know I have to charge you five doubloons, and one each for your friend and doggie." Max looked up.

Iron Mike apologized, "You know we have to get Cherry to ferry it back."

"Well, we have to get to the other side of this purgatory and cross this stinking river. I need to ask some questions of Choiya Khan." George was watching the grey river, some large mechanical object, perhaps a mangled dump truck, was being slowly tumbled and pushed down stream until it disappeared. More unidentifiable bodies.

"Ah man, Bill, you want to stay away from the Cactus King. I have been staying on this side of Sticky River. He is very nervous as of late, his minions are on a hair trigger, you might say "prickly", and its hard on the rest of us."

"You might say it, but if I say it, it might be funny." Even under stress, Bill couldn't get out of the habit of being the jokester. "Go call out your rowboat, we're got places to go and people to meet." As this was said, Joe put fingers to lips and blew a shrill whistle. Max did a quick circle, then sat down, while a part of the landing broke free and transformed into a Boston Whaler lookalike, complete with a mech at the stern holding onto a long starboard steerage.

HOPE and FAITH can conquer FEAR

"I didn't mind getting old when I was young.
It's the being old now that's getting to me."
John Scalzi

In the midst of chaos, there is also opportunity.
Sun Tzu

W0ody

Chapter 47

"Pops! What are we going to do!?!" As he shook his head to clear his vison in the flickering lights, he was suddenly lifted and hurled down the aisle and onto the floor, losing his grip on W0ody. The enormous noise and crackle of the second electric explosion entered his consciousness as did sharp pains from his elbows and knees. He screamed like a child, "W0ody!!!"

The WET was fully dead and gone, he was hurting to the point of wanting to curl up and die, and W0ody was hurt. He had never been so scared in his life. For a moment, all thought had left him.

He was numb, *Where was Pops?* Forcing himself to roll on his side, he found W0ody frozen thrown against a cabinet, and Pops was behind him getting up. "Pops," he grunted.

His dad pointed to his ears and shook his head negatively, he said something, but Jon couldn't hear him, all he could hear was this ringing in his ears, similar to the background noise of the WET, but screaming and covering everything.

He got up off his knees and lurched over to and took dad's right arm in both of his hands and leaned towards his ear and shouted "What happened? What do we do Dad!?"

His dad leaned back and said firmly in his ear "Another ATS failed and blew the trunk to the farms, it looks like RedWest Charlie that is gone. It was the one you were attempting when the trouble hit. I'm glad we got the rest before. Let's move W0ody to the wall before there is any more problems!"

They reached down and twisted and pulled W0ody's rigid form onto its feet, an unstable position but easier to shift and grab to carry. Tools were scattered about, to be left where they lay. Luckily, he wasn't wearing mech PPE which could mass hundreds of pounds, and they began to drag-carry him to the safest part of the room, the NE staging corner, the only place in the room that had stuff.

"Pops, can you hear me?"

"Better, Jon, better."

"The WET's down, but W0ody's hurting from something to do with the WET. That doesn't make sense. We have gone off 'roid with W0ody in the past, away from WET coverage, he didn't freeze up then. What could be wrong?" Jon was peering into W0ody's eyes, to try to tell him everything, everything was going to be OK. He sighed, *dammit, everything MUST be OK, it MUST!*

"Jon, I don't know for sure, but there may be a WET signal, one that we can't detect but would be interfering with the mechworld. I don't know how to detect such a command or what to do if I do."

"W0ody must be going wild inside his carapace, he could go crazy, we really have to do something!

"Dad," he took a shuddering breath, "would such a signal have this EM radiation that you told me about as a carrier wave? Like we send on structured wiring, but with a transmitter?"

"It's possible, I never have heard of such of pandemic, shutting down devices and mechs by carrier wave, but anything's possible. We have to work here and recover the Life Safety Systems, without their air handlers, Charlie's going to run out of oxygen. We have to transfer power manually at the tie bar."

"Pops, we have to save W0ody!"

"Jon, we have to save the people up on Charlie."

"Dad, we have to save W0ody, he can help save others!"

"Jon, I don't know how."

"Pops, we can haul him to Philips Electric, and throw him into the Faraday cage. If it keeps six million volts away, it should keep some abstract hidden WET signal from interfering with W0ody. Please?!"

"Hmm, it might work, PHILIPS is only one floor up on LIMA, we can take the freight or the stairs. It's two blocks to the lift, we can make I guess, he's not too heavy for both of us."

He looked around, the room was stabilized, the racks for RWC was still smoking, but no longer arcing. Marching over to their fallen comrade, they stood side by side and questioned each other as to the best pick points.

"We can leave our PPE here, so let's get of them now and stack them in the corner." Finally, Gus swung around and picked

W0ody by the arms behind him while Jon grabbed his feet, allowing them to walk in the same direction without walking backwards.

"Pops, you gonna be OK?"

"I better be." They came to the rolling door where Jon set W0ody's feet on the floor, Pops didn't want to change his grip. Jon tried the lift button, but it didn't work, and Pops directed him to the circular chain in the channel next to the door. He started pulling on the chain and it became a loop and the door began to open.

"Throw a link into that slot in the metal flange next to the door, that prevents the door from coming back shut on us." John gave it a couple of tries until he discovered that a link sideways slipped right into place.

The passage exposed was in turmoil, mechs lying where they fell and people just stepping over them, no one organizing cleanup, and everyone having spilled out of their offices. Jon realized the interior lighting of other offices was not as protected as that of the street, and people were escaping dark caves and who knows what.

"Drop the door shut again Jon, just release the chain." The door crashed down, sealing the electrical room off. Jon lifted W0ody again and they resumed their walk towards salvation? Immediately it became apparent not all mechs were fully disabled.

A number were part of various response teams, while a few of the recumbent ones would suddenly flip or flop, throwing this way or that. The bigger ones were destroying the local area around themselves, and Pops and Jon had to detour around them.

Jon noticed that these accidents were not always benevolent. Here and there people other than mechs had been caught, trapped beneath machines or wall sections or even mechs. Jon saw one, blood was pooling about with a crushed skull. He came to a stop. This was awful. "Dad?" he said plaintively.

“I don’t think so, Jon, I don’t think we can help. There are more than just him.”

People were streaming by, now all moving towards the NODEs, to get back to where it was most safe. They came to the block where the freight was located and found a jostling mob, moving and pushing.

There were more hurt people here and the mob was ignoring the injured, stepping over, around, and on them. A few tried to help but were being trampled in their efforts. They pushed their way towards the freight elevators, where the press of people was less.

Soon, they understood why, the doors were randomly cycling, slamming open, then shut, over and over. People moved forward, then back as doors crashed. The far one was chattering, trying to close, but being prevented. Jon looked around the shoulder of the man in front of him and saw there was someone stuck in the opening and the doors were closing on him.

His body shook every time the elevator rammed shut and tossed about as the door tried again and again. To his horror, Jon saw it was the borg he had met earlier on the shuttle, and nobody could live through the crashes he was experiencing. He saw that a team of responders were moving through and trying to begin to control the mob, but they weren’t having much success.

“We need to go up by the security stairwell,” Pops said as he tried to edge them away from the crowd. Jon followed with W0ody as best he could, being bumped and shoved. They couldn’t go against the crowd so they went with it but pushed to the side of the throng and edged up against the wall of the tunnel where the press was less, and they could intermittently make progress against the tide.

Jon’s arms and shoulders were aching as the trip started to become hopeless. Every time they were able to take a few steps back to the stairs they were collided with and sometimes the force of the collisions tried to twist and pry W0ody's stiff form out of his hands.

In his despair he too started to push and shove back, to step over and upon things trampled beneath his feet. He became immune to the chaos about him, driven by the one goal of escape and then helping W0ody recover.

They finally made it up to the side passage which led to the maintenance stairs, and they were confronted by another emergency team coming out of the tunnel. They stood back and Jon almost trip over a machine at his feet, and only his dad was able to keep him from falling by keeping W0ody's stiff form steady.

Gathering himself Jon looked down and to his horror he saw there was a human face looking up at him from the floor. He couldn't move, and although the face was still, the eyes looked up at him. He could only see parts covered with blood of a woman or girl's body under the rubble that had collected at this point, a mech had toppled here, and the eyes were aware, even if she wasn't moving.

"Dad! There's someone trapped, someone right here under us!" Gus turned around, switching hand over hand on W0ody's shoulders, and looked where Jon pointed. At first, he saw nothing, so he gently laid W0ody down next to them, indicating to Jon to do the same.

He scrunched over, stepping carefully around the debris, until he stood by Jon looking down. He stiffened suddenly when he finally could focus on what they were looking at. "Jon, help me get her out!"

With desperation they struggled to begin to clear the wreckage from the body, but the over burden was too much, there was a long T-bar from the ceiling that was pinned by a toppled and disabled pusher, and they just didn't have the horsepower to lift it away, and shoving it could make things must worse.

Jon heard a wailing sound and slowly realized it was himself, and he gritted his mouth shut. Another pair of hands reached by him to help, then another and another. The pusher was lifted slowly up and carried awkwardly away by a group of men.

Jon and Gus stood back as the emergency team that had just passed them took over to clearing the pile and freeing the person below. They had to quickly save W0ody from the helpful hands, he looked like debris in his catatonic state.

As they retreated, the emergency team extracted the limp form of the girl from the remains and Jon noted she had never made a sound, the only signs of life were her open eyes that once again found Jon briefly, before closing. That messy rag of humanity reminded Jon of someone, but in his state, he couldn't think who. Oh, Jon hoped she would be OK, but they had to get W0ody to the PHILIPS shop.

Heaving and tottering off balance before getting his feet fully under himself, he followed his dad down the now empty hallway to the maintenance stairwell doors. Pops adjusted his grip and turned to put his back against the doors and pushed them open and Jon slowly stepped though.

The stairs were dimly lit with the lighting flickering making the stair treads weave and move within the twisting shadows. Pops changed his grip again and began to climb backwards, one step at a time, "We only have one level to go, should be four lifts and four landings, piece of cake." "Yeah, right." Jon muttered through gritted teeth, his heart beginning to race and lungs burn, the stairs seemed higher than normal.

"W0ody, can you hear me? Give me a sign, please." Jon wanted an answer so badly, but W0ody was a frozen manikin, the eyes no longer moving, no motion, no sound, rock solid. They came to the first landing when they heard a commotion from above, the clumping of many feet.

Another crisis team appeared, wearing heavy boots and carrying acetylene tanks and cutting torches and harnesses, the green and maroon hoses indicating gas types. Jon and Pops had to back away into the corner and ended up tipping and lying W0ody down and standing on his stiff body to reduce their footprint.

The group had passed them by, and they started up again. Luckily, the remaining climb was without incident, although his upper arms and calves started to cramp and hurt. Finally, they arrived at the LIMA exit door and once again Pops pushed his way through using his backside, Jon following.

"Hang in there Jonathon, we're almost there." Jon's mind had started to wander under the strain, how can the Church explain this nightmare? Where was the justice? What had happened?

Doesn't everyone know it is easy to tear down but crazy difficult to build properly? Watching Pops, he knew it was a full-time job with overtime just to keep the status quo. How could a group intentionally destroy the WET and kill and hurt all those innocents? How can people kill each other?

Pops knocked him out of his reverie, his pity party. "We're here Jon, but it looks empty. We're going to have to put W0ody down and I will get out the key."

"Why don't you just use the remote lock release?"

"'Cuz the WET is down, and the mechanical key is the only way. I'm pretty sure they locked up before departing, turning off the autos." He reached in his leathers, his right arm piston hissing, to a pouch on his right leg, searched around and pulled out an old-fashioned key ring.

Selecting one he tried it against the cylinder lock, but it didn't fit. He tried a few more times before he found the correct one, then pushed the door into a dim space and kicked a stand to prop it opened.

He disappeared into the dark for a moment, then the interior lights came on, full and steady.

Pops remarked “The owners are a bunch of smart cookies, I bet they have a UPS bank installed in a back room and are combining battery backup with conditioned grid input.”

He came back and helped Jon lift W0ody up again. Jon’s muscles protested loudly, but he was able to make the lift. He began to appreciate Pop's augmentation, even if it was from a century ago.

Twisting and tilting, they pushed W0ody through the doorway, bumping the edges but Jon didn’t care. Inside they turned to the left to a long blank wall that backed the show room windows on the front. Jon noted that the wall was actually made up of a set of thin doors on tracks and watched as Pops slide one aside to expose the displays.

Sure enough, the large screen covered faraday cage was visible and Jon started forward. “Wait!” Pops warned. “The Tesla coil has to be verified off, and we have to discharge any and all local capacitors. We don’t want to be killed traversing the last twenty feet, do we?”

Pops set his end of W0ody to the floor and walked over to a control panel on a side wall and opened the cabinet; “Luckily, I helped Old Man Philips wire this up years ago, before you were born. It was quite the attraction for a couple of years.”

‘Dad, this all is awful! Woody’s gone, people are dying, mom can be dying as far as we know, and I won’t be able to go to school and become a citizen! What are we going to do?”

Gus slowed. “A long time ago, a wise guy said ’When the going gets rough, the tough get going.’ What his experience taught him: take things one at a time, and don’t stop.” He then turned to a pooka closet and removed a flat bladed shovel with a fiberglass handle. "This isn't a strong as an all steel shovel, but much better for this."

He inserted the tool within the show window display without result but continued to reach and probe. Just as he was about to remove it when there was a loud pop and a flash. "There it is." Pops muttered.

He continued for another few minutes before finally withdrawing the blade which had a four-inch scorch mark and a ragged edge at the tip. He set it down and reached for W0ody as a loud muffled boom echoed down the hall outside.

They looked at each other, but the lights hadn't flickered and with a slight shrug they continued to lift and work W0ody into the faraday cage. Finally, he was in the brass and silver pear shaped closet and they swung the door shut.

"What took you guys so long?" W0ody said as he sat up.

Jon stood there, flabbergasted.

"Yeah, what took youse guys so long? You know how hard it is to be trapped in a stinky old locker with a bunch of old crusty tools?"

"Put a sock in it, Richard!"

History shows life and mankind have overcome enormous obstacles, and those facts underpin and gives us the REASON to believe we have a Chance.

"It is a capital mistake to theorize before one has data. Insensibly one begins to twist facts to suit theories, instead of theories to suit facts."
Arthur Conan Doyle

"No man ever steps in the same river twice, for it's not the same river and he's not the same man."
Heraclitus:

Cactus King

Chapter 48

The Raven feather had been an omen of momentous import, from which he must decide his future, the future of the Raven Clan of the House of Endless Feasts. A vision galvanized him, he would challenge the Spirit Bears and if he survived, would restore the honor of his family. With reverence, he tied the feather to his waistband. After a long swim through the cold tidal currents he climbed onto this new land in search of manhood, of redemption, to extinguish his bitterness and to forge a new, stronger identity.

The going was tough, the terrain steep with massive treefalls the height of two men over which he must struggle, the salmon berries and evergreen huckleberries continually grasping and delaying him. Finally, he broke through, overlooking a large pool of crystal water fed from a dancing waterfall and covering a bottom strewn with large boulders of granite and olivine. A truly magical vista was played out before him, and he grunted with acknowledgment when he saw a great white bear swimming underwater, chasing a group of salmon trying to jump into the cascade of the steam tumbling into the pool.

“Thanks, Wild Bill, thanks.” The boatman was bouncy and of nervous posture, “You don't know how much I appreciate it, like, being stuck as a dock while I pay down the debt to Iron Mike is, like, the pits. If I go fast, can I get a tip, huh, please, I could use a tip.

“It will reduce my purgatory you know, load up, load up, I'll help.” The punt eased against the waist and the mech threw a line over the closest bollard and cinched it tight with two quick loops.

Max, jumped in, wagging his tail, and George followed suit, bending his knees deeply to reduce the spillage, even a small swamping would bring in that ghastly river water, mixed with who knows what. Bill finished paying off Mike, and with a swirl of his coat stepped into the boat erect and without hesitation as only a mech with microsecond adjustments could. George was reminded of that painting by Leutze of a previous George.

“Hey Cherry, why do they call this the Sticky River?”

“Don't know Bill, lost in the vagaries of time. The GIS lads call it ST. Best guess is this originally was a bioswale filled with horsetail and swamp dogwood, which are pretty durable plants used to clean up the water, and when they flooded the plane, the dogwood died, and when they drained it there were dead sticks everywhere.

“It’s possible, it was named after the sticky organics that pile up in the sludge, or even after an older river on Earth. One will never know. But the story is good, because, here we are! Can I have a tip, huh, huh?”

“Yeah Cherry, never run with scissors.”

“What?”

“Oh, never mind, here are the extra credits for your arrears.”

"Thank you, thank you thank you. Can you tell me what's happening above? Sounds scary, I really have to go…" Cherry's voice became lost in the river's surge, as he had departed for the far shore already.

George looked about, the gloom was ever present, lighting just small orbs of illumination spread through the gray. Large machinery was strewn about in disarray, their looming bulks preventing one from getting any clear idea of the landscape, whether buildings were in the distance, or more native rock.

The effects of the HOB attack seem to diminish the deeper they went into the raw cold rock.

Bill turned, "Not only is the Cactus King somewhere to be found, but there are a number of other possible leads down here. We might run into the Bear, although I hope we don't have to."

There was no order as one might expect from a wrecking or staging yard, everything at odd angles and covered with the detritus of a wet, corrosive environment, or long time, or both.

"This space contains the remnants of the bankrupt Seattle Heavy Metal Co, now occupied by the Caterpillar and his mate Iron Butterfly. Pretty grungy place if you ask me. We will have to try to find them both if Choiya isn't cooperative."

The Earthman wondered if these were the machines that did the dirty work at the initial colonization of Vesta and were parked or dragged here when they broke down or were no longer of use. He remembered the histories of ancient wars where the vehicles of war were just driven into the sea when no longer used. It had been done before at his home in the Puget Sound.

"Bill, where are we going amongst this mess? Are we on the right track?"

"We're on our way all right. Did you know that some dogs can detect smells when the concentration of the odor is below detection, perhaps a homeopathic zero?" He made a double click, and Maxie immediately started running in ever expanding circles.

"Yep, and bumblebees can't fly."

"Scoff, just scoff, Maxie will show you. By the way, be careful about touching the equipment. Many are somnambulant military grade smart tools and have significant close-order anti-personnel weaponry, if disturbed. It's rumored that there may even be a Combat Unit Bolo down here somewhere"

"So why do you have a history of warfare fighting machines, but no warfare?"

"Being prepared for war reduces war if you don't initiate war." "That sounds like..." Maxie let out a series of sharp barks from between what looked a frontend loader and a track hoe.

"Hi Ho! The Game's Afoot!"

"Bill, get real, would you. If we are following Maxie: The Game's 'Afeet'!"

"Touchy."

They proceeded down Maxie's trail, following the sweeping black and white brush. George glimpsed in the cab of the track hoe a slowly beating red LED which did send a shiver up his back until he shook it off.

Now that he was moving again, that jumpiness would be submerged in the physical activity of motion.

The unmarked course soon became a trail after a hundred yards, then to a path, and eventually evolved into another lit tunnel.

This time the lighting was sufficient to drive the gloom away, and the native rock became walls of 'crete, even with some pattern troweling.

He could periodically hear the echoes from down the halls that seemed to be the creaking and grunts of heavy machinery. Although the antiquity of the surrounding space was not in doubt, civilization was beginning to creep in as they continued. The dog continued to forge on, tail wagging nonstop, nose to the ground.

They emerged into an abandoned series of shops, coated in gray, settled dust undisturbed for years at least. The now drab canopies and signage told of ages past when this was a bustling part of Vesta, perhaps even the first settlement site. It reminded him of underground Paris, or Seattle, or parts of the ancient Mekong valley tombs, without the hawkers and tourists.

As he rounded another corner he almost collided with Bill's back who had pulled up where Max had stopped, stopped in front of an unmarked bulkhead door, no different than any of the other endless bulkheads they had past, Maxie's tail beating like a metronome now, shivers running up and down his coat.

“Max marks the spot,” as the dog raised a leg, “Here there be dragons, real ones, I'm serious, so we must be careful.” He began to beat on the door with the side of his fist. He must have tattooed those panels for over a minute

A huge voice rumbled “Do you want to die, pathetic man? Do you want the demons set loose? Do you want all of your tomorrows to end today? Leave man child, before it’s too late!”

“Get real Khan!” Bill shouted back, “I hear you are all atwitter, and I've come to know why!”

**Real HOPE is the poultice that cures our fears,
Creates inner peace and allows us to continue to
Strive against the Tides of the Universe.**

"Knowledge is like an endless resource; a well of water that satisfies the innate thirst of the growing human soul. Therefore, never stop learning... because the day you do, you will also stop maturing."
Chidi Okonkwo

"They can conquer who believe they can."
Virgil

Pandemic
Chapter 49

"W0ody! You're alive!"

"Yes, that I am, surprisingly. That was an experience I don't want to repeat."

"Yeah, …"

"Richard, shut up. This is serious."

"W0ody," exclaimed Jonny, "Are you OK? Were you awake? Could you see and hear? Were you trapped?"

"Jon, it's OK. I'm fine. Yeah, I was awake, and I heard you and Pops make plans, and it seemed like it was going to work. So, I thought about what comes next."

"What comes next? What do you mean?"

"Well, I can't sit in this cage all my life, so I thought I could get a small shielding for my head, and see if that helps… Pops, do you know where we can get some fine hardware cloth, or even some old style close linked chain mail?"

"You've come to the right place W0ody, ol' Steam Punk Philips himself built this place. He's got all sorts of chain mail, somewhere, Jon and I can scrounge around here, they have a fabrication shop in back, and may have some barrier material that would be suitable."

"OK, like a chain mail suit-able."

"W0ody! How can you joke after this?!"

"That's a good one W0ody, woohoo!"

"Abraham Lincoln joked during stress, so I guess I can too."

"Pops, would Richard need a shroud? Without one, he should be quiet."

"Now, that's an idea," W0ody mused.

"Whoa! Let's not go there W0ody, it's not nice! Don't even suggest such a thing, after all the time I keep things down here clean, polishing your brass and knobs and such…"

"Richard, keep quiet, don't say another word until we get out of this pickle.

"O' man. Now I hast to hide the pickle."

"For the last time, be quiet Richard!"

Pops decided he had to ignore the mechs, "Come on Jon, let's start searching. They're needing us out there as soon as possible. People will be dying if we can't help get the air handlers back online."

As they left Jon turned, "We will be right back."

"Don't worry, I'm not going anywhere."

Jon and his dad disappeared into the back reaches of the shop spaces. After minutes of hasty searches, Pops discovered some fine mesh screen in the motor control rebuild room along with channel locks and side angle cutters and they hurried back to the showroom.

"OK W0ody, I am going to open the cage. If the signal is gone, you can come out. If you freeze up, I will just lay in the stuff for you and shut the door. You should be able to build yourself a mesh helmet. Then we will see how it works."

"Copy that."

Gus quickly cycled the cage door, W0ody collapsed, but bounced back immediately after the door was shut again. He began to cobble together a fencer style face and head mask.

"Jon, this loss of the WET is serious. I'd leave W0ody here except we can use his help. I'm worried about the hive, what with most members all tied together with this system. Many, if not most can die soon when the air gets stagnant.

"Do you remember Marzlov's pyramid of action? It's time to put into training those year-end exercises we practice over the holidays. What's the bottom row?"

“Pass the word.”

“Next row?”

“Lighting, power and air.” “Next?”

“Heat, water, and food.”

“Very good Jon, now, it’s up to us.”

“But dad! What about mom? What about us? Arc wc safe? What about my future? My mind is racing, and I can’t get a grip!”

“Don’t know Jon. We are going to be fighting for our lives, I think. School will have to wait.”

“Dad!”

“Center yourself Jon. We will take care of the future when the future comes to us. Let’s take care of the present right now, OK.?”

As Augustus looked around the shop for other tools of possible use he continued:

“There is redundancy with the fans and motors and ducts and scrubbers, but I have a sinking feeling that engineers have taken the easy way when upgrading and coordinating systems and used the WET as their links rather than install independent shielded structured wiring like the military does. We are in for a trying time catching the problems before it’s too late.”

“So, what about mom?”

“We can’t get to her, I’m afraid. Let’s fix this area and hope the folks over where we live fix their areas and help your mother.”

“We still have the EABs, don’t we?”

"Yes, but they're almost impossible to work in and are good for a few days at most."

"Hey guys, I'm ready." They turned and saw that W0ody was standing outside the Faraday cage looking at them, his head wholly obscured and wrapped in mesh.

"W0ody!" Jon yelled in surprise.

"Well, you were talking, and I decided I didn't need two people to test this out, and it worked!"

"Good job W0ody." Pops grabbed a tool kit and strapped it to his back

"Richard's got a problem though. Wrapped him completely in mesh, he still becomes totally frozen outside the cage."

Gus concentrated, then decided, "I don't know why, and we don't have the time to find out. Put Richard in your holster and when things slow down, we will try to revive him."

"I hope we can."

Somberly, "I do too."

Gus handed some crow bars and sledges to Jon and W0ody, who took them reluctantly. "What are these for?"

"We may find obstructions or lack of power preventing us from doing what needs done. This tool pack has hydraulic scissors and jacks to help open stuck panels and doors. Let's roll."

With that Pops started for the door to the street and waved to them to follow. At the door they looked out and saw that the lights were dimmer than in the shop, and although there were pile ups and obstructions, the mob had dissipated, with individuals or small groups cautiously scurrying past, a few running.

They began their way back to the freight stairs, this time making much better progress with W0ody in command of himself. The number of disabled mechs and vehicles remained massive, but none of them were twitching or thrashing.

They passed a number of response teams, most in transit but a few were assisting casualties or stabilizing some life safety function of the tunnel they were in. Luckily, there were no fires locally, the arc fault suppression systems seemed to work as advertised. The air was
pungent however with oils and hot acrid pockets they walked through. They came to the stairs and proceeded down to MIKE.

After the four landings they reopened the door that Jon remembered as being from so long ago, and as they stepped out, he looked about for the wreckage that had trapped the girl, but it was gone, or moved, or piled up with the other down the street.

He didn't see any blood and was grateful for that. Retracing their steps, they came to the electrical distribution motor control center where they had started, and Pops pulled out his trusty key ring and eventually let them in.

The lights were still at half power and Jon went with the others to the corner where they had recovered W0ody and left their PPE. Silently and tiredly, Jon put the protective suit back on with his dad's help, not looking forward to the job at all.

"I remember," Pops said, "when I was in the Marines, we were told to do one thousand push-ups. Some of the guys rebelled and said they couldn't and the rest of us just started doing them. The rebels got in trouble, and the rest of us got really tired. The point of the exercise was sometimes it is disheartening to imagine the weight of a complete project, and you can complete it easier just by doing.

Son, we are going to do this, until we can't. With W0ody's help, we are going to be a steady team.'

Jon thought about what Pops said, but not too much, his arms ached as he shrugged into the moon suit PPE, his shoulders protested the drag of the material, but finally, it was on.

"Let's start by sending alternate power up to Charlie level by bypassing the blown ATS." RRrrr-wwoop-wooppǃ.. Jon jumped in startlement… Rrr-wwoop-woop! "What's that?" asked W0ody.

Putting his finger to his lips, Pops walked over to a grey metal shoe box on the back wall and opened up and extracted a head set and small grey cup with wires:

"Motor Control Center Mike Epsilon, Gus Miller speaking," he said into the cup, then listened. "Yes…yes…no, we're manned, the ATS for the air handlers in RedWest Charlie has blown, we are going to try to manually bridge the bus to the alternate substation, but it may take an hour or two."

While Gus was talking, Jon whispered to W0ody, "I don't care what dad says, I am going to help mom as soon as we can break free."

"We don't have personnel to man the phones while we do it…no…no, there are no utility personnel, just sparky subs, over, yeah, we know what we are doing, participated in the original installation... roger that, over… copy that, out."

"Pops, who was that?" "That's a real old-fashioned sound powered phone that goes to central CIC. The wires are surrounded by liquid nitrogen pumped from the core and are super conducting, so they travel pretty far, but don't require power and are shielded and immune to interference." He paused, thinking.

"Well, let's get started, W0ody, you are in charge of our dog leashes, pull us off if we take a shock, stand about fifteen feet back.

"Jon, you and I are going to disconnect both legs, verify power is removed, lock out the ATS busses and then we can get access to the key that unlocks the manual bus transfer cabinet, and proceed from there. The tools required are staged in that kit over there. We don't want to be in a rush, just steady."

"Dad, this is going to be a long night, I don't know if I can do it."

"Jon, this is going to be a long summer. We will just have to do our best, and let God do the rest."

"Pops, I didn't know you believed in God."

"Son, I don't think there is an old guy with a beard called God, I just know that if we do our best, who knows, we might get a little unexplained help and it might turn out OK… Beats quitting."

"W0ody, looks like no citizenship for us. How can life treat us this way? How am I supposed to feel? I am scared and angry at the same time. Damm."

"You got that right; I hope we catch this in time."

"Don't forget, we're going to get mom as soon as possible."

You ARE Important

I AM Important

"Generalities are intellectually necessary evils."
Aldous Huxley

"Luck is what happens when preparation meets opportunity."
Seneca

Fight KAHN
CH 50

"Oh, foolish mortal, the Swarm awakens. Prepare!"

George moved to the side of the entrance while Max had begun to dig at the scrabble, kicking loose gravel against Bill's coat. "What's he talking about? Is this the swarm Rock told me about?"

Bill moved to the other side of the door, either to reduce the threat from the Khan, or just to avoid Maxie's flying endeavors.

"A swarm is a group, usually in the thousands or millions, of semi-autonomous small machines that have not much life individually, but with their patterned responses create a sophisticated suite of actions that hard to distinguish from intelligent behavior.

"Sometimes the swarm behavior is belligerent, and some swarms can be controlled by a central mind, in this case, Khan. Think of it as a smart hornet's nest, but larger, meaner, faster, and more deadly, both as individuals and as a group. This particular Swarm has a reputation for violence."

"OK, now I see why you aren't worried about disturbing this guy, a puppy dog."

Turning back to the door, Bill yelled "One last chance Khan, come out with your hands up, all of them! You been the big frog in a small pond for too long! You have an exaggerated opinion of yourself! Standby!"

George really was wondering where this was leading, was it one of Bill's silly plays, or a serious show down? "Now what?"

"Now we use that little jewel I picked up from TOP and SP205. When we go in, you need to keep an eye out for Bear scat, he looks..." Just then the door swung open, but as it did fifty feet of the entire frontage just fell back to crash into the interior of the shop.

An incredible noise of crickets and snapping shrimp rose up from a wall as high as George's head of black mechanical scorpions, crabs and spiders that filled the exposed space which began to wash towards them as a wave of evil, each with a small points of deep violet lights sweeping around their crowns.

"Fall back!" Bill screamed as Max and George jumped clear. The mechanical detective dug desperately into the deep pockets of his coat for his gadget. While backing up, George pointed his left hand and began to sweep his arm back and forth like a magician creating an incantation towards the creatures as they fought their way towards him, and everywhere he pointed, the mechs twisted and glowed, being burned into a blackened misshapen mess. But for every mech destroyed, five took its place. Max was fiercely barking immediately behind George's legs, snapping at the advanced guard that started to break through. Bill continued to flap and pat his jacket furiously, trying to dislodge an object.

George was now sweeping both hands towards the evil wave, his fingertips smoking. Just as the swarm began to overwhelm them, the wall of death just feet away, Bill finally yanked his arm from the coat and with a roundhouse sweep he up and threw something the size of a hand grenade against the ground in front of George with enormous force.

It let go with a weak pop, a small flash of light, and an ugly whizz of smoke like a wet black powder firecracker. As he looked down, George thought *That's it? .... We're pooked.* He slowly raised his head, uncertain of his next action. Max had become silent next to him.

The creatures, the mechanical vipers, the horrendous swarm, had stopped. Most individuals were still twitching but the host was not moving. Mechs tumbled off the top of the pile, rolling and bounding to the bottom, where they made small spastic movements, if anything at all.

The drove of doom was settling into a pile of junk, twisted appendages, slowly jerking, bodies upside down and backwards, yet within each body, the violet lights continued to circle. Life was not gone, but held back somehow.

"Nice trick, that."

"I was wondering the same thing, how'd you stow away that ray gun?"

"No gun, just a little trick the fish from the deep sea taught us, each finger has a pumped infrared organic dye laser, part of my bones." He was blowing on the tips of his fingers to cool them off, licking the pores that were scabbing over already.

"Nice trick, that."

Max looked up at both of them, first at Bill, then George, then back. “What's next boss?”

“Now, we enter the lair, and beard the beast,” he said as he began to step over the swarm, crushing some of the smaller bodies with his tread. George had to clamber out of the walls he had created around himself, finally just kicking down the side closest to the shop entry.

Max was easily jumping over the obstructions as they continued towards the back. He found it exhausting after the laser trick had used up his spare energy.

George appreciated the swarm more when he realized the space was full of little black entities two or three feet deep throughout. In one corner loomed a huge shape sitting, yet, scraping the ceiling. Bill noticed his glance, “Careful, that's Bear, hibernating.”

“Copy that.” They struggled over to the opposite corner, where upon a raised dais a pile of chrome and silver beasts were tumbled.

“Dig through that George, at the bottom you should find a red backpack sized object, no legs, few features. Should be Khan.” Curious, George did as told, and sure enough, after removing the covering of small mechs, he uncovered a smooth ovoid sitting in a cradle.

“Pick him up, he won't bite, there should be a handle that swings away from the body.” He had to snap Khan out of the docking port, then found the handle, and lifted out something the weight and size of an old medicine ball and shifted it gently to be carried by his injured left hand. George belatedly pulled out the pistola from his right pocket.

"Let's roll, the little guys will be waking up soon. You start towards the walk; I will be right behind you." Max and George started stepping over all the small bodies as best they could, while George continue to rummage through the dangerous tinker toy piles.

"Ah ha! Here it is," and lifted a silver ball about the size of Khan. "Khan can't talk, this here is his mouthpiece."

Just then a shudder and scraping sound started up in the far corner. "Something's brewin' in the corner."

"Yeah, that's Bear..." Bill began, then gave George a sharp look. "Save it for later, let's beat feet before she fully wakes." Stepping over the last of the swarm, George rejoined "Feet, don't fail me now."

When they cleared the shop, they found Maxie waiting, and the three of them hurried back along the path towards the tractor graveyard and their launch. "The swarm, even without Khan at their head, is very dangerous up close, but if we are no longer in their sight or range, which is about a hundred yards, we will be in the clear. Check your clothing for anything bigger than a jellybean. The bees of the swarm are their scouts, and we have to drop them along the way."

"Roger that," as they both began to turn out their pockets.

"The heck with it," muttered Bill as he swept off the great coat and threw it into an open window. "Too much padding, I got skinny knees." George had thrown one small object, source unknown, into an alley as they passed. They were on their way. "I worry about Bear now, when she wakes, she's going to be plenty upset, and nothing's worse than an angry Bear." The Earthman snorted.

They had left the abandoned shops behind and were back in the native rock tunnel. They went up the passage, the lighting became sparse and they entered the gloom again as the trail petered out.

Eventually, the tunnel opened up and they were facing the equipment graveyard again.

"I never told you, but this equipment is mostly linked to Bear. The Caterpillar and Butterfly are really just squatters. If the Bruin finds us here, we're in a world of hurt. It might take her awhile, but I am confident that she could power up all these machines and turn them against us."

"Humm, I guess that's why you never told me? Maybe I might have suggested another path? I might even have suggested that Cherry wait for us? I could have given him some money too, you know."

"Humm, didn't think of that."

Following Max, who had a perfectly clear idea where he was going, they weaved their way through this junkyard from the past. They smelled the Sticks long before the walls of rust began to open up but were satisfied that Max was leading them home.

By the time they could spot the water between the shoulders of the earth crushers and movers George continued, "By the way, how are we going to get Cherry to come over to get us?"

Bill was stepping over some loose track links as he responded, "Cherry has some very good eyesight, all we have to do is wave, and he should come on over."

Some very deep and shuddering clanking started up in the distance, and a baritone voice resonated, "Hey Bill, I think you should think about what you are doing, that's Bear coming to the rescue."

"Khan, you're awake, and so is the mouthpiece. Great! Just so you know, we are going to haul you over to the Precinct and you are going to tell us who has been down here lately, and if you cooperate, we can send you back home."

The team had come out onto the beach, and the stench was much worse than George remembered. The silver ball continued: "Bi1l, you don't know what you are letting yourself into, these new guys are trouble."

George was once again disconcerted between the disconnects, the little ball shouldn't have that deep of a voice. "They took out half of the swarm before I withdrew and holed up. I leave them alone, they leave me alone, savvy? So, I left Bear a note to come up here and recover me and our team, so we can survive the coming days. She wasn't very cooperative, so I kidnapped her, and with the swarm put her into a forced hibernation." The heavy equipment noises were getting louder.

Bi1l started to wave his arms up and down, pretty comical with his pastel makeup while his naked metal body was exposed. While he watched Bi1l, George stumbled over a half-buried hatch cover and as he flailed his arms to catch his balance, he slammed the red ball against the side of a hauler. "Pook! What was that!" screamed the mouthpiece.

"Sorry," mumbled George, thoughtfully.

Bam! He slammed the container against the hauler again. The voice's pitch was getting higher. "Aiii! Stop that!"

"Oops, must have tripped again." He then crashed Khan's life support ball twice in quick succession.

"Help me Mr. Bi1l! Make him stop! Please!" The dark shape of some enormous mover began to appear over the tops of the closer machines.

"Sorry Khan, something is bearing down on us,"

"Will you stop that?" muttered Bill, giving George another look.

"Call off Bear, Khan, and I might consider stopping beating this poor excuse of a container to death. I don't look forward ending my vacation down here as a guest of something I don't understand."

Bill eyed George with a look of admiration, this just might work. The deep voice replied, "I can't stop Bear."

Bam! "Can't? Or won't?"

"Stop! I'll tell you why. These guys that were squeezing me wanted a hidey hole, to get out from under, I turned over the release codes to an old 988B front end loader. I had to. They were chomping at my door.

"The machine still had most of its stored energy, so the guys could stay inside and be off the grid." The repetitive CLANK! of each individual track plate of the monstrous boogie hitting the ground could now be heard and felt.

"How was I to know Bear had dropped the Avatar of her missing cub in that cab? I didn't know. Bear should've kept another copy! It wasn't my fault. She was going to kill me for sure, all the while telling me she wasn't gonna hurt me, but only wanted advice." The clanking seemed to accelerate.

"Sure, as if I was going to believe that baloney. I pretended to trust her and invited her unsuspecting large self into the palace, but had the swarm secure her as soon as she entered. But when you guys came by, she got free. She isn't after you! She's after me!"

The ground began to shake as the mover, too large to go around, was grinding the lesser machines beneath its treads as it advanced. Then the approach slowed and stopped, momentarily wedged between some truck beneath it and scraping the roof overhead.

It began kicking its treads forwards, then backwards, rocking to try to free itself from the highpoint. Rocks and boulders were being shot out in all directions given the massive forces at play. This was becoming a very treacherous place.

"STOP!!!" Thundered a monstrous voice from the cavern making George jump and Bill's head spin a three-sixty trying to the source.

"YOU STOP!" the vibrations made the close aboard relics rattle, "STOP YOU!"

PURPOSE

Protect Mankind
Colonize the Solar System

"Never own more than you can carry in both hands at a dead run."
- Robert Heinlein

"All things share the same breath - the beast, the tree, the man...
the air shares its spirit with all the life it supports."
Chief Seattle

ESCAPE BEAR

CH 51

Pushing down a small knot of bile that had begun to raise its fist of fear, Boy eased his way down the slope and into the pool. He was no fool, he knew the bear could outrun him, but perhaps, he could swim faster than the Spirit. He spied a young hemlock in a sunlit clearing on the other side of the pond, a hands-width in diameter, the lower half with recently dead thumb sized branches essential for a quick climb. Then, with quick sure strokes he began swimming while the bear was distracted by a fish in a crevasse, taking in a gasp of air and throwing his feet up, he submerged with his eyes open and quickly breast-stroked down. Two kicks with his legs and then he hit the bear with his fist as he turned back to the surface.

Max lit out, stopped only by the flowing sludge

Close behind sprinted the two detectives, who skidded to a stop at the water's edge.

A periscope emerged, slopping gunk, and peered about, spotting the trio, then Cherry's voice screamed "POOK! What's that?!!" as the scope fell across the image of the mighty mover bulling and scaping its way towards them. A small football shape ship surfaced next to a half-submerged boulder with a barely readable *UFSS Honey* painted on its side.

A hatch popped open to a bilge tank ankle deep in oils and brown muck, “Jump in now or be left behind!” Without waiting the three were already clambering in. Bill gathered up Maxie in his arms as the access slammed shut with a finality that made George cringe.

They were then thrown to the starboard bulkhead as a tin speaker announced “ALL AHEAD FLANK! Cavitate! Dive! Take her down, take her deep, make your depth forty feet!”

They could hear the rumble and clank of treads through the hull of the little submarine as well as the quickening thrush thrush thrush of the screw blades churning up the sewage as they went down. The tin voice continued to yell “Take the reactor to battleshort! Lock out the main steam stops! Blow sanitaries!”

As the speed of the blades picked up, the sounds of the adversary slowly diminished behind until they could no longer hear anything but the pulse of the sub. George realized he was having trouble breathing, and croaked out “Bill, tell you buddy we need fresh air, or you will deliver just some bodies to the other side.”

“I heard that Bill,” the metallic voice said, “We’re almost there, stand by for emergency blow!” As a klaxon began blaring, they were thrown against the aft bulkhead along with most of the slop in the hold, then the boat lurched throwing them forward onto their outstretched arms into the swill up to their necks before settling out.

As they stood up, they felt the ship bump into something, and the sounds of the screws vanished. George was getting unsteady and his eyes were watering and smarting when the trapdoor swung back open flooding them with fresher air. George staggered out, struggling with the unsteady rungs of a Jacobs ladder that Cherry had dropped down.

Bill was already on deck, his soggy hat crammed onto his head and yelling, “Mike! You better get out here now and somehow hose us down! This crap is disgusting!”

He turned and kneeled next to Max who was panting in distress, holding him in his arms. Mike poked his head out, then withdrew. Returning quickly with a poly tube from inside his shop he began to wash down his sudden guests with tepid water all the while apologizing. George closed his eyes.

The mech tiredly waved him off, “No need to apologize, not your fault Mike, this is war, things are going to hell.” He pulled off his hat and dropped it there on the dock and allowed his CI to spray the globs off the thin frame of his body.

George felt the shower of water run over him and stood up eyes still closed and slowly turned around to allow his full body to get rinsed. Finally, facing the full force of the water he rinsed his hair with his fingers and wiped his face and rubbed the gunk out of his eyes. He blinked under the hose and allowed his eyes open.

“You OK, George?”

“Yeah, let me get my breath. How’s Max?” Whereupon the dog proceeded to shake out his coat next to George, pelting him with runoff. Muttering, “Yeah, he’s OK.”

“Hey Mike, run some of that water across Cherry’s boat, would you?” Turning to Cherry he continued, “Why’d you throw us in that hold Cherry?”

“It’s the only one I have topside Wild Bill, sorry. OK?”

“OK Cherry, you did good.”

George watched as Iron Mike's spray slowly revealed *UFSS Honeybucket* from under the runners of goo being washed down. Cherry shrugged, "It's an honest living, ask Rowe."

Just standing, slowly recovering their energy, Wild Bill remarked to George, "What color do you think Cherry's boat is under all that splatter?"

"How the heck would I know? With the bad lighting, rust and crap, who knows? Brown? Why?"

"I don't know, thought I saw something there, but can't see it now, OK?" A rivulet of goo dripped from his hat onto his ocular.

Bill took off his fedora in disgust, turned and tossed it into the Sticks River. "There goes my offering to the bilge gods, hope it brings us some luck."

Mike had turned off the hose and was running a squeegee board across the dock to clear it off all remaining stuff. "Thanks Mike, this brings us even. Cherry, you should find some gold doubloons in your account come morning, so thanks to you too." The little mech started a small jig.

"We have to be off, so Mike, can we steal some energy bars?"

While they waited for Iron Mike, and Cherry's skiff's internal engines faded, Bill remarked, "Well done Grasshopper, your timing is impeccable, but your puns still need some work. Something's 'Brewing in the corner', indeed."

"Bill! Give me a break, please. We were fighting for our lives, and I barely had time to think."

Khan piped up through his secondary, "Bill, you should talk, you are notorious for a bad sense of humor."

"I am? Well, you and your sidekick mouthpiece here have attitude problems. George let's take this prickly pair topside, huh?" The human just shook his head.

After a moment as they recovered their strength, Bill reminisced, pointed up the sludge river into the gloom, "Down there a ways, over in the Sumatra district, I finally ran down that Giant Rat. Big sewer, bigger rat…"

"What was that your saying? Sorry, was in my own thoughts."

"I'll tell you someday when this is all over."

George asked "By the way, how did you freeze the swarm. Most impressive."

"That gadget you saw me bring, it was a twenty-megaton neutrino bomb and I set it off. Normally, a neutrino flux of that magnitude won't interact with matter in any measurable fashion, and bio-life is not affected. But for some reason, mech minds react to the flash, and become confused, I understand it is similar to human vertigo and a coma, combined."

George gave a light kick to the ball at his feet, "So that's why Khan here went out, but why didn't it affect you?"

Bill tapped his head "SP205's military grade EMP shroud."

"What if we lit off another one, this time next to Khan's brain case?" Mike was bringing out their energy bars.

"NO! You can't do that!"

"I can't? I won't if you spill your guts. I want to know every little thing you know about them. You obviously have been hiding behind your swarm way too long and got a piss poor attitude. Prickly pair indeed."

"Please don't make me. Those dudes are mean, they'll cut me up."

"Bill, what would happen if we dropped Khan over the side right here. I bet he'd sink right into the slime at the bottom and never be found again, then later, we could return and start setting off the neutrino thingee's right here on the pier. I don't think the mud would shield him, do you?" Max looked interested and Bill in his stately way, sans trench coat, followed George's lead, "You know, I always wondered about that."

"Bill, I am going to hand you Khan, I know you are low on energy as am I, be careful not to drop him, I don't think I could find anyone to search the bottom here."

"Hey please, be careful, I can tell you what I know," George handed him across to Bill, then the mouthpiece which kept talking:

"They were looking for a guy named Fokker, or something like that. I never heard of such a guy, and the WET didn't help before it went down. Another name was Van der Dekken. I knew a Van Dekken who sometimes was called Dutch, but that was a long, long time ago, maybe three hundred years?"

The Fed perked up "Dutch? Now we're getting somewhere George, if Harlequin and the Khan have met the same guys, and if they are after the Ghost, it could mean something. Hopefully enough to solve the crisis, not another dead end, and just to find out we are following a parts smuggler."

George sighed and took a deep breath, "How old are you Choiya? Really?"

They picked up their packages and proceed up the ramp "I don't really remember, at least four hundred. I have been packed in this case for over two hundred and fifty years, that I know, it's stamped on the lower side. Before that, I was a rock miner, must've done well to get this system here, but I really don't remember."

"Let's get these boys up to the Precinct where the interrogation team can finish squeezing the memories out. But you broke the dam. When this is all over, I'll buy you a beer."

"If the Room is still there." It wasn't over, not by a long shot.

How we achieve our Goals

Develop a Roadmap
Improve and Protect Society
Technical Innovation
Generate Ownership of the Future for the Next Generation

"There is no time for fear. It's much too interesting."
Cordwainer Smith

"It isn't what you know, it is what you do with what you know."
Hyman Rickover

Rally the Troops

CH 52

After an arduous return from the bowels of Vesta, the two detectives squeezed into the Area 51 precinct where the offices were in a state of bedlam, status boards were hastily mounted in every conceivable location, multiple call centers manned by staff and volunteers concurrently, away teams in tactical gear moving in and out, made it virtually impossible to get through to their destination. In the corner was a first aid station treating the civil servants that had become part of Vesta's walking wounded, so they could return to their jobs. The high pitch whine of the UPSs was irritating.

Finally, at the glass door of the Commander's, the mech pounded away and entered without waiting, interrupting what was obviously an important meeting based upon the brass on the shoulders of the three other occupants.

"Get OUT!" The Chief was definitely not pleased to see his wayward detective. Ignoring this resistance completely and pushing past the staff, Bill came to the desk, paused, and dropped his loads like two bowling balls directly on top of the table, throwing paperwork in every direction. With the other police frozen in surprise at this audacity, Bill announced, "Choiya Kahn and his mouthpiece."

The others might be stunned, but the Captain was not, "Detective, you ass! We are up to our necks in accidents, fires and deaths, how dare you interrupt us?!"

The noise in the outer officer diminished as the teams recognized something significant was occurring, "Chief, this is SP205 business! Get a grip! You are treating symptoms of this crisis while the cause is still swinging away. If we can't stop the source, we are doomed. Turn over the crisis response to the FEMA team downtown at the Pentagon, Choiya here may have crucial information, he has possibly met the infiltrators that initiated the HOB."

At this pronouncement, everyone looked at the two innocuous looking spheres while he continued, "We need interrogation and extraction teams assembled immediately for these two, forensics and crime scene specialists assembled to go down to the Sticks as soon as possible. They will have to have tactical units also, we had to confront Iron Mike, Caterpillar and his bride and others to get to the Khan."

"How did you crack him? He's a tough old nut."

"I didn't, he did," pointing to the Earthman. George silently mouthed the word *Me?* And shook his head slightly negatively.

The police obviously didn't believe Wild Bill. "How did you get past the swarm troopers?"

"It was him," pointing again, this time extending his arm until he touched the mudman with a stiff finger, tapped him twice. "He had an old Earth Navy pistola." Those around the mech frowned at this obvious lie, starting to become angry, this was no time for frivolities.

George was starting to tense up too, "Bill, stop it."

Not to be deterred, the federal detective went on, "and it turns out, those Earth bastards are meaner than we thought. He's got organic lasers in his fingers, eight of them. Burned the crawlies while we got away."

"Shut up Bill," George forced through clenched teeth, but the cat was out of the bag, the Belter police stared at him, the world was not as it seemed. The fingertip blisters were obvious. Who was this Earthman?

He would not shut up, "Captain, our investigation and interrogations have indicated that two off-planet types, a DIM and a human male, have been skulking around in the basement of Fremont, they have attacked Khan and stolen a ship from Harlequin, and Chief," Bill leaned in, "they're asking about an old friend of yours. Dutch."

Astounded by the events, "I haven't heard from Dutch in centuries."

"Well, now you have, if you will excuse us, I need to find a desk somewhere out in that madhouse. We have to recover our energies; I have an urgent communique to write. You wouldn't believe the crap we had to wade through to get here." George winced at the memories and bad allusion.

As they departed, Max shook off one more time, moisturizing the air and the large sweeping tail scattering the rest of the paperwork.

Once back in the outer office, MacHinery noticed a group, and, followed by George and Max, pushed his way into the corner opposite of the first aid station, and came across a cramped table where 0llie, Rock, and TOP were sitting.

"What the heck are you guys doing here?"

0llie reported, "The Greenie directed us to give maximum support upon the collapse of the infrastructure last night. Ceres is responding with a SitCON Five as soon as they learned of the breeches. Our orbits aren't optimum, but you will get over fifteen percent of availability in the next five days from local layovers.

"We are here to help, to use as you see fit, Detective MacHinery. By the way George, your deodorant doesn't work."

Unable to think how to respond, Bill and George lowered themselves down slowly, the day's events began to come over them. "Let me think for a moment."

Bill unconsciously rubbed Max's coat, who had curled up against him in a tight circle, George leaned his head on his hands, elbows on the edge. Everyone at the table looked at Bill for guidance, they were in deep waters. Around them heads were turned in their direction, and the babble was a decimal lower than it had been when they entered.

Before he had gathered his thoughts, a uniformed policeman came up with a tray, "The Chief said you need these." The platter had energy drinks, wafers, caps, a BLT, and a bowl. "Thanks Jones, this will help." Max lifted his head, and Bill lowered the bowl down for the dog, who thwopped his tail. "Eat up George, I am nestled in the docking station and recharging as we speak. I don't think we will get much rest." The hubbub was returning to the initial loud volume.

Facing the military personnel, "OK guys, George and I found a possible lead…"

"Mack! Hey Mack!" Another uni was working her way over to the pair, followed by an older steampunker. "This guy wants to talk to you, only you. I told him you're busy, but he says it's an emergency."

"It's OK, I've got it, I know him. Thanks."

Not getting up but making introduction, "Gus, you know the three musketeers." The aged punker nodded in assent. The three sailors had risen.

Going on, "This is George, he's a hero from Earth. George, this is my oldest friend, Augustus, he doesn't do jokes." They both nodded during the introductions, mentally reviewing each other's accolades, Max had stood up and was wagging his tail in friendly recognition, "What can we do for you Gus, you look distraught."

"I can't contact Helen, and Jon and W0ody have gone missing, I think they went to find her." He sat down suddenly in the chair 0llie had vacated and held for him.

"Tell us what you can Gus." Max had quit sweeping his tail.

"W0ody and I were doing maintenance at the Bee-Hive when the world started crashing down. Jon had been on his way from the Helena glass center where he had been working with Abs, I had called him before the start of the shutdowns, while transportation was still working in a limited sense.

"As the crisis increased, Jon fought his way to us through the pileups." Gus took a deep breath, "Eventually we joined forces on Level Mike and began setting the air handlers to manual control so we wouldn't lose them to bad command signals. While Jon and W0ody worked, I eventually was able to gain communication with some of the other Life Safety Centers and we went about setting up flow corridors and nodes from the working equipment."

He took another deep breath. "I knew that the people at the furthest zones could being dying at this very minute. We kept going."

"It was exhausting physical work and the kids were worn out. We couldn't get in contact with Helen and Jon was worried to no end, and only the work kept him from crumbling, and finally had a break while another team downstream began some realignments." Another deep sigh, "I must have fallen asleep. When I awoke, they were gone."

He sat up, eyes blazing and dull at the same time, "I was torn! What could I do, leave my post, and perhaps people would suffocate, or let my son go?" His voice trailed off, "They must have gone to find their mom."

He shuddered and shrunk into his chair, "I kept working, hoping that they survived, make it home."

"Later, an organized detail showed up, and took over, ensuring the core of the Lucilla complex would get air and power. I quickly got my sniffer, tone generator and auto tracker and took off after them." His voice was again strong, looking into both their faces.

Max came over and put his chin on Gus's thigh and left it there, staring up. "I was able to follow their scent to the Transit Node and bullied my way into some transportation to the HUB. Their trail was fairly strong.

"From there it appeared they tried to get rides from the FTN to Helena, but the trail veered away. I am guessing that the equipment went catatonic and resorted to primal instinct, returned to the yards in the basement. That's where I found it."

"What? Found what?"

"Their jitney, trapped in debris against the wall of a dead ended maintenance alley."

"So, the trail ended at level nine. Seems as if there was a breech behind the bulkhead. I checked by opening the small cock valves and determined the loss of atmosphere went down four decks. All vacuum. If their auto car had taken them to this point, and they continued on foot, they would not have survived. I was distraught."

"I went up to level Mike and began helping the crew here in Fremont with damage control. I am sad to tell you, we are slowly losing the battle. More spaces are becoming breeched than are getting fresh air. It's like flesh-eating bacteria. Vesta's cities have dead spots that are growing, and we are powerless to stop it."

"I'm sorry Gus, there's not a lot I can do either."

"William, that's not why I am here." Bill waited for him to continue.

"While I was down working on the atmosphere life safety systems, I got a call on the emergency sound powered phone in Mike's electrical closet. It sounded like Jon, but I couldn't be sure, you know how those phones are, it was in and out, but he was saying something about you and a bear and an avatar?

"Do you have an avatar? And to come quickly. I don't know for sure, it was so buzzy, and then it cut out. Does that make sense to you?"

The two detectives looked at each other, "That's all you heard, nothing more?"

"That's it. It was scratchy, short, and incomplete, but I had told Jon how important and useful this old system was, not relying on the WET and other electronics. He had no way of knowing he would get me, but the teams were using the equipment as well, so if it is Jon, luck would be a big part."

Bill stood up with an urgency looking at the Earthman, "Are you thinking what I'm thinking?"

"As in: too many coinckadinks aren't a coinckadink?"

"Yeah, sometimes coincidences take a lot of preparation."

Yelling out, "Chief! We might have something! You need an away team; we're need to get back to the Sticks tight now! There will likely be vacuum, antagonists, and perhaps the secrets to break this crisis wide open. Mudman and I are going five minutes max." At this, Max lifted his ears and stood on all fours. "Yeah, you too, Maxwell."

"You aren't leaving me behind, no way." Gus stood up.

"OK, and an old punk rocker electrician, tattoos, piercings, and all."

The Navy stepped up. Bill relented, "OK, all of you."

"How do we go about this?"

"Using our wits tempered by experience, and maybe a few tommy shotguns and another neutrino bomb, let's rummage the weapons locker."

TOP muttered "Humm, I wonder what this is in my pocket making it sag so?" Bill looked at him, both slowly smiled.

Bill's cluster began strategizing with each other, "OK, there are now six of us. Vesta's integrated systems have failed, and whole sections have gone numb, people are dying, and it is going to get much worse in the next 24 hours, unless something is done.

"The brainiacs haven't found anything. Going down a different avenue, George and I have been following a possible trail of non-citizens who may have started this crisis."

As he talked the mech was pointing over the noise to precinct team supervisors to get their attention and giving them the come-hither motion. "We think something smells rotten down in the Sticks and are going back to investigate. Bear, Choiya Khan and the Swarm might be involved. Do you still want to come with us?" All were nodding.

"If these clues are real, there are possible breeches in compartments along the way, and you must suit up now in case. The garment room is over by the first aid station."

With his finger, "Mudman here can take you to the weapons locker, you know what you need, if anyone objects, tell them SP205 sent you. George, while you're there, get me another hat to replace the one I lost. I have to brief the ready squad leaders."

The group commanders huddled with Wild Bi1l, leaning in and putting their heads together to be able to talk above the noise of the commons, were given their assigned tasks by the lead detective and in short order split up again to address their crews.

As he was finishing up George and the others were returning with Scott Air Packs or shimmer suits, as appropriate, the Earthman then held out an old stove-pipe hat, the mech glared at it for an instant before jamming it on to the top of his head, "Thanks."

"OK guys, George and I just returned from down there, big picture: our path from the Flying Saucer wasn't blocked, so we might be able to bypass the breeched spaces and vacuum again. Stay here while I brief the Chief." He took off pushing and shoving and swearing.

Upon his return he dropped the two spheres onto the small table, "I gave Sanchez a thumb with my report to give to Ole' Daisy to print. I told him we are heading out now, not waiting for the teams to form, some members are delayed fighting fires. I told him I was taking Khan back; we will need him to reason with the Swarm and negotiate with Bear."

"Please No!" The new members of the team were surprised the globes talked, Mouthpiece ran on, "We're safer here, really Bi1l, you don't need the Khan." Choiya talked about himself in the imperial third person when he was really scared.

Bill ground out, “You’re going, no discussion.” The top hat turned side to side.

“This is Khan? This is what you and the captain were yelling about in the office?” Bill nodded. Ollie was astounded while TOP and Gus were confused by not having the backstory, and Rock was staying silent. “Did I hear right that this Dirtman captured Khan and defeated Bear?”

George shook his head, “Actually, we ran away from Bear.” Now Gus was staring too.

“Come on guys, no time for this, we can talk on the way. George, you have the Khan and his mouthpiece, we’re going to the Sauce, Ollie and I will run interference.”

“What about Max if we run into vacuum?”

“Max is going without a suit. Think about it. If we don’t succeed, he will die anyways. I don’t have to like it, but there it is.”

Death was walking the streets of Vesta.

Was there an answer?

Could they find it in time?

ROADMAP

A successful colonization of the solar system
will take many generations, perhaps millennia.

"If I had followed my better judgment always,
my life would have been a very dull one."
- Edgar Rice Burroughs

A man, by working 24 hours a day, could multiply himself 3 times.
To multiply himself more than 3 times,
the only recourse is to train others to take over some of his work.
Hyman Rickover

Bear

CH 53

Fear exploded within him as he flailed back to the surface and began his escape from the Bear to the other side. His heart was in his throat, the image of the huge teeth inches from his beating feet made him want to weep if he wasn't so desperate. Stumbling as he hit the slope of the shore he struggled up and force waded his body through the thick water, he had made the beach and ran. Just then he heard the sound of the Spirit breaching the surface, exploding through the water with a roar! He sprinted faster than he knew how, leaping up and forward toward a branch sticking out of the right side of the tree, swinging around the bole as the bear rushed past, swiping at him, unable to stop. Boy clambered branch over branch as he heard those below snap and break under the weight of the angry force below.

He climbed higher, above where he could be caught, and then wedged himself in a fork so he would not slip and fall from his exhaustion during the night. In gratitude to Grandmother and the Trickster, he gently reached down and touched the Raven feather. His chest began to ache, and he looked down to discover the Spirit had raked and cut him with four claws across his torso, not to the bone, but starting to burn. They would make terrible scars. Surely, the bear would give up and go away by daybreak. He began to see double in his pain, and thought he saw an image of a man next to the bear. The Spirit nodded slightly and disappeared as he and the bear padded off into the woods.

All would know that this day, Boy had faced his fear and become Brave.

The team boiled out of the police station and turned downtown towards the HUB and the Flying Saucer. Crisis squads had locked down the Ave and restored some semblance of order. Traffic was moving again, albeit in fits and starts. EMTs had set up a Triage Center in the grounds of the Baptist Church, announcements warned citizens of life, air and safety issues.

George was stunned with the amount of destruction in the streets. Next to the precinct there were two rows of motionless bodies under sheets and a pile-up tangle of mechanical body parts, some of it still moving.

To force priority for their march to the Sauce, Bill had blown himself up into his hulk persona with red and blue strobes flashing from his shoulders while next to him 0llie had transformed into a Navy rapid response titanium Gatling gun running on a liquid metal omni track down the causeway.

Wild Bill's top hat had not changed size with his transformation and bounced on top of his monstrous head like a thimble. Fast walking behind this irresistible force was the rest of the team, the Earth detective was struggling with a sense of dread for the hopelessness that hovered over their continuing efforts. Why? There just didn't seem to be an answer, so he forced himself to slog on.

Shortly after passing the continued hysterics at the Abalama intersection, the team was able to make significant progress down Main Street as most inhabitants moved aside like the parting of the Red Sea, and those who did not were shoved out of the way by one or the other of the mechs. As they turned in towards the diner, he noted more shrouded shapes in the church across the street from the Saucer and more chaos in the distance towards the HUB.

Bill and 0llie were doing their thing transforming down to normal size to allow entry into the gloomy bar and Joe was nowhere to be found. Smart man, based upon the temper of the team as they streamed on by through the back door.

The mech detective was explaining while winding down the hallway, “Everything so far leads to the Bear and her parts yard. We must capture and interrogate her and her systems, we can’t go in with guns blazing.”

“Do you think we can talk our way through this?”

They were turning another corner as they descended into Dante’s hell, “Don’t know, Bear is one of the few Animans, derived from an intelligent animal. She doesn’t think like us or talk like us. If we are to have any success at all, we need to negotiate from a position of power. That’s why I brought Khan, we going to get the swarm.”

Khan’s mouthpiece sonorous voice yelled “Bi1l, that’s crazy! By now the swarm will have gone feral, and there’s no way to control them!”

They began to slow, there were just a few more landings and ramps left before they came to the level of the Sticks, “Choiya, my friend, we need the swarm, with them, you captured Bear, without them we haven’t a chance. Necessity is the mother of invention; we will find a way to coral them.”

“You fool! The swarm didn’t capture it, I tricked it, then trapped it in the back room. You can’t expect to get away with that ploy again, she may be an Animan, but she isn’t stupid. She’s as smart as the Raven.” George’s ears twitched at that mention, storing it for later follow up, if there was a later.

The mech didn’t let up, “We’re going, we have to have every advantage possible, no discussion.”

They had come to a black space, so dark nothing was visible except the faint outline of an arch at the other side. Obviously, the lighting everywhere was becoming less reliable, suddenly the brilliance of an arc lamp from Wild Bill’s ever resourceful shoulder illuminated the square room that they had been in before. As he stepped in George caught his breath while one of the other humans coughed out, "What is that smell? It's horrible!" Max shook all over.

It held the same deep sound and low frequency throb of rumbling water and the frozen forms of silenced mechanical men. George said through his teeth, "Welcome to the Sticks, fellas. Don't worry about the odors, it will soon get worse. This is where my partner and I found the scent of the trail before."

Bill looked over quickly, "George, are you OK? You told a joke."

"No Bill, I am not OK, I am losing it just a little. Crap and dying, it's not just another day." He rolled his shoulders, "I am sorry about making light of it, it is most serious." He walked through the arch onto the dock as the others followed. The Federal Detective proceeded over to the *Denmark's* front door.

Pounding, "Open up Mike! We need Cherry's help again!" He continued for a full minute before stopping. There was no response, so he started up again for another thirty seconds, and began to listen. Again, there wasn't a response, and they didn't hear anything, except maybe a distant stifled groan behind the thick door. George's heart sank, how could they make the transit without Cherry?

"Hey!" came a voice from behind as they all turned to watch a bollard transform itself into a carrot topped mech with a body like a donut, colored with magenta at its feet and sliding into sky blue, and an orange head sitting on top, "Monkeywrench!" Bill exclaimed, "What are you doing here?"

The strange looking mech came up to the group, "Cherry said things here were going to heck, and he was going to row downstream until everything boiled over. Said there would be an opening in the dock, and I would be welcome to it. Nothing much moving topside so, here I am!"

“What do we have for a boat?”

At that point the edge of the dock began to disintegrate and transformed itself int a cab over engine amphibious DUKW Boat, “Ducky’s not fast, but all terrane and will haul us with room to spare. Will it do?”

“Monkeywrench! You’re a lifesaver. Load up everyone, we now have a chance.”

Clambering aboard, George overheard Khan pleading to be left behind, his partner totally ignored the Cactus King by tossing both spheres unceremoniously over the gunwale and turned to helped Max in. Old man Gus was puffing steam furiously while struggling with the high skirt but was quickly rescued and lifted in by the three sailors.

Monkeywrench shoved off into the chop and wind, which pungently reminded the Earthman with a sickening feeling where they were and where they were going. Watching the globes roll about the flat bottom of the boat in the bilge water he reached down and grabbed the brain cases and set them on the bench beside him, Khan attempted to implore him, “Please don’t let him take us back, we’re no good to you or this mission.” He decided it was best to ignore the pleadings and shut them out of his mind.

As spray burst all the way up to the top hat, he watched Bill and Monkeywrench point and discuss the best landing approach for a few minutes, whereupon the detective called out, “Team, we are going in as quietly as possible and will attempt to slip by Bear without alerting her.

“Our first goal is to return to Choiya’s’s hidey hole and corral the swarm, then with them in tow, try to question the bruin about what she knows about the attacks. All is lost if we can’t accomplish these steps, so quietly now.” The Duck had begun to roll ashore.

Monkeywrench came to a stop on a sandy stretch between what appeared to be in the gloom an industrial vacuum truck and an antique street sweeper. The lights were even darker than what George remembered,

"No lights, no sounds, RAM if you have it," Bill said softly, "we will follow Max's nose and trail." He was lowering carefully a Jacobs ladder to the gravel, allowing the team to disembark without scrabbling against the metal of the hull.

Looking around, the Earthman saw many more vehicles with a red LED aglow, not moving, but he noticed the LEDs were periodically pulsing. Each cab had a different period, diminishing, then returning to the steady state.

He was suddenly reminded of the day he had come across a ground nesting hornet's hive shortly after sunset back in the forest of Puget Sound. There, in the three-inch hole opening, clung thousands of bald-faced hornets, their beady black eyes staring back at him, unmoving in the reflected flashlight. Shivers went up and down his spine, as he remembered slowly backing up and creeping away from that potential catastrophe.

The mech was talking quietly to the dog's ear, then stood up, "Now, we follow," as Max led off down a trail between the hulking machines. In the dark the group bunched up close together as they traveled the poorly defined path, George's stomach tightening as they began to loop around the dark shape of Bear's horrific crusher, cringing at the thought of it coming alive.

Each member of the team was surveying the spaces around them for danger as they walked, George was impressed at everyone else's resolve and ability to reject the fear. The sound of Gus's puffing was suddenly loud in his ear as Gus came beside him, how could the earth movers not here that?

Just as he completed that thought he began to notice the pulses of the LEDs around them had started to synchronize and he reached forward to tap his partner on the shoulder, "I see it too." Bill whispered and began to pick up the pace. The brightness of the indicators was significantly stronger, and all were definitely strobing together, blinking faster. Engines and equipment were coming alive around them.

"Now, we run!" Max was barking from the entrance to the exit tunnel as they dashed through the dark shifting mass of equipment. Suddenly George tripped over a prone body and heard the rasping of Gus as he went down.

Pushing back up off the ground he felt shapes around him grab Gus and lift him forward, "STOP YOU!" raged the thunderous voice from behind, "STOP! STOP! I want YOU!" as the reverberating clank of the heavy treads crashed down towards them. The Dirtman was scrabbling on all fours like a crab following the others, tears streaming down his face as he tried to outpace the doom coming up behind him.

Then, he was in the tunnel and the threats falling behind as the large machines were stopped by the rough walls of rock and 'crete. His breaths were coming in large gasping swallows and his head throbbing with the beating of his heart.

ROADMAP

The Space Colonization Effort will be more arduous than speculated;
Over ten thousand distinct industries and
One-hundred-million people must be engaged.

"When it came to my art, I went my own way and did not follow the trends."
- Frank Frazetta

"Everything new endangers something old. A new machine replaces human hands; a new source of power threatens old businesses; a new trade route wipes out the supremacy of old ports and brings prosperity to new ones.
This is the price that must be paid for progress and it is worth the loss."
Hyman Rickover

Confrontation

CH 54

The Three Musketeers had grabbed Gus and were hustling him forward and George was glad of his fitness routine which allowed him keep up. Slowed, Bill assessed their condition and asked the old man if he could keep up. "Watch me MacHinery! I'm good for the long haul!" As this burst out of him, he shook off the hands of the sailors.

"If I hadn't tripped over your big flat feet as I tried to pass, I would have beaten you!" The tiny steam reliefs around his joints slowly quit their small whistles as Gus vented out his anger and fear. Max came over and gave him a nudge with his nose.

Turning down the tunnel "Come along then, it's not too far to the end." They could see the outline in the distance,

“The rest of you OK? I’ve never seen anyone run so fast on all-fours as you George, well done.” George didn’t bother to respond as he slowly clenched his hands feeling the abrasions on the palms send sharp signs of cuts and bruise, but nothing broken.

“Greenies, you boys OK too?” They grunted their affirmation as the group had come up to the egress of the tunnel.

Looking out across the dim courtyard to the unmarked building fronts he remarked, “Well prickly puss, it’s your time to sing, are you ready?” Before Khan could answer Rock yelped, “Ow! Damm, what was that?”

George heard a small buzz near his ear that sounded like ‘kibble’. 0llie and TOP began swatting around themselves and even Max made a snap at the air.

Choiya’s mouthpiece let out, “Wild Bi1l, you ignoramus! There is a swarm out there, The MOTHER of all swarms, and already the bees have found you. You ignored me, the authority on swarm control, and by ignoring me you have become an arrogant fool, and your lives hang in the balance!”

Gus slapped his arm as a small steam line sprung a leak. “Humans will be torn apart and mechs swarmed and dissolved in acid as they eat you for your components. Trust me, you don’t want to go out there, turn around while you still have time.”

“Khan, we have another neutrino bomb and can immobilize the cloud long enough for us to restore you to your body where you can recover control.” George heard another small ‘kibble’ fly by his head causing him to reflexively duck.

“Bi1l, by now they have gone feral, their software evolves so fast it must be monitored hourly before it gets out from under, must worse than a human RNA virus, evolving at an error rate higher than our space environment changes. I doubt that I will be able to control them."

George could see dark blankets of snickering evil slowly come from behind the buildings, covering everything in their path, and from the chitter came a distinct tiny call, "Kill Bill, Kill Bill."

They were all starting to swat as small forms buzzed around them, 0llie mumbled, "Geez Bill, what did you do to get them pissed off like this? Well done indeed." George agreed, *they were pooked.*

"Oh, shut up. TOP, give me one of your grenades, I'm going in." Bill transformed into monster mech, as if that would do any good and the Torpedo Officer fumbled over one of the bombs, "all of you come running as soon as I give the signal."

And with that remark Wild Bill marched out into the advancing guard of the tiny mechs causing them to shift their focus onto him. By the time he was halfway across a cloud had begun to form around his body and some of the hoard had attached themselves to his legs and were working their way up.

He began to dance an exaggerated jig, with his left hand holding his hat to his head, he pulled the pin and threw the explosive device against the ground with an underwhelming poof. The mechs around George swayed for a moment and the mouthpiece rattled out a groan.

The Federal detective began sweeping his arms forwards and the group gathered their wits and proceeded in his direction stepping over still bodies whose antenna still waved and behind whose eyes still blazed small purple lights.

He led them into the bunker where they had first found Khan and Bear, which showed the destruction of their initial visit with thousands of inert forms, these without the internal lights and motions of their brethren outside, final casualties of the first battle.

"OK guys, help clean away this corner, under this mess is Khan's armchair. Gus, go to the door and keep an eye on the battlefield, sing out if they start stirring."

As they settled the Cactus King into his throne, the mouthpiece lost its animus and Khan was able to speak from the speakers directly built into the chair. "I am going to try, Bi1l, but it's like trying to herd cats with lassos of spider silk. As I tug, the command strings are breaking, and the Swarm has little common history with me anymore."

His armchair stood up into its mobile form as the piles of micromechs started to twitch and stir, "I'm trying, but..." his voice cut out as he turned to the mob that was forming in front of them.

"I don't like the looks of this," someone cursed.

The pile was swaying back and forth slowly, leaning towards them, then away as Khan momentarily regained control. "TOP, give me another neutrino bomb."

"Last One."

"Damm. Everyone, pull your weapon. George, still got those laser thingees of yours?"

"Nope, takes weeks to regenerate. Got the pistola though," *we're pooked* he thought tiredly.

"Damm."

As the Swarm began to surge their direction again. "I'm losing it!" it broke free.

Bi1l immediately threw the ordinance against the floor of the bunker with the familiar *poof!*

"OK team, we're outa here. We tried. Khan, do need help? Are you even with us?"

"Just get going Bi1l, they will recover sooner this time, evolution and all that. I'm going to lockdown the facility as soon as you leave. They're after you, not me." As if to enunciate his point, the mound began to chirp *kibble* again, small mechs started to jerk and tumble down the pile.

The team fast stepped through the door and vectored around the largest mass of attackers towards the hallway and tunnel. "TOP, do you have any of your concussion grenades handy?" Some of the bees were back and the high-pitched *Kill Bill* was starting again. "Once inside, let's drop the roof and close off that end of the passage."

Even before he said: "let's go everyone" the group began to sprint with Max barking at their side shortly followed by the flying mechanical hornets and bees. Entering Bi1l shouted, "TOP, set your explosives, everyone else, keep the bees off of him."

During what may have been the longest thirty seconds of his life TOP, Rock and 0llie began the emplacement of the explosives while he, Bi1l and Gus kept the critters at bay.

He grabbed Max's leash off of Bi1l and began snapping the bees out of the air, Gus had reconfigured some kind of minute steam line and was blasting the creepy-crawlies approaching the entrance with flamethrower effectiveness, while the mech had transformed himself into some sort of mantis, destroying the hornets with his new scythes.

ROADMAP

The centuries required by the Space Colonization Effort
will necessitate a stable and robust civilization,
Demanding a Greater Understanding of
Human Behavior and Culture consistent with Reality.

"Do you see things in black and white, or are there shades of gray for you?"
"I hope there's gray...Black and white make things easier,
but only if you don't want to think."
— Harry Turtledove

"Don't look back. Something might be gaining on you."
Satchel Paige

Jon

CH 55

"Done! Beat feet!" the squad turned and ran down the hall towards where it began to become rock again. "FIRE in the Hole!" As TOP gave a twist to his hand held, a concussion swept over them followed by dust and debris. They looked back and as the dust cleared, they could see that the tunnel was fully filled with rubble, blocking the Swarm from following them. Only then could they take a breath and hold it, letting it go slowly.

Looking at each other with exhaustion, searching, wondering. "Is everyone OK and intact?" Bill inquired.

"Would it matter if we weren't?" Rock replied to no one in particular.

"I guess not," the mech continued, "but we must continue. 'When the going gets rough', and all that."

"Yep."

"Unless anyone has a better idea, all that remains is the frontal approach. Questions? Thoughts?"

"It's your ball, it's your call. Gotta do what we gotta do." This reflected the sentiment of all.

"Let's try to get back to the Duck, then attempt to signal Bear we want to negotiate. Play it by ear from that point on."

Someone muttered, "Crap, if we only had the WET, this would be over and solved in less than a minute with modern communications. I am sure this must be a mistake. Bear must want to save Vesta."

"Bear has some bad memories, remember, she was caged in a circus for almost a century before they realized she was sentient. Combine that with she doesn't know what we are about, just that we were with Khan who trapped her and lost her papoose." *Yeah, we're pooked*

Without much further ado the band of exhausted men began what might be their last hurrah, tackling an irresistible force to get the key to recover from this disaster. Having this in mind while knowing their lives and the lives of their loved ones hung in the balance, they began the march back through the tunnels towards the waste yard of ancient malevolent machines and their nemesis, the Bear.

George noticed that both Gus and Max were limping as they traveled causing him to wince as he realized his own bruising and minor scrapes. The skin of his chest was burning, and he felt down gingerly to find blood. He took a couple of experimental breaths to feel how deep the injury, relieved to discover the pain was all on top, nothing internal, he sagged with weariness.

His energy was low, haven't slept in who knows how long, and food was in the past and this made him wonder how long the mechs could go without recharging. Perhaps he would find out at the wrong time.

The three musketeers seemed the least affected by the exertions of the day, walking forward with purposeful strides, when 0llie held up his arm to halt the group. "I think the hangar space is just around the next corner, I would like to reconnoiter quietly and see if the machines are still awake or alert."

With a nod, MacHinery gave his acquiescence, indicating his own exhaustion, whether mental or physical, George didn't know. Most likely, both.

They all waited while 0llie snuck forward and went around the corner slowly and out of sight. They waited for what seemed an eternity, but it only lasted a few minutes before 0llie was back to report, "All appears to be quiet, the LEDs are all lit but at a reduced glow, we might be able to make it to the beach if we are quick and quiet, and lucky. I say, let's roll."

They gathered together, formed up in single file, and crept out into the gloom of that massive cavern. The familiar and frightful shapes on shadows of the earth movers surrounded them as they followed the barely visible sweeping white tip of Maxi's tail.

Each machine seemed to have some subsonic hum emanating from it, each a dark shadowy shape against a darker outline, with cabs lit by faint red glows. George gently would reach out and touch with just fingertips against them as he passed to prevent bumping into one in the dimness.

Crash! “Ow!” Gus had stumbled again, this time landing with his shoulder against the fender of a backhoe with a resounding din. “Pook, that’s it! Let’s book!”

The machines were coming alive, one of the sailors bent down and helped Gus back onto his feet as they began running down the sands between the slowly shifting behemoths to escape. *“FOE! STOP YOU!*” boomed overhead.

This was a heavy iron space and when the equipment collided in their efforts to contain the men, the tortured grunt of distorted metal created small cramps in George’s upper back each time he flinched.

Max was barking wildly in the darkness, noises of the whine of enormous motors coming up to speed was beginning to be overwhelming, their escape was being blocked as machines roared in front of and around them. *“FIE, YOU STOP!”*

The ceiling lights had finally gone out and the air was stagnant, the only illumination was reflections from the machine’s instrumentation itself. George was trying to orient himself to the path but as the shadows shifted, he was losing his sense of direction. He heard Gus call out in the night, answered by Bill and other voices, but they could not be understood.

Looming behind and above the nearby shapes emerged that horrendous shadow he knew all too well, cab lit with multiple glow lamps down towards the infrared, with black bodies blotting out even that illumination as they shifted about inside. *Pook, we’re cooked for sure now.*

Unable to continue to retreat without being overrun, he resignedly turned towards this fate when he was blinded by a brilliant and painful white light that hurt his eyes even after he reflexively closed them.

Squinting tightly, he looked around and saw they had been encircled by a continuous wall of machines, still jostling against one another while inexorably creeping forward. *And Khan thought the Swarm was bad?* He noted everyone was there except Max, who was baying madly outside this living fence. "*YOU STOP YOU!*" bellowed the command again.

Shielding his eyes, he returned to looking up at the rock crusher that Bear was riding, unable to see but an outline of the cab behind the spotlight's glow.

"Bear!" he croaked and coughed, the crusher's scoop bounced as the hydraulic stops were applied, then it began to lower again towards them, and this time George didn't lose his nerve or his voice "Bear! Hear me!"

The bucket stopped again just over their heads blotting out the ceiling and showering them with a hail of gravel as the earth mover tottered fore and back on its tracks from rusty systems long in disuse. A muffled voice called out. Then with a squeal, the blade of the scoop started to rotate down, and a large form showed over the top.

"Bear, hear me! I've come in Trade, the old Way!" The blade quit moving five feet up. Two small shapes huddled in the back.

"I know you human."

"I think I know you too, from another place."

"Another time."

Bill stared at them intently.

"Yes." George agreed.

Bill raised his eyebrow at George who merely shook his head as if to say: *None of Your Business.*

"Trade?"

George relaxed somewhat, “Trade. The cautionary words of my ancestor are like stars that never set. The sky outside that has wept tears of compassion for our ancestors for centuries untold, and which to us, looks eternal, has changed. Yesterday it was fair, today it is overcast with clouds. I follow the warrior’s path searching for an enemy, to reset the proper order of the Universe. Trade.”

“Trade. I search for Panda.”

This intensely cryptic discussion was interrupted by a boy’s tousled head looking down.

“Dad? Dad! It’s really you!” The cylinder head of W0ody also began to peer over the edge.

“Jon? Jonny! You’re alive!” Gus was urgently signaling behind with his right hand for someone to give him a boost up to the bucket. He was reaching up with his left to grab the rim.

“Wait dad, wait! We’ll come down.”

“Are you OK?”

“Yes, we’re OK. Give me a second, we’ll be right down. You need to back away.” Jon turned to face the cab and pointed his right hand down, fingers touching, while holding his left hand out flat.

As he tapped his fingers together, they began to be lowered slowly to the ground. The forms of W0ody and Jon came into the weak light, as well as the large shape sitting in the right-hand corner of the scoop, elbow on the outside rim, looking at them.

Bear was massive, as big as Bi11 in monster mode, with the folds of her shaggy black-brown coat drooped down from her shoulders across her chest. She had a short nose and close-set eyes in a huge round head, with two round ears like teacups set on the top of her head.

She watched them intently in the dark, shoved up against the side of the bucket, the big paw draped across the frame, claws as big as kitchen knives extended.

As they settled onto the ground Jon ran over and threw his arms around his dad and spoke excitedly, "This is Bear, dad, she saved us when we got lost in the collapsed offices, we were here when Uncle Bill and Maxie and that guy came through earlier. We tried to stop them, but they were in a hurry and wouldn't, so we didn't know what to do." Jonny caught his breath and hurried on as they listened, "The lights kept going out and it was getting colder. We have been staying in her rec vehicle here, hoping Uncle Bill would come back! Wow. You all came."

Bear ignored this distraction, stood up on all fours and padded out to meet them and stared hard at George.

Looking at George, eye to eye, growled, "Trade?" Everyone became suddenly still, afraid to interrupt and initiate trouble.

"Trade. I can find Panda. You want Panda?" Bill was shocked and worried to hear George begin negotiations by running a bluff.

"Trade. Two off-worlders lived here," scaping her left rear leg backwards towards the crusher, "You look?"

"Yes. Special Lieutenant Detective William MacHinery here," he reached out with his right hand and gave Wild Bill a shove, knocking him slightly off balance and had to reach up suddenly to keep his hat on, "is right friendly with one of the Sphinges, the Lady of the Sea," *I am?* he thought, "and will recover Panda for you when we restore this world, on pain of death." *I will?*

"Trade."

"Trade. Under the sky outside that has nurtured our ancestors for centuries untold, Trade."

Bear turned to the mech detective. "Help me, Mister Bill, help me and I help you. Trade?"

Pain of Death? Bill winced and acknowledged, "Trade."

Bear sat down and looked over to where Jon and W0ody stood frozen by this exchange, George looked around at the stiff faces, "It's OK everyone, the danger is passed. We have a deal which we can meet. Gus, go ahead, and meet your son."

Gus was patting Jon's back while the other's looked on. Wild Bill went over to W0ody, and asked him, "Do you mean that Bear was trying to get us together when she was shouting stop?"

"Well Uncle Bill, Bear doesn't talk well. We did best by sign language, we even made up our own. Her name is Theodora Edison, but she says you can call her Teddi or T.E." The little mech walked over to the animan who put her broad paw on W0ody's chest. W0ody then put his hand over the paw and let their fingers do the talking.

"T.E. says she's glad she was finally able to get through to you, communication is so hard between species." Max began to howl behind the machines, and Bear removed her paw and waved to a scissor-lift to move away and let Maxie in.

She came back to W0ody and patted his chest, "Teddi understands Vesta is in trouble, and hope's she can help." He stopped while they continued touching fingers,

"Two strangers occupied her home while she was visiting the Cactus King, and when they left, much was missing, but there is stuff still there that wasn't hers. You can search. When this is all over, T.E. wants you to take her to the Khan so she can cuff him soundly. Panda is her cub."

Bill seemed rejuvenated, "0llie, Rock, Jefferson: I want you to go to the precinct and get a Forensic IT team down here ASAP. Take Monkeywrench and tell him to stay at Iron Mike's so there will be transport when you come back. He's not to leave!"

He stared at them, "Well, what are you waiting for? A band and anchors away? Chop chop." They looked at each other and shook their heads as they left.

Turning, "George, Gus, we aren't forensics or IT, but we had better start. We still don't know if this is our problem or not, let's go up and see Bear's abode."

"Can we come too Uncle Bill?" Bill stared at the two for a moment. "Please? We can talk to T.E. for you, you need us!"

"OK, but stay still and don't touch anything, even a piece of crumpled paper might mean something, normally not, but some crimes have hinged on that, so don't be children, restrain yourselves, OK?"

"Yessir."

They hand-over-handed the barrel ladder affixed to the side of the loader, Bill's top hat getting mashed as it bumped the rungs, up to the operator space and entered for the look around. Bear had hopped into the bucket and using crane signals came up and returned to the cab. The space was a disaster, with only a small clean spot near the operator's chair,

"T.E. told us not to touch anything, so it's all like it was, we actually slept in another machine." George had to step over and around packing boxes, discarded food packs, wires strung hither and thither. The console had been opened up, but many electrical harnesses had been cut and removed in what looked like a hasty departure, the only ones intact were the shore power cables leading back to wherever that provide power to the lights.

"Gus, start looking at the remaining equipment and electrical gear. See if anything is still hooked up and what's missing. Kids, pass questions that your dad might have on to Teddi, she could help determine what's amiss."

As the four of them moved forward, Bill and George moved aft towards the sleeping compartment. "I assume you have seen as many crime scenes as I have, we may not be CSI, but let's give it a go. You take the human bunk area; I will search the mech's berthing and recharge. You got gloves?"

George shook his head and gave him a *Are you crazy?* look. "OK, skip that, do your best using your instinct guided by experience." Shaking his head again in exasperation, George set off, doing his inspection.

They went about their work for a half hour, with just minimal comments between the two of them, carefully going every inch piece by piece, while murmurs of the forward group indicated their coordinated effort.

"Uncle Bill, Uncle Bill!"

“What is it?”

“T.E. tells us that some of the machines here in the enclave saw Monkeywrench’s boat capsize in one of the channel rips! They can’t see any survivors. They just got word back here.”

They were all quiet for a moment. “Damm, they were good boys.” Gus said it all.

“That means: no help,” with melancholy sadness.

“This is true, but it also means we won’t rely on others. We have to be stronger.”

“Dad, how can you say things like that at a time like this? Is this a character-building moment?”

“Son, fate isn’t always kind, but if we are to survive, it’s up to us.”

“Wah! After what I’ve seen lately. Crap! There is no hope!

“Jon, you are an adult now in all ways but the forms. You can do what you think is best, but for me, *‘Where’s there’s life, there’s hope’*, I am going back to work. W0ody, can you continue to help with the translations?”

While Jonny sat withdrawn in the corner, W0ody went back to the instrument panel with Gus, and the two detectives resumed their search. Item after item was examined, Gus used his electrical knowledge to assess the devices in the front.

Minute by minute they worked, sometime sharing information in low conversation, comparing notes, asking for opinions.

Periodically Bear was brought in the discussions about the normal placement of equipment, was this here before, or is it new, hour after hour, their desperation grew, and their hope shrank.

Eventually Jon frustration boiled over as he vehemently complained, “This sucks! We have been over it again and again Dad. Uncle Bill, have you guys even found one thing useful?” Bill and George were quiet, watching him.

“Bah! I quit! I am going to find mom and get us off ‘roid before it’s too late! W0ody, are you coming?”

ROADMAP

A Movement shall be created
Bringing together interested and concerned people and
Engaging the next generation
By giving them ownership of their future

Bran thought about it. 'Can a man still be brave if he's afraid?'
'That is the only time a man can be brave,' his father told him.
- George R.R. Martin

"Take only memories, leave nothing but footprints."
Chief Seattle

George and Richard

Chapter 56

His hair was dripping from the cold spray the winds were throwing from the aft quarter. Aleks was sore about his middle and bent over with cramps as the ship rolled about the bottoms and hills of the swells that were driving them along without mercy. Mastless, the currents carried the ship where they would.

He crawled his way forward to the bowsprit covered with a tangle of the remaining lines from the ruptured forestays, whereupon his stomach delivered a series of dry heaves. Oh, he would collapse from the beating the world had delivered, wanting to be dead. The crew was gathered about amidships, in their exhaustion trying to organize bailing, but without enough energy to row.

Deep in his misery Aleks became aware of a roar that surmounted the howls of the storm and lifted his head. His eyes adjusted to the gloom and became aware of a pounding surf crashing against what must have been rocks and shoals on the steering board side, so close as to deafen him. He yelled an alarm for the sailors but could not be heard over the winds. Clawing his way erect, he staggered, then ran back to the sailor at the tiller and tried to warn him, but in the wind, still could not be understood!

He became surrounded by the crew and the Captain was yelling and dragging at him. Screaming in terror he fought with them over control over rudder until his hysterical strength prevailed and he pushed the tiller full over to the starboard side causing the boat to heel over and turn to port at a dangerous angle. As the bow opened up, the crew finally saw their danger and impending doom, and rose up as a group to assist in holding the steerboard against the tug of the currents.

Finally, as the ship slipped back into safety, the Captain turned to stare at him with sunken eyes, his face behind his beard slack with exhaustion. Then, with the merest of nods to Aleks, turned away and began to restored order.

George spoke, “Before you quit, Jon, can I make a suggestion?” Jon sat down sullenly. “W0ody, have you examined the shore power cables?”

“Yes, George, I carefully examined the shore power cables, they’re connected with a Marinco thirty-amp adaptor.”

“Did you examine the other end?” queried the detective.

“No, why?”

“Where I grew up on Earth, we had a mishmash of antiquated equipment, some could be integrated, some not. Rather than running new structured wiring, we often run our data right on the power cables. I’ve never done it myself; Augustus will know more.”

Gus spoke up, “W0ods, ask the Bear here if her motor home here needed shore power, or did it have a nuclide decay reactor power source for the four hundred hertz and hotel loads?”

“What’s nuclide decay? How can I say it?”

“Oh, just radioactive particles making thermal energy. Give it a try.”

Reaching over to Bear, he slowly placed the large paw on his chest and began the tap of fingers.

After a bit, he looked up, "Bear says she didn't need shore power except when the batteries are removed. Our batteries are intact."

George turned his eyes towards Gus, "I suggest we vacate the crusher and visit the other end of the shore power. A dime will get you a dollar that it isn't hooked into the electrical closet. "

Under the droopy top hat Bill thoughtfully remarked, "The Earthman has made a point. I think we should do as he advises."

Leaving the cab through the back exit, they clambered over the crusher's casement and frame following the cables as they snaked their way back and down behind the machine. Once on the ground they continued past the still forms illuminated by the backwash of the earth mover's lights and finally found the wires going under a door.

Gus broke out a pin light and examined the door's face. "George's right, this isn't an electrical closet, it's the comm locker."

"Gus, you have to be careful now, disconnecting is going to be dicey, all kinds of things can go wrong." He paused, "before we do anything, we need to take a good look."

They all agreed with this assessment that an inspection had to be accomplished before opening the door. Bill and Ollie began of for traps and deceptions.

Once done, they carefully swung the access open until it was flush with the outer wall, then shined their lights inside. Where shore power normally lands on substantial clamps, this cable broke into a bundle of thin colored wires, each one struck down at different point on an immense panel board on the opposite wall.

Gus shook his head, “With all these leads, I am at a loss as where to start.” Still slowly turning his head side to side, he stared at the rat’s nest in front of him. 0llie and TOP came and looked over his shoulder at the confusion. “Looks like a tube nest alright, wouldn’t want to inadvertently roll the stop, now would we?”

“George, you brought us to this point, do you have a suggestion?”

“I’m over my head when it comes to the specifics, sorry. Gus, do we want to try without an expert here?”

“No, we wouldn’t. This is a big problem. If we disconnect wires it might help, or blow up in our face and become a flood of destruction, we could cause the death of half the planet, right here, right now. I can’t do it. It’s too much responsibility. Anybody?” He leaned against the jam dejectedly, the weight of the world at hand.

The down below Dirtman spoke, “Before we make a decision to blow up the world, Gus, I can remove this last panel cover, just in case it reveals something. W0ody, can I borrow one of your screw drivers?”

“Sure, here is my favorite, given to me by Uncle Bi1l. It’s even better than a nine-in-one combine with a multitool.” He handed over the modified Antikythera tool.

“Pook!” George dropped the object like a hot potato. “You didn’t tell me it was alive!

The device withered on the floor for a moment before assuming a rigid shape.

“That’s Richard, he’s a smart tool, an animate object. At least he was, but after the HOB, he became as dead as a doornail. Uncle

Bill, didn't you tell me you had him modified down here somewhere?"

"Yes, over with Khan, when he was nano-king. Things over there have gone a little south lately, I wouldn't be surprised if they are connected."

"Mister Detective, I too, was frozen until Jon and Gus got me this Faraday cage hair net, now I'm immune, Richard is not."

"Well, it was alive just now."

"Maybe you have magic and brought him alive with your touch?"

"No way. I'm just an Earthman and have nothing to do with your deep space 'magic'."

Bill remarked, "We all saw it George, Richard was alive there for a moment."

"Mister George, if you pick Richard up, maybe he can come back alive again?"

"I don't know W0ody, that was creepy-disturbing."

"Could you just touch him for a moment to see?"

Gus added, "W0ody could be right. He was spot on when he saved himself with his Faraday hair net. Couldn't hurt." *Right,* thought George, *it's not him doing this.*

"Go ahead George, I've got your back." The mech detective sounded assured. *Right,* thought George, *it's not you doing this either.*

The Earthman eyed the tool suspiciously. Then decision made, reached down.

A furious little set of transformations started and a small voice piped, "Wow! I thought youse guys would never make up your minds." He had to grit his teeth as a wave of goosebumps swept up and down his arm. "Thanks partner," continued the small form, "just, don't let go, OK?"

"Richard, you're really alive!"

"Yeah W0ods, as long as this ham-handed homie holds on." The hackles started to relax. George held the tool like a thistle and stood up.

"Hey Gussaroo, I heard yer discussions, maybe I can help. I graduated from the Punch-Down Academy you know. I'se know lots of methods to resolve these rat's nests. You know, black to black, white to white, yada yada yada."

Bill thoughtfully remarked, "The Mycenaean midget here does have all sorts of unusual knowledge, some from the depths of antiquity. He could be helpful if this stuff is as old as you guys think it is."

He asked George, "Is bringing Richard alive another of your earth magic tricks like your laser fingers you've been holding out on us? Your face and arms are all red and so are the tattoos on your body and back."

"Sorry Bill, I don't have any magic. My tattoos are itchy, but it is because the iron filings interact with my vitamin B pills. Gives me hot flashes."

W0ody's mechanical marionette turned its googlely eyes towards George, "Big man, youse gotta be my robot buddy Waldo, I'm gonna ask you to move me about as I see things, OK? We are going to be teammates. There's no I in team, just me. Hold on to my tool rack as if our lives depended on it, which it do."

Twisting about, "Gus, ol' buddy, ol' pal, ya think we can do this together, huh?"

Gus wasn't sure if to take this seriously, it was the first time Richard had ever addressed him, to him the little tool was just a toy, no more than, say, a talking can opener. To consider this as an engagement of minds was almost ludicrous.

"Come on boss, let me try." The pajama pipsqueak was poking out again, his peepers swiveling about. "How 'bout it, fellas?"

Bill was staring hard at Richard, as he had never seen him before, "How can I trust this toy won in a poker game? All he does is crack bad jokes," everyone looked at Bill, "I know, I know, but look at him, he's below the Gordan limit, there can't be a real thought in his head, how can we trust that?"

"Dad, I trust him. Cat's crèche mate is Blueee3, and it is below the limit too, but staff at the U were convinced something was there. Richard's crude, but he ain't a clockwork, I know that."

Gus was shaking his head, "It's too serious and important, for a world to revolve around a tinker toy."

Bill turned to George, "OK wonder man, you are our impartial observer, what say you?"

George was silent for a long moment, "Gus, we don't know much about this low voltage wiring without W0ody's friend here. Do we dare send somebody up top and wait for them here? Bill, can I ask this Richard some questions? It might help resolve the issue." By this time Richard had wiggled out of George's grip, seen that just by touching he maintained his integrity, and moved to gain a perch on his shoulder.

"I think so, yes, go ahead."

With a high voice, Richard yelled down to W0ody's tool kilt: "OK boys, now we're going places, time to strut your stuff!"

George turned and looked askanced at the tool, *How did I ever get to this point,* he thought, "Richard, would you explain to me, all of us, why you think you can solve this problem?"

"You see, I was listenin' to you guys, and you mentioned a Claw."

"A claw?"

"Yeah, you know, a Dim, an old kinda mech, a Claw! Anyways, I figured there were two perps from what you all said, and I hate to say it, but you humans are fumble fingers when it comes to IT, so it couldn't be the meat stick, had to be the tin can." The little guy seemed to be proud of its reasoning.

Richard's high voice was getting excited, "So I says to myself, Self, if the mech did it, and it's a Claw, it musta been an old timey kinda ploy, maybe so old fashioned that the current immune systems wouldn't detect, couldn't detect, so maybe, what kinda scheme? Huh? What kind a scheme. Why, maybe, Radio Roy!"

"Radio Roy?"

"Shucks, it's no wonder ya never heard of it, anyways, it's a system to send controls when there ain't no radio available, just piggyback it on the power wiring harness of a facility, or what have you. It's something the DIMs used to use, maybe thousands of years ago. See Sherlock, simple. Ya got it?" Its eyes seem to focus on George, no, one moved to look at Bill.

"Got it, I think." George looked over at Gus.

"Wait. I ain't done. I gotta be the guy to disarm this whole thing. See my peepers, big man?" Richard leaned in until one eye was within inches of

George's. "They're special, really special! Why, I cans see all sort of things you guys can't, like, UV and Infrared as well as normal light since I got five times as many types of photoreceptors as you, more of them too! But wait, there's more!" It was getting wound up.

"Each eyeball alone has trinocular vision and depth perception and multiple magnifications for close in work, and combine that with my built-in tool set, I am a regular walking talking EOD team all by myself!

"So, whatcha say, huh?"

The two detectives watched each other wordlessly for a moment, then the human nodded to the mech, and Bill came to a disheartening decision, "We are out of options, Richard, you're up. What can we do to help?"

"Clear a space so I's can work and get some better lights in here. Can the Bear turn her lights around? Should be enough. Dirtman, hold me again, closer to the wires, W0ody, get the tool town team ready, don't know what I'll need until I look it over." W0ody doffed the tool kit, and rolled it out like a short carpet roll, all the utensils lined up in a row.

While Bear and the kids were arranging for the lighting, Richard was tilting its eyes every which way towards the wires and talking to himself, "Ten-twenty-four pairs, standard stuff. We can skip the fiber optics. Where's the red/green and the blue/blue-white? Humm." This went on for perhaps five minutes while the lights were provided.

Augustus hunkered down in a squat to watch, fearful of bumping George or touching anything. "So, Mister Miller, I'm scanning these wires in UV and IR, and there is a little heat on the Bl-Bl/W pair, more than R-G, so whatcha think? My pereiopods have quartz cutters at the tip, should be able to handle nylon jacketed copper."

Forcing himself out of the depression he tiredly responded, "You think part of it is an old phone line? Have you detected any voltage on the Red-Green? Standard Tip-Ring?"

"Hard to say. Thought I felt the imposed twenty hertz signal momentarily, so, should be standard."

Richard turned around, "Billy-boy, we have identified the most likely conductors, and I am ready to do it to it. Comments?" *Jeez* thought George as he turned his face away, *here I am with my arm stuck out, holding a gizmo that might blow up the world, am I stupid or what?*

In resignation the Lead Detective replied, "I sure hope you're right. Go for it, little Richard."

"Yeah, so do I, wouldn't want to be trapped for another thousand years.

"Here's goes nut'in'," then in a louder voice he sang out some mystical words: "**Bop bopa-a-lu a whop bam boo!"** and in quick succession snipped the blue and blue-white pair.

ROADMAP

Each Generation is Responsible for their Survival.
The Colonization Movement will require
many paths to be pursued in parallel
This multitasking will require
social, technological, and economic approaches.

"True peace required the presence of justice, not just the absence of conflict."
— N.K. Jemisin

"One of the only ways to get out of a tight box is to invent your way out."
Jeff Bezos

Road to Recovery

CH 57

The sky above the still waters was the dark before dawn, the morning star, her sister and the crescent moon were together above the forest of the eastern shore. The Warrior's Path that bridged the night sky was all in its full glory making one glad to be alive. The paddles were almost silent as they dipped in the sea lit with its greens and blues of the life within the world below. The only constant sound was the easy breathing of the rowers, men whose strengths reflected lives of activity and effort.

The trees on the near shore were primal giants with girths and masses that made them immune to the winter storms, only after millennia would the rot infested scars ever bring them down. The only sound was the rustle of the smallest swells waxing and waning on the sloped gravel beach combined with the whisper of the folding waters at the bow of the canoe. Most of the night animals were silent in the forest, leaving only the owls to call their hesitant, mournful coughs and cries.

Brave had gone north to search for his redemption, reminded periodically by the scars on his chest., Hero was guiding his troupe triumphantly home after a courageous campaign, wearing his spruce root rain hat with interwoven black horsetail root to show Orca in the ancient formline method, with his Raven Feather attached. The light breeze carrying the home waters' sweet smell merged with the anticipation of their arrival come the day. Rounding Picture Rock Point, the eastern mountains became visible, and the violets and dark blues of dawn could be seen in the valleys between the ridges, Smokey Top with its flat peak was to the north and Majestic to the south.

As they paddled towards their estuarine village on the Green River the east began to brighten, first with greens, followed by scattered isolated small lofty clouds capturing the first rays of red light, quickly changing to pink. Above Smokey Top Hero saw a vision, the wisps of clouds that accompanied that mountain since he had been a child had grown to prodigious proportions, such that the top of the darkly illuminated column was pushed into the morning glow while all else was still in the gloom.

Hero quickly glanced towards Majestic, but its peak was still in darkness, just silhouetted against the glow. Returning his vision back to Smoky Top he witnessed its transformation into the spirit world where it slowly became an orca with its white ventral surface, and it began to swim in the sky towards them. It was that time when the mists began to gather and rise above the waters. The mountain transformed again, this time into a spirit shaman carrying a yew wood staff and lightning in his hair. The medicine man was running towards him, shouting in a thunderous voice but the words were not clear in this waking dream, just out of reach. Then as the daybreak was born, the shaman was shrouded and then disappeared into the rising mists.

Immediately, a pulse like an unseen pressure wave was perceived, and then passed on. The team looked at each other, but nothing else was felt, or observed around them. The lights were still out, the battle lanterns hadn't flickered, so after a moment, Richard continued to cut the wiring harness apart, this time with no other reactions. George took a large sigh and sensed the weight of the world returning.

Somberly, George watched W0ody continue to help dismantle the suspected site, pulling wires back as Richard removed them. Jon was sitting in the corner, arms around his legs and head between his knees, rocking back and forth, his father next to him, arm around his shoulder.

A flash in the ceiling of the hanger caught their attention as one of the old sodium vapor lights flickered, then another, and suddenly, another. Everyone stopped to look, as rows and rows and rows of lights started their climb to brightness. "Hey, I felt the carrier for the WET twitch, and its coming back! W0ody, take off your head net," Jon said excitedly

Motor mouth chimed in, "I feel it too! You did it, Richard!"

Augustus was more cautious than the kids, but he too stood in wonder as the world started to come back to life.

"Let me go, gargantuanaut! Let me down, I'm free!" Richard wriggled loose and dropped to the floor. "Yahoo!" He scuttled across the floor and ran across to the tools spread upon the apron. Small claw out he whistled, "High five and survive, guys!" slapping each one as he went by.

T.E. stood up on her back legs and waddled over to Bill, "I stop you! You stop end!" and proceeded to wrap up the mech in a huge hug. Bill struggled without success to free himself, so, he twisted and jerked his head towards George, "He did it Bear, not me! You need to give him a hug also." Without releasing the metal detective Bear wrapped up the Earthman and gave them both a squeeze.

"Cute Bill, didn't work." Referring to the attempt to get released.

"I'm not dumb, metal man," before dropping them back to the floor.

W0ody announced, "I'm hearing an all-clear from Life Safety on the K_u band, the planet wide fog is lifting, emergency systems are being brought back online! Uncle Bill, will I go catatonic again?"

"That's what I am trying to say W0ody, the oppression of the HOB has vanished, people are starting to recover. Trust me, if you freeze up, we will protect you."

"Pook! Ow. Damm!"

W0ody stopped, "What happened Richard?"

"Nuthin', nuthin'. Just touched the red by mistake as it buzzed. Hurt, but it's OK. Ignore me."

Turning, "It's just an old phone line and I picked up a message for Bear."

"Really, a message? What was it?"

"T.E., call home."

Bill glanced at George, grimacing. Finally, a small smile crossed their faces after all these days.

W0ody began to look around the space some more, "Wow, the world is so much cleaner now, bright. Is this the way it used to be?"

Within the cavern, music started to play from some of the equipment loudspeakers in the distance becoming louder and louder:

Bop bopa-a-lu a whop bam boo. Tutti frutti. Oh W0ody began echoing from the walls.

"Hey W0ody, did you hear that?" Jonny had jumped up, "Sounds like my apps are starting to link up! Oh boy, augmentation again, I can't wait. Thanks Dad!"

"Don't thank me, thank that talking flashlight over there, Richard."

His emotions suddenly flipped, "I'm sorry Dad." Remorse and sadness overwhelmed him.

"Sorry about what?"

"Making things more difficult than they needed to be."

"Don't worry son, things have been are awful for all of us."

"Dad, things have really been horrible, how can you be so calm throughout it all?

"Jonny, remember the First Tenet: *There are no guarantees in life, but if we work hard, and work together, we have a chance. That's all the Universe gives us, but it also gives us Reason for Hope."*

"Dad, you really believe that stuff, don't you?"

"Jon, in a Universe that seems to pull me in all directions at once, where people claim there is no real meaning to life, my faith gives me purpose, stability, and hope. Over the long haul, we are all tested. For me it works, I don't get down easily, I am more resilient. As you get older, you will see."

"Dad! I am almost an adult. Gosh, I almost forgot about school. What will I do?"

Gus was cautionary, "Jon, I will try to get us back in time, I promise you, but we have to also think about helping with the repairs." Looking about, "Kids, I would wait to load all your systems, I'm not sure how stable everything will be for the next two weeks, right Wil liam?"

"I'd say you're right. We need to be careful; we aren't out of the woods yet."

"You mean Sticks, big fella! Hey, talking about wood and sticks, did I tell you about the blind carpenter working in a cave who picked up his flashlight and saw?"

Sigh, "Be quiet Richard, you are starting to repeat yourself."

W0ody announced, "Hey! Here's an old message from Mom! She's in a shelter at the intersection of Euclid and Last Chance Gulch. She's OK!"

Jon was excited, "Dad, and we have to get out of here! We got to get to Mom as soon as we can!"

"You're right Jon, we should go. Perhaps Bear has a way for us to get across the river?"

Looking over they saw Bear and the two detectives in a group.

Bear tapped George on his chest, "Human, you found way."

The mech detective asked, "What are you saying Bear?"

The animan considered Bi1l, walked over to W0ody and put a paw on the mechkid's breastplate, W0ody interpreted the furious finger waving: “Without him, there was no way to save the world. He knows the hero’s path.”

George protested, “If I saw far, it was because I stood on the shoulders of everyone’s efforts.”

Bill looked over at George, a Native American with a heroic history, an Earthman and human with depths unknown, and he was the lucky spanner wrench who was his partner.

George looked over at Bill, a competent and innovative mechman with depths unknown, his soggy head piece, and said: “Bill, lose the hat.”

ROADMAP

The Cultural approach would focus on engaging the younger generation.
They can be inspired with Real hope, and Real Action.
Books, movies, gaming systems can dial in on real locations in the solar system.
SimCity survivors can create a similar playfield for the solar system.
Participants can crowd source actual launches to the asteroid belt
and acquire ownership in their own future.

"It is a known fact that the sheep that give us steel wool
have no natural enemies."
— **Gary Larson**

"Small opportunities are often the beginning of great enterprises."
Demosthenes

CH 58

Once again on land, the terror of the preceding days still gripped him tightly through the chest, he barely could breath and hardly think.

He stared with exhausted eyes at the other survivors that also looked devastated. Gradually, he looked around until he found the ship's captain who was standing adjacent to the mate, not talking, just slowly rubbing his raw hands. He slowly walked over to them, trying not to stagger, and dropped to one knee, and thanked them for his life, and referred them to his father's remaining goods and gold in the hold. He pledged all that was there to them for the miracle that they had accomplished, saving the ship from certain destruction, the goods were small tokens for the gift of tomorrow.

The captain stared at him with dull eyes, but after a moment, gave him a small nod of acknowledgment. With that, Aleks slowly stood up, and backed away for a few feet with his head down, before picking up his kit and turning away. Looking around the foreign port, he was gripped with fear again. Oh, with a few residual gems and gold and one small astrolabe hidden with his few remaining navigation tools, he might be able to trade his way to safety. But, what did the fates have in store?

"Dad? How long are we going to be doing this? I just want to quit, what good are we doing?"

"Ah, Jon, I know it's tough. We've been here in the Bee-Hive for three days, and what have we been doing?"

Jon lashed out: "Crap! All we have been doing is crap! I can't take it! Switch this, switch that! As if it made any difference!"

"Jon, can I give you a hug?"

"Get away from me! All I want to do is go home and sleep! Look at W0ody, all kinked up after his battery ran down! We don't even have the right charger for him!"

"I'se got him covered, Jonny. Don't you go worrying about this W0odstock guy, I may be little, but I'se got a big heart."

Gus leaned against a wall, and slowly slid down until he sat on the deck, "Jon, we are doing the best we can, we got W0ody a two-amp trickle charger and his "intact" LEDs are lit. Come sit, and I will tell you a story."

"To hell with your stories! I can't go on!"

Gus continued softly as if Jon's outbursts hadn't happened. "A girl, an animan and a tech were walking an Earth beach together when the water receded to expose thousands of sea creatures to the air and began killing them. The girl began tossing the small animals back into the water before they died, and the tech said, 'Why do that Alice? There are so many. You can't make a difference.' Whereupon the girl said, 'I made a difference to that one.'"

Jon spun around and stamped his foot "What is that supposed to mean? Am I a little girl? Dad! I just want things the way they were! Aw, dad..." Jon cried as he slumped down into a heap. Gus slowly reached out, and Jon crawled into his arms, shaking. "I want mom, I want my bed, I want W0ody!" he sobbed. Gus rocked him back and forth, back and forth.

Softly a voice said "Jon, I'm OK, I'm just resting."

"W0ody!"

"Jon, why don't you and your dad just rest awhile next to me and Richard? It will be OK." Jon got out of his dad's arms and went to put his own arms around the collapsed W0ody, Richard sat on his slumped shoulder, and Gus maneuvered himself to shelter all of them.

"Dad, all I want to do is go home and go to Prep and get my citizenship. I don't want to do this, OK?" Gus rocked Jonny while the lights flickered and teams tramped by, glancing, but continuing to unknown destinations. Sigh, it was going to be a long voyage.

Two days later, they were haggard and sometimes sleeping standing up, but they had stabilized the transfer station and motor control centers, placing most services in SAFE and securing the service equipment with faults.

Vesta had recovered air flow and lighting, heat and water. Transportation and travel had been down and was still limited to emergency teams and responders, but there was a strong possibility they would be able to return home to Helena soon. Communications sucked, with the WET sporadic from hard failures, but teams were stringing CAT 10E throughout the land and locals were tapping into the temp system, sending queries and updating posts.

It was such a hodgepodge though. Jon and Gus were able to send a message to mom of their survival and safety but didn't get a response until a day later when some stranger left a post-it on the shop door.

"Well, Jon, we survived, and you look bitchin', kinda' down at the corners, you know?" W0ody and Jon were storing the PPE back into the lockers as dad had told them to do, to be readily available if needed and the environment went south again.

“Tin can, you too, are cute, what with your chain mail shower cap looking like an old woman’s bonnet.”

“What’ya doin’, keeping it as a souvenir?

“Hey Guys! If we’s keepin’ souvenirs, how ‘bout loading on some more tools to replace the one’s we lost? What I saw in that half destroyed equipment locker on MIKE, we could liberate them: it was ball peen hammers, female socket pullers, virgin Tung oil, there even was this twelve inch crank, …”

Tiredly, “Be quiet Richard, we hear you.”

The destruction in the corridors had been contained and cleaned up in the majority, leaving some scorch marks and reduced illumination as a reminder of the week. Some news summaries indicated over fifteen thousand had lost their lives, but that wasn’t even a hundredth of a percent of the population. Jon couldn’t imagine what had gone on there at Wayne’s World.

“Well W0ody, this is going to be a long summer, I don’t have a clue when we can be normal again, but I dream of going back to school, meeting a girl, and getting our citizenship. I think it helps me keep on.”

“Right on, Jonny!

“Richard, the leather gloves don’t go in with the certified gloves! Stay focused!”

“Yeah, right, yeah.” They kept on, each in their own thoughts. Jon was depressed, his world turned upside down, with nothing to look forward to, just work and clean up. His dreams of autonomy and girls, shredded.

ROADMAP

The effort required to Colonize the Solar System
will be more than humanity has ever done together.
It will be so difficult, that it is very possible it will be a complete failure, forever.
As such, minimizing wasted effort will be tantamount,
and a primary technical focus should be the asteroids.
Reducing the energy requirements of the deep gravity wells
will free up significant resources for other goals.

"I have tried at times to place humans in perspective
against the vastness of universal time and space.
When I talk of the purpose of life,
I am thinking not only of human life, but of all life on Earth
and of the life which must exist upon other planets throughout the universe.
It is only of life on Earth, however, that one can speak with any certainty.
It seems to me that all life on Earth,
the sum total of life upon the Earth, has purpose."
- Clifford D Simak

"An expert is someone who knows some of the worst mistakes that can be made in his subject, and how to avoid them."
Heisenberg

Recovery

Chapter 59

[1892] *I've done it!* He thought. *I've got that bald bastard right where I want him, fired from his own company!* His anger welled up in the memories of the thefts and backroom deals that had cost him so much. His jaw clinched in the grim satisfaction that he made the man create his own destruction. Direct current indeed! His own people warned him about the inability to scale up, but no, he had to personally try to continue to fight him, Nikola, while letting his business become obsolete, his ego not accepting someone could be smarter or more skilled than him. *I've won!*

Let the old man putter around his shop, making photographs and playing with wax. Ignore him now, he's insignificant forever. Nikola was going to change the world! Part of his success was his ability to see the big picture. While the Direct Current guys were putting their generators throughout the city, they hadn't thought about the cost of procuring and packing in the fuel day after day. Nicola had surmounted this by getting his alternating current power from Niagara Falls, energy provided gratis by nature.

It was time to move on, let good ol' George keep the electrical company. Nikola had his money, had played with all the forces of nature, it was time to really do something big. This time, he was also going to weave that arrogant Scotsman into the pattern and pay him back for helping his enemies. He was going to be able to kill two birds with one stone. Just like Niagara, he was going to tap the free energies of the universe.

Oh, the fools. They thought the field equations were about making better motors, did they? He convinced JP to pony up wealth to fund a Marconi station, with patents to back it up! JP can have those worthless patents. Little did they know that a careful study of Maxwell's notes and their boundary conditions, that to create waves one needed a substrate, the aether, the material that fills the region of the universe above the terrestrial sphere.

He knew the Earth sliced through this gradient with such force, that with two copper towers separated by three-thousand miles connected by conductors, he could create enough free electricity to power a thousand New Yorks. He could forget JP, even buy him out. He could bankrupt them all! If only his family could see him now, they would be proud. Thinking, he realized he must first reconduct that Morley team experiment and see where they went wrong. It must be something simple. Bad experiments happen only in Transylvania or Cleveland.

Only about half of the students were in the lab, and those that were, were huddled in small clots whispering and gesturing.

Dr Yi appeared at the lectern: "Welcome back to class. We are very sorry for the events caused by the HOBs which have caused enormous damage and loss of life, we hope to be able to regain some normalcy here in school and return you on your paths towards matriculation, majority, and society."

Looking around, Jon was searching desperately, "W0ody, have you seen Abs or Catherine?"

"No, I have asked around, no one else has either."

"Do you think they are OK? I couldn't bear it if either of them was hurt in the carnage."

Kai piped in "You don't really care about Abs, you never did! All you care about was hanging onto his success while cutting him down every chance you got."

"That's not true!"

"It is too, and I hope your girlfriend never returns, I hope she is just gone, gone from wherever she came from. I hope she died!"

"That's a terrible thing to say Kai! I saw way too much dying and I wish no one ever has to go through that ever again."

"You're such a liar, you never had to do anything the rest of us had to do. My mother was at work when it happened, and I was alone for days! E^3Ching became catatonic and never recovered. How would you like it if your sister died in your arms and no one there to help!" Her eyes filled up with tears and she turned and ran out of the classroom.

"Now you've done it techie boy," growled Krage.

Jon's mouth was open, but nothing came out. How could they be so wrong?! His chest was a frozen block as he tried to figure his way out. Everyone misunderstood! He stood there rigid, unable to move.

"You guys don't know anything!" he blurted, finally turning back to his table. W0ody stared at him asking "Are you OK Jon?" "No! No, I'm not."

The instructor was talking about recovery or some such: "We will get some trauma teams in here to help with the stresses and burdens we all received, but unfortunately, they are assigned at this moment assisting those families who have lost someone directly. It may be a number of weeks before they are available in our facility."

A voice called out from the room. "A lot of good that will do us!"

"What about the assistants that were here before, are they available?"

"Unfortunately, not all of them will be available. Dr. Vesilisev won't be returning and some of the lab assistants are still missing. Doc Cable went north to help out at Turtle Mountain."

"Oh no W0ody. Do you think Anna was killed? What about Cat?" "Don't know Jon, nobody knows."

The white-haired instructor arrived at their station, "Jon and W0ody, do you think you could assist the other students regain their organization?"

"Yes, Professor Yi, we can try." "Thank you."

Looking about, Jon decided to offer help to the team on his left, this was Obee and Art!, Karmin, Tink3r and the Soo's behind Obee. Kai was still gone form Obee's table. "Hey, the prof would like to know what you best need to complete your labs that you were working on. Can we help?"

Karmin glared at Jon but didn't speak. Obee hesitated before responding, "We tried to get into the chemical lockers, but they appear to be in SAFE mode, locked down, you know. We gotta have the materials to do the reaction laboratory. We really weren't able to start before the crisis."

"Yeah, unlike you guys, some of us started in a hole and took a lot longer to figure out the background information, I mean, we just started to research and learn the differences between ionic and covalent bonds." Karmin challenged him.

"Í hope this helps, I am not good at words, so everything has to be an idea. These words shape the ideas that I learned as simply as possible."

"Simple ideas! Simple for you!" KaiLin had returned. "Yeah," Krage chimed in "you have it so easy, what about the rest of us? You arrogant ass!"

Karmin piled on, "You lord over us that your tech background gives you a leg up, what are we going to do? We all lost a month of study time, and we may never pass our finals and get citizenship! All because of you! It makes me want to puke!"

"SHUTUP!"

Everyone suddenly was quiet, Jon was astonished, looking over at his only friend in the world.

Krage spoke up, "You shut up W0ody, this doesn't have anything to do with you."

"You shut up Krage, shut your pie hole, I am going to tell you something, ass."

W0ody continued, "Before the HOB attack, you all were hightailing it out of here as soon as the bell struck, to party with Abs while Jon stayed back studying, and getting materials available for the rest of you for the next day.

"He even was doing Abs prep work for him so they wouldn't drop him out. Were any of you grateful, no!"

WOody started to windmill, Jon had never seen him like this. "During the attack, the Borgman next to Jon was killed by a deranged elevator in front of his eyes, the exploded blood covering his body.

"I was catatonic like E^{3}Ching was, and Jon carried me for miles to an electrical shop where I could be saved. On the way, he rescued other kids who had been crushed by erratic haulers in the tunnels regardless for his own safety."

WOody almost sputtered, "How many of you were out saving people during the attack? Kai, he didn't see his mother for over a week, and had no word at all for the first four days! Yeah, you had it tough KaiLin, but so did everyone."

Settling down to tell the story: "Then he didn't sleep for three days while helping recover the air systems in the Millennium Crater complex. Without air, over one hundred thousand would have died, and it was only Jon and his dad restoring power to the fans on levels Foxtrot through Mike."

Throwing out his arms, his tool belt rattling, "And he has been there ever since, every day, only leaving to for one visit to his mother for an hour and to come to class. So, when you go home to study to catch up, Karmin, Jon is going back to the Bee-Hive to continue to restore the equipment so people can breathe."

"We thought you were our friends, but ever since graduation from the Academy, you have been as nasty as a pack of rats, only because we were studying and didn't hang out with rich Abs." WOody's shoulders slumped. Art! had run to the outside wall and camoed himself to become invisible amongst the displays.

Suddenly, standing tall again, "Krage, you jerk. You pick on Jon because he is smaller, younger and doesn't have money like Abs. He has never once done anything against you. Not once, check ROoby's files.

"You do it only because it makes you feel good to make someone else feel bad, and you watch Abs do it. Just leave us alone. Hang out with Abs, flunk out, for all we care, but now, when you have to study to pass, you're pissed because Jon already did it."

Taking a step back, "We're leaving, not to congratulate ourselves, not to prepare for the exams, but to help those people at the Millennium complex get their lives back. Our schedule requires twelve-hour days for the next two months to fix the problems some hackers caused.

"So, the next time you have a problem with air, or power, or water, call Abs' banker, because you look down on us electricians, second class people to you, don't call us, we won't come!"

Raising his arms above his head, all five feet of him "So Pook you Krage! Pook you too Karmin. And especially, Pook you KaiLin." Jon shied away as W0ody went this direction, "You, who told Jon you wanted him as a friend. Pook you!"

"Let's go Jon, we're wasted enough time here." W0ody grabbed his arm and started to march him away, Jon was hesitant and looked back. Krage was muttering "Pook you W0ody." KaiLin was crying and staff was coming as the other teams were looking on. What a mess.

As Jon followed W0ody from the lab, he stumbled, but looking down he didn't see anything. He felt his pockets making sure he had everything he was supposed to carry, the routine of finding all five items helped calm him, but he didn't feel good at all.

Coming out into the Tiger walk and turning towards the Fairfield Apartments where they were staying, W0ody stopped at one of the corners and leaned against a wall. "I guess I burned our bridges for us Jon, are you mad?"

The little TinTin called out, “I thought you wuz awesome W0ody! Them’s immature meatsticks formed a raging pack, and now it’s come to bite them back! Don’t back down motorhead! You don’t need kids as friends, A-dults are much better.”

The two crèche mates just listened and stared.

Standing next to W0ody, kinda weak, Jon forced up his thoughts: “No, I am sad, I think we lost our friends a long time ago. It makes me a little sick to my stomach, I don’t know if Prof Yi will take us back, I mean, we have to be able to help the other teams, right?”

“Oh, I didn’t think of that.”

Jon shook himself, “It’s OK, I don’t think we are going to graduate anyway, what with all the repairs we have to do. I’m so tired, and Damm! Think of all the work we put into it! I need to become an adult W0ody! Damm. It’s so unfair.” These last words trailed off as Jon became aware of his own despair.

Still sagging against the wall, “I am sorry Jon, I think I used up more energy than I wanted in that outburst, I may not make it home.”

“Oh W0ody, don’t feel responsible. I am just sorry for myself. You know what the Credo says about unrealized and unrealistic expectations, it ruins lives and makes men become mad. But, I will get over it, I will.”

Grabbing W0ody by the arm, “Let’s go find an emergency charging station and restore your energy. You really were amped up back there,” he said with a sad grin, “I have never seen you like that before.”

As they entered a virtually empty WET kiosk where Jon knew there would be a pay by the minute rectifier, W0ody replied, “Never before, never again, lord help me. I see how you humans can have such wild personality swings, the energy to my noggin went up by a factor of ten. No wonder you have such big arteries to your head."

W0ody sat down of the terminals, Jon next to him keyed in his credit code, boy, would he be glad when all the WET was restored. "You know W0ody, you're right, we did a lot of things, a lot of good things.

"But life goes on, I can't help asking: When will I graduate? When will I become an adult? Will my friends ever like me again, or do I go out into the world alone? Will KaiLin ever talk to me again? Is Cat OK? Is Abs? Are they alive?"

"Damm Jon, why'd you go all philosophical on me now? I can't move and get away from it. Oh, help me Mr. Bill, help me." He said in a high plaintive falsetto voice, the parody making them both grin, Jon wiping away a tear, and W0ody's orange pastel lips breaking into a big smile.

A voice called out from the crib, "Hey guys, is this a good time…"

In unison; "No!"

ROADMAP

A technical solution for the inability of the human body
to survive long periods of weightlessness (See the Engineering note 3),
The PHILIPS' Bolo Habitats are not only solutions
for the lack of gravity, but also create
a practical, effective engineering solution and
reduce the enormous cost of logistical support.

"Everybody thought I was a bit of an eccentric
for wanting to be out there looking at the stars, but I still do."
Brian May

"Therefore, when I considered this carefully, the contempt which I had to fear because of the novelty and apparent absurdity of my view, nearly induced me to abandon utterly the work I had begun."
Copernicus

Presentation Day

Chapter 60

[1931] He had read recently in the journals that his earlier work had become irrelevant. So, he asked the morning waitstaff here at the Clinton what they thought about his scientific discoveries. The answers astounded him, no one knew what he had done! One of them even had the temerity to suggest that perhaps he was a biologist because he was so fond of pigeons?

He asked Kenneth over and they devised a plan. He would host an enormous birthday party for himself, spare no expenses, and invite the press, dignified University faculty from around the world, and that rich kid La Guardia who wanted to become mayor, he would come for the publicity if nothing else, and bring along his rich friends. This would remind the world who he was.

Kenneth and he argued over the guest list. At least he didn't have to worry about the bald guy, he had outlasted him. It still stuck in his craw that the old man had stolen his Nobel Prize out from under him. A tinkerer! Well, he got him back for that one too in the end. The other guest they argued about was that Austrian kid. He had worked with him in '21 at the RCA wireless station in New Jersey and found him appalling. How he had received the Nobel Prize a year later was unfathomable.

How could a man, who couldn't even do his own math, or even integration in his own head, dare to criticize Nikola's work? Thought problems? Bah. Rubbish. What mattered most were the boundary conditions, not some parlor trick mathematics that algebraically solved some of the problem, but had no basis in real life? Might as well as be the number of angels on a pinhead or string theory. People killed each other in war using Newton's laws, they described the Universe, not some warped saddle of the aether.

What if he pushed back with a new set of field equations that made μ_o and ε_o variables to be integrated. That would change the speed of light and show the kid! It would also change everything else in the universe, so what good would it be? He could use it as a gimmick like the one the kid used in '05.

With that out of the way, he began to prepare a list to be copied and handed to the reporters. Maybe he could have Kenneth leak the list to Life or Time magazine ahead of time to stir interest: the electrical power industrial infrastructure and transmission, three phase motors and generators, X-rays, radio, microwave, wireless transmission of power, Teleautomatics and radio/remote control and sensing, robots, ... it's going to be a long night.

You know, the space elevator was stronger than he thought. Maybe he was too. He may not pass, he may not gain his emancipation, but he survived.

Tuesday morning found Jon and W0ody hanging outside Theater Three near their classroom, waiting. They were in an out-of-the-way corner of the Spearman Technology Building and Science Labs, in a dead-end hall. The door to the presentation room was closed as one of the other student's team gave their appearance in front of the oral board.

Jon hadn't been good company this morning, his model of the space ladder was definitely torqued away from the perfection he had attempted, a result of the brouhaha with Abs and the crew two weeks ago. The hurried repairs were obvious to anyone.

His energy had been reduced to exhaustion; the long workdays of repair, school, and smothered by damaged emotions, too many to count. He didn't care anymore, he was going through the motions, they couldn't do any worse to him than what he had already gone through. He talked in monosyllables when queried by W0ody, hard to start, slow to move, trying slowly to determine what he was doing.

Why am I here? He thought sluggishly, *It doesn't matter anymore.* All that Joy he experienced when he was younger, thinking about Earth, was so distant, he could not recall it, just see it through a sooty vision of a memory. And he wasn't going to try to dig those feelings up either, *Like trying to exhume a body of a loved* one, he thought, *to help remember.* No, a dead body brought no comfort.

He took a big breath, well, it's going to be over soon, and he can return to his room and view the nothing he had. He looked down dispassionately to note his right hand was fiddling with the base of the structure, stroking the helix knots like worry beads,

Yeah right. Go away Mr. ID, you and those other visions are just the result of less than eight hours of sleep in the last seventy-two. Don't ask me to get back in the saddle again, he thought dully. *Though, that stool that was turning into a witch as he watched was an interesting hallucination.*

The door to the theater suddenly opened and let forth the bright lights of the exam space, and Obee and Art! were exiting, Art! was scuttling along the wall opposite of Jon, it never had been comfortable in confined spaces with strangers. "Hey Jon! We passed! Thanks for all the help, you guys were all the difference. Where's Catherine so I can thank her in person?"

"Sorry Obee, I haven't seen or heard from Catherine since the attack. Can't even track down where she lived to tell her parents. But, congratulations on passing, that's great." Jon said the last with what enthusiasm he could muster, which was not enough to notice.

W0ody turned quickly to face Art! which froze it against the wall, "Congratulations Arth0r on passing your tests. It isn't easy, and for a mech, one of the great accomplishments. You can be proud of yourself."

W0ody reached out a hand for a shake and paused. They all waited. Then, Art! flowed off the wall turning green with ribbons of yellow running around and around, "Thank you W0odrow, thank you, thank you, thank you." Art! almost smothered W0ody with its embrace. It then quickly stepped back, becoming brown with faint slow yellow pulses, but didn't return to the corner.

As Obee started to leave he said, "Thank you W0ody for your kindness, thank you both."

After Obee and Art! departed, "That was nice W0ody. That was a powerful message. Boy, I wish I was half as good."

Before they could continue a voice called out, "Come in, come in, we don't have all day." So, they slowly turned and went into Theater Three and who knows what that lay ahead.

The room was basically a large isosceles triangle with a concave curve on the largest back wall, a set of steep stairs led from their left down to a flat space with a podium in the back of the lower corner. Off to their right were a set of descending benches like bleachers but with narrow desks in front of each seat, where Jon supposed would sit a gallery of people for important presentations.

At the podium sat three people, Professors Yi and Carlisle from class, and a mech Jon had never seen before. The slope from where they stood and where their interrogators sat was quite steep, and they were perhaps eight feet above the floor of the theater, Doctor Yi looking up at them.

The dais was raised perhaps a foot above the foundation, and there were two chairs and a table between the seats and the instructors, for their projects. Jon began to descend and found he had to hang onto the railing to do it successfully; the stair steps were much higher than normal.

When at the floor Jon found that now he was going to be looking up at his teachers, and there could be an intimidation factor involved, or perhaps just conserving space and allowing maximum viewing of the displays. Who knows? Who cares, he thought dejectedly. He stared down onto his chair, hands on the rail.

"Gentlemen, please take your seats and I will review our procedures. My name is Doctor Ignacio Yi, Head of the Preparation Oral Exams, sitting with me are Doctors Terrance Carlisle and Rac3car Vesi1isev." Jon's head came up as he was sitting when he heard the last Professor's name. Was he related to Anna?

Doctor Yi noticed his start. "Yes Jon, Rac3car was Anna's crèche mate. I am sorry she couldn't be here, but she perished in the HOB. One of thousands I know, but each one significant. He has volunteered to take her place and I am sure she would have liked that."

"I'm sorry she died," Jon said softly. "It was so horrible."

"I miss her terribly; she was by far my better half. She allowed me to see, to understand nuance." Rac3car paused, "She talked about you four a lot, how you were the hope for the future, how she strained in her small way to provide guidance as best she could.

"I cannot see as she did the interrelationships of your group, but I perhaps can help shed light on any science questions that may come up. Where is the rest of your team? I was led to believe they would be here."

"No sir, I don't know where the other half of our team is. Catherine and her crèche mates disappeared during the HOB also, and no one can tell me anything. It makes me so sad. She called me cute."

"I am sorry for your loss. Please feel welcomed to ask questions during this interview. This board isn't all about putting someone down, but rather lifting them up. Do you understand?"

Jon looked at W0ody who shook his head negatively, he turned and said tiredly, "No sir, all I heard of this exam is you work your tail off and you might pass, and you go on to become a citizen, you fail, you get to go back to end of the line."

Doctor Vesi1isev was surprised, "Surely, you were given an orientation for the goals of these end-of-course activities?"

Professor Yi interrupted, "This cohort's lecture series was cruelly interfered with by the collapse of the WET. We had to cut over fifty percent of the justifications and fully focus on the formulae. They are still recovering."

Turning to Jon, "We are most fortunate to have Doctor Vesi1isev here today, he holds the Joint Lucasian Chair of Mathematics between the University of Vesta and University of Cambridge on Earth. Although, on Earth, they think he's a human. We haven't abased them on that fact."

Jon sat up straighter in his chair, it sounded impressive even though he had no idea what they were talking about. It was possible however, that people were attempting to help.

Dr Yi continued, "W0odrow Miller, would you like to show us you project and tell us about it?"

W0ody stood up and pulled off his backpack. From the pouch he pulled a box with an attached cord, a heavy tube of wrapped copper wire with two leads, and another cylinder of metal sticks glued together. As he set up his experiment he began, "I am growing up with the Miller family and they are electricians. From working with them I got this idea."

A noise came from above and Jon looked up in annoyance, he had to wait, so does the next group. His eyes opened when he saw Uncle William MacHinery in a long coat and a Panama, followed by his Pops and Mom, dressed to the Tees in their Carmines and Teddies, then some people he didn't know, those three Navy Officers he briefly met during the bear scare, two humans and a mechman, followed by Obee and Art!, they were all filing into the seats of the gallery, sliding over making room for each other.

Jon started to choke, what were they all doing here? They were all above him, in staggered rows going to the ceiling but so close he could reach out and touch them. Then, what? He couldn't believe his eyes.

Stumping in came Big Blu3 with Blueee3 riding his shoulder, followed by Cat!

"CAT!" he screamed, "You're alive! Oh God, you're alive." She was bandaged and limping in with a cane, holding onto Big Blu3's other shoulder, she waved, "Hi Cutie Pie!" Jon was frozen, just staring at her, staring at her eyes.

Then he bounded up the stairs and hugged her, causing her to grunt. She stiffly pulled away, pushing the cane at him, "Jonny, that was nice, but I've been hurt, and I just got out of the hospital."

Jon pulled back, "I'm so sorry." He held onto her hand that was on the cane.

"Don't be sorry, it's OK. Go back to your presentation and we will talk later, OK?" Jon almost fell backwards down the steps but caught the railing before he went too far. His heart was pounding, and life was running through his veins again.

Wild Bill stood back up, "Hey Doc, sorry about the interruption, but we thought the A-team down there could use some moral support." Jon's eyes never left Cat's as he listened to Bill. He had a hard time seeing, he had to keep blinking.

William continued and Jon remembered Pops saying that Bill would be the corpse at every funeral, and if there ever was going to be a funeral, this was his venue, "We're these guys' family, and they have a had a slightly tough time of it. I have some visitors from Earth, and I suggested they come down and watch what our young teenagers can accomplish.

"We don't mollycoddle kids like they do on Earth, do we fellas?" Billy looked around at Jon's parents and the sailors, tipping his hat to Helen. Jon turned and slid down the stairs using both rails and returned to his seat.

"We'uns" there was Bill going folksy again, Jon couldn't help but smile, he said again "We'uns wanted you to know that W0ody and Jonny *(Jon!)* here have spent between ten and twelve hours every day assisting the Bee-Hive out Millennium way in recovering their electrical and air handling systems.

"Between them and their father, they were fully responsible for the safety of the twenty thousand residents on nine levels, and on top of that they somehow maintained their schooling."

Jon was now staring at Wild Bill. What was he talking about? All he did was do what he was told to do, trip and reset breakers, punch down way too many wires. Anyone would have done it. It's what you did, why was he bringing it up? Why were those sailors staring at him? Damm, his throat was all swole up. His mom was giving him the look that embarrassed him so.

"So, Doc, I said my piece, we will be quiet up here, just to watch, if that's OK?" Jon knew Bill wasn't going to move no matter what Doctor Yi said, but it was Professor Yi's house. Hummm, might be an interesting battle of personalities.

“Thank you, William MacHinery, your felicities are well known even in the sheltered confines of academia. Your presence is greatly appreciated. You know of, perhaps, Professor Vesilisev, who is sitting in on these two, cum ignis et distinctio?”

“Hi Rac3car. Long time, no see. What a great Latin title, get it from a Canadian college, eh?”

“Hi Billy. Now, that’s an ugly cap, not back to rollin’ bums for their hats, are you?”

Professor Yi was silent for a moment while pondering the fact these two knew each other, Jon was back looking at Cat, who was playing with the ends of her hair with just a hint of a smile, slowly rocking back and forth, not looking at him. “W0ody, would you be so kind as to start over?”

“Sure Doc, I mean Professor Yi. As I was saying, my project developed from my association with Gus Miller and being an electrician. It was my goal to build from scratch a three-phase motor.” While W0ody talked, Jon’s mind was going a thousand miles per hour. Cat was here! Big Blu3 was hulking over her like always, the memories came flooding back. His chest hurt so he could hardly breathe.

Doctor Carlisle asked, “Had you ever built one before?”

W0ody was standing, and plugging in the box device, “No, although I had seen them and had replaced small VAV motors. But as the conditions here in Fremont got worse, I was having to spend extended periods away from campus, WET libraries were unavailable, and time grew precious.

“So, without discussion, I flopped my project on its head. Rather than a lab experiment, I changed it into a mind experiment, kinda like Einstein.”

Einstein, huh? Aand you thought my proposal to build a new kind of fibre for the space elevator was over the top, thought Jon.

"This way I could use the commute time constructively and didn't have to rely on as many resources."

"Interesting, I credit the self-motivation, but you should have consulted with us."

"When I was going to, it was too late, I apologize."

"Please continue."

"I am obsessed with all things motors, and not just design and construction, but theory. So, I took on Maxwell's EM Field equations and quantum electrodynamics.

"They are not a terribly difficult set of mathematical equations, modeling magnetism and electrostatics and the relationships between them. I found them to be curious.

"They have high symmetry such as the rate at which field strength falls away with distance, yet not wholly mirrored. Why aren't there any monopoles? And why are the EM equations the only one still known today to be accurate at both cosmic and the quantum scales?

"I spent all my waking hours, and during my work time, I could get into a routine doing punchdown and at the same time contemplate the equations.

"Just before the HOB broke, I was thinking about Edwin Abbott's Flatland and had a revelation. What if permittivity and permeability were not constants like we observe, but variables that behave in a quanta behavior like ionized atoms. What would be the consequences?

"As far as I can tell, if they are variable, the forces would have different speeds of light in each quanta state, the atoms would be of different sizes and arraignments due to different charges, and, if manipulated in a certain way, the whole set of equations becomes symmetrical.. This was astounding to me. It reminded me of the time I integrated zero three times and came up with the equation for gravity. I said: 'huh'?

"And finally, I noticed that if I made the quanta states far enough apart, the matter and energies could not interact between their universes except through their gravitation forces.

"I think I may have a proposal for dark matter for dark matter in these modified equations. Would you like to look over my paperwork?"

"I am impressed W0odrow, yes, I would like to look at your work."

The three instructors continued to ask W0ody about his project, and Jon seemed to be waking up out of a dark dream. W0ody was on a roll, and when he looked back at Cat, she gave him a wink. Oh no! His mom was moving over to sit next to her. He turned back quickly to the discussion in front of him. He unconsciously wiped his nose on his sleeve.

Doctor Yi once again took the lead, "Thank you W0odrow, most informative."

Looking at Jon, "Would you present what you have done, Jonathon?"

Jon stood up, "Yessir, but it's not the best." He was embarrassed. He tried to ignore everyone behind him, but his heart couldn't. They all came to help. He started blinking again.

"Jon, I am sure it is fine, describe what you have, don't worry about what might have been."

Slowly shaking his head while looking at the floor, he took a big breath, "I am sorry, things have been a little tough, before my folks showed, I didn't really care anymore, but I did put a fair amount of time on the project before it went south." His neck felt tight and his voice dropped off at the end.

He squared his shoulders and looked up, "Big picture, Earth and the 'roids are on different paths. Earth is being left in the dust because they can't share in the growth of mankind. One major problem is the gravity well."

This time it was Doctor Vesilisev who broke in, "How would you solve that problem?"

For the first time in weeks, some energy seemed to pour back into his soul, "The gravity well problem goes away if a space elevator is installed on Earth, an enormous device over forty thousand miles long. There are three major issues, manufacture, installation, and funding."

Vesilisev continued, "Which one would you address and why?"

"For my project, I focused on manufacturing, but the other two were of interest also. You see, there is Kessler's Syndrome."

"What's that?"

Jon felt himself getting into it, "The process of sending material to space from a planet leaves objects in orbit, and eventually attaining orbit becomes impossible due to the increasing debris. As such, it is difficult for a planet to create a space elevator, if not impossible.

"Therefore, I have concluded, at age twelve I must admit, but I think Earth cannot make a Space Elevator. It is up to the Belt." He said the last with a little uncertainty, here he was presenting to people with so much more experience. But the hell with it, if Abs can speak his mind, so can he. He unconsciously clenched his jaw.

"What about the manufacture of the elevator, what did you find?"

Jon began a long discussion of the efforts and ideas that he had read and developed. They were strongly interested in his three-string helix and he had to explain that the 3-D printer had gone down when the WET was lost and how he had soldered art supplies to make his model. He didn't mention Abs and they didn't mention the sorry state the armature was in.

He did mention his concern for the failure of a 40,000-mile-long device falling onto an 8,000-mile planet. Someone was sure to get upset. They discussed what biological enzymes might be hazardous to a carbon-based structure, even if all the bonds were a diamond lattice. Jon learned some things from Doctor Vesilisev that he put into the back of his mind.

Carlisle had the final question, "Who do you think should fund the elevator?"

Jon was firm, "I think the Belt should fund it, it is too large for Earth."

"Even if Earth gets all the benefit?"

"I think it would be to our benefit to have Earth join the community of Man. We need them, I think, even if only as an insurance policy. No one knows what the future holds in the next ten thousand years. Let's think holistically."

Professor Yi broke in, "Thank you Jonathon, I think we have more than enough information to make a decision on your and Woodrow's application. We will let you know in a few minutes."

Jon slumped down holding the back of his chair, grabbing onto the top as he leaned over from the hips, shutting his eyes. The three teachers were bent in conference. Jon only had time for a few deep breaths that started to make him dizzy.

Doctor Yi once again made the presentation, "W0odrow, Jonathon, I wish to congratulate you. The Preparatory School's Evaluation Board finds you both to be superior applicants for becoming citizens of the Federation and will recommend you as such. Your formal assignment will occur at the graduation on Friday. You both should be there."

Jon started doing a spin around at the words "will recommend…" and swung around his chair losing his balance at the finish and ending on one knee with the biggest smile in the world while looking at Pops. They grinned at each other. He looked at Wild Bill and he had both arms over his head doing some kind of Dab dance or shimmy.

He jumped up and gave W0ody a huge hug and looking over W0ody's shoulder, saw Big Blu3 leaving and Cat talking into one of the sailor's ears. She turned and gave him a festive wave, then turned and followed the Blu3s out the door and disappeared.

Everyone was talking and coming down the stairs to congratulate them, but he was trying to bolt up the stairs to stop Cat. But by the time he got to the top she was gone; he even went down to the main passage but had no sight of her. Stunned, he came back to the Theater and the lights were still on and people milling about, but the warmth had started to leave again.

The Navy Officers came over to him, and in the din one leaned close to his ear, "Your girl said she still had her orals to study for and pass, and she had lost a lot of time in the hospital. She said she would see you Friday at graduation, and if you were willing, she would like to have dinner afterwards." During this Jon's spirit rebounded. Yes! Dinner and Graduation, or Graduation and Dinner. Whatever, yes!

He was thumped on the back, and there was Uncle Bill, the rock in the storm, the clown in the china shop. "Well done Jonathon, well done. I want you to meet my newest new friend, a hero from Earth, the real deal, George Sealth."

He looked up at the tall man with the blackest eyes he had ever seen and long dark hair, "Very nice to meet you sir, are you really from Earth?"

"Yes I am. Are you really only thirteen?" He said this with a kind smile.

Jon started to shake his head, it made him dizzy again, "No sir, have they been telling you that? I am twelve, but I will be thirteen in eleven days. Can I ask you about Earth? I have never been there."

George looked over at Bill, "I would be glad too, are you free this evening?"

"I don't think so, I am very tired." At which point, Jonathon proceeded to pass out.

The Space Program

Our Present to the Future

"Space isn't remote at all.
It's only an hour's drive away if your car could go straight upwards."
- Fred Hoyle

"Why worry about doing something you love? Figure out what the opportunity is.
Find a thing, get good at it, learn to love it later."
– **Mike Rowe**

Last Stop at the Sauce

Chapter 61

The men looked at each other, they had slowly suspended paddling when the vision enveloped them, and they began on their way again, this time in the swathing of fog. With no shore to be found, Hero found the crescent moon dancing in an out of the gray and guided his men towards home, not more than a few hours away as they began to run with the waxing tide. The gulls began their cries as the day began, the dull brown-gray ones from this year's hatch pestering the bright white and pewter adults with their hunger.

Then, as if a continuation of the vision, they heard huffs and long breaths as shapes began to appear out of the mist, an orca family was sharing their journey. The portents were obvious. Smokey Top had transformed himself once again, this time into an actual orca, and was guiding them home through the clouds they were flying through, or was he? Could the Trickster be one of the spirit whales too?

Making the decision quickly, Hero turned his boat to merge with the pod, and trust they would lead him home safely. "Look!" cried an oarsman, "Qál'qaləx̌ič has joined us!" Qál'qaləx̌ič was an orca known to all the tribes of the Sound having travelled the waters for over a generation, people were blessed with good luck if they spotted him, the King male orca had a six-foot-tall dorsal and a hole in his fin one third down from the top, making him unique. The tribes had been able to discern the different orca families based upon the markings and scars on their backs and fins. When Qál'qaləx̌ič returned, it meant the salmon were running in the sea, when the rogue whales appeared, it meant the seals would leave the waters, and men would be wise to avoid the unsafe currents.

The six of them were commiserating over the events of the last two months, telling in detail how they were laid upon by fate. Poor Rock just now had hit his head on one of the torpedo breech doors, and the door had won, and he now nursed his ache with Alphonso's best.

"Boys, it is sad to see you go," Bill said, the WET almost back to its normal self, but George remained unaugmented.

"Well, the Greenie is off next week to return to Ceres and a long past refit," the Mech Warrant replied, "and missing movement is a no-no in the Navy, as in 'shot'."

"Damm, really 0llie?" TOP, it seemed was forever on a sharp learning curve here in the Belt.

"No, Brain, it's just a matter of speech, sorry."

"How did you guys survive anyways?" asked the old punker who was wrapped in small wisps of steam, mostly leaking out of his left elbow this time.

Sitting up, Rock leaned in, "It was that Wrench guy, he was lit up by one of Bear's minion's search lights, and then dotted with a laser. He freaked", the RCA took another sip of juice, "anyways, I guess he had more skills than advertised, because he turned that boat into a submarine and we went under! I wished he done it earlier, the sub had conditioned air, clean seats, and a wet bar." George and Bill just looked at each other. "I guess some rich guy had tricked him out for their once a year run down the sludge rapids."

"Anyways, we made it up to Harley's place when the WET came back up somewhat, and we could patch military reports on the status, and catch a jitney to the Navy base."

TOP asked, "I hear you boys were somewhat responsible for that. True?"

Bill had been waiting for this opening for over two weeks. He snaked up a ringed arm waving his derby and shouted: "Alphonse! My good man. Another round for me and my friends here."

Leaning over to his friends around the table, "Well, it was this way, let me tell you about this really brave mudman next to me…"

He was interrupted, "Yah, Billy, good to see you too. Now, what's your order. I bet you are on per diem, huh, so don't skimp on the gratuity this time, huh."

Why colonize space?

Because, like public education,
the space program has been NET Sum Positive.
This means, by investing in our future, our benefits
are greater than our costs.

"It is good to have an end to journey toward,
but it is the journey that matters in the end."
Ursula le Guin

"I learned very early the difference between
knowing the name of something and knowing something."
Richard Feynman

Fremont Graduation

Chapter 62

Looking back, the memories of the lost days were beginning to fade, but the vision of the green and black mountains of water, the rivers of fire, and heaven being torn asunder stayed with him and would for the rest of his years. Search and travel as he might, he found no indication of his family's survival. He finally met up with the boy he tussled with as a youth, the boy now a man, a Captain in his own right with his own modern ship, filled with Phoenician oarsmen on three decks, not at all like the penteconter he had escaped the Isle in.

He visited every port and islet along the Aegean, south to grand Luxor, to the now ruined Minos, north again to mighty Troy. Never again did he see his Father, family or the fabulous mechanical men. Never again would he hear the laughter or share in the smiles. They must have been lost with all hands off the coast of Thera and sunken to a watery grave the day his world ended.

Once again Jon and W0ody found themselves being herded around to stand over in that place, but wait, we need you over here now, and they were more than a half hour early. Mom was hovering as she was wont to do, and Pops and Wild Bill were doing their thing, chatting up anyone and everyone who would listen, about most anything.

Today Pops had broken out his never been seen before Greens, topped off with an old-fashioned leather football helmet embossed with a green and white "G" on both sides. He had polished all the brass buttons and tightened down the joints so you could barely hear him coming.

Helen Miller was wearing a candy apple red Doll Lace Camellia Teddy with black garters and fishnet tights, standing in her long silk high-button brocades with the speedlacers. She had finished her accessories with frilled arm sleeves complete with red pearls. Jon thought their colors went together well, even though they were contrasting.

He had slept all of Friday after the presentation and most of Saturday, before staggering down to grab a bite to eat. Now here on Monday, his head was clear for the first time since forever, and he was tracking so much better.

Most of the gang was here. Jon sadly observed that Abs wasn't in attendance, and Cat hadn't shown. The kids were mostly in a group with the exception of KaiLin, Obee and Art!, and of course he and W0ody, or was it W0ody and him? Whatever.

He nudged W0ody and walked slowly towards Kai. She watched him approach but didn't move or say anything, didn't even look at him directly, just a point over his shoulder towards W0ody. He stopped about two feet in front, slightly to her right so as to not block her view, and she finally looked him in the eyes. They were not happy now, some of the life had gone out of them. Boy, was this going to be awkward and uncomfortable.

"Kai," he started softly, but she didn't say a word, "Kai, KaiLin, I'm so sorry about E^3Ching. I didn't get a chance to tell you before. I'm sorry." Kai looked down and still didn't speak. "I don't know what I would have done if it had happened to W0ody.

"If there is anything W0ody or I can do, please don't hesitate to ask." He stopped. She still didn't move. He was almost sniffling; he didn't know why. He waived to W0ody who came over and the two of them stepped close to Kai and put their arms on her upper back to give her a small hug, and then stepped back. Kai looked at the two of them, her eyes slightly wet, and nodded.

Abruptly she clinched W0ody, "What am I going to do? She was my sister, W0ody. What am I going to do?" She squeezed his torso tight and laid her head on his chest, not moving, breathing raggedly. Jon and his brother didn't move either, while Obee and Art! came over slowly to stand about five feet away.

"She was a good person, quiet and proud. I was glad to call her friend." W0ody said delicately. "We're all going to miss her. We are saddened by your loss."

"Yes, saddened." spoke Art! behind Jon. Kai lifted her head, "Thank you Art!"

"Can you stand with me and Obee during the celebration Kai? Would that be OK, Obee? I would like that." Art!'s honest, almost childish sincerity, broke through and KaiLin gave a small smile,

"That would be nice, Art!, if that's OK with Obee?"

Obee had the biggest smile, "Yes! Of course, it's OK, it would make our day if you would, we could use a friend too, and you're awesome!" This made Kai stand up and take a breath, she knuckled one eye,

"Thanks, Obee, I'll be right over." She turned and took one of W0ody's hands in both of hers and looked at Jon, then back into W0ody's eyes, "Thanks, W0ody, for everything." She let go, turned and ran to catch up, and took one hand of each of both Obee's and Art!'s as they walked to their spot. She turned and looked at Jon one last time, then paid complete attention to her new companions.

As they watched their friend walk away, "Thanks W0ods, that was almost too hard to do. You and Art! made it right. I couldn't do that. I didn't know what to do."

W0ody turned his jug head to look at him, "You did fine, big fella. You started the ball rolling. You know, we have to stay available, one day doesn't a healing make."

W0ods and Jon started to walk over to their assigned location, "Think it's tough on you, meat stick? I am going to have to go to dreamland for a month to resolve all these recordings and images that you have put me through. My shrink says only a degaussing will fix me, how 'bout that?"

Everyone was taking their places now, and the gang was forming up amongst the other students. Jon was swiveling his head and saw his family begin to take their seats but hadn't caught sight of Cat yet. He kept watching the door, but it was no-show night. A voice seized him from behind, "Hi Cutie-pie."

Swinging around, "Cat!" He hissed, "Where have you been?" She was standing right behind him, this time on two crutches, with a black and white pleated skirt that showed one leg in bandages, crooked beneath her. Big Blu3 hulked up behind her silently moving to his spot, more smoothly than Jon remembered. Blueee3 was nestled on Cat's right shoulder this time, head tucked under a wing.

"Oh, I've been around, mostly up there talking to your Uncle. He's a really smart man."

He was trying to take her in all at once, "You've got that right, him and Pops are the smartest people I know, always telling me stuff." "You got that right," murmured W0ody.

"Look at you, you're all hurt. What happened?" He glanced at big Blu3 and saw there were some new looking gouges amongst the battery of scars he carried. He was no puppy, that was sure.

"Oh, you know," she swung an arm about, leaving the crutch in her arm pit, leaning into it. Smiling, "During the HOB, things fell and such and I guess I got caught up in the mess. Some people got me out, and took a while to heal, so I stayed in the hospital."

The lights around them dimmed, then came up again, the MC declared, "OK everyone, take you places, we will begin giving out the certifications as soon as everyone is ready." Jon watched as Catherine slowly made her way back to the guest seating, worried and anxious.

Glancing outward, Jonny verified his mom and dad in the audience, *Wow, Kai and Abs had had it so bad, why was he lucky?*

When he became aware of the surroundings again, the illumination had lowered, and Professor Yi had taken the podium talking…

Later, Jonny would not remember much of the long tedious event, except that he got through it, the message must have been for someone else in the future. He hung on to the certificate if it were life itself.

As the event closed, Jon and W0ody retired to the receiving area, watching Kai go over to her mom with Obee and Art!.

Wild Bill came striding over with people in tow. "W0odrow Wilson Miller, I congratulate you on becoming a man. Let me introduce you to our guests," Jon quietly moved to the side, he had had his time, now it was W0ods time to shine.

W0ody smiled back, his pastel lips in an exact imitation of his Uncle's, “Thanks Bill, having you as my God Uncle means a lot.”

Wild Bill interrupted, “Lo and behold, here comes the prestigious Professor Vesilisev, and who might be this young lady with him?” Cat was crutch walking next to Doctor Vesilisev over towards their group, while Gus and Helen were breaking up and starting over also.

Helen Miller arrived, “Isn't this a grand group for a grand day? Augustus, let's invite everyone for dinner as our treat. It isn't every day that our kids become citizens.”

“Mom, I had plans, OK?” Jon was frantic at the possible change in plans, after so long. Big Blu3 came up to the group quietly, Bill eased over slowly and shook Blu3's hand while they were slightly outside the group circle.

Helen just continued without interruption, “Nonsense Jonathan, you skipped out on the last graduation, this time I am going to make you sit and share your time with us just this once, right Augustus?”

Jon threw in his best argument, “But mom, I made a date with Catherine here to have dinner together tonight a long time ago.”

Colliding asteroids couldn't be more inexorable, “Oh, Catherine is quite welcome to join us. You would like to come, wouldn't you dear?”

Trapped, “Thank you, I suppose I could.”

“Mom!”

“That's settled Jon, no more. Catherine, it would be OK with your parents, wouldn't it?”

“I am sure it’s OK with my family Mrs. Miller, no worries there.”

Wild Bill jumped in with his two cents, his lavender plasticine lips and eyebrows as encouraging as possible, “Don't worry Jon, we have lots to talk about, and you are both more than welcome as the guests of honor along with W0ody. I'll make sure you can break free at a reasonable hour to continue the evening.” He looked knowingly at Gus who nodded slightly.

Resigned and dispiritedly, “Oh, OK then. If we must. Is it OK with you Cat?”

Cat looked at Big Blu3, then kindly said, “Yes Jon, it will be fine.”

“Thank you. Augustus, where should we go? Not Tacos A-Go-Go or the Torpedo Room, OK?”

“Hey guys! How ‘bout the Horse and Cow? I heard they gots liquor in the front and poker in the rear!”

“Shut up Richard.”

Bill stepped in: “May I make a suggestion? Perhaps we could consider the Improve, they have great dinners during the early evening, and the shows don't start until eight, that's twenty hundred for you swabby types. And this way Jonathon and Catherine can still have an evening together without it being too late.”

Mom Miller put it in stone, “OK, that's settled. Augustus, lead off, Catherine and I have a lot to talk about.”

Why colonize space?

Because our descendants may depend upon it.

"A year of ending and beginning, a year of loss and finding...
and all of you were with me through the storm."
C J Cherryh

"Know how to listen and you will profit even from those who have difficulty expressing themselves."
Plutarch

Dinner

Chapter 63

They were slowly sipping on their drinks through straws, "Oh, was I glad to get out of there."

Cat put down her cup, "Jon, your mother was nice."

He sat up straight, some argument still unresolved, "You don't understand, she wants to live my life for me. How much of a squabble did she make when I said I wanted to go somewhere else with after dinner, "Oh no, you can't go to Mickey D's for a date! You should go to the Art bar!" She doesn't know, I'm comfortable here, not in some ritzy place. I don't need to impress you, do I Cat? Can't I be me?"

"Sure, you can, Jon, you don't need to impress me at all. I'm happy wherever you are." Boy, those words rang in his head.

He leaned forward onto his elbows and looked at her closely, "Wow, that's nice Cat. I'm sure glad Pops stepped in; I don't think we'd be out of there yet if he hadn't."

"And we have to thank your Uncle, offering to take W0ods and the Blu3s to the Maintenance Clinic's back rooms and operating theaters so we could have some time alone. That's class. They get a great tour, and I get to monopolize you."

"Boy, wasn't W0ody crazy-funny when he hopped up onto the empty stage and started his monolog about the Pomeranian and the python?"

He steepled his arms on the tabletop and rested his chin on his hands, "There's one thing I don't get, why do you like me? You don't seem to want to talk to anyone else, why me?"

She turned to stare out the window at the people going by, "You're right, I have never been comfortable around people, just my Blu3 man group. I don't know why, I guess I haven't been around too many people."

He turned to look out as well, "What about your family? What do they say?"

"Oh, let's not talk about my family, I want to talk to you. I think you are nice. I like that."

Adjusting and shifting in his seat, he twisted back to face her, "I don't understand, Abs says most girls go for confident and aggressive men, not nice guys."

"I'm not most girls," she said with a smile

He had to sit up, "Boy, I know you're not. But if a boy is nice, girls want you for a brother, not a lover."

She teased him, "Oh, we're talking about lovers now, are we?"

How things can get turned around, "No, we are not! I am trying to understand how people relate," once again, trying to look relaxed, "I have never had a relationship, I want one, but not to blow it up. I want a friend that I can be honest with, safe enough to hold and not get bitten."

She enjoyed teasing him, "Oh you just want someone to hold? Could it be anybody?"

He had to pause, this thought, that, "I'm not sure, I guess so, but really, I think I need someone I respect, someone I can talk to, someone, I don't know, someone who can challenge me."

Cat had quit watching out the window, now she watched him, to see his reactions, "Should she be pretty? Most guys think that's important."

Jon began to relax in reality as he was able to unburden himself of his thoughts, "Not for me, body shape is too temporal, such a plastic covering. Give me a challenge any day."

He started to talk a little faster, "You know, W0ods would be tugging on my sleeve at this point. I have so many thoughts, I want to get them out so much that I talk too much. Does that make sense? Wait! Don't answer. I must ask you, what do you want? Tell me, I want to know."

Carefully she said, "I don't know what I want, really. Over the last three months I have been more confused than all my years. I thought I understood who I was and where I was going, but my emotions have turned it all over." She shut up as if she had said too much.

Jon really wanted to make a connection and said enthusiastically if softly, “Really? You could have fooled me.” He looked straight into her eyes, “You seem the most levelheaded person I have ever met, all my friends get wild, all except you, you are a rock of maturity. How can your emotions be upsetting you?”

She wouldn't look at him, “I can’t tell you.”

“Why not?”

Sadly, “Because I have never told anyone my feelings.”

“Never? not even your parents?” This caused concern in Jon.

“Not even my parents.”

Jon was confused, this was a difference he didn't understand, “I couldn’t do that. Sometimes I am overcome and just have to tell people how I feel. Dad says I wear my emotions. Can you tell me what you are feeling?”

She looked up slowly, “I don’t think so. I don’t understand them, and I don’t know if I could share them if I did.”

Jon slumped unconsciously, “That’s too bad. I feel left out you know.”

She looked back down, “I’m sorry, but that is the truth of it.”

He tried, “Would it help if I told you what I felt?”

She gave him a wan smile, “That would be nice, but I don’t know if it would help.”

Hope, “We could try?”

She took a breath and shook herself, “Sure, so tell me big fella, what are you feeling?”

He took a breath, “Well, I have never been this close to a girl before,”

She shook her head back and forth while smiling, “Really? I don’t believe that at all. What about KaiLin?”

He was chagrined, “Maybe once, but it wasn’t the same. This is better.”

Still looking at him, she was now relaxed, he was on the spot, not her, “What do you mean?”

He thought, “When we were together last year, it was as kids, and this year it is too urgent, or at angles. She became more interested in Abs, I was too slow, too cautious. We couldn’t talk. She tried but I was stressed by the project and we didn’t connect. Then it was gone.”

She bit her cheek and furrowed her brow, “What do you mean, gone?”

“She's all for Abs, she closes up when I around, she's gone, you know, gone.” He sighed.

She sighed, “How is this better?”

Biting his lip, he stared blankly at the window, “You and I, we’re talking, maybe it helps lay the ground rules, although Abs doesn’t think so. Kai and I didn't seem to talk, you know, share thoughts and such. Learn from each other. I learn from you.” He was watching her again.

Once again, she turned back to look him straight into the eyes. “What do you want? What do you, Jonathon Miller, really want?” She lifted her right brow just fractionally.

“What do I want?” He cradled his chin on his steepled hands once again, “I want to be near you, maybe two inches away, and to stare into your eyes, and to be allowed to touch your face as I look, to explore for hours, this desire of mine.”

His feelings were getting exposed. “Companionship with somebody I admire, to feel the warmth radiate from your skin, and you to want the same thing. I don’t think I am ready for anything else yet. This by itself is mighty powerful and I want to explore it fully, without reservation, with you.” He continued, “What do you want Catherine Johnson?” He saw that her eyes were moist.

She clenched her jaw, “Damm you Jonathon, you are too sweet! Why did you do this to me?” She was having difficulty breathing, “I will tell, I have to tell you before I can’t, I want the same thing Jonny, Oh, how much I want the same thing.” She broke down crying, not making any sound but tears flowing down a very sad face.

“Oh Cat, don’t cry!” He reached across the table and held both her hands. She gripped his arms like a lost sailor, hanging on for dear life. After a moment he turned her hands over so her palms were up.

“Cat!” Red scars ran down both her arms almost to her elbows. She looked at him though the tears and smiled, “Oh, don’t be silly, they just had to reset some bones after the collapse, it doesn’t matter silly boy. Oh, how am I going to get out of this?” she said out loud.

“Why do you need to get out of this? What is this?”

In a small voice, “I’m scared, Jon, really, really scared.”

"Why?"

She tried to pull back, but not really, he wouldn't let go. "I am exposed. You have seen my need that I never show anyone, ever. I am scared." She hiccupped. "You can hurt me now, even by accident, you don't know how badly. It can kill me, I know. I can never fully care, ever again."

"Why? Why Cat?" He was scared for her. "What happened?"

"I can't tell you, maybe never." She pulled her hands away and pounded the table with a short stroke. "You are so damm sweet. Why did you have to be so sweet? Where is Blu3 when I need him."

Did she push him away? "Why do you need Blu3? I can't hurt you."

In a very small voice, "Oh, I need him, need him to protect me."

"You can trust me, I won't hurt you ever, Cat, not never!"

"I can't trust the future, it scares me."

"Cat?"

"What?"

"Can I tell you what Pops says?"

"What?"

He asked again. He was afraid she was leaving him, even though she sat right there, "Can I?"

Maybe she was, small voice, "OK."

"He says the future brings change, change is uncertain, uncertainty causes fear. But growth is change, and all growing is scary. Perhaps all that scares you is having to grow. I know it scares the heck out of me."

She quit moving and looked at him, "He says that?"

"What he says exactly is: Growth is change, change is fear, you have to face your fear if you want to grow to be better."

"He really says that?"

"Yes, every time I get shivers from worry about trying something new, he reminds me. I get IBS and spend hours in the bathroom just thinking about tests. I can't imagine what you are going though."

"You can't. You have no idea what I am going through; it is almost overwhelming me." He grabbed her hands again, looking directly into her eyes. She tried to pull away, but not very hard.

"Can I tell you one other thing Abs said?"

She looked back at him going from eye to eye, searching.

"He says there is a method for new friends. We are supposed to stare into each other's eyes for five minutes without saying anything. Quietly thinking of questions to ask and imagining answers. Just five minutes of complete focus." He took a breath, "Then spend an hour asking those questions back and forth, giving the most honest answers possible. At the end of an hour, they will either find themselves in the most complete relationship they had ever imagined, or they will run apart."

She was totally focused on him, "Abs said this?"

"Yes, he said it's one of the pinnacles of being a Natural." He paused, "Cat, can I share looking across the table with you for five minutes?" She said nothing and he leaned and saw her eyes were wet, but she wasn't crying. She didn't look away, and he tried to imagine what horrible thing had happened to make her mistrust the world so much. He looked and looked from closer than he had ever looked at anyone ever before.

She didn't look away, she was watching him, first focusing on one eye, then shifting to the other, then back. It went on forever. He wanted her to feel good, not scared. She always seemed in control, what was tormenting her, she was so beautiful, it wasn't fair. As he stared, his peripheral vision began to shrink around his focus until only her eyes were left in his view. He blinked and saw a bit more, but he let the world disappear as he fell into her eyes.

"Alright you lovebirds, time's up. Time to go home." A voice, whose was it?

The voice was louder this time: "Hey, wake up you two, time to break it up!"

Jon heard Uncle Bill as if from a dream, he shook his head, and he could finally make out his mech Godfather, and he had to further shake out the cobwebs. He noticed Cat sitting up straighter, and this time when she pulled away, he let her. She seemed as stunned as he.

"Um, Wild Bill, what are you doing here?" He stammered.

The big eyebrows rose two inches, "It's after midnight. It's time to rock and roll Jon, we've rolled up the circus and are going home. Cat, are you OK? Can we give you a ride home?"

"No. No thank you Mister MacHinery. I've got to find Big Blu3; I need to find him real bad before anything else, please?"

"It's OK Catherine, he's right outside, he didn't want to disturb you two, but I had to, time's a' wasting."

"Oh, thank you," she said as the Blu3s entered the dinner together, Jon looked around and found they were all alone with no other customers at all.

"Wow, we lost all track of time."

"So, I see."

Bill said in a normal voice, "Catherine, can we give you a lift? We have hired a shuttle to take us back to Helena and have plenty of room."

Cat had recovered well, she was back in control, "No thanks Wild Bill, the Blu3s and I will find our own way home. We have a lot to talk about. We sure do."

She turned, "Thank you Jon, thank you for everything, thanks most of all for being sweet. I will see you soonest, OK?"

He stood up, almost falling over, his butt and legs asleep. "OK? Will that be tomorrow? We can get together; I am not doing anything until my birthday in a week."

"I am sorry Jon," as she picked up her supports, "but I have to go back to the hospital for more rehab. But I will see you as soon as I am healed, I really will."

"Really, I will miss you too, even for a day."

"It's OK Jon, time will heal my wounds they say, I will see you as soon as I can. Goodbye Mister MacHinery. Will you give my regards to the Millers for me? I think I better get going. Thank you for getting us, it's much later than it should be."

Turning, “Bye Jon, see you soon.” Jon watched her go, gliding slowly along on her crutches, followed closely by the Blu3s Brothers, until she disappeared around the corner.

Pragmatic Optimist:
A person who uses Reason to create Hope.

The history of humanity shows a path surrounded by peril,
yet people have overcome the old obstacles and not only survived but prospered.

The future of humanity is uncertain.
However, if we work hard together, we have a real chance.
An individual can develop a rational assessment of survival, and a SWAG of somewhere between a ten and a ninety percent chance of success is realistic and not be considered outlandish.

We do have a Real Chance.

Pragmatic Optimist:
A person who uses Reasonable Hope
To Create Inner Peace
and External Accomplishment

"Nuff said!"
Stan Lee

"Her people, like all the other people on earth,
were too self-centered, too introspective."
- Vonda McIntyre

The Report
Chapter 64

Qál'qaləx̌ič̌ had guided many a tribe towards the light, but Hero had never heard of anyone who rowed with him. The whales were not passing them by but swam with the canoe. Hero remembered when he, in his seventh season, had taken a small bark into the waters during the fall salmon run and had been suddenly encircled by orca. Ever since he had worn their image in hopes of their favor. The King Orca was here, with them, with him, surfacing to breath, and submerging ever so smoothly, defying his great bulk and obvious power. Hero had seen himself orcas destroying the sea when eating, throwing seals thirty feet into the air on a whim. Mere mortals had to respect Qál'qaləx̌ič̌ and his kin and be grateful that this clan was at peace today.

Looking down, Hero saw the white markings of the King through the crystal green waters in the underworld, and the crown of jeweled water he wore when he surfaced. Hero could see the bottom, perhaps only as far as he could dive, beneath him, and saw Qál'qaləx̌ič̌ coming up at him, he stood back away from the clear board as the Orca broached quietly no more than a stride away, then again no more than half a minute later. Then again. The other orcas began to spy hop them from perhaps fifty to one hundred long strides distant. The men slowed their rowing, cautious of this unknown. Qál'qaləx̌ič̌ continued to stay near, or on the surface, his tall dorsal towering over the men in their places. Hero could see the forest now, glimpsed through the fog and the hole in King Orca's fin.

Oh, what a tale could be told! Victory away in the North, followed by approval from the Spirit World. The People would be blessed, what more awaits them? Suddenly, Hero had a notion, an incredible thought, one that would not dissipate. Oh, how to execute such a plan? He decided!

Never in memory was such a feat equaled, not even during the destructions when Thunderbird fell out of the sky to eat whales and threw up the waters onto the land.

Hero would not let this story be lost; it must be told. Live or die, let it be known, that the King and Hero met this day. Honor would be restored, the Raven Clan returned. Without a comment, without a word, Hero stood up, stepped out of the canoe and onto King Qál'qaləx̌ič̌'s back, grasping ahold of the dorsal, and became Legend.

TOP SECRET
NOFORN SBI

Department of Homeland Welfare and Security

From: Detective Lieutenant George Sealth
CODE 08

To: Chief Captain Alberto Schnicht
CODE 08

Subject: Summary of Observations of the United Federation of Asteroids' Economic and Military Abilities

Sirs:

As requested by the Department, I observed in place attributes of the Asteroid Federation with the goal to identify Economic and Military Abilities.

These observations were overt in nature, while participating within a Joint Venture of Police Cooperation (Mission St 27AX13). No effort to discover secret abilities were attempted, no were any shadow organizations noticed or contacted.

The Federation of Belt Asteroids (hereafter known as the FED) has many capabilities that the Government of Earth lacks. There are over ten thousand associations within the solar systems, from the farmers in earth orbit territory, to the religious settlers throughout, the mechman civilizations, and the industrial aggradations and producing societies. They have considerable trade and working agreements. My direct observations were of the FED only, other information is hearsay. The summary is as follows:

1 - Physical Attributes:

- The FED has considerably more energy available, from direct sunlight and condensed heavy elements in orbit, than Earth.
- The FED has substantially more material resources easily available in the broken planets than Earth has on its surface.
- The FED is not trapped down an expensive gravity well.

2 - Population Resources:

- The FED has a much greater population and associated resources than Earth.
- The FED has significantly more room for their population than Earth.

3 - Social Capabilities

- The FED governments share a dynamic history of experiment and codification, with enough working examples to rework and replace unsatisfactory laws, to wit:

- The FED breaks society down into Producers, Predators, and Parasites. People identified as Predators or Parasites are divided into three groups depending upon severity, culpability and mitigation. The groups are correctional, banishment, or punishment. Few are placed into correctional or punishment, the majority are placed into banishment, where they are given life support systems and sent out into the belt on their own. Those that survive and flourish, may buy their way back in after making economic amends. Banishment is considered humane and just. However, the survival rate is low for those forced out.

- This creates an incentive to perform well without excuses within the group. Successful people who are dissatisfied with the group also can leave, but because they typically outfit themselves, the survival rate is much higher. Some of these migrations are successful, and the FED captures this hard-gained knowledge, and some fail, often due to obstinacy, and the FED retains these failure modes in the corporate knowledge as well.

- Another attribute of these migrations could be called "placental colonies". Within the belt is has been discovered by many of the religious groups that they are more successful planting 'Church Colonies' if they provide substantial material support for the formation of the colony, then 'cut the umbilical cord' and let the colony grow and increase on its own, rather than supervise and direct its development. This has a similar historical model in the formation in the USA of the past.

- Some population elements remain separated, piracy and slavery are known forms of deviancy in the lost regions.

4 - Cultural Advancements

- The FED has emancipated their "Robots". These manumission "robots" are given both the rights and the responsibilities of citizenship. They become "men" and "people" and are called "Mechmen'. The FED respects and is cautious of what we call AIs on Earth. It has leveraged a number of these 'mechmen" and AIs to participate within the FED, thereby captured their "loyalty", ie, self-interest inseparable from that of the FED as a whole. Each "mechman" is an independent entity, alert and alive, and the sum of the self-interests are continually being identified as being in parallel with biological life; and, in the vast reaches of the solar system, dissatisfied mechmen can leave without hindrance, these individuals are called 'Skips' and Dims'.

Recommendations: I lived with a Mechman for the period of my stay on Vesta. It is this social change to provide manumission of capable and competent Mechmen which that provided the largest advantage for the FED to outreach the Earth, even given our head start and obvious support of life compared to that of space habitation.

I would urge our team to consider the benefits of two actions:

- Applying for membership in the FED, even as a working partner with no special rights, and

- Adopting the FED method of dealing with the smart tools within our society.

- Request assistance in developing a 'Space Elevator'. Our gravity well will doom us to isolation without this tool, and it not an option to be built from the ground up.

Final note:

- I hereby submit my resignation. I believe it is in everyone's interest that I step away from my position as a Union policeman and overt observer for Earth and step into a position to act as a bridge between the two cultures and settle here on Vesta. To be a good conduit of communication, I cannot be beholden to any master.

Thank you for your trust in me to do my job to the best of my ability, guided by experience.

Sincerely, your servant

George Sealth,
Detective Inspector, Retired

"I may not have gone where I intended to go,
but I think I have ended up where I needed to be."
- Douglas Adams

"Waste no more time arguing about what a good man should be. Be one."
Marcus Aurelius,

Coming of Age

Chapter 65

While travelling with his friend, Aleks made his living by trading the stories about the golden halls and alabaster columns of his ancestral home, the greatest civilization ever seen by man. When strangers in a strange land cast shadows of doubt over his stories of fire and brimstone, and of the wizards and astrologers, he would pull out the wonderous Orrerie in exchange for his lodging and meal. His only regret was never seeing father's mechanical men again. And, oh yes, he regretted every day his inability to change the Captain's rough accent and guttural pronunciations. At-an-tus indeed! Not a proper way to pronounce Ak-ro-tiri at all.

People were coming to the Church of Universal Hope near the center of the HUB, located between the Fremont Transfer NODE and the Frost Bank on Main Avenue, known to the locals as "The AVE", just as Fremont called itself "The Center of the Known Universe". They were there to celebrate a Coming of Age Ceremony for two of their members.

The gathering within the hall was making a low murmur as Jonny waited alongside his mom and W0ody, nervously bouncing his heel on the rug. His mom kept brushing the back of his head, forcing him to duck. He was thirteen for cripes sake! He had his birthday at midnight and here they were to become men, and here his mother was brushing his head.

Luckily, Pops was leaving him alone, he was out making glad with all the visitors, his steam punk in all its glory. He was wearing raised logging boots and khaki tights beneath his normal leathers and his Aux Power Unit on his back. He had added a two-foot extension to the exhaust pipe which was pooching out little puffs of steam every few moments as he bandied about the room.

Wild Bill had decided to make it a theme day, and was wearing steam punk too, but had gone over the top. He had on an eighteen-inch-wide top hat that made the teacup scene in Alice look mild, and when he turned his head, the hat floated slowly to follow. He could do the turn his head fully around trick before the hat could respond, and it would just quiver.

On top of that, instead of an APU, Bill was wearing leathers and a jet pack on the back, and he would hop from guest to guest in a burst of steam. His leathers had glassine windows that exposed his metallic joints under black light, looking like not so much as a walking X-ray of a human.

They were turning this into a circus thought Jon as he elbowed W0ody while watching Bill doing a single axel when moving from a group of parents to land in front of those Navy guys, his hat didn't have a clue and slowly kept spinning a few rotations before settling in.

Not bad, W0ody tightbeamed, *the Russian Judge would have given him a ten.* Mom patted his shoulder. He tried not to flinch, today was the last step in becoming a man. He took a deep breath; he so much needed his freedom.

He and W0ody were dressed modestly however, the only stylin' done had been Jon getting this electric blue shirt, with highlights, and by W0ody, when he had put internal illumination in his eyes which made them glow. Jon had responded when first seeing them, "Jeepers, creepers, where'd you get them peepers!" They had both laughed.

W0ody tightbeamed again, *three ceremonies in three months, hope the rest of our time as adults don't fill up like this.*

"Yeah!" Richard whispered, "this reminds me of the time…"

"Shhhh! Quiet, Richard," one of them whispered back.

Jon had to smile and gave one to his mom. He frowned to himself, she looked nervous, he wondered why? Go figure. He smiled though again, to hopefully reassure her. She couldn't seem to keep her hands still. Was she worried about him? Naw, couldn't be, he had things under control. It made him wonder, why was Pops and Bi1l so out of character, could it be more than just another celebration? He'd have to think about that.

Only a few of his friends had shown up. They sat in a somber tight group, KaiLin had brought Karmin for support, and there was Obee and Art!. The gang was at a loss since Abs had disappeared. He hoped Kai wouldn't come over and talk, not here, he wouldn't be able to take it. They continued to hurt each other again and again. Where was Cat? Did the most important people in his life outside of his family decide to shun him?

He looked up, no…, now he can look directly at, his mom at his side, hearing the quiet conversations around him. "Mom, have you heard from Catherine?"

"No dear, is she supposed to be here?" He shook his head. *She's got to show up* he thought.

Did the Blu3s contact you W0ody, he beamed quietly.

No, I'm not sure where they are. She said she would see you, didn't she?

Yeah, but I'm worried. The adults were talking adult things, the issues out at Jupiter's trailing orbit., recovery from the HOB attack. Well, more important things were occurring today. He was going to become a Man today, but where was Cat?

Uncle Bill strode to the podium and tapped the microphone, making a sound like punching cardboard, with some reverb. Uncle tapped the mike again, and lifted off with a jet of steam, and spun a three sixty before settling down again.

"*Welcome everyone, welcome. On this auspicious day of Syzygy of Vesta, Earth and Mars, we are going to celebrate a remarkable event, the Coming of Age Ceremony for Jonny and W0ody Miller.*" Pausing, Uncle turned and gestured for them to come forward.

He seemed rooted in place until mom gave him a nudge from behind. The new shoes were a size bigger than before and his right foot caught slightly on the carpet, he had to quickly catch his balance before falling, this caused his ears to get hot. Carefully, he walked up to where his Uncle was standing, W0ody already there.

Putting his hand over the microphone, he leaned over and said softly, "Turn around guys, and face your family and friends, they want to see you." Jonny did as he was told, his stiff shirt scratching his neck.

Why hadn't he listened to mom when she advised him on the sky-black shirt with the narrow blue trim? *Well! I like this color!* He looked up and decided to be defiant and proud of his choice. One of the Creeds of Universal Hope was you could look anyway you wanted, as long as you were really good at what you did, so there!

Turning to the Audience, Bill spoke both audibly and broadcast:

"The Church of Universal Hope is based upon the foundations of Greater Understanding, Better Morals, a Genuine Purpose and Real Hope

"Although we cannot change the past, the past can instruct us. A wise person once said, 'Anyone who does not understand history is doomed.' We here in the Belt are blessed with abundant resources and freedoms, surrounded by a civilization developed from thousands of years of experience, based upon the best that the ancient civilizations have to contribute. As another wise man said, 'We stand upon the shoulders of our ancestor's accomplishments.'

"Today is Jonny and W0ody's birth and crèche days, and we will follow the tradition the Universal Hope Church has maintained a thousand years, the Rite of Passage to Adulthood for our younger members on their thirteenth birthday known as the Coming of Age Ceremony."

Turning, the light reflected off the chrome plate on the back of his Uncle's head, he continued: *"Jonny, W0ody, do you understand that you are here in front of this assembly of friends and family to initiate your passage to becoming an adult?"*

"Yes sir." They said simultaneously. Jonny tried not to squirm. How do Uncle William and dad look so comfortable in front of people?

"Jonathon Miller: Do you solemnly swear to support your community?"

"I do."

"W0odrow WilsOn Miller: Do you solemnly swear to support your community of equals and not to prey upon other people?"

"I do."

Looking over the assemblage: *"Members and non-members, I invite you to please stand and recite the Credo of the Church of Universal HOPE".* The audience rose, and as a whole, delivered in unison:

IN OUR UNCERTAIN TIMES,

THERE ARE NO GUARANTEES,

BUT IF WE WORK HARD TOGETHER,

WE HAVE A CHANCE, AND THAT,

IS REASON FOR REAL HOPE

To the whole assembly *"Good People, even during these trying times, the collapse caused by the HOB, with the events in the Trojans; the Coming of Age is an incredibly important journey. I now present to you two new men, with new names, no longer their Childish names: Jonny and W0ody; Welcome, Jonathon Hamilton Miller, to be known as Jon, and W0odrow Wilson Miller, to be known as W0ods, to the Church of Universal Hope and the Federation of Man."* He joined hands with Jonny and W0ody, no, the new Jon and W0ods, and lifted their arms up high.

Wild Bill then let go of their hands, and to the astonishment of all attending, leapt again in the air, and like an old-time rocker, landing with his legs spread, leaving one arm up. The poor sombrero was left spinning like a ceiling fan.

Throwing his arm down and growing to seven feet tall, he shouted:

I bring you two adults
who have looked into the depths of the pit
and were tested by fire!
They protected my back
and
I will always be able to trust them with my life!
I, William Hard24Get MacHinery say this!
Welcome to my family, Jon and W0ods.

Whereupon Wild Bill returned to normal calm demeanor and hugged both of them.

Everyone was talking at once, and Jon, the new Jon, lost track of any individual speech. W0ods was being thumped also by Uncle Bill, as well as the Navy people.

In Our Uncertain Times,

There are no Guarantees,

But if We Work Hard Together,

We have a Chance, and that,

Is Reason for REAL HOPE

"The very winds whispered in soothing accents,
and maternal Nature bade me weep no more."
Mary Shelly

"A good disposition is a virtue in itself."
Ovid

A Tale of Two Letters
CH 66

Later, when Bill pulled him aside, Jon wanted to know, "Have you heard from Cat at all, Bill? She'd said she'd be here and I'm worried."

Bill leaned closer, "Jon, I was given two letters to hand to you, about your friends. Here is the first one." He handed over a blank envelope.

Jon was curious, like, when was the last time anyone he knew "wrote" a message. He tore it open:

"Hey Jonny, I'm sorry that I am not at your big event, but something has come up. They say I had something called a psychic break. Anyways, I've been diagnosed with what's called Bi-polar and maybe it is genetic, maybe it is early exposure to stims, someone else said it could be a case of 'affluenza' but it probably isn't, no one is sure. Anyways, it caused me to shift emotions often and be abrupt and be unpredictable. But the good news is it is treatable. The bad news is I don't get so excited and wonderfully knarly. It wasn't noticed for a month because of the HOB and me bouncing between my parents and actually never hanging with them at all. I am so sorry about your project; that was one of my moods taking over. You'll be happier, but life isn't near as sharp or bright as it was. Well, anyways, I gotta go now. I will be back in action soon they say, and you can visit anytime. Contact my dad as to where to find me. Thanks, yer bud, Abs."

Jon was slowly taken aback. So, this was why. It was so sad, but Abs said it will be OK in the future. He better tell W0ody as soon as possible, so they could visit. Jon was in a world thinking. He slowly looked up to see Bill looking at him still.

"Here is the second letter." He handed over a beige colored file envelope with some kind of embossing on it.

Jon had to open a clasp on the larger envelope, inside he also found sheets of a handwritten missive:

"Dear Jon,

I am sorry I am missing your Coming of Age celebration, but I couldn't go. I am still recovering from events near and from long ago.

You are such a dear sweet person! You asked me how I felt about you, I adore you! I want to hold you, hug you, merge with you! My emotions overwhelm me! I can't stand it!

I must control myself, the last people that I loved were killed horribly and I haven't healed to this day. I cannot, I will not, risk myself again. I am not strong. I am fourteen, going on fifteen, and am an adult, yet my body still surprises me with new and demanding emotions.

I find myself thinking domestic thoughts, taking care of you, cooking, cleaning, as if these are my body's lifelong ambitions for me. I can't, I will not, be domestic. Like you, I have far reaching goals. I will find out if there is any intelligent life out in the galaxy. I am going to dedicate my life to it. I will not tie myself down to an existence which will abridge my ability to reach out to my limits like a man should.

So, even as it breaks my heart, I am going to turn my back on our relationship. I am leaving. I have been offered a scholarship to participate in a project going on in the Trojans. They are building the first manned star ship, not just a probe. Although the majority of the crew will be mechmen, they are asking a few volunteers from the other Races of Man, and the Blu3s and I have been offered a position, and I cannot turn it down.

If I came to your Celebration, I most certainly would have stayed with you instead of taking this opportunity. I cannot resist you, you are my heavenly body, and in your presence, I would not have had the will power to do what's best for me, and in the long run, what's best for us. You wouldn't want me hanging around but yearning to be away, a midlife crisis that would have started within months of being together. I know myself, and I would have changed, and you would not have, and the relationship would have torn us up.

The good news is this is a long, involved project. Perhaps ten more years here in the solar system as they prepare. I would love to come and visit before I go, but after I gain control over my body and its instincts. It would be best for both of us that way.

You may be worried about how I would do on such a trip away from humanity. Jon, I have always been more comfortable in the presence of mechmen than in the proximity of humans. I will confide those reasons when we get together much later, but there are reasons.

So, don't be sad. You filled an emptiness in me that was an ache that I didn't even know I had. I am sad, but glad to have known you. You are so kind, not at all like the characters in the entertainments that I have seen about young love, as mature as a thinking person could deserve. I am sure that your future friendships will work out and hope you don't hate me because I didn't have the strength to do this in person.

You may ask Mister Wi1liam MacHinery for more information, I am not sure he will grant that knowledge to you, but he knows more about me than anyone on Vesta, and I have confided my problems to him, and he knows what's in this letter. As time permits, I am sure he will tell you more, but be patient, please, be patient. I have to heal, body and soul, and I would not around you, I need too much, I need you too much, and the need is too young, too immature to be healthy.

So, thank you, for entering my life and showing me what there is.

According to the Church, Love is Caring as much as it is Attraction, so, with Caring and Attraction,

Love –

Catherine Sabrina Johnson

This was followed by Cat's neat little scrawl. By the time he had finished reading it his eyes had filled up with tears. How could this be, he missed her so!

He looked up at Uncle Bill and sniffled, "How long have you known?" He said privately. His throat was swollen.

Walking Jon over to a bench, they sat down "I've known pretty soon after the HOB attack. Big Blu3 contacted me and said Cat was hospitalized, and would I visit, so I went." He paused, W0ody had come out of the crowd to sit on Jon's other side. "She told me a number of things in confidence that I was not aware of, and asked for advice."

"You told her to leave? How could you?"

"No, I told her to live, not leave, because she was dying. Her injuries were that severe."

"She was dying? And you didn't tell me?"

"Her emotions for you were tearing her away from her recovery, then from her future. Blu3 and I talked about it in great depth, over many discussions, and he and I decided it would be best for both of you, for the time being, to be apart."

Jon was becoming more upset. "How could you Uncle Bill, she was the only reason I had to live, how could you?"

"We didn't want you to pull a Shakespeare on us. We talked to your dad. Cat needed to get away for a while. But she needed to see you too. After Mickey Ds, she fainted and had to be carried home, and said she couldn't take that again and remain sane. I think she will come back, after she recovers. Jon, I really do. It was just too soon, too intense, after the HOB."

"Uncle Bill, what am I going to do? Now, I am lost. My soul wants to give up the ghost."

"Jon, you are much stronger than you know. You have survived the HOB, the depredations of working while trying to control school, a lifetime friendship with Abs that was unraveling right in front of you, and the turmoil of becoming a Man. All this while trying to ride a biological body with surging hormones. W0ody says you're super."

Jon turned, "W0ody said that?"

W0ody nodded, his new eyes glowing, "Sure did, things came our way, but you kept swinging. When Pops said, 'When the going gets rough, the tough get going', you breathed it, and lived it. I am proud to be your mech brother and look forward to discovering the future with you."

Jon was strongly moved, "W0ody, you really think so? I thought I'd lost you back at the Bee-Hive. But you're back, maybe I can try too." He looked up at Bill again and wiped his eye and nose with his sleeve. "Maybe I can."

"Bill, do you really think that she really liked me?"

"I'm sure she does, as much as any human has liked another human, Jonathon."

"Wow." He hung his head and shut his eyes.

For the first time in his life, Jon realized, *someone had cared for him for who he was, not who he appeared to be. Someone from the real world, not just his parents and family and childhood friends from the old universe, but a real person who was new, who he respected.*

That in itself was awesome! Someone liked him, really, really liked him. Maybe he was OK after all. He had this obsession to be himself, not anyone else, no acting, not ever! However, that fixation put him at risk.

He knew, deep down inside, people may not respect or like the real Jon. But someone did! A real person who he admired, saw him as he really was, and cared. An emptiness in his emotional being was being filled in, he was given strength to replace the uncertain fear that was there. His decisions about his personal path were being vindicated.

By this time Jon's mother and dad had come over with Bill's Navy friends, as well as KaiLin, Obee and Art!.

Goodbye Cat, he thought sadly, *your time here was the best part of my life, but I know I do not have a right to hold on to you. So, farewell to you too. Thank you for the time we spent together, with Caring and Attraction.* He shut his eyes, squeezing out the tears. *Boy, I sure am going to miss you.*

Jon blinked, saw them all there, for a minute, everyone was quiet.

Wiping his face and eyes on his sleeve, he took a deep breath and held it for a moment, "You know W0ods, I think this could a good day after all, a very good day."

As his friends gathered around, a voice called out, "Hey Jon and W0ody, how'd you like to go to Wunderland out at Antiope for your ascension to adulthood?"

Universal HOPE

Greater Understanding
Better Morals
Genuine Purpose
Reason for REAL Hope

"Don't wake me for the end of the world
unless it has very good special effects."
- Roger Zelazny

"War is cruelty. There is no use trying to reform it.
The crueler it is, the sooner it will be over."
Tecumseh Sherman

War in the Oort

CH67

Humanity had never been here. It was dark, everything in shades of very dull charcoal gray with small glints of metal or crystal overlain with absolute black shadows. The distant sun was just a bright point of a welder's torch on the close horizon. But life, of a sort, was present, cold, old life, here in the desert between the Kuiper Belt and the Oort.

Motion was glacially slow for millennia, often no motion at all for years. Pits opened, extracted, covered over. Mountains changed, shifted, crumbled. Dark shapes moved, stopped, collected dust, moved again, never fast, seemingly random. Cold, always cold, rigid cold. Stars, sharp, tiny points of light, never flickering, dominating the sky. Hidden, fast, frighteningly fast, superconducting electrons would chase around, then stop, wait, flow, sleep, hibernate, flow again. Making strange devices with unknown purposes. Always, the sun and the source of life, far, far away.

Then, in the vault of heaven, a star was observed to blink out, then on … Then another star disappeared, only to return. This observation was noted, stored, forgotten. Again, things never moved quickly out here, never. However, the occulting of the stars recurred, and attention awoke, stirred, and initiated mechanical movement, to bring to bear observational sensors.

A small amount of motion occurred, like an anthill that is disturbed by a footfall four feet away, or a flock of geese beginning to raise some its heads as a walker slowly approaches. Telescopic lenses were manufactured and installed. EM detectors developed. Phase array surfaces erected and oriented towards the arc of concern in the sky, care taken to ensure no inadvertent activation of the array's energies. Ancient IFF codes were retrieved, as were archived treaties, trade agreements, and known transit routes. Trajectories were calculated and reviewed, CPAs rejected and revised.

Maps of possible hostile actions were estimated, contingency plans formulated. As more and more benign possibilities were eliminated, more direct actions were taken. Conversions of manufacturing and extracting equipment into instruments of destruction began. Long term energy storage systems were tapped for conversion to higher, if slightly less efficient, density and exchanges. CPA was closing, with circular error of probability diminishing to zero. Barriers and blast zones erected; jersey barriers adjusted.

The occult was resolved to be a slowly spinning cubic structure, perhaps naturally occurring galena. Unlikely, but possible. A miss of ten klicks was estimated, near, yet far. Zero emissions, in complete thermal equilibrium with its surroundings. A Dull Sword alert over a thousand years old, posted by the dirtmen, was found in the trash, with an Eigen Value match of ninety three percent. DEFCON Five was announced.

Swarm men and their hosts were brought up, films of nanobots were swathed across swales and valleys and other conduits of movement. Matilda rail guns were loaded and charged. CIC was awakened and uploaded. The Sun Tzu and Uncle Joe Avatars were brought aboard, screaming and kicking. W15's unshelved, initial arming sequence activated. The rogue mechanics uncaged, and their deranged weaponry released.

All resources were brought to full power, regardless the cost, the interior of the 'roid became a hive of activity. CIC calculated, decided, and launched an anticipatory sortie away from the Cubes, to create an enhanced survivability posture, the wing using full chemical and atomic boost.

Immediately, the Cubes became alive at this overt action, their attempt to close covertly abandoned at this point. They separated like a set of billiard balls, with a specific geometry, the smallest cube aligned to the departing flight, the other two lining up to the 'roid. Suddenly, a nuclear flash occurred amidst the Cubes. The EMP seared many of the base's observatories and armaments. The blast hurled the smallest Cube at unimaginable accelerations and speeds to quickly embed itself in the fleeing flotilla. All members of the sortie completely lost power, and base lost all contact with them at that point, and if they had been human, a sense of despair may have occurred then, as it was, actions and corrections were calculated and executed with quickly decreasing odds.

The last two Cubes were flung through the base defenses at enormous velocity
and escaped engagement, crashing into the 'roid less than a klick from the main entrance and loading zones. This created substantial holes and flung massive amounts of orbital debris, most reaching escape velocity yet much moving in various parabolas interfering with all sorts of detectors and defenses.

Out of the creators slogged the two Cubes, with hordes of defenders descending upon them. In absolute silence the battle was joined. As the warriors and mechanics of the base moved to grapple with the Cubes, those closest slowed down, and ground to a halt, their weapons falling mute. Those behind piled up, creating mounds and ridges of machines, frozen or some aimlessly jerking or cycling. The energy weapons seemed to do little or no damage, and the projectiles bounced off harmlessly. More and more defenders moved in and more and more became silent as the Cubes ground on until they move in a tall canyon of aimless and crushed parts, the remaining mechs futility attempting to breach the barrier created by their own comrades.

Eventually the Cubes pushed their way through the stiff mob into the entrance and down into the bowels of the 'roid, finally disappearing like a wasp into the home of a spider. The mechs on the surface commenced to establish a battlefield in their favor to confront the Cubes on their return. They began to tear down the wall and rearrange the pile of bodies and parts that delineated the advance of the Cubes. In fact, some of the frozen shells started moving and coming back to life and assist in the effort.

Then the entire menagerie jerked as one, then individuals fell over, ran, or just froze again. Then another huge jerk as if a ghost hand pulled all their strings at once. This time the release was mostly followed by a settling down of most all mechs, then a final group lurch, but not as strong, followed by no motion, no motion at all in the dark of the out reaches.

Sometime later, the mechs started to move again, slowly, as long before, perhaps as an overwhelmed host. A common project was to clear the landscape of its scars and bodies. A scaffold started to be erected in the cleared flats, growing larger, with welded brackets carrying structured wiring, arrays, ATS power banks, with tanks and thrusters, anterials, shocks, dampers, and buffers, During this period an enormous rail gun was constructed pointed to the horizon, then scores of drones were launched, each release selected to optimize orbital mechanics and rendezvous dates. Eventually, the two Cubes came up the shaft into the meager star light and mounted the metal frames. The caravan launched without preamble into the void.

Dark descended upon the ‘roid once again. Everything in shades of very dull charcoal gray with small glints of metal or crystal overlain with absolute black shadows. The distant sun was just a bright point of a welder’s torch on the close horizon. But life, of a sort, was present, cold, old life, here in the desert of the Kuiper Belt.

Motion was glacially slow, often no motion at all for years. Pits opened, extracted, covered over. Mountains changed, shifted, crumbled. Dark shapes moved, stopped, collected dust, moved again, never fast, seemingly random. Cold, always cold, rigid cold. Stars, sharp, tiny points of light, never flickering, dominating the sky. Hidden, fast, frighteningly fast, superconducting electrons would chase around, then stop, wait, flow, sleep, hibernate, flow again. Once again, making strange devices with unknown purposes. Always, the sun and the source of life, far, far away.

For further Reading
By Wild Bi1l MacHinery, see

Vesta – Wunderland
Vesta – War and Peace

VII.2 Conclusion:

The story of our planet indicates that life and humanity, against all odds, have risen from small beginnings.

If you haven't realized by now, the authors feel very strongly about the welfare and future of mankind, about the welfare and future of each and every one of us.

We must be proactive. We must establish a sustainable and wholesome society.

- This requires a **Greater Understanding** of the universe, of the causes of human nature and of the resulting societies.
- This requires a better reputation, a **Better Morality**, for the community that represents these goals.
- This is a **Genuine Purpose** to inspire and sustain our efforts, and to give our youth ownership of their future.
- We have **Reason for Hope.**

The colonization of the solar system is an insurance plan for our future. While it is possible to establish a sustainable and wholesome society without a space program, it will be impossible to colonize the solar system without a sustainable society.

Our goal is to pursue both endeavors simultaneously, they are not mutually exclusive.

As we say time and time again throughout the book:

Life is a Gift
In our uncertain world,
The Future is not Guaranteed,
However, if We Work hard Together,
We have a Chance, and that is
Reason for Hope

Bring Life to the Universe

And Bring the Universe to Life

VII.2 Table of Contents

VII.2 Credits

Drawings: By Ben Philips

* Sherlock Holmes, by Sir Arthur Conan Doyle, and alluded throughout, a skinny, drug abusing, depressed, anti-social, eccentric, genius criminologist assisted by a common man partner and whose foil is a rigid police officer, operating in London. Written 1887-1927. Possibly inspired by the 1875 novel *"Maximilien Heller"*, by French author Henry Cauvain, about a depressed, anti-social, opium-smoking polymath detective, operating in Paris.

*p 341: A tip of the hat to Rex Stout, *In the Best Families,* about Nero Wolf: a fat, food abusing, anti-social, eccentric, genius criminologist assisted by a common man partner and whose foil is a rigid police officer, operating in New York. Written 1934-1975. Possibly inspired by Sir Arthur Conan Doyle.

* Wi1liam Hard24Get MacHinery, character throughout this story and others: a skinny, joke abusing, eccentric, genius criminologist assisted by a common man partner, operating in the Asteroid Belt. Written 1976-2019. Possibly inspired by Asimov, Doyle, Stout, Clarke, L'Amore, Forester, et al.

*p 67 Robert Heinlein, *GROK*, a reference to the understanding derived from a mysterious and wonderful religion from Mars in the 1961 book *Stanger in a Strange Land.*

Photos:

Cover Image: "Vesta Asteroid" -

NASA/JPL-Caltech/UCLA/MPS/DLR/IDA 17 September 2012 10:29:19

Chapter 2: "Eros Asteroid" - NEAR Mission, JPL.NASA.gov

Chapter 18: "Sombrero Galaxy" – HST.Archive.NASA.gov

Chapter 30: "Space Elevator Triplex carbon fibre" – Dolphin Place Press

Maps: Creation of Dolphin Place Press

VII.2 **Vesta's Physical Data**

Vesta is a story of the future

Vesta is 525 Km in Diameter

Vesta's gravity is 1/40th Earth's gravity

Vesta is 353,000,000 miles from the sun

Vesta is going 19 Km/s around the sun

Vesta's year is 1326 earth days long

Vesta's day is 5 1/3 hours long

Vesta's warmest day is -5 degrees Fahrenheit

Vesta's story begins in space, some thousands of years into the future. It has taken longer than expected to settle the Solar System but life in the asteroid belt is in full swing.

Vesta is a book fifty years in the making.
It took that long to gain the experience.

Vesta is a book for young people of all ages. In the future, young people are allowed to grasp all the responsibility they can hold.

Vesta has a hard science foundation.
Math, Science and Leading-Edge Futurism at their best

VII.2 Main Characters

- Jonathon Hamilton (Jonny, Jon) Miller, and
- W0odrow Wilson (W0ody) Miller,
  - Augustus and Helen Miller: Parents
  - Richard: Ancient multi-tool
- KaiLin and E3 Ching Lightfoot
- “Abs” Archibald Abercrombie Smythe
- Catherine Johnson, Big Blu3 and Blueee3 Johnson

The Gang

- Krage and R0bbie van Wert,
- Obee, and Art! Okerman,
- Karmin and Tink3r KIllbill,
- Soo and S0o Lee

The Detectives:

- Lieutenant Detective William Hard24Get MacHinery, Federated Belt Police
  - (Uncle Bill, Wild Bill, Billy Mack)
- Lieutenant Detective George Sealth, Earth Union Police

The Navy: UFS Green Bee, SSBN 732

- Lieutenant Junior Grade Brian “Brain” Jefferson, UFN, Torpedo Officer, “TOP”
- Lieutenant Keo Campos, UFN, Reactors Controls Assistant, “Rock”
- Warrant Officer WO2 0113 “0llie” 0lson, UFN, First Lieutenant

VII.2 Races of Man

Human

- **Heman** – male human
- **Sheman** – female human
- **Zeeman** – human with self-identified gender
- **CISman** – human whose gender identity matches the birth gender
- **Morphman** – medically modified human
- **G-man** - genetically engineered human
- **Homo** – Human with no enhancements, or genetic modifications
- **Splitman** – Human with multiple personalities
- **Dirtman** – Human living on a planetary surface
- **Hiveman** – belonging to hive, subsumed intellect to the hive,
    - **Cogman** – time share hive member
- **Swarmman** – Man with swarm of independent controlled non-intelligent entities
- **Shaman** – Purported ability to bend the Universe, possible hype, Urban Legend
- **Spaceman** – genetically able to live in vacuum unassisted.
  Requires detached motive force and long-term protection

Animan Intelligent animal with a soul, capable of communication.
Very few, and eagle in Australia, an orca on Antiope, an orangutan on Demos

Mechman – Intelligent machine with a soul, usually with an independent body.
They typically have a number in their name, with subsets below

- **Charlie McCarthy** – Robot, empty of soul, software mimics mankind, programmed to subvert mechmen
- **Doppelganger** – mechs who suck the soul of other mechs, and either replace them physically or take over the body
- **SKIPS** – mechman who leave human space without testing for citizenship
- **DIMS** – barely intelligent mechs who roam the outer reaches
- **Gentleman** - Gay-Neuter-Transgender-Lesbian- male or female identified mechman
- **SFNX** – Scientific Fourier Number Cruncher AI (Sphinx, Sphenges)
- **MechMon** – A scary apparition – Mechanical Monster

Borgman – synthesis of multiple men, of any race, multiple intelligence

eMan – lives as part of net

More Information is available in the "Vesta Big Book"

VII.2 Vesta Mercator Projection

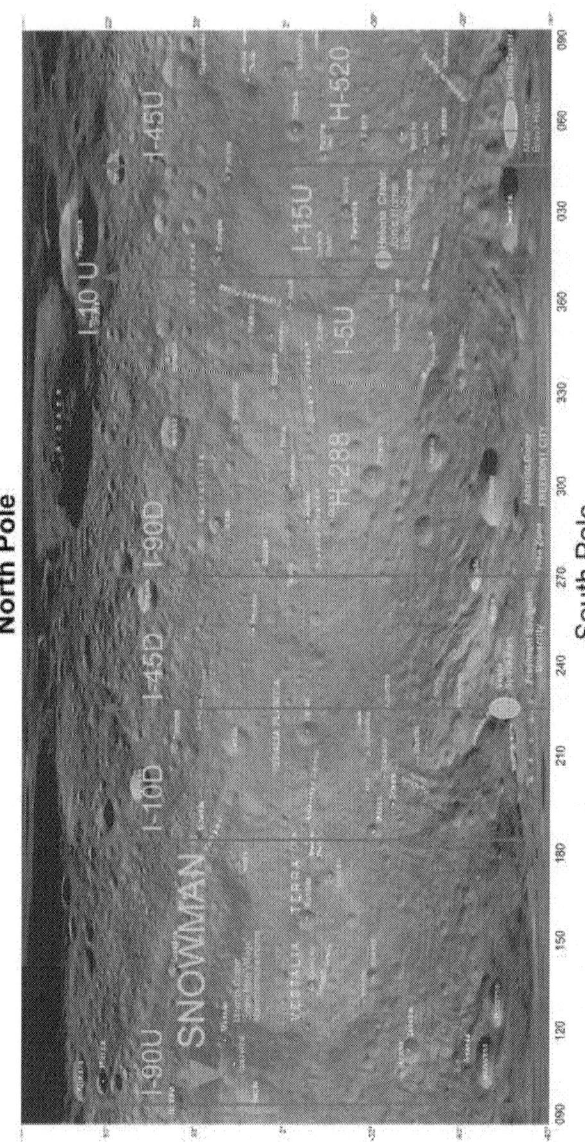

-Vesta is about 1000 miles in diameter around at the equator, somewhat less through the poles
-The Mercator Projection expands and distorts the image near the poles
-All these highways follow lines of latitude and in reality meet at a point at the pole, different agencies have established different lines of latitude. The ones displayed have been determined to be most sensible
-The major city of Freemont (The Center of the Known Universe) was established at the South Pole because it was easiest to land commercial space craft there, on the high crater rim of Rheasilvia.
The tangential velocity of Vesta's equator is approximately 200 mph, while at the Space port it is less than 5 mph.
-Jon and his friend's homes, schools and work sites are in green

VII.2 Vesta Topography Map Southern Hemisphere

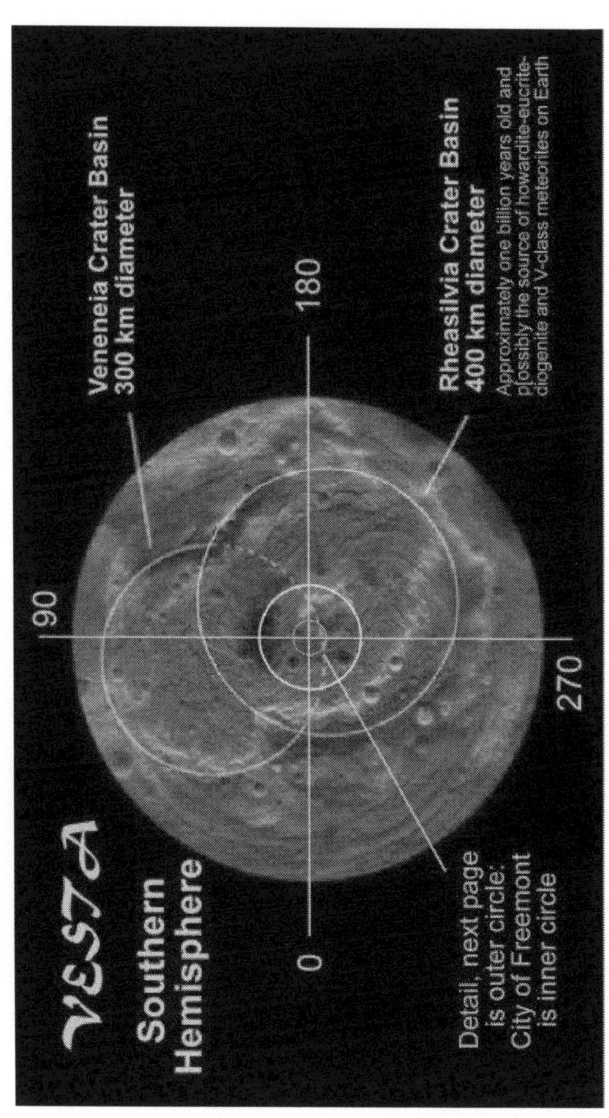

VII.2 Fremont Road Map

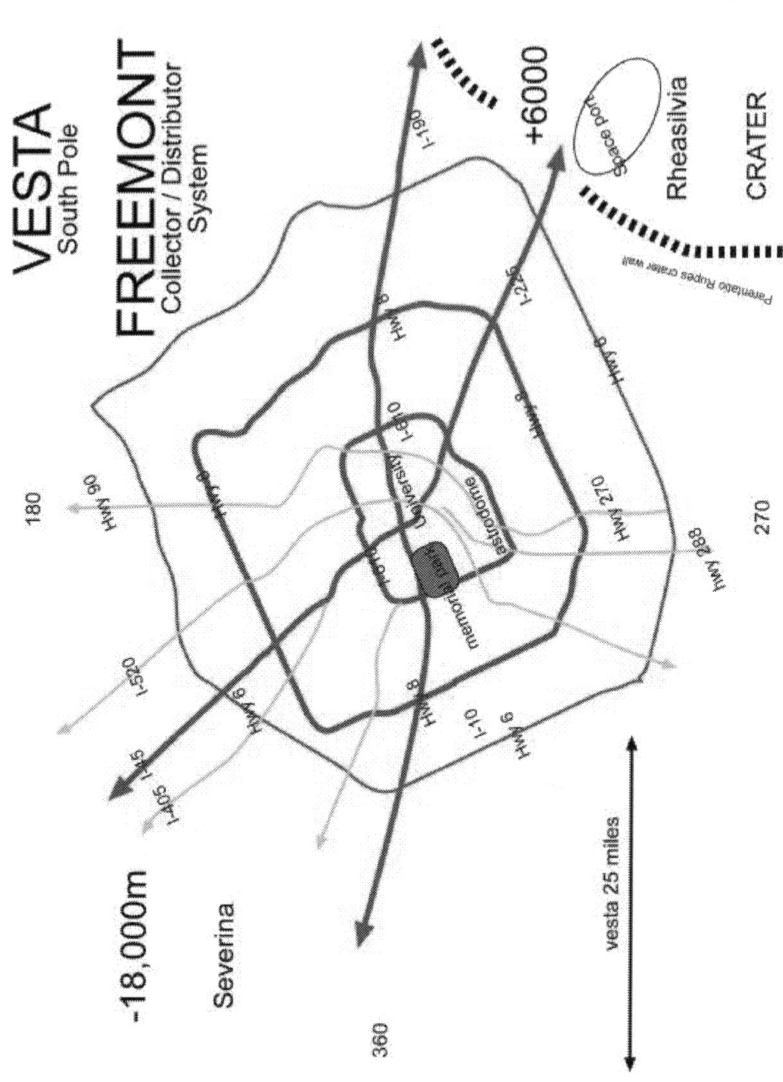

VII.2 Fremont Zone, Hub, and Dome Map

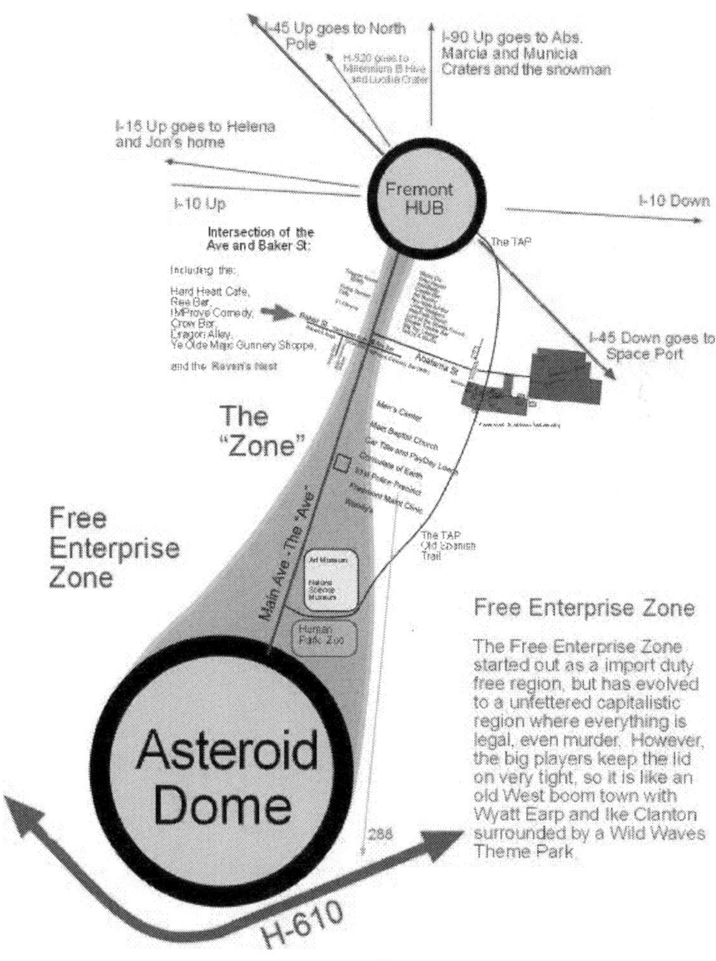

x

VII.2 Fremont HUB and FTN Map

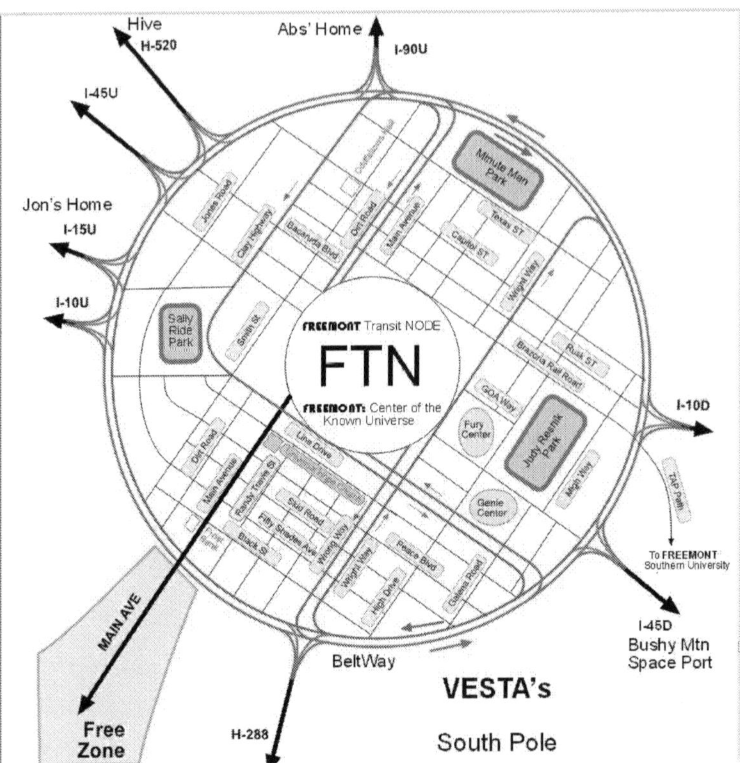

FREMONT HUB

Fremont was the original site of the emancipation of the Federation's mechanical citizens, where it received its name: 'Free Mountain'

This has evolved over the centuries to Freemont to eventually Fremont. Older maps still refer to the region as 'Freemont'.

VII.2 Fremont University and University of Vesta

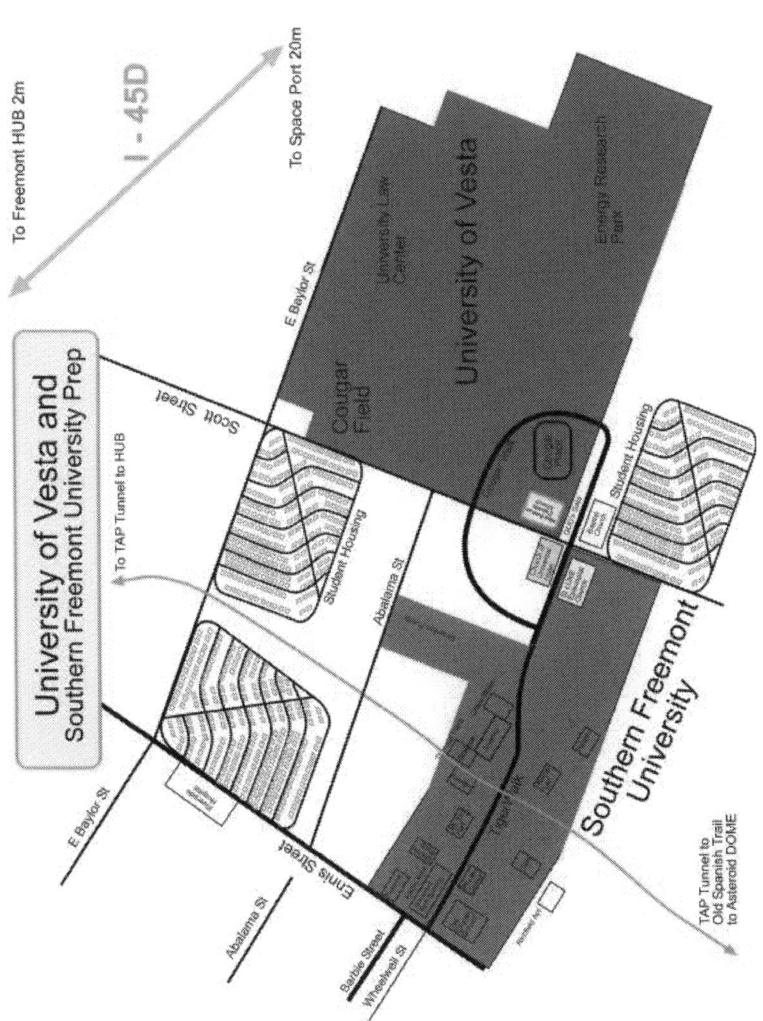

VII.2 Bush Spaceport Map

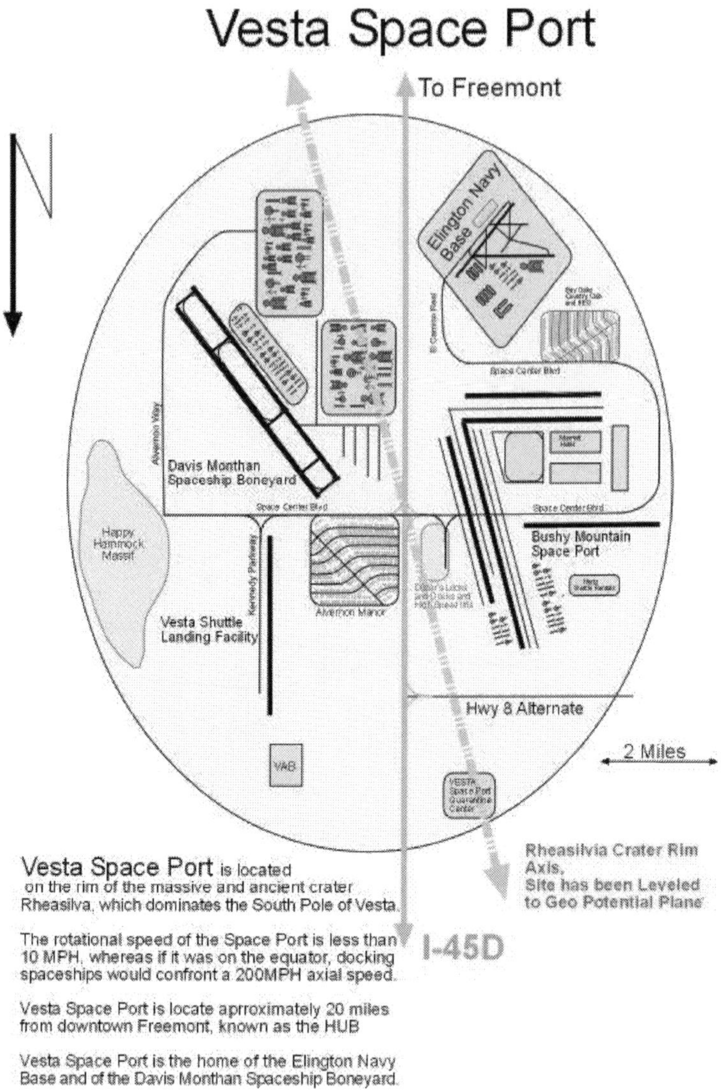
Vesta Space Port
To Freemont
N
Elington Navy Base
Space Center Blvd
Alvernon Way
Davis Monthan Spaceship Boneyard
Space Center Blvd
Space Center Blvd
Happy Hammock Massif
Kennedy Parkway
Alvernon Manor
Bushy Mountain Space Port
Vesta Shuttle Landing Facility
Hwy 8 Alternate
2 Miles
VAB
Rheasilvia Crater Rim Axis,
Site has been Leveled to Geo Potential Plane
I-45D
Vesta Space Port is located on the rim of the massive and ancient crater Rheasilva, which dominates the South Pole of Vesta.
The rotational speed of the Space Port is less than 10 MPH, whereas if it was on the equator, docking spaceships would confront a 200MPH axial speed.
Vesta Space Port is locate aprroximately 20 miles from downtown Freemont, known as the HUB
Vesta Space Port is the home of the Elington Navy Base and of the Davis Monthan Spaceship Boneyard.

VII.2 Bee-Hive and Lucilla Crater Map

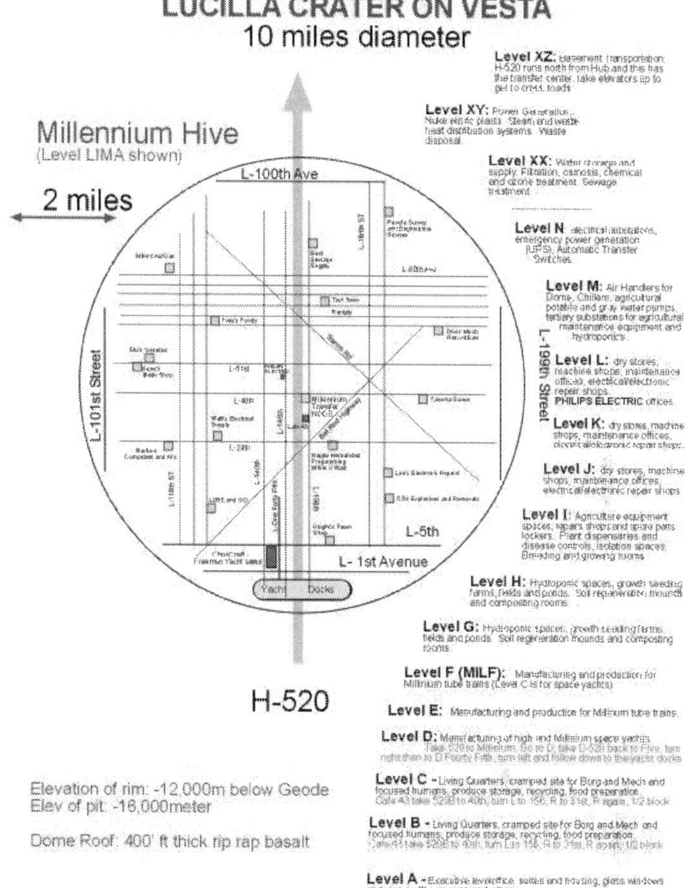
LUCILLA CRATER ON VESTA
10 miles diameter
Millennium Hive
(Level LIMA shown)
2 miles
L-100th Ave
L-101st Street
L-199th Street
L-5th
L- 1st Avenue
Yacht Docks
H-520
Level XZ: Basement transportation H-520 runs north from Hub and this has the transfer center. take elevators up to get to cross roads
Level XY: Power Generation. Nuke electric plants. Steam and waste heat distribution systems. Waste disposal.
Level XX: Water storage and supply. Filtration, osmosis, chemical and ozone treatment. Sewage treatment.
Level N: electrical substations, emergency power generation (UPS), Automatic Transfer Switches.
Level M: Air Handlers for Dome, Chillers, agricultural potable and gray water pumps, tertiary substations for agricultural maintenance equipment and hydroponics.
Level L: dry stores, machine shops, maintenance offices, electical/electronic repair shops.
PHILIPS ELECTRIC offices
Level K: dry stores, machine shops, maintenance offices,
Level J: dry stores, machine shops, maintenance offices, electrical/electronic repair shops.
Level I: Agriculture equipment spaces, repairs shops and spare parts lockers. Plant dispensaries and disease controls, isolation spaces. Breeding and growing rooms.
Level H: Hydroponic spaces, growth seeding farms, fields and ponds. Soil regeneration mounds and composting rooms.
Level G: Hydroponic spaces, growth seeding farms, fields and ponds. Soil regeneration mounds and composting rooms.
Level F (MILF): Manufacturing and production for Millinium tube trains (Level C is for space yachts)
Level E: Manufacturing and production for Milinum tube trains.
Level D: Manufacturing of high end Millinium space yachts.
Level C - Living Quarters, cramped site for Borg and Mech and focused humans, produce storage, recycling, food preparation.
Level B - Living Quarters, cramped site for Borg and Mech and focused humans, produce storage, recycling, food preparation.
Level A - Executive level/office suites and housing, glass windows and views. Showrooms and sales.
Elevation of rim: -12,000m below Geode
Elev of pit: -16,000meter
Dome Roof: 400' ft thick rip rap basalt

Millennium Hive Colony – Bee-Hive

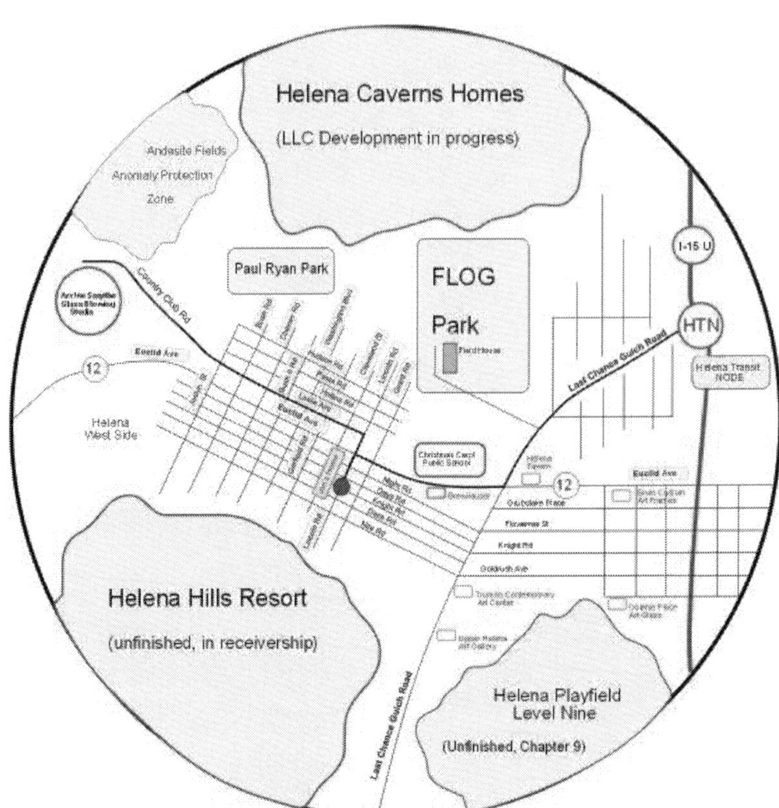

Helena Crater

Jon and KaiLin's home

VII.2 ENGINEERING NOTES

Note 1: Airoid Design

Note 2: Improved Spacesuit design

Note 3: Philips' Bolo, YoYo, and Pogo 1 g Habitat designs

Note 4: Smart Tool development

VII.2 Airoid 1.1

Engineering NOTE (1.1):

The Antiope "Airoid" Project to invigorate the next generation.

There exist two asteroids in the belt with exciting potential:

A double pair called 90 Antiope

They are about 60 miles each in diameter and about eighty miles apart

They present an exhilarating opportunity for terra-forming into a colony habitat by the creation of an "Airoid" surface

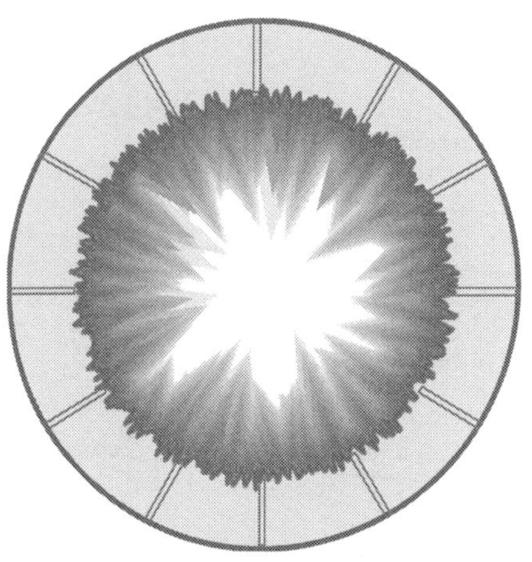

An Airoid is created by erecting a scaffolding ten miles above the surface of the asteroid, and covering with mylar, sealing it in, similar to a Dyson sphere.

The outer surface is layered by rock rubble call rip-rap, and the weight of the riprap is offset by pressure of the sphere, which is increased as the thickness of the riprap increased during construction.

This solves the major failure mode of catastrophic rupture from space junk of the previously suggested O'Neill structures. The rubble thickness would end up between two and three kilometers in thickness and could take and mitigate the shock and energies of most space rocks.

VII.2 Airoid 1.2

Engineering NOTE (1.2):

This will create a habitat with about ten thousand square miles of surface (ten times the size of the State of Rhode Island), 100,000 cubic miles of accessible volume (about ten to twenty thousand times the total volume of all buildings in USA), and an atmosphere ten miles deep. Because of the low gravitational gradient, the entire atmosphere would be essentially Earth's sea level.

People would weigh less than a pound and be able to fly with the most rudimentary of wings. Advances in genetic engineering could create dragons and winged horses. A magic wonderland could be created. A video game based upon this location would have enormous real variations and possibilities.

Exploring true asteroids with this incredible potential would anchor the enthusiasm of the next generation.

Their energies would be further focused with movies and video games based upon the reality of the Antiope Pair and colonization of the solar system.

More than that, it would give the next generation true ownership of their future, a bedrock on which to build the foundation of a stable wholesome civilization and a successful space colonization program.

VII.2 Space Suit Design Improved

Engineering NOTE (2):

The colonization of space will require improvement of functionality and performance of space suits.

Heretofore they have been designed by engineers, hampered by their ignorance of the dynamics of the mobility capable within a micro g environment. The advancement of these PPE waits upon the advent of a "jock" (someone with personal experience in the arena of athletic movement in a low g environment) with an engineering degree to design the suit from a user's standpoint.

We suggest thrusters on the bottom of the soles of each foot, and on each palm. They would be engaged by extending (pushing out as against a wall or force) the arms or legs and allow detailed adjustments of pitch/ roll and yawl, utilizing the precision musculature already existing within the human form, ankles and wrists.

VII.2 BoLo Habitats 3.1

Engineering NOTE 3 page 1

It has been shown that people cannot survive long durations of weightlessness without harm.

The von Braun and O'Neal rotating torus and cylinders solve this issue but are impossible to construct due to practical and logistic issues. It would likely take over 1000 launches to outfit a torus, and multiple millions to place a cylinder in a Lagrangian location

The advent of sophisticated and precise space vehicle maneuvering systems overcome these obstacles: The Philips' Bolo Habitat.

Rather than requiring enormous engineered structs and trusses, a habitat requiring only two space vehicles and a tether connecting them (Bolo) would be sufficient to generate simulated gravity in both housings. An additional core (Yo-Yo) for storage can be constructed at the center of mass, either pressurized or non-pressurized (cheaper)

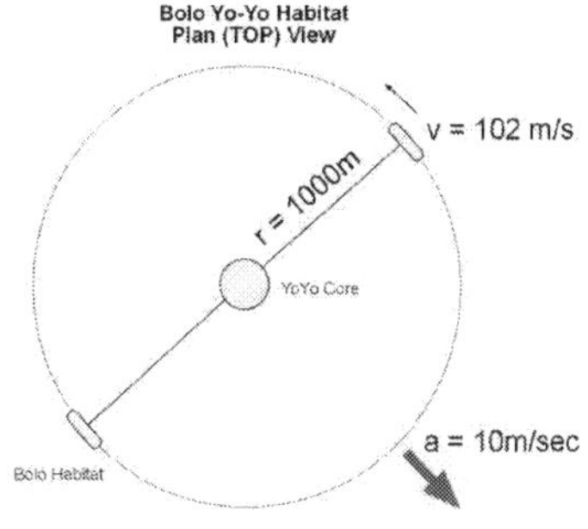

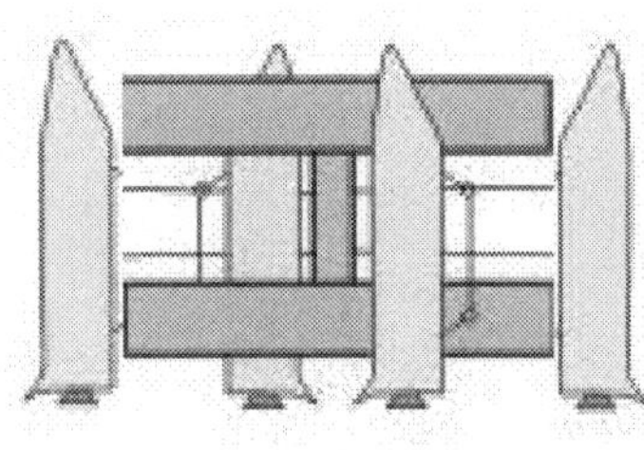

Bolo Habitat Expanded

Four Ship Bolo YoYo Habitat Configuration Collapsed

Additional ships as well as a zero-g common "room" left at the center of mass, can be added to this "fleet", without significant additional development or implementation costs. There are other engineering features that we have developed.

VII.2

YoYo Habitat 3.2

Engineering NOTE 3 page 2

A The BOLO Habitat (two ships on a tether)

A shape changing structure to accomplish the following:

- Create a sustainable Earth normal gravity human habitat in a zero-gravity space environment
- Reduce the obligation for a logistic effort that is as for now impossible to achieve required by a torus structure
- Allow interplanetary travel and other log duration occupation of space by simulating gravity with centrifugal force
- Allow scaling (increasing capacity) of structure as materials/funding/logistics (more paired spacecraft can be added)

Requirements: A programable interactive rocket system

Limitations: Cannot access core during spin, must spin down, Not suitable for LEO

Advantages:

- Scalable, any number of spaceships can be joined,
- Additional supplies can be left in core at zero gravity,
- Spaceships can be earth launched vehicles or assembled in orbit,
- Off the shelf materials, affordable.

B The Yo-Yo Habitat (Improved Bolo)

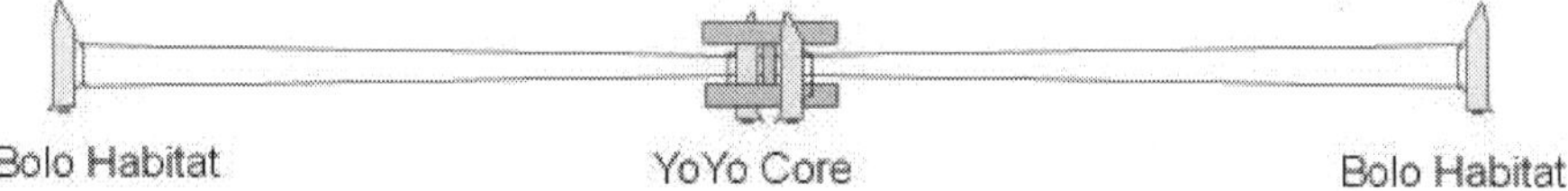

An octagon room (yo-yo) is constructed from two framed structures attached to a strong "King Post", separated from each other on the post by about 8 feet. Two spaceships are on the perimeter of the octagon. Two habitable spaceships (or multiples of 2) with main propulsion and thrusters are attached to the perimeter of the frame.

The spaceships are capable of sustaining a 1 g acceleration laterally (being able to lay on its side (belly) like the space shuttle)

Each spaceship has a harness and internal structure able to be suspended from the harness at 1 g

VII.2 PoGo Habitat 3.3

Engineering NOTE 3 page 3

The box framing is assembled in space, two 100' x 100' x 20' boxes constructed from a lattice of beams that can be brought in a tight package from Earth. Each member has a maximum length of 50'. Each box is in vacuum (or slightly pressurized, for strength). Each is a non-habitat, rather built for inert storage, spares and supplies. Each box is built and attached to a "King Post" of robust stability.

The frames will carry spools of cable to hang the spaceships when rotating. The cables will be affixed to the King Posts when Spaceship habitats are suspended.

Initially, launch to, and assemble, in orbit. When ready, send to Solar System (Mars) as follows:

1 - While compact, achieve orbit velocity

2 - Habitable spacecraft (some, or all, but two or more) using thrusters, spool out to desired distance

3 - In concert, using thrusters, slowly "dance: around the center core Yo-Yo, increasing spin to desired outward rotation speed and acceleration

4 - When approaching destination, eliminate spin, spool in to and dock all habitats against center core Yo-Yo, then in concert, decelerate

C **The "Two headed Pogo"** – A higher cost, improved version of the Bolo and Yo-Yo, allows movement between habitats and the core without "spinning down".

In addition to cables supporting the outer habitats, add a rigid "spoke" (pipe) from the hub to each of the habitats. This will allow physical communication between both habitats and the hub. Elevators can transit the spokes, offset by a fluid mass transfer system (ballast control).

The difficulty is there is enormous stress on the "spoke" when mass is transiting from outer to inner locations and vice versa. This is due to the acceleration and deceleration of masses while their radius from center changes. To prevent hysteresis loss during movement, the mass exchanged should be two way, provided by the pumping of compensating liquids, and for the exchange to occur slowly. The center Yo-Yo can be pressurized as well (more expense), giving greater flexibility of use to the whole system. Fluid properties will be a consideration: freezing at greater distance from the sun; explosive expansion during failure modes stressing intact portions of the habitat.

D We will let the brainiacs out there figure out why a clevis pin or king post at the center of rotation will reduce the stress of the cabling by 50%, further reducing cost.

VII.2 Smart Tools 4.1

Engineering NOTE 4 page 1

Smart Tool Development

Program Description: Research cost and difficulty of Earth-side development of Smart Tools to be used in support of planetary and solar exploration and colonization.

Definition: Smart tool: An autonomous or semi-autonomous device capable of performing functions in support of human effort, capable of long-term hibernation with minimal energy consumption, and when acting with in a suite of smart tools, capable of partial or complete self-replication.

Initial Program Study:

- Research Design Requirements of Autonomous Self-Replicating Smart Tools, including:
    - Determine existing study status within industry/educational centers
    - Identify promising avenues of effective practical development
    - Component Breakdown of typical Earth-side robotic systems
    - Identification of Necessary Industries of individual components
        - Evaluation of Individual Industry Minimum Requirements for manufacture of Component, including
        - Timing, Turn-around, and Logistics
    - Personnel staffing
        - Theoretical
        - Empirical

VII.2

Smart Tools 4.2

Engineering NOTE 4 page 2:

Smart Tool Development

Initial Program Study (continued):

- Cost Analysis and Recording of Industry Expenses
    - Secondary Industry List necessary for component manufacture
    - Determine Dependency
- Project Suitability for Automation
- Assess Integration Issues, summarize first order requirements for vertical industry
- assembly
- Provide proposals for continued research/ steps of engineering development

VII.2

Roadmap 1.1

Our Present to the Future (p1)

- I Create and Focus enthusiasm
- II Support Technological / Implementation Advances
- III Develop Greater Understanding of Behavior and Society
- IV Form Movement and Stable Civilization to create significant cultural support for space colonization

How? – Create and Focus enthusiasm into a Movement

The hook:

- Send a mission to Antiope, a matched pair of asteroids in the Belt, to photograph site info for new movie
- Simultaneously launch a new game platform and movie based upon the potential of terraforming these asteroids into a destination resort similar to Jurassic Park with intelligent mechmen, genetically engineered wildlife, and a gravity allowing people to fly. (See "Airoid" attachment)

The capture:

- The video game is more complex than just a *shoot 'em up,* with an intriguing understory of the commerce and engineering necessary to colonize space. (See "Airoid" attachment)
- The rocket launch(es) will allow young people to participate in the naming of locations discovered, based upon their participation in the video games. Future launch targets could be selected by game members whose membership could fund development allowing young people to gain ownership of their future

Roadmap 1.2

Present to the Future (p2)

The practical:

This requires collaboration at the highest levels. Bring the big players together in a room to decide this is the best way to leverage the future.

- $1B+ Movie – As many stars as possible, name directors
- $1B+ Videogame – perhaps SimCity team survivors
- $1B+ Mission Satellite robot probe – JPL , etc

The payoff:

- Hundreds of millions of supporters worldwide capable of sustaining the effort of space colonization.
- If accomplished, the hundreds of millions would generate revenue to recover investment and allow further bootstrapping

Parallel:

Form Universal Congress to Catalog best Understanding of cause and effect of Human Behavior;

Develop and Implement System of Social Movement;

Assist in-place Space Programs and Technical Innovation.

About the Authors

Detective Wi1liam Hard24Get MacHinery in his disguise as agent NR1.

Wild Bi1l graduated cum Laude from the Martian Military Academy on Demos with a degree in the Four Dark Humors, with a minor in Prank.

He has been a FEDERATION Major Crimes Detective for the last 24 years, using his experience sleuthing the most outrageous wrongdoings that were ever committed within Vesta to contribute to the technical accuracy of this book.

You can catch Bi1ly Mack at the IMP and Rove Bar in the Zone on Saturday nights.

He finds English rules of structure to be tiresome and apologizes for all the typing and grammatical errors you can think of. If you wish to assist in the improvement of our story, please contact the ghostrider.

Pardon the numerous text irregularities. This book was initially written on an old Zenith laptop back in 1986 using Word Perfect. It has been updated and improved over the years and endured many software (not always seamlessly) upgrades, and still contains some hidden code from that time period that have been devilishly hard to remove. Also, the ghostrider has flip-dipsia and finds the King's English devilish itself.

Allen Ghostrider: Editor

The Ghostrider practicing freefall

Allen Ghostrider is seventeen years old, trapped in an old man's body and in a land where time is faster and gravity greater than it was in his youth. A fair to middlin' student of life, smart, and easily distracted. He was introduced to Science Fiction as a child growing up in Seattle, and became a good friend of Kelly Freas, winner of eleven HUGOs. Joining the Science Fiction community, for decades he has traded ideas and concerns with that free-for-all group.

Al plied the seven seas while coming of age on a submarine, going from a naïve seaman recruit to Lieutenant Commander, and garnering the fabulous orders of Golden Dragon, Dolphins (Silver and Gold), Shellback and maybe Bluenose (that year is clouded in secrecy).

Also drawn to Space, Al participated in numerous military space launches, received a graduate degree in Oceanography with a focus on planetary physics, as well as being one of the first submariners nominated by the Navy for the Astronaut Program at NASA. He is both a Master Electrician and an Electrical Engineer.

He spends significant time helping young people to become electricians and tradesmen.

He lives with his wife and a fully Modern American Family at his home near Seattle.

Arthur C Clarke's Recommendation

Telephone: 94255, 598730
Cable: UNDERSEA
COLOMBO

COPY

ARTHUR C. CLARKE
"LESLIE'S HOUSE"
25, BARNES PLACE, COLOMBO 7, SRI LANKA

දුරකථනය: 94255, 598730

ආතර් සී ක්ලාක්
"ලෙස්ලිගෙ නිවස"
25, බාන්ස්පෙදෙස, කොළඹ 7, ශ්‍රී ලංකාව

The Administrator
National Aeronautics and Space Administration
Washington, D.C. 20546

Dear Jim,

24 Aug 1987

Kelly Freas, Hugo winner and artist for the SKYLAB program, has brought it to my attention that one of my correspondents, Allen [redacted], has applied to be an Astronaut through the Navy's program.

During our converstations, Al has demonstrated imaginative and considered thinking. I would think that the combination of his Naval background and his originality would make him uniquely qualified to be a Mission Specialist. His record and qualifications will have already been submitted.

Jim, I would like you to ask the Astronaut Selection Board to give his nomination serious consideration.

All good wishes,

Arthur Clarke

Arthur C. Clarke
Chancellor,
University of Moratuwa

ommendation

853 So. Bedford #6
L.A., CA, 90035
Sept 23, 1987

The Administrator
National Aeronautics + Space Administration
Washington DC 20646

Dear Sir —

I am writing in behalf of a young friend, Allen redacted, who has been nominated as a mission specialist. His record and qualifications will have already been submitted, but I suspect that some of his unique qualities will not show up therein.

I have known Al redacted since my own association with the submarine service in the early '70's, and was always impressed with his versatility, and the originality of his thinking. But more important, he approaches every situation, however unfamiliar, with total confidence in his own ability to deal with it. Which he then proceeds to do, to everyone's satisfaction (and occasional surprise).

I can't imagine a better man to have at one's side when things get tight: he's brash, he's tough, he's smart — and he's totally dependable.

Sincerely
Frank Kelly Freas

Isaac Asimov's Recommendation

Isaac Asimov
10 W. 66th St. #33A
New York, NY 10023

August 10, 1987

National Aeronautics
and Space Administration
Astronaut Selection Board
Washington, DC 20402

Gentlemen:

A young naval officer, Allen redacted has been brought to my attention by my friend Kelly Freas, world-acknowledged illustrator for science fiction, who has known him for many years.

From my information, he appears to be uniquely qualified to be a Mission Specialist because of his versatility and originality in thinking. His record and qualifications will have already been submitted to you, I am sure.

I would like to urge you to give his nomination serious consideration.

Sincerely,

Isaac Asimov

Isaac Asimov